# LEGACY
## OF THE
# GODS

# BLURB

**I was lost and alone until they found me. Ruthless. Killers. Bikers.**

Now I belong to them. But after what they did to me, we have a long way to go before forgiveness.

Someone is screwing with the Jackal's motorcycle club business. They know what we are. Who we are. Always one step ahead. And they won't stop until we're six feet under.

It's time to fulfil my legacy. Become who I was born to be. Embrace my mates. Destroy our enemies; family or foe. Because no one takes what's mine. No one.

***Legacy of the Gods** is book 3 in the **Jackals Wrath MC series** (**Operation Isis**) featuring a stubborn, yet strong heroine and four badass, haunted bikers as love interests. If you love shifters, fated mates, Egyptian mythology, urban fantasy and romantic suspense, this is the series for you! This book contains dark elements with trigger warnings, suitable for 18+ readers.*

Legacy of the Gods (Operation Isis #3) © Copyright 2022 Skyler Andra
Cover art by Dark Imaginarium Art & Design.
Chapter vector art by Eerilyfair Design.

All rights reserved under the International and Pan-American Copyright Conventions. No part of this book may be reproduced or transmitted in any form or by any means, electronic or mechanical, including photocopying, recording, or by any information storage and retrieval system, without permission in writing from the publisher/author.

This is a work of fiction. Names, places, characters and incidents are either the product of the author's imagination or are used fictitiously, and any resemblance to any actual persons, living or dead, organizations, events or locales is entirely coincidental.

Warning: the unauthorized reproduction or distribution of this copyrighted work is illegal. Criminal copyright infringement, including infringement without monetary gain, is investigated by the FBI and is punishable by up to 5 years in prison and a fine of $250,000.

❦ Created with Vellum

*Just wanted to say a lil' thanks to all my ARC reviewers and some special ladies who have helped with this series.
Huge thank you to:
1. Kerry, my gal for military chats. I'll never forget the Chair Force!
2. Kelly, my go-to gal for all things nursing and my incredible Beta reader.
3. Special little thank you to Ines for reading these notes and acknowledging them :)*

# OPERATION SERIES UNIVERSE

Welcome to my "Operation" series, featuring a world of godly avatars. **What's an avatar?** They're humans embodied with the power and characteristics of their patron god. For example:

- Ares (God of War) is a hot-head ex army soldier.
- Hermes (God of Thieves, Travel & 50 other things) is a slippery and fun ex-thief.
- Eros (God of Love) is a former Phone Sex Worker who runs from love.
- Hades (God of Underworld) is lonely, cold, and hard until he meets Persephone in the bubbly and warm Autumn.

This isn't a re-telling of the gods' story, this is my unique spin on the mythology.

**OPERATION CUPID**
Completed reverse harem mythology romance.

1. Battlefield Love
2. Quicksilver Love
3. Awakened Love

OPERATION SERIES UNIVERSE

3.5 Stupid Cupid - a Valentine's short story

**OPERATION HADES**
Completed fated mates romance.

1. Lady of the Underworld
2. Lord of the Underworld
3. Rulers of the Underworld
4. Return to the Underworld

**JACKAL'S WRATH MC (Operation Isis)**
Reverse harem paranormal motorcycle club romance with shifters.

0.5 Prophecy of the Gods (prequel) - exclusive to newsletter subscribers
1. Curse of the Gods
2. Captive of the Gods
3. Legacy of the Gods
4. Wrath of the Gods - coming 2022

**BLOOD DEBT MAFIA (Operation Anubis)** Paranormal mafia arranged marriage romance.

0.5 Falling for the Mafia (prequel) - coming 2022
1. Married to the Mafia - coming 2022

More gods series planned! Stay tuned.

GRAB A FREE BOOK

One last thing before you jump into the book. Sign up to my newsletter here to grab an exclusive *reader's only* ebook copy of the prequel if you haven't already got it, **Prophecy of the Gods**.

## GRAB A FREE BOOK

https://dl.bookfunnel.com/1hwipcn67p

# CHAPTER 1

## *A*aliyah

IT STARTED WITH BLOOD, and it would end with blood. War launched between the Jackals and Wolves, an ambush on a drug shipment the first act of aggression. Casualties fell on both sides, me being one of them, my brother another. I survived, thanks to scrappy backyard surgery from the Jackal's doctor. My dick of a brother pushed through four bullet wounds, thanks to the help of demons and dark magick.

Edgy from thinking about my brother, I gripped Castor's waist tighter from my bitch-position on his bike. His warmth soaked into me, steering away my fears and the chill crawling through me.

Mysterious players entered the fray with the Jackals, paid for by a shadowy enemy, muddying the waters and confusing the avatars. My allies defeated one threat, staging a fake drug delivery, capturing three hostages, and executing a traitor.

Cleared of guilt, I earned the Jackal's trust, and agreed to remain with them until all threats were neutralized. I didn't know how long that would be or if I'd even want to go home after all this. My life felt insignificant without the avatars in it. But there was still that niggling doubt, the voice inside me that persuaded me to leave them behind, that they were more trouble than they were worth. I'd already lost two people I loved through biker clubs. Adopted my daughter out to shield her from that life.

Blind to our enemy, the Jackals and I were vulnerable to more attacks and couldn't mount an offensive strategy to curb their efforts. In the meantime, the avatars focused on defending their club from ongoing threats and continued their hunt for the real enemy. I hoped this would finally lead to the identity of my father's murderer, because only then would I be able to repay the blood taken from me.

The gods led us to this moment, and they would see us through to the end, whether we lived or died. There'd always be another human to take over as their avatars. Trapped by the curse for thousands of years, the gods were getting edgy and impatient for freedom, and they placed enormous responsibility and trust in Slade, Zethan, Castor, Alaric, and me to break the curse binding us together. Castor bore the brunt of that responsibility, but now that I was here, I could help ease that burden and contribute to his research. I was backed by a goddess of magick, after all.

Castor's bike roared louder as it rolled into his garage, where he parked it and killed the engine. I reluctantly released my grasp of his stomach when he kicked the stand down, and I dismounted.

The trench coat concealing my awkwardly folded wings got caught on his footpeg, jerked off my shoulders, and fell to the stained pavement. Wings that refused to tuck into my damn back no matter how much sex I had with Castor. Squeaks accompanied the garage door's descent, and my eyes shot to the neighboring properties across the road.

"Shit." I bent down to scoop up the coat and threw it over my shoulders.

Castor gave me his signature secretive smile as the door creaked shut. He extended a bruised hand, marked from enforcing his fists on the captives.

"Here, dark sorceress." That deep and rich timbre knocked me on my ass with what little balance I possessed.

Goddess. This dark, enigmatic criminal should be charged for doing such things to my body and making me puddle at his feet. My heart punched my mind in the throat and shut that bitch up.

I accepted his hand, and he hefted me to my feet, steadying me as I rocked against his firm chest. Extra weight from my vivid new appendages put me off balance, and I felt like a waddling pregnant woman. The fabric of my coat caught on my wing, scraping it, and I wriggled, trying to shake it loose. Never accept a dare from Castor to shift. The last two days I was stuck with these heavy-ass things.

Castor unclipped my helmet for me and brushed stray hair over my ear. Blood flowed in a heated rush to parts that demanded to be touched.

Paranoid, I asked, "Do you think your neighbors saw me?"

His devastating eyes roamed over me ravenously. "Mrs. Beatrix at number twenty-one is a nosey neighbor. Very disapproving of a *dirty biker* living opposite her." His impish smirk teased me.

I slapped at him. "Shut up. I'm serious."

He chuckled, and my bond went taut with need. "To her credit, she's the best guard dog I've got. Calls her best friend around the corner to gossip if anyone comes snooping." He tapped his head. "And I hear every word of it."

"Aren't you lucky?" I squinted my eyes and gave him a mock smile for teasing me. "Jim at number six is stoned all the time. Smurf, the little Chihuahua at number three, barks at anything. And Mr. Balfor at number four is deaf. None of them can be relied on to protect my apartment. Thieves broke in and stole my laptop and TV."

"I can help you with that." Castor grinned, tapping his head again.

"*Please*. My laptop has my graduation photos and some of my dad's last birthday party." The thought had me going silent for a moment.

"Consider it done." Castor's knuckles skimmed along my arm.

What he'd said snapped back into my head. I paused, hesitant to take another step after his answer. "Wait. Are you shitting me? Has anyone come snooping?"

"A few cops showed up after your dad died," he admitted. "One tried to plant a gun in my back garden."

What the fuck? Dirty-assed cops. Was there anyone decent in the police force these days?

"I took care of it and warned the others. The cops didn't get far after that, especially when they obtained warrants and searched our houses." He scrubbed his scruffy jaw, stubbled from all the research we'd been doing in the Great Library of Thoth. Oh, and all the sex had kept him too busy for man care. "I wasn't fast enough to save Slade."

Heat in my body dissipated in an instant. I caught Castor's hand, drawing it from his face, clasping it tightly. "We'll find evidence to exonerate him."

Castor's expression remained unsure, and he scratched the outside of his hand with his thumb. "C'mon, dark sorceress. Let's go inside." He dragged me to the door, tugged it open and gestured for me to go first.

A couple of days ago, I bargained Slade's ass to move out of the rough and ready clubhouse and stay in better comfort. I proposed Castor's place as the most ideal, simply because I couldn't trust myself not ending up in the Jackal's president's bed if I stayed with him. Zethan was scratched off the list because of the curse, and I didn't want to risk being choked if I bedded at Alaric's house. Reluctantly, Slade agreed to let me stay with Castor. At last, I could finally get some privacy and freedom from guards following me around all the time. Escape from the constant smell of oil, fuel, grease, alcohol, and sweaty asses of thirty noisy men.

Castor's reluctance nagged at the bond. He liked his space and didn't want me to crowd it, yet I just invited myself into his life and felt awful for giving him no choice. Ever since, a part of him felt distant, a little cold, and detached, like he hid something from me again. Every time we took two steps forward, we seemed to take another back. It made me doubt that he or the rest of the avatars were right for me. I didn't want to be privy to every emotion, and I sure as hell didn't want to know they kept things from me. Bikers weren't exactly loyal to their women, and the club came first. I sure as shit wasn't settling for second best again.

Still, I owed Castor thanks for being a good sport. "Thanks for letting me stay with you. I know I put you on the spot the other day with Slade."

Castor's arm came around my back, drawing me flat to his chest, and a pleased shiver played down my spine. "You're my woman. Your home is with me." The possessive edge to his voice warmed me from head to toe.

Despite reassuring me, smudges on his end of the bond concealed something. I wanted to know what it was but didn't want to pry. He'd tell me when he was ready. If it was another woman, I'd barbeque his ass, because I was not sharing, nor was I letting him go down the path of my father or brother with having a mistress.

Keen for some banter to lighten up his mystery, I stretched up and seductively whispered in his ear, "You might regret saying that when I decorate your sofa or bed with pink cushions." I finished with a playful bite to his lobe, feeding more blood to my southern borders.

"Oh, no you don't." He lifted me over his shoulder to carry me caveman-style inside, and I giggled.

Pain lanced down my wings as they caught on the doorframe, canceling any arousal. Shit, those things were annoying. Two damn days. Itchy as hell and right where I couldn't reach, aching between my shoulder blades. The weight pulled on my muscles, straining them to the point of a constant backache. Made sleeping very difficult.

"Fuck. Sorry, dark sorceress." Castor gently returned me to my feet, rubbing the edges of my wings, dulling the pain.

I groaned and leaned my head back. "Keep doing that and make it up to me, you brute." My nipples hardened at his dark chuckle.

Castor forced me to shuffle sideways, edging me inside his foyer, his hands never leaving my shoulders. Once inside, he took my hand, grabbed the suitcase Zethan had dropped off earlier today in his van, and led me along his hallway.

I wasn't sure what to expect as my boots tapped on the polished oak floors. Messy like his clubhouse desk, packed with books, whisky glasses, and magical items? Smelling like herbs, candle wax, and incense? Completely the opposite. Freakishly neat and clean. Stormy gray walls contrasting with lighter ones. A movie poster from the seventies and weird art on his wall. A guitar and speaker beside his leather sofa. Minibar in the corner of his living room. A motorcycle wheel mounted to his wall. Massive TV on a wooden stand.

Two plush recliners that I wanted to drop into and snuggle. An everyday bachelor pad. At least it wasn't filled with weird sex swings, poles or toys … although, I bet his bedroom was. Dark Daddy must be into toy play.

We moved into his kitchen, where he deposited my suitcase full of the clothes he brought me. Antique furniture, including a dining table, bookshelves, and wine cabinet featured in the dining room.

"It's nice," I admired.

"Nice?" Castor teased, wrapping his arms around me, enveloping me in his radiant warmth. His hands settled at the curve of my back in a comforting pressure. He pulled an alluring, exciting hunger from me, which my heart demanded I explore, but my mind warned me of the consequences.

"Nice for an enforcer," I joked. "Although, I expected whips and chains." A reference to his weird sex contraption on the wall of his bedroom at Thoth's library, where he strapped me in and fucked me upside down.

He chuckled, breathing hot and heavy in my ear. "That's just for the bedroom. And you wouldn't have the heart for it."

I nudged him with my ass, playfully teasing, hoping he'd lift me on the counter and take me to alleviate the dark need his touch sparked. "You got a red room, huh? A dungeon downstairs too?"

I didn't really know what that was, but my friends at the hospital told me about a patient who came in with a sex toy stuck up her vaginal cavity from some Dom and sub play. Red rooms, BDSM, whips, and chains were the topics of conversation at the water cooler for the next few days. Learned *a lot* from those chats.

Castor was into his Dark Daddy and dominance play, so I assumed he might be into that too. I was eager to explore. Whips … maybe not. A light spank? *Hell, yeah.*

He scratched the back of his neck. "I wanted to wait a month or so before introducing you to that."

I snorted and smacked him for joking with me. "Good one!"

"I'm serious." *Fuck.* He led me to a wall on the far side and jerked his head at it. "Open it, dark sorceress."

I quirked an eyebrow. "Open what? It's a wall?"

"Panic room," he corrected, and my stomach sank. "I want you to hide down here if anything ever happens. If your brother ever tracks you here. We've all got a basement for protection. Perk of the job."

Tricky Castor always had a ploy up his sleeve. Bikers should always be prepared for their enemies. *Goddess.* Nowhere felt safe anymore, not even with the Jackals. But I was safest with the avatars, four incredibly powerful servants of the gods.

Eager to practice my skills, I summoned the detection magick he taught me to use, seeking out any spells on the wall. Wards beneath my fingertips tingled on my skin.

"Aten," I whispered the Sun god's name, calling upon his light to illuminate the concealed hieroglyphs. Dark symbols of birds, snakes, eyes, and people glowed golden, crackled, and burned red into the wall.

"Good," Castor crooned over my shoulder, and shivers wracked my body. "Now remove the wards."

I swept my vertical hands outwards. "Teti."

Fire razed the wards, and they sizzled and spat embers. Ash fluttered to the floor, vanishing before it burned the wood. An outline of a door formed, gaining clarity, forming a heavy, wooden frame with an iron handle.

Castor massaged my shoulders and kissed the sensitive skin behind my ears. "Good girl."

His magick unlocked the basement door and cast it open

with a stubborn groan, telling me it hadn't been opened in a while. Hand clasped in mine, he took me downstairs for a tour. Another snap of power flicked the lights on, producing a hard, red blush. Musty and stale air encouraged me to sneeze. This place hadn't seen fresh air in goddess knows how long.

At the bottom of the steps, my wings shot outward at the sight in front of me. An antique four-poster bed made of solid damn wood with a mattress sheathed in red satin. How the fuck did he even get that thing down here? Never mind. Magick, probably. A gold stand with various kinky-looking devices dangling on it; feathers, tassels, collars, handcuffs, wristbands, silk ties, red ropes, and blindfolds. I swallowed at the long leather rods that looked like horse whips. Ten blinks later, my eyes jumped to the dark, leather-studded sofa with a side table covered in crystal glasses and decanters filled with colored alcohol. A rod on the wall with more dangling items I didn't recognize or want to know what the heck they were used for.

"I thought you said this was a panic room." I tried to make light of it, but it came out nervous and stuttered.

"It serves multiple purposes," he explained, magick curling from his finger to summon a compartment from the wall packed with guns and knives.

Fuck me, I shouldn't have joked about the dungeon. He really owned a red room that doubled as a defense pit. All this was a little intimidating.

I swallowed at the thick, nervous lump in my throat. After the BDSM water cooler chats, I bought some erotic fiction books to cure my ignorance. Talk about eyes being opened from those. Some of the kink aroused me, like the control Castor demonstrated, or the gentle tying up, blindfolding, and elimination of senses to heighten pleasure. But I drew the line at having my mouth bound, my body contorted into weird-ass positions, tied up by shibari rope or forced to wear and do humiliating actions.

Wow. Castor really threw me in the deep end. Uncomfortable with the daunting number of toys, I turned to look at him. "Maybe I should stay with Slade."

CHAPTER 2

*𝒜*aliyah

"It's not entirely what it looks like." Castor nestled his hand on my hip and inched me over to a blue porcelain vase with blossoms and a peacock. "Most of these are collector items. This is a Ming Dynasty vase from the fourteenth century." His fingers traced the ancient relic reverently.

Visiting Thoth's Great Library opened my eyes to all kinds of ancient wonders. Scribes, papyrus scrolls, reed pens, sandstone carvings and pyramids, the Nile River, dates, Kushari, and more.

Castor's finger pointed to the opposite wall where a glass cabinet stored more sensual toys. "Those bad boys were owned by Sultan Osman of the Ottoman Empire in 1301. I don't use them." By bad boys, he meant the set of horse whips, which made me cringe thinking of the dirty old Sultan and his courtesans. Castor leaned in to whisper the rest, "But those over there on the rack? They're fair game, baby."

My pussy throbbed at his promise, echoing in my g-spot and core. I wanted him and it burned like a fire inside of me, raging out of control. I reminded myself that this wasn't a forever relationship. Once I was clear of these men and the mate bond, I wouldn't be influenced by its sway. Then I could return to my regular life and not have a curse dictate whom I wanted to be with. For now, though, I'd enjoy his company, have fun while it lasted, and take what I needed sexually, so long as he was cool with it. Although, something told me Castor wouldn't be the kind of man I could walk away from. His touch corrupted me, made me forget my misgivings, left my heart a mess.

His strong hand roamed down to cup the globe of my ass. "Don't worry, when I have you warmed up and begging, you'll want to use them."

"Nice try, Dark Daddy." I shrugged him off to examine two samurai swords mounted on the wall. "A little bossy play is fun, but I'm not sure I'm down with all this weird BDSM shit." Important to set my limits from the start. I might be most comfortable with him of all the Jackal avatars, and I trusted him to dominate the play, but I wasn't confident with the rest.

Castor slid a possessive arm around my neck and shoulders. "They were owned by Kusunoki Masashiage."

I glanced up at him with a kicked-up eyebrow. "Who?"

"Only one of the most famous samurais of all time." He said it like I should know who the hell that was.

I flicked up my other eyebrow. "Did anyone ever tell you, you're a geek?"

"Nerd, actually." Castor's throaty laugh brushed my ear. "A geek is passionate about a particular topic. A nerd is passionate about learning."

I snorted at him. "This is why I don't challenge the avatar of Wisdom."

Still a *geek*. Surprising for a biker. Not surprising for the wise, curious, and experimental avatar of Thoth and a former solicitor. No wonder he liked all this kinky crap and its creepy Sultan history.

"I think I need a drink." I started for the staircase, even though I could have grabbed one from the stand near the leather sofa. I didn't want to stay down here longer than necessary.

Castor rushed to catch me by the wrist and spin me back to face him. "If you don't want to come down here, we don't have to. I built it for several reasons. Privacy. Screams." He waggled an eyebrow at me. "The good kind."

*Thank fuck for that!* For a moment there, he had me worried that he was into torture sex. But that didn't comfort me.

"Security for my antiques." He flung out his finger as he counted. "And there's enough food stored in the cupboard for a month-long siege."

"Siege?" My eyes must have swelled to the size of teacups.

"It's just a precaution." He clamped his hands on his hips, and yep, my gaze dipped there, to the tapered waist, the solid, strong, pelvis and thighs. "I told you I had some nasty people after me when I prosecuted them."

"Nastier than Danny?" I shot back.

He snorted. "On par."

"Maybe I should stay with Slade."

"He's just as popular with the criminals."

I stepped forward to hit Castor in the stomach with my palms. "Not funny."

His arms banded around my back. "If you're not comfortable in this room, there's sixty-three Kama Sutra positions to explore in my bedroom." He shrugged, trying to put me at ease. "Or The Art of the Bedchamber, Chinese Sexual Yoga." He wickedly wagged his heavy brows.

I coughed into my hand. Goddess. Of course, the avatar of Thoth was familiar with every sexual practice of every culture. By the sounds of it, he was going to keep me very busy in the bedroom. What a lucky girl I'd be while we dealt with my brother and his club.

"I'm not reassured the Kama Sutra will protect us from gangs," I said, trying to joke but only half feeling it.

His thumbs swept over my face. "I'll be content doing whatever you want and being with you. You don't know how glad I am to have my mate." The singing along our link supported that. Except it ducked behind the dark smudge to hide.

I coughed again. "No, you won't."

Dark Daddy liked complete control, and that included telling me how and when to get off. We were going to fuck his way. Every single time.

Disappointment stung Castor's end of the mate bond. Another mate unwilling to experiment and fulfil his deepest desires. Fuck, I hated to be compared to Liz, and hated even more that I disheartened him. Goddess, sometimes I wished I didn't have insight into my mates' hearts.

All this was too much, too soon. With Slade, I knew what I would get. Fire, passion, a storm. Things were different with Castor. He was a mystery shrouded in darkness. Alluring as hell but intimidating at the same time. The nurse in me was scientific, practical, and assessing. The unknown scared me a little.

*Fuck, Aaliyah. Stop it. Slam the fucking brakes on those thoughts.*

I couldn't cultivate a relationship with the avatars. Couldn't think about where things were headed. How close I felt to them. Where I wanted it to go next. This couldn't evolve into anything real. It couldn't last. Wouldn't work. They were bikers and killed to protect their interests. I was a nurse and saved lives. Opposite ends of the spectrum. I'd not leave a legacy of blood.

I side-stepped Castor and climbed the stairs, wanting to put this room and his darkest desires out of my mind. Back in the kitchen, I grabbed my suitcase, waiting for him to reappear.

He took a few minutes as if he needed to compose himself, then plodded slowly up the stairs. At the top landing, he paused, bracing his hand in the doorway. "Aaliyah—"

"This is heavy," I cut him off. "Can I put it in my room?"

He sighed, shut the door, and ran a hand over the wall, reinstating his magical protection wards. "It's down here."

He grabbed my suitcase from me, and I followed him down a hallway off the dining room.

He slid open the third door on the right. "I made up this room for you."

I entered and studied it as he set down my belongings. Floral pattern quilt on a queen-sized bed. Lace and mahogany curtains. Nightstand with a beautiful lamp with a naked female with wings holding up the base. Fluffy pillows and a throw on the bed.

"Nice decorations." I pumped a soft and luxurious pillow. "Getting in touch with your feminine side?"

Castor's throaty laugh weakened my knees. "I'm a mind reader." He pressed two fingers to his temples. "Got ahead of you on the redecorating."

I thumped a fist on my thigh. "Damn!" I scanned the ceiling. "I had such huge plans. Pinks, flowers, candles."

"No chance, woman." He poked me in the stomach, and I giggled. "In all seriousness, my mom stays here when she visits."

No mention of his dad. "Just your mom?"

"He took off when I was three, and she raised me as a single parent." The heartbreak in his voice told me not to ask about his father, so I respected that.

"When will I get to meet her?" *Goddess, Aaliyah.* Jumping the gun there.

His hum buzzed through me. "When you learn to tuck your wings in."

"Touché." Couldn't meet a parent like this.

"There's a bathroom at the end of the hallway." Castor moved back to the doorway as if he intended to give me privacy. "You're welcome to sleep in here or with me. Whatever you choose."

Longing, thick and heavy, tugged at our connection. He wanted me by his side, warm and in his arms. Fucking me into delirium and unconsciousness. Listening to my breathing as I slept. The thump of my heart in my chest as he leaned on mine. I wanted all that too.

More than that, I appreciated he gave me a choice when Dark Daddy could have had his way and ordered me into his bed. Castor offered compromise, unlike Slade, who clubbed me over the head like a caveman and drove me crazy. Probably why Castor and I got along so well.

Hell, everything moved so fast with the Jackals. Infiltrator and resident of their shelter. From enemy to sleeping with them to their captive, all the way to being their mate and staying with them. We'd completely by-passed the dating stage and jumped right into being lovers, and it felt strange. Wrong almost, yet so right at the same time. That was how they rolled. Part of me wanted to put the brakes on and say, *"Whoa, let me catch up and sort out my feelings."* But the Jackals lived every day as if it were their last, and as their mate, I didn't get that luxury.

*Ride or die, bitch,* my heart warned me.

"I'll let you settle in." Castor's deflation stung me.

Hell. I didn't want to lie alone in bed either. I wanted my dark, sexy, mysterious man by my side. A hard chest to lean on. Strong arms holding me tight. "I choose both. A room of my own and one to share with you."

His face lit up with a dark, devious grin as he scooped me into his arms. "My greedy little dark sorceress!"

# CHAPTER 3

*S*lade

SHIT KEPT GOING from bad to worse for us, and we couldn't catch a break. Half a million dollars down, a batch of drugs that we couldn't offload thanks to undercutting. Ambushed twice, one member of the Jackals dead, one traitor executed, and stuck without a drug runner. F.U.C.K.E.D. My ass was sore from being pummeled by our enemies known and unknown. Storms, lightning, fire, lava, hurricanes all pulsed in my blood, a torrent desperate to lay waste to those cunts toying with my club.

I lifted my arms and swung and crossed them over each other, stretching my bunched, corded muscles. My leather cut creaked from the motion, growing tighter by the day as my body swelled with my building rage. Knots crisscrossed my back, neck, and shoulders. Pent-up tension ready to fucking burst if I didn't take down my mounting enemies. I needed a massage, sex, a punching bag, a goddamn enemy to scorch. Anything to work out the escalating pressure.

My ears pricked, my jackal hearing detecting a soft sound. Laughter. Bright. Warm. Like the first patter of rain that soothed the summer heat. My mate. Castor brought Aaliyah to the club this morning for church. The burn and pull in my muscles eased, and I lowered my arms. Listening to her converse with Zethan and Alaric, I rubbed the spot on my chest where all her fire sat. Passion, urgency, desire. A blaze that dulled after we fucked, and she realized her second mistake. Anger pooled in my gut at her regret. If I wasn't such an ass, she'd be staying with me, in my bed, keeping me warm instead of damn Castor. Lucky bastard.

Regret burned a hole in my stomach. Instinct had me protect the club and my brothers over my woman. Any president would have done the same in my place. In hindsight, I should have listened to Castor and Zethan, and given her the benefit of the doubt first. Checked out her alibis, gathered evidence, fit the entire picture together before coming to any conclusion. But I was no solicitor like Castor and definitely no police officer like Zethan. Didn't finish high school. Brash and impulsive, my mind went to the worst-case scenario, and it may have cost me my relationship with Aaliyah.

I forked my fingers and jabbed at the pressure between my brows. My jackal wanted to control and dominate her. Make her submit to us. But she didn't submit. This fight to win her back wouldn't be easy. The feisty woman already bargained my ass off. Convincing her that I was a good mate, that I trusted her, cared for her, and wanted to protect and love her, would test my limits. My skeleton would rot in the ground before she forgave me.

Fuck. Meanwhile, my goddamn balls were petrifying. At thirty-two, I wasn't getting younger, and longed to have a kid. But at this rate, I'd never be able to put a baby in her belly. I needed my woman and that was it. I'd not stop until I made her mine. Bring on the fireworks, mountain rides, fucking picnics. Every stop pulled out to win her back.

My gaze fell to the blue box on the edge of my desk. A start, at least. I was keen to see how she responded to the gesture.

"Reg calling," my phone announced, dragging my mind along a bed of nails as it came back to focus on club business.

Last prick I wanted to hear from when all he seemed to deliver lately was bad news. My headache tripled, and I rubbed my forehead.

"Yeah?" I answered the call.

"Hey, Slade." I didn't like the defeat in his tone.

"What the fuck is it now?" My patience ran thin last time he delivered bad news. At this point, it was non-existent and my temper high.

Reg failed me twice, let the Wolves ambush him and my club, then failed to sell the batch of Pharaoh we'd reclaimed from the distributor of Hellfire MC. A mistake he'd not repeat a third time. I'd kill him if he fucked me over again.

Reg's stutter set my nerves on edge. "Shit, Slade. I don't know any other way to say this."

"Spit it out!" I barked down the phone, clutching the edge of my desk, bracing for more shit news.

"A ... a competitor has entered the market." Fucker was a few words away from being dead.

I pulled the phone away, ready to crush it. News I'd been dreading for the last three weeks. My pulse stuttered, burning with the fire from the pits of Hell my god commanded.

"It gets worse," Reg had the nerve to continue. "They're selling the gold at half the price." Gold was our code word for Pharaoh.

Some fucker cut into our market, and when I found out who, he wouldn't take another fucking breath. "Who's the ballsy cunt?"

We couldn't afford for a competitor to take over our number-one position in the market. Pharaoh was the most popular recreational drug for the last two years. Earnings from that single product alone shot us to the top five clubs in Australia in terms of money, power, and influence. A spot we weren't about to vacate for some dumb prick who stole from us. Our enemies would pay for stealing our recipe and intellectual property.

"We … errr… don't know who it is," Reg squeaked. "I've had my guys look into it. They can't find where it's manufactured or who's selling it."

Fuck. Reg was so nervous, he'd stopped using the code.

"Use the damn code," I commanded. We designed it to protect us if the feds listened in to us. I scrubbed my tense, aching jaw. "Fuck, Reg, you're fucking me up the ass in more than one way."

"Leave it with me, Slade," Reg stumbled over his words. "I'll get you a name, I swear."

"Do what I pay you for, Reg!" My voice filled with the deadly promise I intended to keep. "Or it's your ass on the line." I hung up on him and hurled my phone at the wall, smashing it into hundreds of pieces.

"Shall I resurrect that?" Zethan smirked. Stealthy bastard stood halfway between my desk and door, carrying two beer bottles.

"Motherfucker," I growled. "You can resurrect something as small as a phone but not a damn person."

He didn't take the insult to heart. Broken pieces of metal and plastic reassembled in his palms until it was whole again. "My god was the one cut to pieces by yours, asshole. Isis resurrected Osiris with the help of Thoth. Inanimate objects are not living, and that's my domain." He set the mended phone in one waiting palm and the chilled beer in another.

"Thanks." Fuck, I'd be up shit creek if I didn't have my second in command.

Over a beer, I informed my VP of my conversation with Reg.

"We need Castor on this pronto to get intel on our competitors," Zethan said. Agreed.

"Castor!" I shouted through the door Zethan left open. "Get your ass in here."

My enforcer appeared a few moments later, crossing his arms and leaning on the wall by my desk. "What's up, Prez?"

I told him what had happened. "Find anything you can. If it's the same cunt who sent the riders, then your channels will probably be blank, but do what you can. This fucker is not going to steal our position in the market. We can't fucking afford that."

"Sure thing, Prez." Castor gave me a solemn, unconvincing nod that twisted my gut in knots. His channels were more silent than an empty football stadium. Someone knew what we were. What we could do. And they fucked with us to destroy us. No other explanation for it.

An alarm went off on my phone. A reminder.

"Everyone in church, now," I growled at Zethan, snatching the orange-ribboned box from my desk and shoving it under my arm.

"You got it." Zethan's ripped form flexed beneath his red flannel as he backed away.

I didn't know why he hid his shredded body beneath the cloth. Sure, he had a few scars. What Jackal didn't? He should be showing that shit off. Chicks loved it. I'd seen the way Aaliyah's eyes lit up when she looked at him, her gaze roaming over his physique. The same way they *roved* over my body.

Outside in the hall, I caught my mate's gaze, giving her my signature cocky smile. The faint glimmer of magick over her shoulder concealed her shifter wings tucked at her back. Woman looked incredible in her dark, tight jeans molded over her yoga-toned pins, and the new leather jacket resting over her shoulders and wings. My jackal growled that Castor bought it for her when I was the gift man. Still, she looked a real Jackal in it. Her glossy, dark hair hung over one shoulder, tempting me to reach out and tug it, dragging her to me for a kiss.

"Mornin', Nurse A." I cupped the back of her neck, claiming what was mine. "Looking beautiful today." My lips burned to seal over hers, but her reluctance shifted along the bond, and I held back. Me. Slade Vincent. Holding fucking back.

My dick stirred at the memory of her acceptance of all the fire and destruction of my god. At her letting me claim her. Then all the fire in my cock went out with a hiss at her words rattled in my head. *The only action you're seeing for a long time is with your hand.* I'd put her through hell, and she was intent on raking me over the coals for it.

"Slade." Her lush, plump lips pulled into a casual, friendly smile. Nothing more. Nothing less. No more fucking Mr. Vincent. Woman left me cold and aching in the hall as she escaped my grasp and filed in behind Alaric. Her vanilla and cherry scent taunted my nose, and I breathed her in, making my balls tighten more.

My throat closed up at the lost fire in her eyes every time she looked at me now. The pitiful howl of my jackal reverberated through every bone. The thought of losing her opened up a gaping wound in the center of my chest. I couldn't lose another mate.

Fuck. Why did I admit defeat? Slade Vincent won every time. I might have lost a few battles, both with the club and

Aaliyah, but I wasn't beaten. Not yet. Not ever. I'd do whatever it took to light that damn fire in her eyes again.

Members crowded in the church room, solemn and quiet since Jaxx's execution. No one blamed me for it. Pitfall of the job. They all knew what they signed up for. If they didn't like it, the dicks knew where the door was.

My asshole tightened. This meeting would be as unpleasant as the last with the news I had to deliver. Fury came on quick, engulfing all other emotions. I swiped at the drink Alaric prepared me and drained it whole.

"Morning. Just wanted to give you an update," I informed my club, voice hoarse, throat raw. "We're in the process of offloading two of our businesses to repay the Pharaoh debt. Sorry, Benny, but I've got to sell Ink It."

I hated to cull any of my businesses, but we needed fast cash, and the tattoo parlor was the most popular in town. We'd had several offers in the past, and judging by them, the parlor was bound to sell for a decent price, and quickly.

"Fuck." Benny slammed his fists against the table.

"We still own Dirty Ink, and you can work there."

"I built Ink It from the ground up, President," the barrel-chested artist whined, sparking fury to lash at my insides.

I cast a glance at Zethan. His solitary nod urged me on like a buoy keeping me afloat amid the stormy sea. Without him, I'd have burned this goddamn room down. Didn't need Benny's bitch'n when the club, everyone's ass was on the line. This action would save us all.

I scraped a hand through my hair. "Once we get back on our feet, we'll try and get it back."

Benny muttered something under his breath. I didn't hear it over the thundering pulse in my ears.

*Just test me, fucker.*

"I'm also scrapping the Myrtleford Bar," I announced.

"Fuck no!" Brix's favorite watering hole.

Dick liked to flirt with our waitresses, give them tips, and hook up with them occasionally. Used our fucking spare club rooms for nookie behind his old lady's back. Had her in here last month, balling her goddamn eyes out. Asshole needed to keep his dick in his pants and obey the oath he swore at his wedding. What good was his word to me if he couldn't keep it with his damn old lady?

Fire stormed through my veins as I raised two palms. "This is best for the club. Unless anyone here has the cash to pump us up." I leveled every member with a challenging stare. "Any bright ideas to keep us afloat?"

No one said jack shit. Just as I expected. Assholes could bitch and moan but never provide a solution. That fell to me as president.

My dry throat ached, and I rubbed at it. Always on the ready, Alaric poured me another drink, and I threw it back. The sting of whisky dulled the other emotions raging within me.

I gave him a nod and went on, "Getting Pharaoh back into production is priority. A dirty cunt copied our recipe and is selling it, undercutting us."

Murmurs swept through the room, stoking the flames banking behind me.

"We're gonna take out this cunt when we find out who he is," I growled. "I won't have this club lose its spot in the club ranks. Got it?"

Everyone nodded in agreement. The club worked hard to get to where we were. Blood, sweat, and fucking tears. No cunt would take that from us. Especially not some gutless fucker who hid in the shadows and got Danny and his mutts, and hitmen to do their dirty work. Snake didn't even have the balls to face us. Balls he'd lose when we finally caught up.

I'd cut them off and shove them so far down his throat, he'd choke on them.

I accepted another finger of whisky, an endless supply Alaric kept on tap for me. "On to the next item of business." I picked up the pale blue box wrapped with an orange ribbon from the lectern.

"Gonna start wearing a dress are ya', President?" Kill Bill triggered rowdy laughter throughout the room.

"Very funny, asshole." I clunked the box on his head in passing. "I want to put this to a vote. I propose to bring in a new prospect."

Everyone's gaze went to Aaliyah as I set the box in front of her. More than a few eyes narrowed with suspicion and doubt. We never welcomed a female into the club before. First time for everything.

She pushed it away, and I growled. "We agreed I'd be a temporary medic."

I shrugged and threw her another smirk. "Changed my mind." I needed an excuse to make her stick around. Something more than a temporary arrangement. She was my mate, and I'd not let her leave easily. Hell, I'd tie her up, throw her back in the cell if necessary. "I'm giving you the choice to stay with us and be a real family. One that doesn't shoot the people you love or betray you."

She choked back a sob. "Slade ..." The words jammed in her throat.

"What do you say, fuckers? Show those hands. Yay or nay."

I counted every hand that shot up. Twenty hands. A few slowly raised. Four remained by their sides. Brix and his little trio of bitches. Majority ruled.

"Excellent." I patted my mate's shoulder, desperate to touch her. Anything, even the tiniest drop. My body was starved for her. "What do you say, Nurse A? Want to join us?

Become one of the family?"

Aaliyah's gaze skimmed across the men at the table, pausing on the disapproving glares, lifting her chin defiantly at them. She plucked the box's lid off, removing a small, black cut with a caduceus symbol and the name Queen Hellhound stitched into the leather. I gave her the title hellhound to honor her father. Queen because she was our damn queen. I wanted to put on the ankh, the symbol of her goddess, Isis, but I couldn't give away her identity. Our secret must remain one. If the rest of the club discovered who we really were, they could use it against us. Team up with other clubs to take us down. Five avatars with the powers of gods were a huge threat to the other clubs. If that happened, I hoped our members were smart enough to choose the winning team. The team that could turn them to ash with a blink of an eye.

"Queen Hellhound," she choked out.

Her face remained cool and neutral, but I felt the twist of pain in her chest as she lifted the leather, turned it, revealing the logo on the back. A snarling Jackal with the words Jackal's Wrath MC embroidered on it. My heart melted when she traced the medicine symbol, lingering on the name, and closed her eyes. Tremors rippled through the bond. Anger. Vengeance. She brought the cut to her nose, sniffing it. Tears streaked down her cheeks as her eyes snapped open.

"What's wrong?" I knelt by her side, my hand on her knee, squeezing.

She swiped at her tears and hiccupped. "Nothing."

Terrible liar. Woman appreciated the nickname as a tribute to her father. Surprise in our link told me that she didn't expect everyone to welcome her when she was from the enemy. Or for me to give her the choice to come on board. Zethan always called me a bull in a china shop. I was the leader, my will unbending like my god's. But that got me nowhere with my mate, and I needed a change of tactic to win her over.

"He was a good man, Aaliyah. We all respected the hellhound." I tightened my grip, desperate to stop my woman's flow of tears. Upsetting my mate tore me up inside.

Several members backed me up with murmurs of support.

Aaliyah clutched the cut to her breast. "Thank you, Slade. Everyone."

"We've never had a woman member before," Brix interrupted, and I burned him with a glare.

Prick was still dirty at Aaliyah for accusing him of leering at her when she went to the ladies' room. I threatened to knock out his fucking teeth if he ever looked at her again. Fucker hadn't glanced her way since.

"Why not?" I asked. "She can ride, shoot, and if you get shot, you'll want her saving your ass."

"I don't want to be a member," Aaliyah defended herself, and I knew it to be another lie. Conflict twisted in her chest. She didn't know which side to choose, us or herself. "So don't get your panties in a knot, Brix."

He flushed red and leaned forward menacingly, making my jackal snarl at the disrespect shown to my woman. "I don't wear fuckin' panties!"

Tension simmered between those two. Aaliyah didn't appreciate the heavy-handed way he guarded her last week. Brix didn't take the scolding and threats very well. Me, personally, I enjoyed the fucking fireworks. My mate was a damn firecracker, and I never wanted to contain those sparks.

"Could have fooled me, Brix." Aaliyah's grip on the cut stiffened. Woman would fit right in with the club just nicely. Could give it as good as she took it. "We can all see your ass crack when you bend over. Definitely some lace there."

Brix glanced around at the other members, and Castor sniggered, initiating a few chuckles and snorts.

Aaliyah leveled a hard glare at her challenger, giving rise to the conflict in her heart. She was torn right down the middle. "I only agreed to stay and be the club's medic until my brother and the Wolves are dealt with." Fuck. Throw me under the bus, woman. Set fire to my peace offering. Roll over with a truck and back it up again. "I don't know if I'll stay beyond that." Her eyes met mine, like blades to my heart. "Don't worry your pretty lacey bows off, Brix."

"Fuck off!" Brix pushed his chair away. "I don't wear bows."

"Yeah? Show us?" Alaric chimed in.

Fuck. I shook my head and covered my eyes as Brix proved his point, unbuttoning his jeans, sliding them down to expose his jocks. No lace. Definitely no bows. Thank fuck. Cotton sporting an extremely small cock.

"Put your goddamn junk away." I snatched Aaliyah's whisky and swallowed it. Fuck. That was a sight I'd never erase from my mind. "We don't need to see that shit."

"She wanted to see a real man." Brix grabbed his almost non-existent crotch, jiggled it, then shoved it back in his jeans. The club howled.

Real man, my ass. Prick cheated on his old lady. Shifters like me didn't do that kind of shit.

"Fuck. On that note." I moved to the podium to grab my gavel. "Church is dismissed."

Everyone leapt from their seats, hooting, laughing, clapping Brix or Aaliyah on the back. She was one of us, all right. No matter what she said. Woman could deny it until she lost her breath. I just had to make her see it.

A loud voice broke through the commotion. "What about a funeral for Jaxx and Tank?" Rusty. How could he defend that fucking traitor?

Everyone stopped in their tracks and spun to face him.

My blood temperature shot up one hundred degrees. "We're having a service for Tank tomorrow." I didn't mention the traitor whose body I'd burned to a cinder. Relished every fucking second of watching it go up in flames. Afterwards, Castor created a spell to make it look like Jaxx's body curled in the freezer out back.

"We should bury him." Fucking Rusty wouldn't let it go.

I squeezed my gavel almost to the snapping point. "That traitorous cunt doesn't deserve a burial or us paying our respects."

"What about his missus?" I twitched with irritation at Rusty's badgering.

"What about her?" I leaned forward, and Rusty glanced away from my murderous glare.

"We should give her some money to look after the kids," Rusty muttered.

"Her filthy husband chose to betray us," I snapped, curling my fingers into a fist to stop myself from flinging my glass across the table and smashing it on the wall. "He probably got paid by Danny to rat on us. She's not getting a fucking cent from us. She's dead to us. Got it?" Club rules. Jaxx took the oath and broke it. Fucker should have thought of his kids before betraying us. "And if I hear of one of you giving her any money, I'll fucking put a bullet through your skull."

I was an unforgiving and ruthless prick when it came to anyone who screwed over the club. Had to be in my role. After Mom was gunned down in front of me, Dad changed, hardened up. He taught me how to rule with a merciless and severe hand. We didn't get to the top six clubs in the country by being sympathetic and kind. Rules were drilled into every member, and they knew the consequences for breaking them. If they betrayed their club, they were dead, and their family on their own. Incentive to remain loyal.

Everyone murmured a *"Yes, President,"* at me, and I unclenched my fists, watching them break away from the room.

Aaliyah waited for everyone but the avatars to leave. Then she stood, carrying the cut, shoving it at my chest and leveling me with a fierce glare. "Don't put me on the spot like that again."

## CHAPTER 4

### *A*aliyah

GUILT WRACKED MY CHEST. It should be me in that box. The riders were after me, ordered to retrieve me for my brother. Deliver me to him so he could personally oversee my slaying. At least, that was the story Zethan fed me. Tank was a casualty, shot and betrayed by Jaxx as the riders brought our truck to a halt.

Bitter day for a send-off. Miserable, gray skies. Growling wind ripping at our hair and clothes, muffling the eulogy and sniffles in the crowd. Solemn faces in the throng listened intently as Slade delivered Tank's tribute. Faces that would liven up back at the club afterparty. Bandanas on the arms of mourners flickered in the breeze. Material with Tank's emblem on it, a military tank with two wrenches behind it. A custom for a biker funeral.

It made me think of the cut Slade designed for me. Perfect

for me. Reflected my medic role. Honored my fallen father. Honored my goddess with the title of queen. Honored me. Fuck, I was emotional after church yesterday from thinking about dad, and snapped at Slade. While the gift was sweet and heartfelt, it was designed to bond me to the club, connect us as family, give me a reason to stay with my mates. I got angry at Slade for giving me another reason to stay when I had to leave. This life wasn't for me. Life with the Jackals was no fairy tale, and would only end badly for me, inviting death for my mates or me. The Wolves stole my ex and father. Leaving the bikers behind was the smarter choice. I'd done it once and had to find the strength to do it again. Except when the time came, I wasn't sure I'd have the resolution.

Every member of Jackal's Wrath MC rode in the funeral procession with his helmet off. Only along the strip of the cemetery, though. Couldn't give the Bathurst Police more reason to arrest them when the Jackals were under enough heat from the cops. Tank's widow, Jess, rode bitch with Slade out of respect for her husband.

I rubbed at my goosebumped arms, freezing in my low-cut dress ... all that I could get on with these damn wings piercing my shoulder blades. Damn things still hadn't absorbed back into my body, forcing Castor to spell them invisible. Shoved under my trench coat, they made me look like a hunchback, but thankfully, only the avatars could see them. Everyone else saw a regular shape of me. Because of my awkward appendages, I hid at the back of the group of mourners, wary of touching anyone with my appendages.

Sorrow hung heavy in the air. I didn't do well with funerals, family member or not. Death was inevitable when working in an emergency room. It never got easier, even after three years of practicing. A unit in my nursing degree prepared us for the difficulty we'd encounter. Hardship faced by patients, sickness, trauma, illness, and death. It cautioned us to put aside our conflict and emotion to perform our duty. Without that distance and detachment, I never would have lasted a day. Every loss hit me hard. I felt like I failed that person in my duty of care.

If it weren't for Isis' counsel reminding me that life was a constant cycle of rebirth and death, I'd have gone crazy. As a fertility goddess, she gave rise to the crops, the water of the Nile, bringing food to sustain life. Osiris, her husband, balanced out death, breaking down the stalks and roots of the harvested crops, giving fertilizer to support new life.

A warm hand squeezed mine. Castor, positioned to my left and looking fine in his dark jeans, buttoned shirt, and cut. A constant source of warmth and support. I leaned my head on his shoulder, inhaling his spicy cologne.

Jealousy stung the mate bond. Two other men surrounding me wanted me close to them too. Wise to the power of the link, I pushed aside the emotion and intensity doing its best to sway me.

*Not today, Satan. Not today.*

Alaric boxed me in on the other side, arms folded behind his back like a soldier standing at ease. His spiny words and lack of trust hurt me. Regret squeezed our connection like a pinched nerve, flaring at every expression of intimacy between Castor and me. Alaric and I agreed to a fresh start. He had so much to make up for and didn't know where to start, what to say to me, and he kept squirming, glancing at me.

Zethan hovered a couple of paces away, leaving my heart lonely and longing for my true mate. He too played me with the phone, fooling me into thinking he wanted to get acquainted. Acts I'd not forgive from the shamed or apologetic sensations failing to lull me back under his spell. He fidgeted as well, rolled his shoulders, and shifted. Golden wisps swept all about him, outlines of humans, faces, bodies, and forms. Souls begging for release, encircling him, pestering him, whispering their pleas. Annoyed, he waved them away, and they'd vanish for a few moments, then creep back to harass him. All in a day's work for the King of the Underworld.

Up at the podium, Slade's wobbling voice called me back to the eulogy. His eyes were swollen and red. Lines grooved his rugged mouth. Smoke and melting steel twisted in his veins. Barely contained rage building to pressure that would explode. His throat clicked as he gave a hard swallow. Unable to get the words out, he finished his speech early, stepping away from the podium. His heartfelt and respectful speech surprised me. I thought he'd say something crude and inappropriate.

Remorse so powerful crashed through him. He blamed himself for Tank's death. Exposing the mole in the club cost him a good man, and he questioned whether it was worth it. Overwhelmed by his grief, he nudged Alaric aside to take position next to me. Heavy breaths heaved out of his chest as if every inhale scratched and burned his lungs. Need to touch me pulled our connection so taut I feared it might snap. A tumultuous storm begging for calm, he needed me as much as I needed him. Both of us were weighed down by our guilt, like shackles on our ankles, dragging us into the watery depths.

Sympathetic to his needs, I took his hand, clasping it between mine, sending a bolt of electricity through me that ended between my legs. He was starved for contact. Hungry for his mate. Hell, so was I. Except I was stubborn and not ready to forgive and forget so easily. The storm within him lowered from a category three to a one. He glanced at me, a grim smile my only thanks. That one look lit the kindling inside my heart. Harsh winds caused by my resistance threatened to blow out the small spark.

The funeral officiant closed the ceremony and ushered everyone to pick up the shovel and toss dirt onto the coffin before it was lowered into the ground. Bury our brother at arms. Slade tugged me over to the wooden casket, collecting the shovel from the officiant and tossing dirt onto the lid. The rest of the club and I followed his lead. Before we moved away, I sent Tank a silent prayer, thanking him for protecting me and the other Jackals two nights ago. Not that it meant anything when he left behind a wife and two kids.

Slowly the crowd dispersed as the ceremony finished. Slade held me there as bikes started, rumbling as they warmed up and roaring as they took off. Per tradition, they revved their bikes for each year Tank was a member of the Jackals, eight in total.

Slade surprised me, clasping the side of my face and leaning down to place a soft, imposing kiss on my lips. Fiery heat scorched my heart and chest. "Thank you, Nurse A," he whispered.

Startled, I moved back, touching my lips. "I'm not ready for that." A kiss wouldn't heal everything he put me through.

"Ride with me?" the Jackal's president proposed with a crooked, half smile. "Keep your old man warm?"

It would take a lot more than charm to break down the walls between us. An apology for starters. I'd given him the wrong impression by taking his hand. The fucking mate bond betrayed my every thought. I had to temper that bitch down just like my heart. I wrapped my jacket tighter over my chest, and marched out of the ceremony, leaving him behind.

Castor jogged to catch up to me. "He's hurting right now. We all are. Slade blames himself for Tank's death."

Tell me something I didn't know. Tank died because my brother wanted me back. Wanted to kill me to justify a turf war. Something I never forgot.

"And I'm not hurting?" I slammed on the brakes to stop in the middle of the cemetery. "Innocent people are dying because of Danny."

Fuck. I cringed. Why was I bringing myself into this equation? This was a tribute for Tank, not an Aaliyah pity fucking party.

"It's not your fault." Castor's hand simmered on my cheek, and I closed my eyes, letting his heat leach into me.

Guilt burned in the pit of my stomach. "Maybe if I stayed with the Wolves ... I could have prevented this." Then my dad might still be alive. Dad would have kept Danny in check. The women he used in his porn and snuff films would be safe and alive. Tank wouldn't have perished. I wouldn't have been a bitch to Slade when he only wanted to thank me for soothing him. Shit. This was all too much.

"Aaliyah, there's no point torturing yourself with what ifs."

Fuck, Castor was right. It was pointless arguing with the avatar of knowledge and wisdom.

Later at the wake, the club partied, celebrating Tank's career with the Jackals. The smell of baked food, salads, roasted meats, and desserts filled my nose. Children squealed from out in the backyard where the club had erected play equipment. Alcohol flowed freely between the adults. Beer glasses clinked. Bikers threw back tumblers of whisky. Kill Bill told funny stories, making the room holler. Tank's wife both cried and laughed at her husband's antics.

I walked through the clubhouse, greeting members as I passed. "Hey, Benny." I smiled as I squeezed past him on the way to the bar.

He grunted in response, and in a sign of solidarity, went

to stand beside Brix with two other members. Men that didn't vote to bring me on as a prospect. Men that glared sourly at me from across the clubhouse, muttering something to each other. Bitching most likely that I was a Savage Wolf.

I was used to being the lone wolf. The only girl in the club. Not a patched member. A wannabe doing everything to win that position and the respect of the club. Pipe dreams. Only allowed to hang out at the club and go on some missions because of who my father was. Always an outsider. History repeating itself. Good thing I didn't plan to stick around too long. Valued myself way too much to accept being treated like dirt.

Alaric stood by my side, keeping my crystal glass topped. One of his radios crackled with a message, but he turned the volume down. After half an hour of guarding me somewhat, he finally summoned the courage to speak to me. "Don't worry about those assholes. Brix bitches about everything."

"Good to know." I'd hardened up to dickheads like that. Encountered them all my life. During my time with my dad's club. At the hospital with arrogant doctors or condescending senior nurses—the newest nurse who got hit with all the abuse.

I clutched a whisky tumbler, turning the crystal back and forth, the light catching the amber liquid. My heart twisted, remembering my father and how much he also loved his drink. I hissed at the sip of liquid burning my throat.

"Still guarding me?" I asked Alaric, eager for some conversation. Anything to strip away the guilt eating away at my stomach for Tank's death.

"Old habits die hard, huh?" He smiled and tossed back his drink.

Liar. That wasn't the real reason he stuck to my side. The mate bond betrayed his desire to talk to me, except he flushed with shame for the way he'd conducted himself. He didn't know how to start up a conversation with me. Wasn't sure if I'd respond to him. The soldier needed me to take the lead.

Shadows of stubble dotted his chin, which was strange for him, since he kept himself so straight and clean. He smelled like fresh linen and soft spices on top of his natural scent of pine and loam. His golden eye glowed as it devoured me everywhere, and my skin tingled all over, basking under the gentle warmth of it, like the first ray of sunlight in Spring.

As a former Air Force serviceman, I assumed he was used to his comrades being injured or dying. Service in the line of duty and all that. Not that it made it any easier with each loss.

"Thought I'd keep you company." Unable to look me in the eye, he tucked his glass behind his back, standing at ease. His dark brown hair stood on end, rather than gelled back like he normally wore it. "Repay the favor from the other night."

"It was nothing." My duty, if anything.

The ambush shook him and sent him spiraling into a PTSD episode. While Slade took care of the traitor, executing him in front of the club, I held back with Alaric, supporting him. Goddess knew, someone as damaged as Alaric needed all the comfort he could get.

"Hey, I know I'm the wildcard of the bunch, and you're probably hesitant after what … happened at the shelter … and what happened last week." His sharp jaw ground on the last word, and I marveled at the strength and definition in it. Like the claw or beak of a hawk. "But I'd really like you to come have dinner with me. I'll show you my astronomy setup. Horus can get me places that a telescope can't."

He smiled on the last bit, an expression I rarely got to

glimpse. Shame really, since he had perfect, pillowy lips that a girl's mouth could fall onto and never return from. Even better teeth. Straight. White. Handsome.

Alaric and I came to an understanding in the back of the truck where I'd healed his injured wing. A fresh start to wipe the slate clean after multiple tense confrontations. I didn't want there to be any more animosity between us. His suspicion and mistrust came from a dark place, and I suspected it was the reason he was damaged and suffering PTSD. Someone or thing had hurt him, and he lost a part of himself. I'd be lying if I said a part of me didn't want to take that man and heal him. I couldn't bear to see the sleek, beautiful hawk caged by memory and ghosts.

"I'd like that." I took another sip to wash away the pleased heat spreading through my chest.

"Good." He grinned and relaxed his stance. Goddess, his smile could knock a girl off her bike and cause her to have an accident. And the man could wield it like a weapon, like Slade deployed his dimples on me. "How about later this week?"

I didn't get to answer when Slade shouted above the hum in the room, "Pipe down, you assholes, I've got something to say." He came to stand beside Tank's widow, Jess, with something tucked under his arm. "On behalf of the club, I'd like to present you with Tank's cut and lifetime membership." Slade pulled her in for a bear hug. "Don't worry, Jess, we'll look after you. We'll keep up Tank's salary, so you don't have to worry about a thing."

Tears spilled down Jess' cheeks as she accepted her husband's cut. She was too overwhelmed to get a word out.

Fuck, that was incredibly generous of Slade, especially with the club's financial troubles. But then again, the Jackals took care of my apartment rent and car payments, and I wasn't even a member. The president could be so kind and generous on the one hand and ruthless on another. He hadn't extended Jaxx's wife the same courtesy. Not that it was any of my business when the club was Slade's to run.

Zethan caught my eye from the corner of the room where he kept his distance, drinking alone and solemn. My heart urged me to go over and keep him company. No, I couldn't. His eyes burned with lament that struck me to the core. He wanted to make things right between us. We were divided as mates when we needed unity to fight the enemy threatening to destroy us.

My heart screamed at me just to get over it. Kiss and fucking make up. But it wasn't that simple. We both broke each other's trust. I infiltrated the shelter and club under false pretenses. He treated me like a criminal he investigated, gifting me a phone, using it to assess my guilt like a damn detective. All the while, I thought he showed me the same kindness and compassion he extended to the women in his shelter. We'd been raw, vulnerable, and open with each other. I told him my shame of adopting my daughter. He spoke of losing his son to heart failure. I felt bruised from sharing my most personal secrets only to be used by him. Rarely did I let anyone see that side of me. Always had to be tough like that. *Don't show anyone your weaknesses, baby girl,* my dad used to tell me. Now I'd shut down on Zethan and locked him out.

Still, Zethan and Castor convinced Slade to give me the benefit of the doubt. Without their backing, I'd be stuck captive inside the cell. They granted me freedom and the chance to show my loyalty when we attended the Summernat biker rally. Because of that, I owed Zethan my gratitude. Jury was out on my feelings for him. The next few weeks might be another story. A fresh start was in order there, too.

He pulled out his phone and typed something. Moments later, my phone buzzed in my pocket. I couldn't bring myself to read or respond to the multiple messages he sent me since I moved in with Castor two days ago. Time and space apart would help me think clearly without the damn mate bond clouding my judgment. Fuck, these four men were going to be my undoing.

## CHAPTER 5

*A*aliyah

**Two Days Later**

"Pass me the spring onion." Castor called me away from staring at the screen of my beeping phone.

The thing hadn't stopped going off since the funeral. Unread messages from Zethan. Like Slade, he also took the loss of Tank hard and needed an outlet. Funny memes or hellhound pics flicked through. Cute little enticements to talk to him.

Castor leaned over me to grab the garnish for the Moroccan stew he prepared for the other avatars. "You ever going to answer him?"

"When I can think straight." Stiff muscles called me down to the yoga mat Castor bought me. Being shot and cooped in the cell were not conducive to a healthy body, and I needed to stretch out my tight, protesting muscles.

Castor flexed his hands, and the screen lit up, characters typing on the dash without being touched. "Stop punishing him. Talk to him. You have to forgive him at some point."

I wasn't ready to forgive or forget just yet. While I performed the downward dog, bending my body into a V, touching the floor with my feet and palms, I thought about his comment. I had three men to forgive. Men who accused me of false motivations. Proving my innocence to them was exhausting. All the back-and-forth arguments. It only took saving Alaric from a gunshot wound, me rescuing the Jackals' asses from lockup in a Canberra police station, and fighting my way out of another ambush to convince them of my innocence and trustworthiness.

Now we were at a stalemate. We were stuck with each other until my brother and his club were dealt with. My heart was a sappy little bitch, skipping through the flowers doing cartwheels, elated to be surrounded by her mates. Fucking flowers and cartwheels! My mind was a bitter, scorned woman, seeking redemption for my father, and fighting the undeniable and intense attraction to these four, unique men. Beyond that, I was a confused mess and didn't know what the future held for me. I had a home to go back to but no job. Based on Slade's actions with the cut and his general habit of steamrolling me, he'd pressure me to stay with them as their prospect, medic, and mate. Time would tell what decision I'd make.

As I moved into a cow pose, my phone beeped as Castor sent a message from my phone with his Thoth magick. Glaring at him, I climbed to my feet and snatched it off him to read it. *"Chat tonight?"*

Shit. Now he locked me into confronting Zethan.

"Fuck, Castor. Thanks a lot." I pressed a hand to my forehead. I wasn't ready. Didn't know what to say to Zethan.

Castor pointed his cooking knife at me. "He convinced Slade to treat you innocent until proven guilty. You owe it to him to hear him out."

I hated that Castor was right. Hated even more that the gods and the curse decided my mates for me. Hated that I had no choice in this. Mostly, I hated that I couldn't tell if my feelings were genuine or a result of the mate bond.

Castor was the kind of guy I'd date. Zethan, too. Alaric had that sweet, romantic appeal if he wasn't so bitter and damaged. Slade, cocky, forceful, not my type at all. But his rugged wildness called to me on a deeper level. I couldn't look past his generosity, his fierce desire to protect me, and the fact that the rough man could be so sweet when he wanted to. In a way, he reminded me of the guy your parents warned you not to date. The bad boy. Girls always married men like their dads. And boy, did Slade resemble my dad.

Castor threw the diced onions into the pot. "You're going to dinner with Alaric. Don't be a fucking hypocrite."

Right again. I hadn't forgiven Alaric, but went easy on him because of his PTSD, while I held it against Zethan. That wasn't fair. I was a hypocrite for more than one reason. I did the same thing as Zethan, misleading and tricking Castor to get information out of him, pretending to be a judge questioning a defendant.

"Fine." I groaned into my hands as I placed them over my face.

Confusion ran through me as I rubbed at the back of my neck. If I looked at it logically, I would have done the same if I were in Zethan's place. Get to know the person and determine their motives. I couldn't blame him for doing his job. Still didn't make it any easier to digest. I'd let him say his piece.

"Go back to your Isis cow pose," Castor teased, sticking two horned fingers on top of his head, mooing at me. "I want to see you work that sexy ass of yours."

I laughed at him. "What about the crane pose?" I got back onto the mat. "That could substitute for an ibis pose?" I slowly tested myself, lifting myself onto two palms. My body rocked from weakness in my core muscles caused by the gunshot and not doing my stretches in weeks. Repair hadn't made them strong, telling me my magick needed a little tweak.

Castor rushed over to catch me on the hip and shoulder before I clumsily rolled headfirst into the ground. "Mmm. That's a mighty fine ass." His hand cracked on my butt, sending a pleasant sting and burn through me. He bit me on the crease of my hip before righting me into a kneel on my shins.

I thumped him back on the arm. "Get back to cooking, Jamie Oliver!"

"Not until I get a kiss." He leaned in, claiming my mouth, drinking in my lips and taste. "Mmm. You taste like honey."

"Ginger beer," I corrected him, my hands roaming up his body, taking in his broad, strong chest.

"Whatever, you wily wench." Demanding fingers knotted in my hair, tugging me closer. "Give me some more of that sugar." His mouth sealed over mine, rough, dragging, scraping. Slow. Oh, so slow. Like he had all the time in the world. I could barely breathe amid the sweeping brush of our lips and his tongue hauling me deeper under his spell. Soft, tempting, and beguiling. More than just a kiss. An assertion of ownership.

I sank my fingers through his dark, curly hair, locking him to me, unable to get enough of him. Electricity charged in my skin as he draped one arm over my shoulder, cupping the back of my neck. Every cell in my body buzzed with new life. I breathed in his spicy cinnamon scent. Clawing hunger crawled through me, and I wanted to straddle his lap. I wanted him to keep going and wipe away the reasons why I shouldn't be doing this. But I was afraid that I got too close to him. Let my guard down. This kiss was a massive reminder of why it was dangerous to fall deeper.

The stew bubbled on the stove, demanding stirring so it didn't burn. It smelled incredible. Beef, potatoes, carrots, and beans in a thick, tomato gravy. Crusty bread baked in the oven, making my mouth water and my stomach growl like a bear waking from hibernation.

Castor groaned, struggling to pull himself away from me. "If we didn't have visitors tonight, I'd fuck you on the counter and eat sticky date sauce from your pussy all night long." His hungry promise crackled through my body and ended between my legs.

"Tempting." I linked my arms behind his neck, not wanting to let him go.

I was dangerously close to falling for this man. Thoughtful and considerate, he brought me clothes and anything else I needed to make my stay satisfying. He offered me comfort and protection in his dark, dangerous biker world, and I knew if any harm found me, he'd do anything to save me. Locked in his maple gaze, I couldn't look away and didn't want to when he stared at me like I meant the world to him. Hell, this man checked so many boxes: intelligent, funny, sexy, respectful, trusting, honest, dominant, and affectionate.

This time, it was just him and me. No puppet strings pulled by the mate bond. These feelings belonged to us. Everything had shifted between us in the space of a week, and my feelings grew by the day.

Despite that, some deep part of me remained unconvinced this was a side effect of the curse and none of it was real. It had my mind and heart in a spin. This whole experience frightened me how he had the power to take control of my mind and body and left me helpless to resist him. Maybe that was why I was adamant to leave once our business with Danny was concluded.

"Come on, dark sorceress." Castor snagged my hand and pulled me to my feet. "Stop trying to seduce me. No more yoga. My dick is so hard watching you shake that ass, it might snap off."

I moved to stand behind him at the counter, arms around his waist, rubbing his groin, teasing him. Bad idea. Touching him made me forget all my doubts. This man called to my heart and soul. Resisting him was like fighting a losing battle. "Maybe I can help alleviate that tension."

We had some fun while riding back from the magick shop in town. I loved the feel of his thick, steely length in my fist. Now I wanted that velvety length wrapped in my mouth.

He ground into my hand and glanced over his shoulder with gleaming, wicked eyes. "Sex magick and cooking. That's a first for me."

I bumped him away from the counter, positioning myself between his legs. Looking up at him under my lashes, I dragged my hand down his stomach, over his hips, along his thighs as I sank to my knees. He let out a surprised breath as I flicked open his jean's button and drew his zipper down. That breath sharpened as I removed his cock and grazed his blunt head with my tongue. A dominant hand settled on my head as I teased his shaft, lapping at him. His groan of need was swallowed as I traced teasing circles on his tip.

"Fuck, dark sorceress." Tremors coursed through his body as he grappled with stirring the stew at the same time.

I sank my mouth over his head, working over his cock. He hissed and thrust himself deeper. Smooth, velvety steel.

"Yeah, like that, baby," he praised as I dragged my lips

over his long, thick, scorching length. "Oh, fuck." He threw his head back and let go of the wooden spoon, all his focus zeroing in on the pleasure echoing down the mate bond.

His arousal made my own ache for his touch. Electric pulses raced through me as he caressed my hair. I swallowed his groan of need as I traced circles on his tip. As if responding to me, I felt the whisper of a finger on my clit, and I jolted and released his cock.

"Just go with it, baby." Castor smiled down at me with drugged, heavy lids. "I never let my girl go without."

Magick touched me, alleviating my burning need. Desperate for my own release, I returned the smile, welcoming his foreign, seductive caress. His power stroked my throbbing bud, and I arched my back, the slight gesture setting me on fire. That one move spread the greedy, hollow ache through my body. Delicate, teasing brushes of my tongue made him twitch fiercely inside my mouth. He stroked the growing pulse between my thighs, making me shudder and cry out over his length.

"Yeah, baby, scream over my cock," Dark Daddy spoke. Deep, dominant, demanding. The triple D.

Strained breaths dragged from Castor's chest as he thrust harder. I sensed his eagerness to feel my pleasure crash over him as he strummed my clit faster, each drag of his magick turning rougher, fiercer, more possessive. He owned my clit, and he knew it. My body purred like a bike engine attuned to his strokes.

His cock was like molten steel in my mouth as I glided over it, working him hard, deep, and fast. The throb in my core deepened as I approached my breaking point. Showing no signs of slowing, he sent me hurtling closer, full speed on a collision course with pleasure. Low, throaty moans told me he was close too, fueling me to bury him deeper and bring him home. Shocks pulsed along my clit as he mercilessly thrummed me with his magick. Aching whimpers exploded over him as my body tensed, my teased orgasm finally arriving at my destination. Shivers wracked his body as he tightened, pumping hot, salty liquid down my throat.

"Fuck, baby, that was incredible." Panting hard, he released my fisted hair, stroking my head and cheek.

I crawled my finger along his slightly ribbed stomach. "Jamie Oliver won't teach you that in a cookbook."

That sexy, throaty laugh of his threatened to throw me back on the bike with him. He clasped my wrist and tugged me to my feet. I reached down to put his bobbing length back in his pants, but he caught my wrist. Firm. Challenging.

"No, dark sorceress," he breathed into my ear, and I fought the tingles shooting from my lobes to my neck. "That was just the entrée. Let Dark Daddy feed you the main course and dessert."

## CHAPTER 6

*Z*ethan

"Fuck, not you, too." Slade removed a huge bunch of roses from the side cart of his bike that outshone the bouquet I clutched. "Rain on my parade, why don't you. Asshole."

Adding to his gifts, he removed three wrapped boxes and two bottles of wine. Going all out to win over our lady's heart, hey? Typical Slade, dripping in gifts, charm, and sex appeal that always won the ladies over. I'd kill to possess an ounce of his confidence. Difficult when I was insecure about being covered in scars.

I chuckled, tucking the bunch of yellow sunflowers under my arm while I hung my helmet on my handlebars. "You're raining on mine."

Last week, Aaliyah conned me into buying Carlie the same flowers for Dylan's birth. Said that yellow represented warmth and happiness. I didn't believe that shit, but I figured the color would remind her of the time we spent together, and the warmth and happiness I longed to give her if she'd let me. Woman hadn't answered my texts in days. Her smile was like the first ray of sunshine after rain. But it was fucking cold under the shadow of her storm.

I tugged at the collar of my buttoned shirt. This was the most dressed-up my mate would ever get me. Suits or jackets weren't my style. Brownie points were on the menu, and I needed as many as I could get out of the doghouse. We all did, except Castor. Wise asshole always knew the right thing to say to placate our mate. A skill I could really use since I wasn't a big talker.

Alaric pulled in behind Slade, all growl on his Chieftain. He alighted from his bike and added to the collection of Aaliyah's gifts with another bouquet of assorted flowers.

"Fuck. We should have coordinated this." I scratched my forehead.

Slade's eyes narrowed to slits as they fell to Alaric's blooms. "Fuck, not you as well." I laughed at how comical his disappointment was.

Alaric hadn't lost his shit-eating grin since scoring dinner with Aaliyah the other day. "Shut your face, bitch! I always bring my mate flowers."

True. He was the gentleman of the three of us. Slade the beast. Me the practical one. Castor the smart one. Smart-ass as well.

"At least you scored a date, asshole." Slade rubbed from his jaw to chin, something he did when stressed. "My dick will be a fossil before our nurse forgives me and lets me out of the doghouse."

Both Alaric and I laughed. Served Slade right for being a fiery bastard and reacting without a clear head. Dude needed to meditate or some shit. Keep calm and not lead with emotion. Constantly lowering him from a destructive storm to a grumble got tiring quickly.

"Laugh it up, dickheads." Slade took the lead to the front door where Castor let us in.

At the sight of Aaliyah in the kitchen slicing the bread fresh out of the oven, I lost my breath. What a fucking vision. Long, curved legs molded in her dark, figure-hugging jeans. A sweatshirt concealed her small waist, but those juicy, wide hips begged to be grabbed. Casual with a hint of sexy. Her top fell below her shoulder blades, allowing her wings to drape unhindered. Silky black hair in a wild mess hung down her back and over her feathers. Her aqua gaze focused on the loaf she sliced.

*Mine.* And I wanted her. A taste of her. Something I'd never get if we couldn't break this curse. Hell on fucking Earth.

"Hey! Hungry?" The nervous tension left her body when her gaze shifted from Slade then Alaric to me.

Eating was the last thing on my mind when my stomach bunched with nerves. I held her stare, trying to get a read on her. Things were awkward between us, and I didn't know where we stood, or if we stood at all.

"That depends on what you're cooking, Nurse A." Slade turned on the charm, diving in first, leaning down, aiming for a sly kiss on the lips that she dodged at the last second. He caught her cheek instead, and his disgruntled twitch shot down our bond. "I got you these. Wasn't sure if you liked red or white wine. Or your favorite chocolate." He recovered well, hiding his dissatisfaction beneath a cool mask and dimpled grin, shoving all his gifts at her.

"Going all out to impress me, hey?" She set aside all the gifts to slip off the card attached to the over-the-top bouquet of roses that put mine and Alaric's to shame.

"For you, anything." Slade winked, laying it on thick.

"Aww, thanks, babe." Castor got in a peck to Slade's cheek. "I'll enjoy the chocolates."

"Don't touch them, you asshole," Slade growled. "They're for her."

Castor chuckled and retreated into the kitchen to grab a weird looking round pot with a flue lid. Some fancy cooking dish.

"I'm not perfect," Aaliyah read from his card. "But I promise to be your partner in crime. Until my last breath." Aaliyah tapped the card against her other hand. "Handwritten too. Thank you. It's very sweet."

"Never took you for a romantic." I punched my president's arm. Never seen him pick up a pen and paper unless it was to sign a contract. That might have also been because he had dyslexia. "Smooth moves."

Appreciation trickled along our link, his sentiment touching her deeply. Who would have thought Slade a charmer? More like a bulldozer. To him, there were no lines to be crossed, and he crossed them like he owned them.

Normally, I would have followed rank in the club, but I held back, rubbing at my stubble and gesturing for Alaric to present his bunch of flowers.

"Smells good." Alaric also laid a kiss on her cheek. Soft. Respectful.

"Aww, you shouldn't have." Aaliyah sniffed his mixed bouquet and clutched them to her chest, a happy blip bumping along our bond.

"Get used to it." Slade clamped two hands on Alaric's shoulders. "This man will spoil you with flowers at every opportunity. Make us assholes look bad on anniversaries."

Anniversaries? *Jesus, Slade. Way to scare her off.*

Aaliyah's eyebrows rose. "I'll need a vase then."

"Or ten." Slade moved to shake Castor's hand and clap him on the back. "Hey, brother."

"Good to see you, Prez."

"Fuck that title shit. Tonight, I'm just Slade."

"Okay, *Just Slade*."

"Smartass." Slade moved around him to sniff at the food Castor set on the dining table. The bear of a man was always hungry. He lifted the lid of a pot to swipe a finger through the stew to taste it. "What fancy-ass shit is this?"

"Moroccan tagine," Castor replied.

Aaliyah's eyes shifted to me. Expectant. Uncertain. "Hey."

"Hey." Despite the risk to us both, I bent down to kiss her cheek, my lips smoking at the contact. "You're looking beautiful." Her hand went to my arm, squeezing lightly, giving me hope that everything would work out. Being this close was dangerous to our lives and my heart. But, hell, my body buzzed with need and uncertainty, tempting me to move in closer and not let go.

She smacked me and withdrew, and instantly I wanted her back. "Bunch of charmers, the lot of you."

Normally, I was a pro at keeping my emotions in check, but my tight grip on control slowly ebbed away. Everything about this woman made me want to lose my head. I wanted to cook her breakfast. Sit her on my bike with me. Rest her on my lap, cuddling. Get her in my damn bed. I couldn't take another second of this doomed fucking relationship tormenting me. Goddamn curse.

"Can we have that chat?" I blurted. "Get it out of the way so dinner isn't awkward."

Muscles in her neck bunched. "Sure." She set aside my bouquet, escorted me into Castor's hallway and into a private room. "What's up?" Her breath came out sharp and hollow. Hell, she was as tense as I was.

I wanted to stroke the lock she brushed out of her eyes, but I kept my hands to myself.

"I know our relationship is strained right now," I started, scratching at my forehead with my thumb. "I just need to know if I'm wasting my time here. You haven't answered my messages. You're angry with me. If you don't want to hear from me anymore, say the word." Fuck. Brutally honest. "Because I don't know what's worse—the pain from being close to you or the pain in my heart from staying away."

My heart struggled to keep a steady beat, and I tensed, bracing for her polite rejection. Nothing I hadn't experienced before. Once women saw my scars, especially on my dick, they ran a mile. Except rejection from my mate was different. That would tear me in two.

She played with her fingers, stretching them. "I've been sorting out my thoughts and feelings without the mate bond complicating things."

"Understandable."

Liz met Alaric first. Then Castor. She didn't have to sort out her feelings all at once. She collected her harem as she went.

Four at once couldn't have been easy on Aaliyah. Four *supposed* enemies. One accused of murdering her father. That shit would mess with your head.

Aaliyah rubbed at her lined forehead, and I wanted to kiss away each crease, ease her worry. "You guys immediately wanted to claim me. I told you I didn't believe in fated mates and wanted a choice. But I'm coming around to the fact that we might be something to each other."

Fuck yeah, we were. Nights ago, she accepted Slade as her mate. Let him claim her in bed. Screamed the fucking clubhouse down. Regret pinched the bond afterward. Didn't change anything.

She scuffed the dark gray carpet with her boot. "If I'm honest, I don't want to date four bikers. I left that life behind after Jimmy died. I want a fairy tale, Zethan. A happy ending, not a horror story. I don't want to worry every minute that you might never come home."

At last, we were getting to the heart of the matter.

Aaliyah's concern about that was a good sign. It meant she saw a future with us. The small sign of hope sent a longing ache through my body.

"Our life isn't for everyone." I swallowed hard. "I understand your misgivings, but I can't promise you a happy ever after or that we'll live until we're eighty."

She nodded, jiggling her leg again and chewing her lip. Fuck. If the woman kept that up, I'd take those lips in mine and suck them.

I focused on what I really wanted to say. "I know I hurt you. This whole situation is a complicated, crazy mess. Like out of a damn drama movie crazy." She cracked a small smile at that. Good. My heart moved into a double beat. I was onto a winner. "I was just doing my duty as VP to back my president, protect my club and brothers from harm."

She jiggled her leg and clasped her hip. "I know. It kind of sucks that my true mate … whatever you are … would do that to me. I'd want that person to have my back. Always." She glanced at her fidgeting fingers. "Even if I was the first one in the wrong."

I understood her reasons and no longer held them against her. That was in the past now. I spiked a hand through my hair. Club membership was for life. We only left through death or being kicked out. Our oath demanded the club come first. Duty first. Women second. Fuck that. My woman was just as important, and I wanted to show her that.

I moved closer, setting her on edge. My fingers twitched, and I afforded myself a single stroke of her silky wing feathers. "I can guarantee to always have your back from now on, if you can forgive me." Disregarding all common sense, I slid my hand into her hair, drawing her face up to mine, placing a deep, heartfelt kiss on her mouth. I savored her taste, her sweetness, the hint of wine and tomato. Fuck me. She tasted even better than I thought. Fighting the onset of cramps and the desire to throw her up against the wall and fuck my apology into her, I pulled away. "Can you forgive me?"

"Give me time." She rubbed my wrist. That was a start, at least. She poked me in the chest, and my hellhound responded, growling pleasantly, wanting to lick her and nibble her neck. "And don't fuck up again. That goes both ways."

I chuckled, diving down for another searing kiss, leaving my lips burning and longing for her when I pushed off her. "C'mon, I'm starving. You hungry?" Her desires were more important than mine in that moment.

"Yeah." She let me take her hand and lead her to the dining table where the other three already sat, beers cold and fresh, food served, steaming bread smothered in melted butter. Slade stroked the seat next to him, dark blue eyes expectant. She smiled knowingly at me and took the seat. My body felt the cool of her departure as I slid in beside Alaric, opposite her.

"Hope you like a bit of spice." Castor scooped some stew onto his spoon and swallowed it.

Slade frowned. He was a simple guy. Meat and potatoes. Caveman. He grunted and munched on the bread.

Alaric was posted around the world and sampled different cuisine.

I didn't mind trying new foods and tasted the stew. Spice burned my tongue and throat, warming me. "It's good."

Aaliyah smiled at me and dipped her bread in the gravy.

Jealousy spiked in my veins as Castor's hand buried under the table, probably going straight to Aaliyah's thigh. My hellhound hearing detected the pluck of her jeans buttons as they came undone. She squeaked and shifted, sharpening my attention. Castor removed his hand and sucked on his finger. I released a pissed off groan beneath my breath. Watching him like that made me want to rip off his head and drink beer from his skull.

Aaliyah stuffed a heaping spoonful in her mouth, chewing fast, swallowing hard. She coughed and lunged for her water, gulping it down.

Castor kept lowering his hand below the table, clearly touching Aaliyah, then bringing his finger to his lips with an amber sauce, licking it. Slade and I side-eyed each other. Alaric glanced between Aaliyah and Castor, frowning, his lips pursed.

"What the fuck are you doing?" Slade asked for the three of us.

"Nothing." Aaliyah's cheeks stained pink as she sat up straight.

"Butterscotch sauce." Castor smiled like the cat that got the fucking cream.

Aaliyah tried to stamp down on her end of the mate bond to hide her embarrassment, while Castor showed it off like he walked around naked. The answer clicked into place with a little digging in the connection. That asshole put butterscotch sauce on her pussy and kept fingering it, swiping a sample to suck.

A bolt of arousal shot straight to my dick and lit that thing up like fireworks on New Year's fucking Eve. I held back the long, deep groan in my throat. So. Fucking. Sexy. I wished I was seated next to her so I could dip my finger in her honey. Damn Castor. Lucky son of a bitch.

"Nurse A, you kinky little minx." Slade lit up with a wicked smile and sat forward, leaning his elbow on the table as he stretched toward her. This kind of fetish was totally up his alley. "I didn't think you had it in you."

Aaliyah's cheeks burned hotter, brighter. Fucking Cute. "Can we talk about something else, please?"

Slade's hand dipped beneath the table, and she squeaked. "Spread your legs and let your old man at that honey."

"You're embarrassing her, Slade," Alaric defended her, trying his hardest to end the conversation.

"What's there to be embarrassed about?" Slade crooked one elbow and held his palm skyward. "She's our mate. Kinky, too." He waggled his eyebrows. "Fuck, Nurse A, you've got me so hot now."

His need raged along the bond like a wildfire consuming everything in sight. The prospect of a mate that would fulfil all his dirty fantasies had his balls tight, his dick hard, and his brain stuck on nothing else. Me fucking too.

Goddammit. I wanted to punch something, knowing I'd never get to tap that sweet pussy or have her mouth on mine for longer than a few seconds. These assholes constantly rubbed it in my face that my true mate was always out of my reach. I hated that they got to be intimate and have their way with her, and I got less than crumbs. She was more my mate than theirs!

Aaliyah giggled and slapped at Slade's hand, making him chuckle. "Stop it!" The way her body hunched in on itself told me she squeezed her thighs shut tight. No one was getting in there without a fight. Not even Castor.

"We're your mates." Slade leaned back in his chair, feigning disappointment as he shot her his signature dimpled grin. "What one tastes, we all taste. Don't go singling one of us out with favoritism."

Nice try, asshole. She wasn't that stupid to fall for his logic.

"You're being crude again, Slade," Alaric reminded him, the warning in his tone ringing like a raised sword. "Not in front of our mate."

"I'm being crude?" Slade raised a mock hand to his chest.

"I'm not the one with butterscotch sauce between my legs, taunting us!"

"For fuck's sake." Besides these circumstances, Alaric would never dare raise his voice to his president. He threw his napkin down and excused himself from the table. Grandpa got a little pissy sometimes when Slade got foul-mouthed with our mate.

Aaliyah held up her hands and climbed out of her chair. "Castor, this is all your fault. I knew this was a bad idea."

"What?" Castor shrugged and grinned. Damn. Lucky. Bastard. What I wouldn't give to have my hand down there to taste her. "Didn't hear you complain earlier."

"Earlier?" Slade perked up. "Fuck, Nurse A, I'm feeling a little left out here. Your old man demands attention now." He patted his lap a few times. "Come sit right here and show me that sugar!"

"Oh, God." Aaliyah beamed even redder as she slapped a hand over her forehead. "I'm going outside for some air."

Outside. With Alaric. Fuck. Yet a-fucking-gain, I'd lost out on some time with her. Fuck this curse!

## CHAPTER 7

*A*laric

CHECK THE PERIMETER. Scan for threats or danger. Listen for unusual movement. Sniff for out-of-place scents. Complete. Everywhere I went, I performed these steps of my inspections. Rituals to calm my edginess. After my return from deployment, nowhere felt safe to me except when I was with my brothers. Even then, I completed the reconnaissance out of habit, to relieve my anxiety and reassure myself I was safe. Otherwise, I couldn't relax and have a good time unless I drowned my soul with alcohol.

Whisky swished in the flask I carried with me. I uncapped it and lifted it to my lips. Smoky, cool spirits washed down my throat, warming it. I needed to clear my head of Slade's inappropriate comment and Castor's filth at the dinner table. Behavior like that would have earned me a slap behind my ears. Utterly disrespectful to our mate. Leave that kinky shit to the bedroom.

Insulted, I took another wash of whisky.

Demons hissed in my ear. *You belong to us.*

Countless bottles of whisky drowned them out, but lately, their voices rose in volume and pitch, and I struggled to contain them. Only one thing had worked to hold them back and block them. *Aaliyah.* Much more than my last mate.

Reminded of Aaliyah, I touched my hand, my fingers, wrist, all the places where she'd touched me several nights ago. Comfort after the ambush on the dummy drug shipment. How could I forget the warm brush of my mate's fingers? The heated swipe of her thumb over my knuckles, the pad of her fingers sweeping across my palm, the clutch of her small hand around my wrist. My intense surge of longing responding to her. The calm that washed over me like a gentle wave lapping at the shore. Our bodies next to each other, thighs and knees touching, my hand in hers. Conversation with her that removed my anxiety and the horrors witnessed at the shoot-out trap in the mountains.

Fuck, I was an absolute asshole to her when she was frightened, confused, and locked in a cell, unsure about her survival and safety. Again, after she saved my life from a fatal gunshot wound. Ungrateful, spiteful prick. Ashamed, I gripped the bottle's neck tighter, leaning on the porch pillar. I'd been raised better than that. Courteous. Polite. Respectful. Follow orders. Aaliyah had agreed to give me a fresh start, but I wouldn't blame her if she changed her mind.

My hawk night vision kicked in, bringing everything into sharper focus. The paved courtyard I helped Castor build. Spa as a central feature on the deck. Small herb garden in raised metal beds. Hundred-year-old trees providing shade to the rear of the yard.

I threw down another gulp of liquor to bury the guilt stinging me. Compassion brought her to forgive me for choking her. Her nursing instincts pushed aside our differences, and she healed my wing, settled my PTSD, my well-being her only concern. The empathy granted me only extended to my mental illness. For the way I'd treated her, I didn't deserve this angel's kindness. Didn't deserve a second of her time.

When she agreed to come to dinner with me, I felt like the luckiest damn son of a bitch. I had to make the night worth it. Show her the real me. The one buried beneath my demons. Because this was the kind of woman I needed in my life. Patient. Comforting. Forgiving. God knew I had a lot to atone for what I'd done.

The back door creaked as it swung open. I expected Slade's heavy tread as he emerged onto the patio for a cigarette and glanced over my shoulder, ready to give him another mouthful for his improper behavior.

Aaliyah closed the screen door as she emerged onto the porch. She paused and rubbed at her arms. Awestruck, I stared at her. Silver moonlight streaked her dark hair and brightened her crystal-blue eyes. Eyes I wanted to fall into and never return from. Shadows caressed her sculpted cheekbones. I'd never seen such a gorgeous woman. Feathers on her wings ruffled in the breeze tickling her hair. She crossed her arms over her chest, drawing my attention to the swell of her full breasts.

"Sorry, am I bothering you?" She stood by the door, respecting my space. "I just needed some air."

The opposite. Yearning stretched down the mate bond, asking her to stay.

"Not at all." I lifted the flask, offering it to her, wanting her lips to touch it, for me to kiss the place they'd last met.

She waved her palm at me. "No, thanks."

Not what she'd said after the ambush. We'd shared quite a few sips of it. Let me taste her sweetness after every swallow. Her vanilla and cherry taste. Remembering it made my balls tighten and my dick harden. I wanted her lips over mine, sucking, flicking her tongue, biting me. Whatever she wanted so long as our mouths connected and our bodies melted into one another, a tangle of limbs and fire.

Strain in her expression told me she must be freezing. I patted my thigh, and she came closer. "Come take my jacket." I bit back the word *baby*.

Her eyes took on a pleased slant as I threw my leather jacket over her shoulders. Desperate to connect with her, I snuck in a sly brush of her plumage. Soft. Silky. Light. She pulled my jacket tightly around her chest but couldn't do the thing up with her wings testing the limit of the fabric.

"Thank you," she said. "That's sweet of you."

Aaliyah's captivating scent flooded my system, overwhelming me. My hawk screeched to fold her under his wing and take her to his nest. Keep her high and safe from any harm on the ground.

"Beautiful night," she said, admiring the almost full moon.

Small talk. We both didn't know how to act around each other. Shame set me on edge, and I fidgeted, wrestling to meet her gaze. Discussing the night or the weather felt like a cheap cop-out when I wanted her in my arms. Unlikely with the tension between us. She might have agreed to come to my place for dinner, but it didn't equal forgiveness by any means, and I didn't expect her to exonerate me.

Ever since I took her for a ride up to Mount Panorama, I couldn't get the woman out of my head. That one touch haunted me just as much as my demons. My body ached for the press of her against my side, the hypnotic lull of her voice, the way she soothed my damn forsaken soul.

Frustrated, I took a long swallow of the alcohol to suppress my urge to take her in my arms and kiss her. Whisper to her that I was sorry. Beg for her forgiveness.

Something told me that wouldn't be anywhere near enough to get her back to my side after what I did.

Stubborn woman didn't back down when the avatars and I confronted her about her role in the Wolves and her presence with us. This powerhouse held her own among us. Pure conviction held fast to catching her father's murderer and exacting justice. Strong, courageous, and as complex as a damn F-35 jet, she never failed to impress me. But her stubborn streak would be the one thing that distanced us. A fortress that would keep me locked out until I proved my worthiness.

She took her place leaning against a post, tipping her head up to the sky, studying the diamond-studded canopy of the galaxy. "How's your arm?"

One of the riders sent after us shot me in the left wing. My second damn wound this past two weeks. After she healed me, I buzzed for days, high on her power. I didn't feel a damn thing since, not a slice of pain, nothing. Her power was that potent, that addictive, and hell, I wanted *more*. Wanted her.

Isis had many facets—healer, mother, protector—and I could only imagine how powerful and raw the fertility goddess inside Aaliyah would be. Fucking electric. Erotic. Out of this damn world. My cock thickened just thinking about her. My blue balls ached, and I threw back more whisky.

"The PTSD is getting worse, isn't it?" Aaliyah's question caught me off guard and I flinched, swallowing down more liquor.

My demons hissed louder. *She won't want you. You belong to us. You're broken. Twisted. Scarred.* I wanted to scream at them, empty my drink on them, set them alight and kill them forever.

"Yeah. I'm worried about my trial," I croaked at her.

"About being locked up again. I don't handle dark, cold, small cells well."

Aaliyah's wings grazed the post as she slid to face me. "Want to talk about it?" Her tone remained neutral and light to avoid making me retreat.

She knew I hid secrets from her. That something happened to me. Something that changed me, scarred me in more ways than one. I didn't want to get into it. Not here or now. Not yet. Didn't want to scare her away, for her to know how really fucked-up I was.

"My symptoms are getting worse." I lifted the flask, inhaling at the swishing, amber liquid, fighting the memory sparking.

My arrival at the ambush. Gunfire triggering me into an episode. I couldn't let that happen again. Next time, I could get myself or my brothers killed. My grip on the bottle tightened. War waged within me to throw and smash the bottle versus smother it to my chest.

"It's crippling me." I sucked in air at divulging my admission. "I can't do my job. Can't be effective for the club. Slade's going to demote me."

"I thought you handled it well. Considering …" Admiration tipped Aaliyah's voice, and I looked up at her, finding her smiling. She quieted the demons saying otherwise, shielding me from their spitting, spear-tipped words.

"I've got to get it under control." Her bruised, red neck flashed in my mind. I hurt her. Strangled her. Zethan banned me from the shelter after Aaliyah stopped staying there. He and Slade assigned me guard duty of her. Proximity where I could harm her again. Every minute she was near, I fought the dark urges, the demons lulling me to hurt her. I swallowed at the thick, hard lump in my throat. "I don't want to injure anyone."

Aaliyah slowly approached me, and I stiffened out of

instinct. "Maybe I can help?" She tapped her short nails against her thighs. "Apply my healing skills? Maybe the goddess can erase those memories and the pain?"

Yet again, this woman offered to help me when she owed me nothing and I owed her everything. For the first time in years, I felt a streak of hope. I didn't think I'd ever escape my horrors or the demons triggering me.

"I've never tried it before, so I don't know if it'll work." She rubbed her fingers along her palms, and I felt the nurse's urge to touch me, comfort me. "I don't want to give you false hope."

I liked that she gave it to me straight. She sure put Slade in his place. Entertaining to watch sometimes, other times uncomfortable when I felt obligated to defend my president.

At this stage, I was getting desperate to give anything a go. Whisky could only keep the demons at bay for so long. Lately their whispers were louder, and pretty soon, their chants would swamp my thoughts.

I couldn't afford to slip up if I had another episode. Mine and my brothers' lives were at stake. The club was the last place that kept me sane and made me feel normal and valuable.

"I'm willing to try," I told her. Anything to be closer to her.

Pleased, she smiled. I closed my eyes at the warm, sweet trust exchanged in our connection. Something that could only build from now on.

"How does Friday work for you?" She wanted to start already? "We can kill two birds with one stone. You make the dinner you promised and show me your astronomy set-up."

The moment I made her mine inched closer, maybe sooner than I anticipated. Hope fluttered in my chest to the beat of my hawk's wings.

I coughed and swallowed, not expecting that. "Sure."

She held out her hand, and I took it, squeezing it, tightening the guilt in my chest. Slade was right. She was more lenient with me, and it made me feel lesser in a way. That I got a pass because of my deteriorating mental state. I hated that she fucking pitied me.

"I don't deserve you," I said. "And I don't want your pity."

"Deserve? We'll see, Alaric." Fuck. Even the way she spoke my name shot right to my cock. Her reassuring smile lit up my chest like an airstrip at night. Lights flashed, guiding me down to land on her heart. A heart I planned to claim, and I wouldn't damn well give up until I did.

"If you let me love you, I'll show you the sky, moon, and stars." I didn't know where the sudden cockiness came from, but I wanted to let her know what was possible between us.

She snorted and shook her head. "Okay, Slade." She misinterpreted my meaning, thinking it was a crude fucking reference, when I meant my love would carry her to the heavens. Old romantic in me. "And I don't pity you, Alaric. I recognize the difference between trauma and being an evil prick like my brother."

Trauma. Fuck. The word was like a crack of thunder shaking a plane mid-flight. My need to correct myself ebbed as a flashback of the ambush hit me. Friday wouldn't be easy for either of us. Secrets would emerge. Horrors she couldn't begin to imagine. The things I saw and endured. Things I did for freedom. She might reconsider me as a mate once she knew what I was capable of. The darkness that lived within me, beckoned me to join it at its depth. Darkness that dragged me down with it every night and made me wake, screaming and coated in sweat. Darkness that caused me to harm the ones I loved.

Aaliyah sensed my discomfort, her hand clasping me tighter, preventing me from slipping into the crevice that swallowed me.

"Horus is a Sky god, right?" Smart change of topic. The nurse in her was accustomed to easing the distress of her patients, and I needed every drop of her comfort.

"That's right." Flights, birds, gods were topics I was happy to discuss. Anything to forget about my PTSD and demons.

She stroked the side of her hand along my feathers. "Can you only fly as a hawk?"

"Nope. The Sky god gave me multiple gifts." I unbuttoned my shirt, drawing her eyes to my exposed chest as I tugged the material off my shoulders and torso.

Her gaze skimmed over the scars across my chest, neck, and arms. Concern burned along the link. She wanted to touch me, reassure me, but I didn't want her sympathy. A flick of my shoulders encouraged large wings to sprout from my shoulder blades. I wanted her to see me. All of me. Scars that ran deep. Where her wings had green, blue, red, and gold feathers, mine were solid gold, tipped with the Eye of Horus at the end.

Aaliyah's fingers went straight for my feathers. "They're beautiful." Habit had me recoiling at her quick movement, and she withdrew, arms falling to her side. "Sorry to startle you."

Heart thumping wildly, I twisted my body to the side, brushing the end of my wing at her, permitting her to explore me. Electricity sparked in my feathers at her soft and respectful brush. I held back a groan at how good it felt to be caressed by my mate. Calm spread through me, and I didn't want her to stop touching me.

She jolted as my wings shivered. "Sorry."

My mate's caress emboldened me, and I took the liberty to capture her hand and set it back on my wing. "That was a good shiver."

"Oh, okay." Warmth stoked our bond from both her blush and me touching her. Residual uncertainty pinched the link.

We didn't know how to behave when our hearts shouted to come together but our minds remained reluctant. "What's it like to fly like this? Is it easier in hawk form?"

I noticed she asked questions when nervous or unsure. The hawk in me absorbed every detail of its mate.

"Birds have better aeronautics than a human with wings," I explained. "Their bones and body are lighter and require less propulsion to get air bound. But it's a lot more fulfilling in human form, since my hawk doesn't experience the same spectrum of emotions."

"Castor said I'm a shifter." She glanced up at the moon. "Am I going to shift into a cow with wings? That'd be weird."

I snorted, hard. Hadn't laughed like that in a while. When I recovered, I replied, "Isis was represented by a falcon in Egyptian art."

I studied Aaliyah, the way she worked her lip between her teeth. Not a nervous reaction, a thinking action. Cute. I liked it. "Can I shift into a bird, like you?"

"You can adopt both forms like me. Want to go for a fly?" The words came out before I knew it. Shit. I wasn't sure if I was ready for that and if she was either.

Her forefinger trailed down the edge of my wing, and I could barely restrain myself from pushing her against the post and kissing her. Not yet. "What if someone sees us?"

I grinned at her, snagging her waist and back in my arm. "I'm the avatar of the Sky god."

"Cocky." She shoved at my chest, and my bird squawked. Yeah, I was feeling more confident around her. She didn't make me feel like an asshole.

"Come on." I pulled her tighter to me, her breasts squishing against my chest, stirring my big guy again.

Hesitant, her fingers rubbed my feathers again, and I let her know how good it felt with a short, sharp groan.

"Let's go then." At her command, I secured her tightly in

my arms, squeezing a sharp breath from her. We floated down the steps to Castor's gloomy backyard.

I started slowly, gauging her reaction, letting her feel the beat of my wings, strong, steady, and secure enough to hold the weight of three people, although someone Slade's size might test me on that number. When she made no protest, I lifted us both six feet into the air, testing what she could handle. As we climbed higher, she buried her face in my chest. The impulse to protect her was too much. My hawk screeched at the way her fingers dug into my shoulders, her warmth soaking into every cell. My body hummed from our closeness. A closeness I didn't think she'd grant me so soon. I groaned as my damaged soul came back to life. This woman would either restore me or break me.

## CHAPTER 8

## $\mathcal{A}$aliyah

THIS SHOULDN'T HAVE FELT SO good. Warm. Protected. Adored. Alaric's arms moved from crushing mine so that his hands skimmed over my hair, and I sighed into his chest. Tingles rippled down my neck and along my spine, pulsing into my wings, encouraging them to spread. He moved his arms to accommodate them, then clutched me tighter around my waist, a bastion of possibility and excitement. Although we hovered low to the ground, I didn't want to remove my face from his chest and look.

Blood flowed to parts it shouldn't. My swollen lips begged for the burn of his. Heat filled the junction between my legs. Being in his arms shouldn't have aroused me, but of all the men who claimed to be my mates, his touch meant the most when he didn't give it as freely. As his mate, I hurt him more than the person who hurt him physically, and it would take time to mend our rift.

I didn't forget tracing the Horus tattoo on his bicep. How I made the move on him, descending on him with a soft and sweet kiss, over too soon. The way he brought me closer, wanting no air to exist between us as he deepened the kiss. How the mate bond conveyed his promise to face his demons to earn the right and permission from Slade to be alone with me again after he choked me.

Alaric inched us higher, and my stomach plummeted. Worried about him dropping me, I instinctively gripped his arm tighter and risked a glance below us. Powerful and dependable wings kept us afloat seven feet off the ground. Wings that were like him. Staunch, committed, and ready to defend.

The Jackals were not the gangsters, murderers or thugs I expected. Alaric was the first one to make me question whether they were the bad guys.

Trust came hard-won with the former military man. Losing it was catastrophic. Winning it back, grueling, and not without sacrifice.

Despite our clashes, I never swayed from my argument or convictions to avenge my father. Nothing had changed there. Except everything had changed between Alaric and me. My determination impressed him. Where I broke his trust and built an insurmountable mountain between us, he took the first step to bridge the divide between us. When one of Danny's men hit me, it was Alaric who placed his hand over my bruise and let me cup his hand. An olive branch that meant a lot to me. We had a long road ahead of us to fully trust each other, but we made that small start.

Alaric smoothed my flicking hair back and tucked my head beneath his chin. Part of me never wanted to leave the comfort of his arms. Another side of me wanted to branch out and explore my own ability. Time would tell which won out. I lifted my cheek to look at him. Breathe him in. Pine, loam. Scents that brought me back to nature.

His heartbeat thumped, each beat conveying how much he missed having a connection to his mate. Holding her. Loving her. Protecting her. He wanted those feelings with me. Yet every time he looked upon me, shame and regret burned in the pit of his stomach. Self-hatred seared along the bond, the reason he drank himself to death every night. Sensing that he gave away too much, he carried us higher, the ground quickly disappearing beneath us. I let him battle his demons. All I could do was support him until he was ready to banish them.

I glanced out over the endless sky. Goddess, this was so freeing, peaceful, and I'd never felt anything like it. Fresh, clear, crisp air. Silence so pure it enveloped me in a blanket. Endless space above us dotted with millions of dazzling stars. Silvery moonlight bathing my skin. Lights twinkling below, the glow illuminating darkened roads, parked vehicles, houses. The highlight, the arms of a gorgeous man wrapped around me.

"It's cold up here." I rubbed at my arms. "You must be freezing without your jacket."

"We're shifters." He chuckled, taking that as an invitation to hold me closer, his hands going underneath the jacket he loaned me, to my back, my bare flesh pressed between my wings. I held back a moan as he rubbed my chilled flesh to bring warmth to it. "We've got thicker skin than a normal human. It will protect you. Just tell it what to do."

Thicker skin? Not thick enough to deflect a bullet. I followed his instruction and shut out the cold beating at me from every direction. A soft fire lit inside of me, warming my entire body, coating it with the same heat, shielding my body. I had so much to learn from my fellow avatars. Without them, I'd be stuck healing people at the hospital. I might never have discovered a new part of my power to blossom. The more time I spent with the Jackals, I felt my power increase, as if the four of them charged me like a battery. Castor expanded my magical knowledge base, tapping the goddess' memories, bringing access to her magical prowess. Now Alaric taught me to master my shifter skills.

I risked a glance over my shoulder. "It's so beautiful up here," I hummed to myself more than anything.

"It's another place I come to clear my head." From the conflict beating in his chest, he must fly a lot.

"I can see why. It's peaceful." I craned my neck to try and see more.

Lit up trucks tracking along the highway out of town. A couple out walking their dog on the sidewalk. People training on the illuminated soccer fields. The ripple of the water flowing in the Macquarie River. Shit. How the hell did I detect that detail? My falcon sight?

"About what Slade said," Alaric started, staring out over the vast expanse of sky, the building cluster of clouds above us. "I apologize for his behavior. I don't like when he objectifies ..."

My ears latched onto the last word he couldn't bring himself to say yet. Disappointment stung deep and I tried to conceal the mate bond from broadcasting it. I didn't want Alaric of all people to know he hurt me. Again.

My voice came out a harsh croak as I attempted a cheap decoy. "I can handle Slade."

Damn Castor for putting me in that embarrassing position. I should never have let Dark Daddy have his way and leave sticky, hot, creamy butterscotch sauce between my thighs. My fault. He'd licked most of it away, but a small portion remained, and I shifted as my legs began to stick together.

Alaric's throaty chuckle poked at the low-burning fire in my stomach. "Yes, you certainly can."

"Don't encourage me." I smacked his chest, and I swore I heard the responding shriek of his hawk. Something deep and ancient scratched at my chest. My falcon? After a few seconds, I shook off the sensation to focus on the conversation.

"Castor has his strange fetishes and Slade his kinky fantasies," Alaric explained. "Zethan and I are the normal ones of the harem."

Good to know. I was just planning to have some fun with Castor while I was here. I didn't plan on staying with the Jackals once the threat to my life was eliminated. No god was going to choose for me or dictate who I ended up with, curse or not.

# CHAPTER 9

## 𝓐aliyah

I CLEARED MY THROAT. "You mentioned you completed military service."

"Air Force." His grim smile suggested a tragedy there.

A pilot. Sexy. Matched his Sky god and his ability to transform into a hawk.

"Our Army compatriots call us the *Chair Force.*" He chuckled. "They tease us that we sit about all day waiting to drop bombs, provide them backup, or deliver materials."

I snorted at the nickname. "What sort of pilot were you? Were you the cocky Maverick from *Top Gun* or reckless Jake Preston in *Fire Birds?*"

Impressed, Alaric's eyebrows shot up. "You know your military movies, huh?"

I shrugged as much as I could in his arms. "My ex used to watch them."

At mentioning that, Alaric's grip on me tightened possessively, and a thrill skated up my spine. I liked that he thought of me as his. More than liked. Every part of me was filled with a reciprocal possessiveness over him.

"I'm neither." His body stiffened. "I'm the Mike Durant of *Black Hawk Down.*"

Eek. *Black Hawk Down.* From my memory, the movie was about an American mission to capture a Somali warlord, but it went horribly wrong. Troops were trapped and stuck in the fight of their life. Mike Durant was a helicopter pilot shot down by a rocket-propelled grenade.

Something told me I wouldn't like the answer to my next question. That it related to Alaric's PTSD. "Your plane was shot down?" I stroked his arm to soothe the sting of memories I knew would hit him.

He looked back out over the swarming clouds surrounding us like soft pillows. His cheek and eye twitched, and we lost some altitude as his wings paused. A single bead of sweat dripped down his forehead. His eyes snapped shut hard as if he relived the flashback. Rocking rumbled the mate bond like an earthquake hit him.

"I don't want to talk about it." He jerked hard, his grip on me faltering.

Panicked that he'd drop me, I rubbed at his chest to bring him out of the memory. "Hey. Hey. Come back to me. You're here with me."

His attention shifted back to me, he blinked a few times, emerging from the memory, and reasserted his hold on my waist. With a slow, deep breath, he cupped my hand and set it over his chest. His heart thudded so hard I was surprised it didn't pound out of his ribcage.

I linked one arm around his neck, leaning my head to his pec, stroking his hairline. The smart thing would be to steer clear of the topic rather than ask more questions. But, hey, I hadn't been a smart woman since I arrived in the Jackals' shelter. "Do you still fly planes?"

"Not for a few years," he answered.

"Tell me more." I had to keep him talking. Anything to stop him descending back into another flashback.

"I flew a C-130J Hercules medium-sized tactical airlifter." He let go of one arm to brush my cheek, and fuck me if it wasn't the sweetest, most gratifying gesture.

None of the other men touched me like Alaric. Reverent and cherished. They handled me rough, dominant, owning, and the change in pace was a pleasant surprise.

"I air-dropped cargo and troops, sometimes provided aerial cover, shooting enemy targets or weapons to protect troops on the ground."

I hated the idea of him in battle. Of him getting hurt. It felt like he traded in one war for another with the MC. "How long did you serve?"

"Eight years." That made Alaric roughly thirty or so in age. I'd never asked. "Born and bred in the Armed Services all the way back to my great grandfather in WWI." That was a long history of military service.

I patted his shoulder. "I bet you made your family proud."

He read between the lines. "Your family weren't proud of you?"

I hung my head. "Dad wanted me to stay with the Wolves. Close to the family business." My chest stung at the real reason I left. Losing Jimmy and adopting Mia out. "But I didn't want a career in an MC. I tried too hard to please my dad. Too hard to be tough. Too hard to earn his praise. And I got burned every time." Just like I feared getting burned with the Jackals.

Alaric sensed my stinging pain and sifted a hand through my hair. This man was making it difficult for me to concentrate, to breathe, to stay mad at him. "You're family now. You're one of us."

Not him too. Slade tried to convince me to stay with the Jackal's cut. When I examined more closely, Alaric's motivation came from a deeper place than wanting me to stay as his mate. He had a very strong sense of family, tradition, and responsibility. This led him to regard both his MC brothers and fellow Air Force personnel as family, and that extended to me as an avatar.

"I just wanted something that was mine, you know?" I said. "Something that my dad or the club couldn't take away from me."

"I've always followed in my family's footsteps ..." A sense of sadness punctuated his words, like he'd wanted his own life but felt obligated too. Seconds later, the regret tainting our link confirmed it. He'd never had a choice. The Jackals were his first choice, the bond of brotherhood he needed. "Serving in the RAAF, I always fought someone else's war for whatever political reason. Territory disputes. Eliminating *supposed* terrorist threats to justify a war with a country for their resources."

Fuck. First time I'd heard this.

"When I served in Afghanistan, the US troops told me they were being used to protect poppy fields seized from the Taliban. Poppy used for opium production to fund the CIA drug cartel."

Dirty bastards. Everyone was corrupt in this world. Even the leaders. No one had clean hands. Blood dripped from the leader's hands.

Maybe I was better off with the Jackals. At least they couldn't lie to me.

"Nobody seems clean anymore," I said. "Not even the governments."

"No more." Alaric's fingers stilled on my back. "Now I

fight for my own cartel, our territory, our goddamn rules. No one's gonna tell us how to live our lives. What country to cheat out of land and resources."

Wow, he was very passionate about this. I couldn't begin to imagine all the corruption he saw and had to keep silent about. I saw a few of my own in my time at the hospital. Despite all the policies saying the contrary, hospital management received kickbacks from pharmaceutical companies to use their products over another company's products. How else did our CEO on a half a million-dollar salary afford a multi-million-dollar vacation home in the South Coast of New South Wales? Recently a Queensland hospital was busted for this very act. Few were innocent these days. The whole world went to hell and would burn there.

My dad never trusted the government. That was one reason he decided to convert his weekend riding club into a business. Crooked politicians busted taking bribes from lobbyists pushing their agenda in parliament and legislation. Anyone who didn't go along with their agenda would get a visit from their police bulldogs, threatening and intimidating them. My father refused to comply and turned outlaw, managing to keep the club alive by getting dirt on the very men who menaced him.

"Shit, listen to me." Alaric ran a hand through his hair. "Sorry. I go off on a tangent sometimes. That was one of the reasons I left the Air Force."

The longing pricking the end of our connection told me he desperately wanted to make amends. So did I. I pretended to be someone else to infiltrate their club. I deserved his mistrust. From here on in, I needed to be myself. Had to show him the real me. The dependable, strong, independent, fierce woman who wielded just as much fire as Slade.

Went both ways. Alaric had to show me behind the curtain too. The haunted man affected by PTSD. I wouldn't force him to tell me what happened to him unless he felt comfortable doing so. That was his business and not mine. Three years of nursing taught me to respect personal boundaries and not to push where I wasn't welcome.

"I'd love to stay like this all night," his voice rumbled, barely above a whisper. "But a chick's gotta leave the nest sometime and learn to fly. Are you comfortable to give it a try?"

My heart pinched with disappointment. Whenever I got too close, he shut me down, pushing me away. Protective instinct. He was going to be a hard egg to crack.

"You ready to take flight, my falcon?" He loosened his grip, prompting me to tighten mine on him.

I glanced down. After my time in the Wolves, the shit I saw, the men I went up against, I'd never considered myself as fearful. Careful, yes. Completing all my checks and balances in my duty as a nurse. Correct doses of medicine. Hit the vein with a canula. Security protocols with dangerous meth patients. But the prospect of flying on my own was a little daunting. Ninety-five percent sure, five percent scared shitless.

"What do I need to do?" I asked.

"Just make those wings work." He pumped his harder, faster, to demonstrate. "You're in control." Sounded easier than it looked. "But I'm taking you lower just to be safe." Scooped in his arms, he carried us closer to the ground.

I liked that he was considerate and protective of me.

Hovering six feet above Castor's backyard, he said, "I'll count you down. Ready?"

"I … I think so." My heart leapt into my throat in uneasiness.

"Three." At Alaric's first count, I forced my wings to beat, creating a whoosh that flung my hair over my shoulder. "Two, one." He slowly let me go.

Instead of keeping me afloat, my wings dropped me and I screamed and plummeted. My heart caught in my throat as my ass hit the ground.

Alaric landed beside me and caught my hand, gently supporting me back to my feet and into his arms. "Did you hurt yourself?" His hands searched my body and I fought off the pain screaming down my pelvic bone and the excitement skittering across my legs.

My healing senses told me nothing was wrong. "I'm fine."

I was determined to conquer this. Furious beats of my wings lifted me back into the air. Puffs of wind tickled and cooled my skin. I was *really* doing it. Arms wide, I propelled myself higher, then sideways, squeaking excitedly as my wings drifted me. Eyes closed, I moved throughout Castor's yard, wind tugging my hair and clothes. Pure serenity.

Given it was my first time, I worried my wings might tire quickly from lack of exerting themselves, and I stuck close to Alaric. Not that I needed to when he swooped protectively around, above and below me. Everywhere. The soldier in him protected his mate like I was a strategic military target needing defense. I wasn't falling on his watch. He let me explore the sky, rising above the fence height, my confidence soaring along with me. Until I tired, slumped, and descended.

Alaric caught me bride-style in his arms, crushed me to his chest and stroked my hair. He captured my hand, rubbing his thumb over the side, and I sighed as he brought it to his burning lips, kissing it. Damn, when he held me like this, he made it hard to not need him. Especially when the fire in his golden eye kindled for me.

"My mate," he whispered in my ear. Tender. Sweet. Scorching with a fever to kiss me. Unable to fight him anymore, I tilted my head to meet his lips, eager to repeat the kiss on the mountain. Our mouths connected, a gentle brush, exploring each other.

The brief peace we found was shattered when my brain dumped me under the ultimate icy water, replaying his cruel words.

*Traitorous mate.*

*Liz would never have betrayed us.*

*You're hiding something, Aaliyah. I'll find out what it is.*

I pulled away and wiped his mark from my lips. Fuck, what was I thinking? I wanted to make things right. I really did. But I couldn't just forget and erase all the shitty things he said and did. Couldn't let him think that he had the right to kiss me after the way he treated me. One flying lesson and a tender kiss wasn't going to wipe it all away. I didn't know what it would take or if things between us could be mended. I'd agree to a truce, a fresh start, not a damn romantic connection. Angry heat pulse in my veins for giving in so easily. This fucking mate bond persuaded me into actions I'd never normally make.

"I'm tired, I said. "Can we go back?"

Disappointment sizzled along the bond.

"Sure." Alaric wrapped me protectively to his body and carried us back to Castor's backyard.

When we landed, I scrunched my nose and broke away, keeping a good four feet between us. "Do you know a useful trick to tuck these things away?"

He flicked his shoulders, and his wings went taut and straight, then shrank into his back. "Command them."

I groaned. "Really? That simple?"

"That simple." He chuckled at me and nodded.

Why didn't Castor know this? I told those bitches who was boss, and finally they retreated into my skin. *Thank fuck.* It had only taken three fricken days. The ache in my back reduced, and I sighed and rolled my stiff shoulders.

"Thanks." I smiled, grateful to finally relieve the constant weight on my back.

Alaric cut off the distance between us, taking my hand in his and placing a kiss on the back of it. So romantic. This damaged, gorgeous man-made me flush all over with aroused heat and indignation.

"I deserve your rejection." Hell, even his determined whisper captured my heart and refused to let go. "I know I don't deserve you for what I've done. But I don't give up. Ever. You're mine. You're ours. And I will find a way to win your heart and claim you."

Fuck. What did a girl say to that kind of steely determination?

## CHAPTER 10

### Slade

NOT THIS A-FUCKING-GAIN. If my VP kept this up, we were about to go head-to-head, and he wouldn't win.

"We need to get those women out of there," Zethan argued as if it would change my mind.

I scratched the bridge of my nose. "I've already canned that idea. Too risky and it could create more complications for us."

Normally I was the risk-taker of the bunch. The wild fucker raging with chaos, but after Tank's death, I was playing it safe.

Zethan's neck muscles bunched as he leaned forward. "Every day we sit around doing nothing, another woman dies at the Wolves' porn studio."

Alaric threw his weight behind his VP with a stiff nod and a larger than usual pour of whisky. Fucker normally backed me. Topic was too close to home. The reason why the asshole got shot when out scouting the Wolves.

That left the vote split down the middle between Castor, Aaliyah and me. Unless he sided with my VP too, which he normally did. I was a few breaths away from meltdown if they overrode me. I already lost one good man this week and didn't plan on losing another.

I glanced at Aaliyah, praying my woman would have my back. Her eyes were cast down, along with her mouth and shoulders. Sensitive topic with her brother and his mangy club.

Castor sat beside her, his hand below the table, placed on her lap. I heard his light strokes on her thigh and felt their soothing calm. After dinner last night, I wasn't able to stop thinking about him dipping his finger in her honey and tasting it. Fucking hot. My balls had ached all night until I relieved myself.

I was in his place not days ago. Next to her. Holding her. I pegged him with a glare. Asshole took full advantage that he was the only one in her good graces. Fuck. Didn't blame him. Hell, I would have taken full advantage and lapped that shit up, too, if it were me.

I pushed that aside to concentrate on the meeting. Avatars were given higher privileges in the club, like attending upper-echelon club meetings. And after the recent leak from Jaxx, I was more selective of whom I let in on important club business. I was not taking any chances in case we had another mole. I invited Aaliyah here as my mate because I needed to win her trust and earn every fucking brownie point I could scrounge. If she decided to prospect with us, I'd fast-track her membership and bring her onboard as a patched member. I wanted her in my club, my family, my bed, and heart. This was non-negotiable, and I wouldn't let her fight me on this. The sooner she came to terms with that, the better.

Bitter, hot resentment boiled inside Zethan. Danny knew how to get to me and my club members. He triggered me with my emotions, Alaric and Zethan with the abused women, and set off Castor by blindsiding him. Toyed with my woman on blaming me for killing her dad. That fucking mutt goaded us, and I was at my fucking limits.

"How many more women will you let die in the meantime?" Zethan refused to back down.

Dark clouds chased through my body, pressure building, lightning charging. I should have taken a few seconds to bring it back down, but he was getting on my goddamn nerves. "I told you, you're not going anywhere near there until we have concrete proof the Wolves have fucked with our business. We've got nothing more to tie them beyond the ambush at Reg's distribution warehouse, and Danny could argue they were trying to rescue his sister."

Aaliyah tapped her lips and nodded. Fuck, not her too. The nurse in her should be supporting me, playing it safe when we had lives and the club to protect. If we lost more men, we'd be weaker physically and financially, burdened by supporting family members of our fallen brothers. A position we couldn't afford right now.

"Our brothers could die if I fire the first shot of war." I had a responsibility to protect my men. And woman. Tank's death was on me. I'd not bear the weight of another tombstone on my goddamn shoulders.

"They already fired the first shot, and it wasn't a goddamn bullet, it was a fucking rocket-launched explosive." Zethan rubbed at the thick, dark circles under his eyes. Dude needed some sleep. "I put forward a vote to take a team of four men to rescue the women being used in the violent porn and snuff films."

Fuck me. I leveled him with a glare that could have lit a wet log on fire. Dick was testing my stretched patience.

"I say aye." Alaric's hand shot up.

Castor leaned back in his chair and pressed his fingertips together. "Sorry, Zeth, but I'm with Prez on this one." Good. For once I got his vote. "What about you, baby?" He gave Aaliyah's bare arm a single brush, and the heat in my body spiked.

Her gaze shot to me, and I softened, taken aback by her solemn and haunted eyes. My body itched to drag her onto my lap, cuddle her, kiss her neck and cheek. She'd gone through hell from her brother, then with us, and she'd handled everything thrown at her, never once breaking. My mate was a strong little thing with a will of steel. Unbreakable. Unshakable. Admiration and respect bloomed in my chest. This was the woman I wanted on our side. A smile crept up her lips at the respect paid to her. The stubborn resistance she wore like armor, cracked down the center, chunks falling off the edges.

It wouldn't be long until we broke it down and she agreed to stay. Permanently. Where she fucking belonged.

"I don't want anyone else to die because of Danny," she whispered, her voice catching.

Fuck, here we go. She was going to side with my VP. I crushed my fingers to my palm. Winds uprooted trees in my mind. Sand lashed at the insides of my skull. I crossed my arms over my thumping chest, holding back my scaling fire, destined to burn through anything in its path.

"But I don't want to put another club member's life in jeopardy." I sat straighter at her words. All the turmoil within me went silent. "Not until you have solid proof that Danny is behind this, and you have a plan to take him and the Wolves down."

"Fuck, man." Zethan scrubbed at his face from his stubbled cheeks to his jaw, a move he made when he was pissy.

Castor rubbed at Aaliyah's nape, and the fire in me roared. She clasped her hand over his, bringing it down to settle in her lap. Fuck. What I wouldn't give for innocent little touches like that from my mate. She showed her support with words, but I wanted her support in other ways too. Lucky, long-beaked damn bastard.

I pegged Zethan with a scowl. "I don't want to hear about this again until we have some answers. Got it?"

I knew the asshole wouldn't give up on this issue. He'd be at me again in a week or if we got another shred of evidence. Abused women were his weakness and trigger. Fucker blamed himself for his sister's death at the hands of her abusive ex. Zethan needed to let that shit rest, otherwise he'd torture himself for the rest of his life, and give me indigestion and stiff muscles in the process. As VP, he had to think of everyone, not himself.

"I mean it, asshole." His green eyes took in the heat of my gaze without so much as a flinch. "You disobey an order and you're fucking out. Think of the club, not just yourself."

I knew what my VP was like. Soft-hearted bastard missed church if he lost a woman at the shelter. Dragged the rest of the Jackals into a bar fight to defend him when he slugged some cunt getting heavy with his missus. Got arrested three times for beating the shit out of abusive husbands that tracked their wives to his shelter. I had to stand by my VP and him me, but I couldn't let him drag us into the fires of hell for busting into Danny's studio and shooting everyone inside. Not until I was one hundred percent certain the Wolves were behind this, and we confirmed who they partnered with. Until then, I had to put my foot down. Tasted bitter at the back of my damn throat, and I hated it as much as him, but lives depended on me. Lives I refused to risk. When we took down the fucking Wolves, they wouldn't see us coming. We'd blindside those mutts the way they did us. Minimize casualties and losses. Maximize destruction to our enemies.

Resentment and disappointment seared the line between us. Zethan made a point to drag the chair along the floor as he stood and stomped out of the room. The rest of the avatars exchanged glances. We clashed many times before and I could handle the bitterness between us, but I didn't appreciate that he speared our mate because she failed to choose his side. Pussy bitch. I'd pull him aside later. Let him cool down first.

My phone buzzed in my pocket. "Unknown caller," it announced. My body stiffened as I slid it from my pocket. Could be that mutt, Danny, calling.

I answered it to check. "Who the fuck is this?"

"Rat Bait," a heavy, smoky voice replied that I didn't recognize. My nerves sparked but didn't set alight. Not Danny. But could be his accomplice. "This Slade? President of the Jackals?"

I wracked my memory for that name. Fucking stood out like herpes on a cock. Other presidents called themselves Gunner, Psycho or Lucifer, not fucking Rat Bait. Jesus. The stuff was deadly. Killed slow, probably like this motherfucker. After a few seconds, the name finally clicked. President of the Unsung Heroes, a club from the South Coast of New South Wales.

"Yeah, it is." My reply prompted Castor to sit up and stare, and Alaric to get edgy and lean his elbows on the table. "What can I do for you, Rat Bait?"

"Your man here pulled me over to say we don't have permission to pass through Newcastle." Rat Bait was disgruntled. That was easy to tell. "But we got approval from your road captain last week."

We didn't have anyone stopping and checking riders as they passed through our territory. It was an honor-based system. Though, we had a few bar and business owners on the take who reported any unusual activity. None reported anything to me.

I set my phone down on the table and hit the speaker button. I wanted my men to hear this. "What man won't let you pass through Newcastle?"

"Calls himself Scar."

"Not one of ours."

"From Hellfire MC." Rat Bait's tone turned rougher. "Said they run this turf. I thought you took control several years back."

*Fucking Hellfire.* Assholes were playing difficult. Revenge for offing their distributor. Cunt had it coming for selling our stolen Pharaoh. This just proved Hellfire were in on the deal. More fuckers to be dealt with. The death pile kept adding up.

"They don't speak for us," I told my fellow president, my voice turning dry and scratchy with my irritation. "Never have, never will. And it's our territory, not theirs." I was dangerously close to getting my VP back in here to open a portal so I could deal with those fucks on the spot. They had no claim to my turf, and I'd fuck with theirs for getting in my way. "Hold on one sec, Rat Bait."

"Sure thing, brother." I heard the click of a lighter as I set the phone on mute. Fire. I'd love to raise hell with some.

"Hawk Boy, the president of the Unsung Heroes is on the line." I told him what was happening. "Did you permit them to pass through Newcastle?"

"Yeah, last week." Alaric's frown lines ran deep. "Spoke to him on Wednesday."

I gave Alaric a nod.

I unmuted the phone. "You there, Rat Bait?"

"Yeah." He breathed out what sounded like smoke, making me crave a cigarette. Coals kindled in my veins just thinking about it.

"Confirmed with my road captain," I replied. "You have permission to cross our territory. I'll be taking it up with Hellfire MC for the inconvenience. Thanks for letting me know. And let me know if they give you any grief on the way back. In the meantime, I'll pay those fuckers a visit."

"Cheers, Slade." The phone went dead.

I tapped the screen of my phone. "Alaric, Castor, and Aaliyah, you're coming with me tomorrow to sort this shit out."

"Roger that, sir." Alaric saluted me. Asshole enjoyed ribbing me.

I snatched the whisky bottle from him. "I'll shove that bottle neck up your ass if you call me that again."

Aaliyah choke-coughed into her hand. Castor did his usual amused smirk.

"You know I'll enjoy that, sir." Alaric stood up and wagged his ass at me.

"Yeah, you would." Licking my lips, I admired his perky, tight ass, remembering better times, where I'd run my hands over it, bitten it, left teeth marks and bruises from spanking him, hard. He sure liked to be fucked from behind, and I liked to give it. Asshole gave good head, too. We hadn't hooked up since we lost Liz. Hawk Boy hadn't seemed interested, despite flirting. Maybe Aaliyah might be the catalyst for kicking things back off again.

"Am I missing something?" Aaliyah bit her lip, and fuck me, I wanted her to be biting mine like that. Better yet, biting my nipples, chest, stomach. Any fucking where so long as her teeth made contact. My dick ached from the torture and anticipation of it.

Maybe this might work to speed things up. I moved slow,

seductive, rising and coming to stand behind Alaric, edging his chair out the way. My palm ran down his ass. "Alaric likes to give it and take it." I spanked, hard, the sound echoing off the walls.

Primal hunger tore down our bond. My mate's eyes fused with heat. I loved that we did that to her. Wanting her even hotter, I licked Alaric's ear, and ran a hand down his chest, stopping over his cock and massaging. She shuddered at his stuttered groan. Yeah, it had been too long for him, and he needed a release. He wasn't like me. His hawk mated for life, so he couldn't bring himself to fuck another woman after we lost her.

"Want some of this, Nurse A?" I growled at her, kneading harder, making Alaric thicken beneath my grip. I played dirty. Anything to entice my little nurse. I'd have her begging for us. Filled and satisfied that she'd never want another man. Never want to leave.

Her eyes hooded. Fuck yeah, she wanted in on the action. Not yet, though. Woman wasn't ready to let go fully and surrender to us yet. One day she'd come for us. Then she'd be ours. No question. No doubt. I'd be the one to make it happen.

"It's yours when you want it." I breathed, hot, heavy over Alaric's neck, laying a few kisses on his hot flesh, affectionate rather than sensual. "Just say the word, sexy." I let my words wrap around her chest like a dirty promise that stole her air.

She struggled to contain her heart rate after that. Her pussy dripped. I could smell it. Woman like the idea of a group of us. I bet she'd run to the ladies to relieve herself after this. Wouldn't be long until she was ours, and our family would be complete, our hearts and souls complete.

"Castor?" She pawed at her hair. "Don't we have some research to do?"

Fuck, no. I was not letting her leave to go fuck that

asshole in his study and offload her growing tension. She stayed at his place. Spent every waking moment with him, researching, practicing magick. That was about to change. Woman owed the rest of us some time.

"Yeah. We've got to test out the spell." I almost laughed at Castor's pathetic excuse to clear out for nookie.

"She'll meet you in a minute," I told him, and he smirked and nodded. Asshole knew I was jealous. I slapped Alaric on the ass, released him, leaving him hard and dry. "Get the fuck out of here."

She leveled me with a stubborn stare as they left. "What do you want to talk about?" Strictly business. Biggest dick shrinkage device.

Oh, the things I wanted to say. Dirty things. But I kept it light, friendly. Using my charm wouldn't work on her anymore. After we had sex last week, she vowed not to let it sway her. Without it, I was powerless. I had to rely on plain old personality and manners. And I had no manners. I was a predator who took what he wanted.

Resisting the urge to pat my leg and encourage her closer, I sat on the table's ledge, a chair's distance from her.

"I'm feeling a little left out, Nurse A," I admitted, laying it out for her. Vulnerable. That was what she wanted. It was the reason she'd let me into her room the other night. She liked it when I opened my heart to her. I'd fucked up by sulking about my ex and it hurt Aaliyah. "I want us to hang out. Spend some quality time together. Go for a ride or something. Take a picnic or some romantic shit."

A flash of sassiness overcame her features, and my jackal arched its back, ready for the challenge. "We're going for a ride tomorrow." Ouch. Woman shot me through the heart. Made it more difficult to get closer to her. Nothing I couldn't handle. I always caught my prey.

I put her back in her place before she could shoot me

down with a Mr. Vincent. "That's business, not pleasure," I reminded her.

Her eyes narrowed as if she suspected I walked her into a trap. "I know what happens when I'm alone with you."

I cocked my head and flashed my dimples. "You scared of the big, bad Jackal?"

She didn't fall for it and wagged a finger at me. Fucking woman wagged at me. I knew where I'd like to put that damn finger. In my mouth. Suck it slow and hard and have her wet for me.

"Stop it, Mr. Vincent." I'd pushed it too far and had to rein it back a bit.

I slid closer to her along the table. "C'mon Nurse A. Give me a chance. Get to know me. You won't regret it." I left it open for her to decide. Being pushy and cocky got me nowhere but blue balls, town population *me*.

I wanted this woman on the back of my bike, arms wrapped around me. Just us two, no Castor. No other men to compete with. I claimed her first, for fuck's sake. She belonged to me. My jackal wouldn't shut up since and I was sick of listening to the love-sick asshole.

"I haven't forgotten that Slade Vincent delivers on his promises." The way she pursed her lips made me want to slide closer, lean down and take her mouth with mine. Make her see how attentive I could be to her needs.

"Then I promise to behave." I raised two palms in the air. "To not kiss you in the first hour."

She smiled, wide and pleased. A break-her-barriers kind of smile. "No kissing at all and you've got a deal. I haven't ridden much out west and want to see the countryside. Oh, and I like soft cheeses, red wine, and berries."

I'd take it. Hell, I'd take anything I could get, scraps included. "You drive a hard bargain, woman."

Fuck, yeah. Slade Vincent won. Every. Single. Time.

# CHAPTER 11

## Castor

"Gear up, bitches," Slade grunted, looking worse for wear at 7AM the next day. He wasn't a morning person, at all. Late nights, plenty of whisky, smoky air, pool tables, and music were his thing. "We've got a four-hour drive ahead of us, and I want to deal with Hellfire and be back before evening."

Alaric, Aaliyah, and I threw our jackets on, ready for the long haul. Zethan stayed behind to man the club in our president's absence. Safety precaution. Zethan was also busy at the shelter, finalizing a fundraiser for his sister Carlie's club. Money funneled into our club, out of the eye of the public and other clubs. We didn't want other clubs to know our business, especially not about the shelter, because it could be used against the women to hurt us.

After yesterday's meeting, our VP kept a low profile, pissed that we didn't back him and save the women Danny abused. We had to be smart about how we dealt with that pyscho. Needed to know who he partnered with. The mysterious background threat feeding him information about how to screw with us and knew how to blind my gift.

I grabbed my riding gloves and slid my hands into them. Winter morning wind bit into my hands and froze them within five minutes on a day like this. Aaliyah geared up beside me, looking a smoking vision in the leather riding gear I got her. Top to toe curvy. Had the outfit custom made for her exact measurements. She let me do the honors and zip up the front of the jacket. I made sure to go real slow as I maneuvered her ample breasts. Cleavage I'd buried my face in last night. Woman was horny as hell after watching Slade tease Alaric.

"Hop on, baby." I patted the back of my bike for her.

"Fuck, no!" Slade barked, throwing his jacket on. A snarling jackal with the word 'President' burning with gold and flames on the back. "She's riding with me."

Someone was a little bitter since she predominantly hung out with me. Didn't blame her when Slade came on so strong. A force of nature. Sheer strength of wind to topple trees. Topple your heart in the process.

Dark Daddy liked his way, but we never pushed beyond her boundaries. I think that was why we got along so well. Why she submitted to me. That, and she respected my thoughtfulness.

"Challenge accepted." I smirked at him. Arguments always broke out between Slade, Zethan, and me when the three of us had dominant, stubborn personalities. Alaric was the only one of us to hang back.

"Ain't nothing to challenge." Slade flashed his classic dimples. "Nurse A loves riding bitch with me."

"How 'bout you get Aaliyah a bike?" Alaric threw out as he sat on his Chieftain, making the suspension bounce. "Then we don't have to listen to you two bitch over it."

"Who's bitch'n?" Slade gave him a wolfish grin.

Aaliyah flashed Alaric an appreciative smile as she stroked the handles of Zethan's Yamaha, sporty and built for speed and maneuvering. I would have thought she was a classic girl, preferring an Enfield like me or Chieftain like Alaric.

"Speaking of bitch." Aaliyah crossed to me, grabbed her helmet from my bike and sauntered over to Alaric's, sliding on behind him.

Argument settled!

Slade clicked his tongue on his cheek as she set her helmet over her head, concealing that beautiful, smug smile just for him.

Impressed, I whistled. Dark Sorceress was a take-no-shit kind of woman and I respected that. A lot. Every time she got knocked down, she got back up, swinging harder, smarter, better. I never met a woman so strong and fierce in the face of adversity. My ex took off at the first sign of trouble in our marriage. Wasn't interested in making it work. Apparently, my best friend's dick solved her heartache. Things wouldn't be like that with Aaliyah. She'd fight for what she believed in. Fight for those she loved until her last breath.

I let my guard down around her. Dangerous. Turbulent. I was terrified to get too close to her and held her at arm's length. The woman possessed the power to corrupt and ruin me, especially after the bond expressed her desire for casual fun with no strings attached the other night. A little slip that crushed the air from me and cut my heart to pieces. Now I didn't know how to react around her and retreated into my shell. I didn't want to get hurt a-fucking-gain after what my ex did to me. I couldn't go through that again.

Slade gave her a crunchy glare. "I'm looking forward to setting you over my knee to punish you for that sassy little mouth of yours."

Aaliyah flipped him the bird and I chuckled, trying to stay upbeat and ignoring the heartache chewing away at my chest. Our president demanded pure control, but she wasn't handing it over. She handled him like he was her Harley Davidson, commanding him left, sliding him right, negotiating him in tricky terrain. Amusing to watch, especially when she humbled him.

I didn't like having to share my woman with three other men, but I did it to make her happy. I'd damn well take full advantage of the extra time I spent with her while it lasted before the others stole the rest of her time. And that would be soon. Knowing Slade, he'd tried to steal more than his fair share, leaving the rest of us to put him back in his place. I just hoped we could all convince her to stay. That she'd finally realize the mate bond didn't manipulate and trick her feelings. That they were real.

Alaric's end of the bond brightened as Aaliyah wrapped her arms around his waist. Honor, appreciation, and contentment that she'd chosen him over the others. His satisfied smile stretched through our connection as he gave her jacketed arm a few strokes and pressed it tighter to his stomach. A law-and-order man, he always let the louder, higher-ranking club personalities take charge with our woman, which often left him with the scraps. Never heard him complain once. I was happy for him. He deserved this. By choosing him, Aaliyah showed she was willing to work things out with him. He started his bike and rolled it out of the garage to warm up.

"Fucker," Slade growled and shoved his helmet down. Someone didn't take defeat well.

My helmet hid my chuckle as I moved out of the garage, waiting for my president, where I'd take the rear to protect him.

I wanted to get this over and done with so I could return

and solve the riddle of the demonic protection of the Wolves and test my recent theory.

***

WE ROLLED up outside the bar my god-highway sources told me belonged to Hellfire MC, where they hid their club beneath the business. Ten miles out of town, we pulled over on the side of the road, allowing Alaric to project his consciousness into pigeons, magpies and ravens to scope out the bar. Two bikes left the premises from an underground parking garage. Views from directly across the street alerted us to the president's arrival.

"Aaliyah, you're coming with us." Slade pushed his kick-stand down.

"Is that wise?" Aaliyah countered. "I just healed from a gunshot wound. Alaric's still healing internally."

Slade tucked his keys in his pocket, scanning the cars driving down the street as if one of them contained her brother. "You're not staying out here exposed. We don't know if Hellfire works for Danny."

I disagreed with Slade's decision to bring her here and put her in danger. But he wanted her with us in case we needed her to heal us. Not my choice to make, and I had to follow an order.

He flicked a finger at her, and she surprisingly came. "Stay by my side." Baring teeth, he brushed her arm and commanded, "At the first sign of trouble, make these cunts shit their pants or worse." He dropped a rough kiss to the top of her head, and her eyelids fluttered. "Do me proud."

"Oh, I'll do you proud." Magic flared through her. Resentful, hot, and bitter, seeking revenge for turning her life upside down.

"That's my little dark sorceress." I gave her ass a quick bump.

Slade smirked, loving the heated emotions rising in her. "Let's get this shit over with so we can head home." He twitched his neck from side to side, his muscles cracking, releasing the building tension.

Alaric took the lead as we sauntered inside, taut, alert, scanning for trouble. Security roved an eye over us, trying to block us from entering, but Slade swept him aside with ease, and the guy stumbled into the wall.

Music thumped deeper inside the bar. Some dive called Juice, owned by Hellfire MC. Smoke hung thick in the air, making it difficult to breathe. I don't think this place ever had an open window or fresh air. Spilled drink residue made my boots stick to the tiled floor. Nuts crunched under my soles. Fuck, this place was a pigsty.

Alaric finished his scan of the room, flashing Slade four fingers, signaling four Hellfire members inside the bar.

Barely legal-aged strippers wandered throughout the crowd, enticing with their slutty outfits, seeking lap dances and tips. Three women worked the stage above, shaking their asses and tits, curving around poles, bending their bodies in incredible ways. Not my idea of a good time. Men sipped at their drinks, leering at the show up on stage, one getting dragged by his tie into a private booth for a lap dance.

When the bartender caught sight of us, he signaled to two other club members in the corner of the strip club. Eyes narrowed. Brows dropped. Mouths tightened. We weren't welcome here, that was clear.

Aaliyah stuck to Slade's side, sandwiched between him and Alaric, with me at the rear. I kept my eyes trained on my president and woman. No one was getting close enough to touch them. Before we entered, I established a magical barrier around them to repel any weapons in case tensions escalated.

Slade left her by Alaric's side, approaching the bar, a towering inferno of menace. "Get me the president of Hellfire!" he bellowed above the music.

The bartender wiped a glass with a tea towel. "No one here like that."

Classic lie. We knew this town. Studied it after we took over the Winter's Devils' region. Knew our new competitors, their territory, business, and club management. I had dirt on every single one of them. If they wanted to start more shit with us, I'd be sending out evidence to the state and federal police. Get these pricks out of our business and off our backs. Put an end to our ever-growing list of enemies.

"Get me Hellfire." Slade lowered his voice to a threatening growl that said this dick had three seconds before he died. "Before I come behind the bar and throw you across it."

The bartender quickly put his glass and rag down. "Wait here." He scurried away through a doorway. Weak sack of shit. If one of our barmen caved so easily, Slade would fire his ass.

Movement out of the corner of my eye set my body on edge.

"Incoming," Alaric warned.

Four Hellfire members approached from every angle to circle us. Hands moved to the guns concealed beneath their cuts.

I tested the shield and it held.

Slade didn't even bother to look at them as he addressed them. "Do anything stupid and you won't be going home tonight."

"You're the ones who're surrounded," the cocky one to the left lipped.

"Where's your pussy of a president?" Slade growled, his bond glowing white-hot. "Hiding like the bitch he is?"

Two men took that as an invitation to teach him a lesson. But three men emerged from a door behind the bar, stopping them. I sized them up. Center – tall, well-built, oozing command, the words President and Devil stamped on his cut. Next, shorter, stockier, deadly, clutching a gun by his groin, my enforcer equivalent. Third, muscled to the hilt, definitely short on brains.

Issues like this were dealt with by meeting on neutral territory, but Slade entered the mouth of hell by walking right into their town and bar.

Hellfire's president's alert eyes dipped to Slade's cut. "You're not welcome here, Jackals." He said the last word as if it tasted like shit. "Get the fuck out of our territory."

Slade put the *fuck you* in his eyes as he pulled his mouth open to one side, showing teeth. "No can do. See, the thing is." He cracked his knuckles. "You've been interfering where you shouldn't, blocking other clubs from passing through *our* territory." His voice hardened as he drove the meaning home.

Violation of the biker code. Clubs had gone to war for less.

Aaliyah held her ground, staring at the men scanning her from head to toe. I kept my hands off her despite wanting her body close to mine if I had to shield her and throw her to the floor, so I took the hits.

Devil smiled smugly. "Ain't your territory no more, Slade. We've claimed it." Arrogant, corrupt, slimy bastard tried to steal our region behind our backs. A place waited for him in hell.

Flames licked at the bond. Slade's gaze set alight with barely restrained turbulence. He needed to stay calm, or he'd escalate the situation. Explode this bar with gunfire and flames.

Slade towered over the punk by a few good inches. His body twitched, every muscle ready to respond to his command to swing and take this wanker down. "Fuck with my territory again, and I'll bring the full force of the Jackals down on your club." His crisp warning burned with the threat it promised.

Devil listened carefully, weighing his options, folding his arms over his chest. "You killed our distributor and smoked our stock. Seems you owe us reparations."

Fuck. I knew this issue would come back to bite us. We tried to warn Slade to leave Hellfire's warehouse alone. Half a million dollars in debt, and unable to repay Hellfire MC for destroyed stock. Slade would never agree to that deal anyway. What he did was justified in his mind. Unfortunately, Hellfire was caught in the middle and lost out.

"We don't owe you shit, cunt," Slade snarled chillingly, standing firm, not letting Devil get a word in edgewise. "You stole a shipment of our Pharaoh and sold it from your warehouse. I took what you owed us."

For that mistake, Slade whacked Hellfire's distributor and burned the stock and warehouse down as retribution. A risky move that threatened more trouble for the club.

Devil shifted. "We didn't steal your shit. Had nothing to do with selling your shit."

"Then your man acted without your orders." Slade's fists clenched. "Far as I'm concerned, the burden and debt fall to you."

The tension swelled as thick as the machine-generated smoke pouring off the empty stage.

"Don't think so, motherfucker. You owe us seven hundred grand." By the deadly look on Devil's face, we weren't getting out of here alive without a fight. We owed cash. Without paying it, we'd pay with our blood instead.

Slade had two options—diffuse the situation or escalate it. In his typical style, he chose the second. "We're not paying you cunts a fucking cent." Muscles in his neck bulged, his jackal barely contained beneath his skin. "And you're gonna stay the fuck out of our business or end up the same as the Winter's Devils, and we'll claim your territory too."

Hellfire's president removed his gun, a Colt pistol, and aimed it at Slade. "Like I said before, this ain't your territory no more. You forfeited it for fucking with us."

My body went rigid. As enforcer, it was my job to carry out the rules within the club and to protect my president's life. This fuck Devil broke the biker code by interfering with our business, and it was down to me to enforce the law. I'd have to disarm this prick and the other two either side of him. Odds not in my favor.

Slade read my tension through the bond and held up his palm at me. He'd handle this. The deadly flash in his eye said nothing would sate him but bloodshed, broken bones, and pain. Moving faster than a regular human, he grabbed Devil's gun, smashing him in the nose with it. A shattering crunch accompanied the break in the music. Devil stumbled back, clutching his broken, bleeding nose. Slade ejected the gun's magazine and pocketed it, cleared the chamber and snapped the weapon in two, tossing it aside. Then he finished Hellfire's president by grabbing him by the hair and kneeing him in the face, knocking him out cold. Mercy by any standard, when he could have slit his throat or pumped a bullet through his skull. A warning for now. Move against us again, and Devil wouldn't live to see another day.

Fire flowed in a heated rush to every part of my body as Slade ordered Alaric, "Get her out of here!"

Unwillingness to leave his president nipped at Alaric's

bond as he obeyed his order and grabbed Aaliyah by the waist and dragged her away from danger, using his back as a shield. Slade might be ruthless, but he was cautious and wouldn't risk his mate's safety after losing the two most important women in his life.

As men descended on them, Aaliyah unclipped the gun Slade gifted her and gave fire at two men coming at them from the side. Non-lethal shots to their legs, and they went down with precision.

*That's my girl.* Pride warmed my chest. My mate could take care of herself.

I took the heat from the stocky bastard, protecting my president, throwing an uppercut to his jaw. His head snapped back and he hit the bar, hard, going down. The other one wasn't so easy. He caught me in the chin, and I staggered back several steps, my head spinning. Next thing I knew, Slade had him raised over his head then flung him over the bar. Bottles and glasses smashed. He didn't get up as Slade hulked, spinning to face any more attackers.

Patrons and strippers screamed at the outbreak of violence, ducking below tables or rushing off stage and out of the crowd, seeking exit. Music screeched to a halt. Strobe lights ceased, but the main lights remained dark.

Gunfire erupted in the bar, bullets chipping at glass, metal, and wood. Heart thundering, I threw Slade to the ground and lifted a table to shield us. It wouldn't hold us for long. A gunman came at us from the side. Slade grabbed a chair and hurled it at the guy's legs, breaking his knees. The gunman screamed and dropped his weapon, toppling into a set of tables and chairs. Another gunman approached from our right.

"Move back," I told Slade. "Get your gun ready. Fire approaching at 11PM." I referred to the direction from which the man approached.

Slade gave me a stiff nod and crawled back across the floor. I counted to three, then gripped the table's leg. Pulse thundering, I flung the table at the man, catching his gun, the impact making his wrist snap and throwing him back into the bar. I roared, rushing forward, snatching the table and ramming it at him, pushing him over the bar. Beer taps cracked and exploded liquid. I smashed his face until he sagged and slid off the bar.

"We've made our point." Slade grabbed me by the cut and dragged me backward. "We're leaving."

Something told me this wouldn't be the last we'd hear from Hellfire. Perhaps Slade should have killed them.

## CHAPTER 12

## Zethan

Fuck, I couldn't believe I contemplated this. A vulnerable tremor swept over me. My finger hovered over the cell button as I propped myself up on one elbow. Deep, pink scars crossed my chest, sides, stomach, and arms. Scars I kept hidden at all costs. I looked away from the camera reflection, biting back my disgust. Frankenstein stared back at me, his body all chopped up, sewed back together, and brought back to life.

I'd never done this before. Never exposed myself like this. Putting myself on the line was a big leap, but she needed to see me. Know me. Love all of me. Fuck knows I couldn't wait another damn day without her. This woman had me so twisted that I'd do just about anything to repair the damage between us. Do anything to make her mine.

Yesterday she had a rough day, with her, Slade, Alaric, and Castor barely getting out alive from their impromptu visit to

Hellfire MC. Reports filtering back to me indicated Slade made his point to the out-of-line club and things had turned testy. Probably not the last we'd hear from those pricks.

That was the last thing I wanted her to see after our last conversation about bikers not being able to deliver her a happily ever after. Who said we couldn't give her that? Just because her dad passed away short of sixty, didn't mean we wouldn't live to grow old, or that a few of her mates wouldn't be there for her. I wanted to show her what a life with me—with us—could be like. I'd text her every damn day, bring a smile to her beautiful face, and tell her I loved her at every opportunity. Because any day might be my last. I'd not waste one with her. Being the avatar of a Death god had taught me the importance of that on top of losing my sister and son.

"To hell with it," I uttered, capturing the snap of my bare chest, loading it into a message, and entering the text. Doubt had me pause and wait to send it. By sending her this, I laid it bare for her. Gave her the chance to respond ... if she responded. Ball was in her fucking court. I hated the loss of control and the pit it opened in my stomach. "Fuck it."

Like a goddamn sucker, I read over the text again. *I'm bare to you.* Christ, I had it bad. Put my heart and soul on the line.

I shot off the bed, needing to get some steam out of my system. I threw on a shirt, jeans, socks, and boots, then marched out of my club bedroom and down the hall. We needed more information from our captives, and I was the only one who could obtain it. I descended the basement's stairs two at a time, alerting our prisoners to my arrival. Manacles clinked as the captives shuffled tensely after witnessing what I'd done to Jaxx several days earlier. Revived him from death several times to let Slade torture him. The for-hire biker men were well trained in torture and hadn't given up their secrets to Castor, despite hours of beating and questioning. Now that Slade deemed them useless to us, the burden fell to me to extract it.

I came to stand in front of the first prisoner. "Any last confessions?"

Fear darkened his gaze as he looked up at me with black and blue eyes. "Fuck off! I'll die before I give you a thing." He spat at my feet. Poor choice. Never goad a Death god.

"A wish this god of Death can grant." I seized him by the hair, forcing his gaze up to me. I'd be the last face he'd see before expiring.

Deadly powers wound around his neck, cutting off his air supply, choking him. He gasped and squirmed, his fingers flexing and extending with the need to scratch his throat. Red flushed across his face as I stole the air from his lungs and body. Blood exploded in his eyeballs.

The last words he gasped were, "Die, motherfucker." Waste of air.

I laughed at him and shoved his limp, lifeless body aside. Time for the fun part. Pale blue mist from his soul drifted from his body, indicating he belonged to the Indian Underworld. Before he departed this world, I captured him in my grasp, sifting through his memory for what I needed.

Once a soul arrived in its afterlife, it would go through a similar process, where it watched a film of every important event in its life. Good, bad, and ugly, known as a life review. A way for a soul to experience the pain and pleasure it inflicted on themselves and others.

The life review was the most arduous and agonizing torture for a soul to relive. Hated the process myself. Had to be done though, in addition to the weighing of the heart ceremony. Information extracted was considered by the Underworld judges in determining what punishment the soul deserved.

The beauty in my case was that the life review showed me

exactly what I needed. Sure, I prematurely took this fuckhead's life to obtain it. Prick was bound for death in a month, anyway. Gunshot to the chest on his next mission. If we hadn't freed him or intervened, that was. Crime didn't pay, after all. Unless balanced with good deeds like we did under instruction from our gods.

I flicked through the captive's memories until I found the one I wanted. Identity of his employer. A calculating man dressed in an expensive suit handing this idiot a packet of cash.

I tightened my grip on the soul, causing him pain, preventing him from going where he needed to go. "Give me a name. *Now.*"

Without his earthy trappings, his ego, pride, etcetera, he gave me the name freely. "Gerald Walsh. He hires out contract killers like me."

"Where can I find him?" I prodded.

"Victoria Street, Kings Cross."

Sydney. Home to mobsters and underworld figures. More fucking mafia pricks to deal with. I'd prefer to avoid that if I could. Protect the club from getting tangled in more drama, mafia hits, and additional enemies. Especially since Castor and I took out mafia associates a few days back.

I scoured the soul's recent memories, pausing on an image of Danny standing beside someone in a suit. A reflection in the visor of one of the riders before they left the warehouse to ambush us. I performed a final scan, viewing the memory from different angles, but couldn't get the complete picture to get more detail on the suit's face.

"Give my regards to Yama." I released the soul, finished my deathly business, and scanned the last two prisoners before sending them to their final resting place.

I didn't enjoy taking lives despite representing the god of Death. Part of the job, though. Enemies needed to be taken out before they posed more danger and harm. Unlike Slade, a force of fucking nature who destroyed and relished that shit. Goddamn lived and breathed it. Seeing his mom gunned down like that had changed him. Brought out a ruthlessness, a savagery only matched by his god.

The two Wolves kept down here begged me with their eyes to release them too. Not yet. Wasn't their time yet. We might need more information or use them as bargaining chips in this war with Danny.

Pleased with my findings, I went back upstairs. Slade let me handle this my way. I'd inform him of the information later. Right now, he prepared for a visit with Tony, our manufacturer of Pharaoh, to sort out our debt. Dealing with cash flow problems put him in a real mood.

Grunts from the club's gym called me to the door. Alaric worked out, doing the bench press, his neck and face bright red from the strain. I entered and advanced to him, taking the weight off his chest when he finished his set. He nodded at me, breathing hard. In the mirror, I watched Aaliyah perform yoga on the mats, admiring her long, toned legs and strong ass. Flexible. Fit. Fine. Fucking incredible.

Flashbacks of her at the dinner table two nights ago burned in my brain. Castor licking butterscotch sauce from her pussy. What I wouldn't have given to be in his place, tasting her. My big guy woke with a renewed hunger. Dammit. I didn't want to be the creep getting a hard-on and leering at her.

The woman lived to make the world a better place for people, down to the smallest detail. Sitting with the abused women on the shelter's porch, tea in hand, letting them get shit off their chests. Animal spotting with Danya, Lesley's daughter at the shelter, making her day. Comforting Alaric after an episode when he'd been an absolute cockhead to her.

Beyond being my mate, destined for me, how could I not be drawn to her?

A dull ache set in as my cock chose that fucking moment to magick the hell off somewhere without my control. I rubbed at the hollowness left behind. Sometimes I didn't notice the damned thing missing for hours, until the pain kicked in or one of the club's members found my dick, shifted into a wooden phallus. Other times, it hurt like a mother from the get-go. All I knew was that I had to find the fucker.

Hiding my cock was totally up Slade's and Alaric's alley. Whenever it dropped off at random intervals or stressful times, they'd find it and play a game of hide and seek. Pricks used it as a tire stopper for Slade's Harley last time. Goddamn drove over it to test its strength. Hurt like nothing else. After I found it, reattached the little shit, I made sure to kick their fucking asses.

"Lost your cock again?" Alaric grinned wolfishly. "Not clogging up the toilet again, is it?"

Asshole stuffed it in the bowl of my private bathroom once. Alerted, he'd be on the lookout now, his mind thinking up a place to stash it, forcing me into a hunt and wasting my time. I glared at him. Not fucking funny. Third time this week the damned thing pulled a no-show. My cock had a life of its own since Aaliyah showed up in our world.

I couldn't help it. Part and parcel of being the avatar of Osiris, the Egyptian god of the Dead and Resurrection. Poor bastard was chopped to pieces and murdered by his brother, Set, who spread the maimed body across the world. Hence, why my dick occasionally went missing, and the reason for my accident, leaving me covered in scars.

"What?" Aaliyah coughed out as she righted herself from the sexy damn pose that dropped me into this position in the first place.

Best I find my appendage fast and not leave it to their mercy. "Nothing," I muttered, scanning the room. "Dick." I smacked him on the back of the head.

Alaric made a run for the leg press, and I knew he was up to something. Prick was lightning fast like his bird and got my wooden cock and pretended to do a lift with it.

Pain from lifting the weight hit the spot where my parts should be and I hunched over, grabbing my crotch. "Fuck!"

"Give it back, you asshole." Aaliyah chuckled as she wrestled Alaric for my business.

"I'll return it for a kiss." He pressed a finger over his cheek.

"You're just as bad as Castor." She pecked him on the cheek. Polite. Soft. Smoldering. Alaric grinned and tossed it to her. "And you're a jerk!" She punched him in the chest and walked back to me, holding out my jewels.

"Thanks." Glowing red, I snatched it, turned and marched from the room. The pain faded somewhat with the proximity of my member to my body, and I breathed out my relief.

Alaric grunted and made a pained cry from inside the gym.

Fuming, I stomped back to my office, leaned on the wall and shoved it over my groin, letting it magically reattach. For the next few moments, I rubbed away the lingering throb until it vanished. It was bad enough that I was maimed, but I had to go through the humiliation too. My brothers were immature dicks. If Aaliyah wasn't in the gym, I'd have gotten into my workout gear and gone a few rounds on the punching bag to let off steam.

Instead, I remembered one of my associates with whom I wanted to make contact. Needed a small favor. I removed my cell and phoned him.

"Zethan, my man," James answered.

For the last two years, he assisted me in getting fake ID

papers to women who needed to escape as well as securing them a rental living space, a car, and safe passage to their new home. Trustworthy and dependable, he could also track down anyone, regardless of where they hid.

"James, I need a favor." Straight to the point. I wasn't exactly a chatty guy. And I didn't want to get stuck on the phone with this asshole for an hour listening to his indigestion problem. "Need you to track someone. A little girl. Adopted about seven years ago. Mother's name is Aaliyah Heller."

Last week, Aaliyah confessed to me that she had a child with her ex who died in an accident. Young, penniless, studying nursing, and not wanting to rely on her family, she adopted out her newborn. Saved her from her father's club and the life that Aaliyah fell into. Heartache in the bond matched my own after her admission. Still hurt to breathe. Deep, soul-crushing regret burned the two of us.

"Anything for you, Zethan." I heard the smile in James' voice.

"Appreciate it," I told him." Send me the bill, not the shelter, okay?"

"Sure."

I hung up as soon as James agreed.

I wasn't sure if Aaliyah ever tried to find the child after giving her up. I hoped to find the family that adopted her daughter. Nothing was more painful than losing a child. If I could help reunite them, even if it was for her to watch her daughter from a distance, then maybe I could bring some peace to her heart. Fill a part of the gaping hole inside her chest.

I never got to see my little man before he passed. I'd give anything to see little Dylan again. To have one moment to hold him, stroke his soft hair, kiss his forehead, and listen to his precocious laugh.

The same might not be said with Aaliyah, and ultimately, the decision rested with her. Once James located the child, I'd tell her, and give her the choice of what she wanted to do. Regardless of her decision, I'd be there for her. I just hoped this gesture didn't blow up in my face.

The buzz in my palm signaled my phone received a new message. Couldn't be James already. Too soon. Aaliyah's name displayed on the screen. My breath caught in my tight chest. Fuck, I was never scared to read a text message before. Not when I'd seen the horror of humanity. Cruelty and indifference of gods. Destruction and deceit of motorcycle clubs. But reading this text message terrified me like nothing else. Rejection by my mate scared me, but I braved it for her.

*Sorry about Alaric,* the first line read. *That wasn't cool.*

Fuck, she pitied me. I didn't need her pity.

I kept reading. *If it makes you feel any better, I gave Alaric the worst nipple cripple. Screamed like a bitch.*

I chuckled. So that was why he cried out. Served the asshole right. A different kind of warmth, softer, glowing, like a fire kicking off in a hearth, spread across my chest. My woman stood up for me. Made up for her voting against me to rescue the tortured women in Danny's studio.

*Thanks for having my back,* I replied to her.

*Any time,* she instantly shot me back with a smiley face.

I wanted this woman even more. She eased all the hell in my life. God knows my soul needed a break from all the anguish dragging it down. Fuck this damn curse keeping us apart.

Another message came through. *I thought naked pics weren't until our third date? Rulebreaker.* Wink face emoji.

I barked out a laugh. Bantering with her took a load off my mind. A desperately needed escape with all the shit the club had to deal with, the tightened funds at the shelter.

*Semi-naked,* I corrected Aaliyah. *Dick pics are a strictly fifth date only deal. Stop trying to chat me up to get one sooner. I'm still waiting for our first date.*

She flashed me back a laughing emoji with tears. *Damn. Way to keep a girl in suspense.*

My dick hardened with anticipation at our flirty exchange. If this was what she was like over text, I imagined what she'd be like alone, in my bed. The fact that she wasn't weirded out by my magicking dick was a good sign. Life ceased being normal when you were the avatar of a god.

*As for the chest pic.* Emoji with bulging love heart eyes. *Hot AF. More, please.*

Christ, this woman twisted me upside down. One minute she was mad and distant, the next teasing, flirting, tempting me to send her more. She had my head, heart, and dick aching with confusion.

*You're beautiful too.* Her message reminded me of when I told her that she was the most beautiful woman I ever saw. *Don't be a stranger. A.*

Fuck, this woman was giving me a second chance. More than I deserved. I'd not let this opportunity slip by. Desperate to see her again, I snatched a pile of paperwork from my desk and bolted from my room.

## CHAPTER 13

### *A*aliyah

I spat out the water I sipped at from the voice that took me by surprise.

"Hi," he interrupted me.

I wasn't expecting him, but he came quickly after my last text. Butterflies filled my stomach. Something about *him* made me nervous. Out of all my supposed mates, he made me uneasy because he said we were doubly fated to be together irrespective of the curse. My head and heart knew it, but the curse chased him away from me.

Or it was the sexy, naked chest pic he'd unexpectedly sent me, and the note, *I'm bare to you*. Fucking hell, talk about taking me by surprise. The promise of laying himself bare to me had me all mushy and smoldering, and I didn't do lovey shit. I didn't expect such a distant, brutal man to be open with me, when bikers like him usually were closed off and emotionally unavailable.

Goddess, his picture flashed in my mind again, heating me all over. Manly scars running down his body gave him that hard-fought warrior edge. Red flannel material teased at a smattering of hair and a gorgeous, fit body beneath it that I wanted to peel back so I could trace every line on his skin. Golden stubble along his brutal jaw begged to prickle beneath my fingertips. Ear-length light hair that I wanted to run my fingers through. Haunted emerald eyes that I wanted to soothe and chase away his pain.

I patted my chest to stop coughing. "Hey. How are you?"

"Glad, now that I'm here." Charmer. Never would have picked this hard, brutal man to have a charismatic bone in his body. Every one of *"my mates"* surprised me in that respect.

Elation tripped through Zethan like he was hit by a live wire and resuscitated from death. He enjoyed my texts and now got lost in my smile. Bright. Beautiful. Just for him, when all I had lately for him were wary, challenging eyes and a hostile, sassy mouth.

Residual embarrassment from the gym incident hid behind the bond, but I glossed over it, wanting to make him feel comfortable. Having a dick that accidentally poofed away couldn't be easy to deal with. Twice now, I'd witnessed this strange phenomenon. I didn't know how they explained that to the rest of the club and hid their status as avatars.

"Feel like a ride to the shelter?" Zethan's desire to be closer ached down the bond like a lonely, melancholy love song that swept me up in its grasp.

He kept his distance since he admitted he gave me the phone to collect intel. Typical ex-cop, treating me like I was one of his criminals under investigation. Only doing his part for his club. The stubborn, fierce side of me wanted to hold it against him, hold onto my anger, because fuck knew I had a lot burning inside of me. At him and Alaric for bringing me to the Jackals. At my deranged fuckwit of a brother. At the gods and curse thrusting the fated mates bullshit onto me and depriving me of a choice in my love life. I swiped a hand through my hair, trying to bring down my emotions. Hell, if I were honest about it, I would do the same in Zethan's position. After everything, the rational part of me was willing to move beyond the phone business. But I was going to make him work for it. Make them all grovel for holding me captive.

I wanted to get out of the clubhouse, quit being idle, and make myself useful. Hiding out at Castor's with my wings left me bored and yearning to get back to nursing or to the shelter to share my gift. Above that, I felt like I sat and waited for Danny or the Wolves to strike again. Waiting sucked.

"Sure thing." I finished my drink and set the glass down. My muscles buzzed with warmth and power from my morning yoga workout.

"I've got Lesley and Danya's papers to move to Western Australia." Zethan held up a stack of paperwork—passports, driver's license, credit cards, additional ID, and rental papers. Everything they needed to start a new life halfway across the country, out of reach of Lesley's creep of an ex-boyfriend who hurt her and the child. "Thought you might like to say goodbye."

I'd bonded with the mother and daughter during my stay at the shelter, and I wished nothing more for them than to have a clean slate. To make a new home, a new life, free of those confines of the emotional and physical abuse they suffered.

I hid my smile behind my glass, adoring that he trusted me to involve me in deeper shelter business. "I'd love to." I tipped out the rest of my water and set the glass in the dishwasher. "It's like you're a mind reader, knowing I need to get out of here."

"If I was a mind reader." Zethan came closer, nudging me with his arm. "I'd have sent you dick pics by now."

I nudged him back, enjoying the feel of his powerfully built and massive arms. "Put your money where your mouth is."

Shit, I shouldn't have flirted with him. Shouldn't have encouraged him. But this man drew me in like a damn moth hypnotized by a flame. Staying away from him, or any of my *supposed mates*, was difficult. Each of them called to a slice of my heart and soul. Locking them out of my heart was as impossible as stopping a meteor from crashing to earth.

And, okay, so I might not have wanted to wait for a fifth date to receive those damn pics. Hell, to wait for any dates. I wanted to see all of him. Know all of him. It frightened me that this lost and broken man affected me the most. He would be the hardest one to walk away from if I decided to leave once the crap with Danny was finished.

Zethan's end of the bond dipped and curled in on itself, responding to my reluctance and uncertainty to stick around. He used his insecurity over his scars and the curse as a shield to keep me away. This man already lost so much and feared he'd lose me, too. Scars could fade over time and were nothing to be ashamed about. Memories weren't so easy to erase.

Regret slashed at my heart at potentially being the one to hurt and break him again. That sappy bitch just wanted to soothe his haunted soul and ease the guilt that destroyed him every single time he closed his eyes. The smart woman in me wanted to run and leave them all behind. But we all had a past. We were all broken in some way or another. Fuck knows I was selfish and left behind a child I couldn't care for, when I should have done everything in my power to love her. That shared pain of loss was what threw Zethan and me together, and he'd be the one to dredge up my past and make me face it when I was a coward.

He wasn't alone in that regard. All my mates feared something. Castor hid from me because he was scared of getting close. Alaric's demons made it difficult for him to trust me. Slade didn't like to lose control, and with me, he'd always battle for it.

Zethan didn't move away from me, and I felt the onset of cramps, but we both refused to step back, as if joined together by a magnet. I brushed away the hair hanging over his eye, my finger skimming his forehead, the heavy lines through it that I wanted to smooth away. His heart was shackled for too long, and it aged him. He needed to let go of some of the baggage he carried before it dragged him down with it. It pained me to watch him juggle it when he didn't need to. What happened to Liz wasn't his fault. He couldn't have saved his sick little boy, Dylan, either. As for his sister's tragic and cruel murder, Zethan needed to put his guilt to rest there too, or else he risked becoming completely like his god. A man lost and held captive to the world of death.

He took the liberty of kissing me, soft, cautious, asking for permission to continue. "Don't leave, Aaliyah." He stroked my cheek, stoking my pleasure and pain. "Don't you ever fucking leave," he growled more insistently, and the possessiveness went straight to my core.

That wasn't his choice to make any more than it was the gods'. I wanted to reply but my throat choked up, the bitch blocking me on purpose.

Words that he said to me days ago resurfaced. *"Aaliyah, that life doesn't exist for you anymore. So long as your brother's alive, you're in danger. Whether he's alive or dead, I won't let my mate go."* To hell with whatever threat Danny posed. I was going to have the fight of my life attempting to leave these four men. With them and my heart.

Zethan groaned with frustration and released my mouth, biting my bottom lip as if punishing me. "Fuck, you're the most stubborn woman I've ever met. It does my head in." He pressed his forehead to mine. "I'll just have to do something to make you want to stay."

"Zethan..." My stiff joints ached as I raised my palm to set it on his rock-hard pec. Despite the ache, I had no intention of moving, wanting nothing more than to stay in his arms. But I was going to fight him on this topic. "You can't ask me to give up my life for you. Would you do the same for me?"

"The only way I leave is death." He snagged my hand and dragged me from the kitchen, ending the conversation.

We bumped into Slade in the hallway, looking worse for wear. Shoulders hitched up near his neck, dark circles under his eyes, and smelling of cigarettes and whisky. "Where are you two going?" he grunted.

"To the shelter," Zethan replied, releasing my hand and separating from me, easing the pain in my stomach and joints. "Got a send-off."

Slade grunted his approval. "Morning, Nurse A." He moved past us and left me feeling cold in his shadow. Something was up there. He never left me without a devilishly sexy smile and dimples.

"Everything okay, Slade?" I turned and called out.

"Nothing I can't handle." He gave me a two-finger salute and entered his office, leaving me concerned for him.

I glanced to Zethan for answers.

"Don't ask," he told me, waving at me to leave, but that didn't ease my worry for Slade. He looked headed for a heart attack or stroke if he didn't stop smoking, drinking, and stressing. That was where I came in, but I doubted the infuriating man would listen to my advice.

Cold winter air wrapped around me outside as we climbed into Zethan's van. Thank God his men went down to my mom's place and retrieved it. I worried my brother's sedative kidnapper might have stolen it and sent it to the chop shop.

Zethan's jaw hardened as he cranked the engine to life. I wanted to soften his stern features with a single stroke of my fingertips. "This will be the last relocation we'll manage for a while." His voice hardened like his jaw.

Guilt burned at the lining of my gut. Zethan didn't need to explain why. Fucking Danny was the reason. Bastard stole a million dollars worth of drugs from the Jackals. Not that I approved of my mates' means of making money, but it funded charitable organizations that supported abused women so I couldn't be too judgy.

Castor told me that their avatars warned them off maintaining a balance, weighing up the bad deeds they conducted through the club with good feats. Otherwise, the gods would throw the club and avatars into chaos. Even old Set had to rein in his destruction at times.

"I'm sorry that my asshole of a brother fucked things up for you." I set my hand on Zethan's thigh, and he stiffened, glancing at it, glaring as if I set his pants ablaze. Right now, I didn't give a shit about the damn curse. He needed my reassurance.

"Don't apologize because your brother is an unhinged psychopath," he growled deep in his chest. "You played no part in this." His eyes radiated caution, as if it took every bit of restraint he possessed not to slide across the seat and put me in his lap.

I fiddled with my fingers, wondering what end Zethan and the Jackals planned for my brother when irrefutable proof connected him to the stolen shipment and second ambush. "What will you do to him when you catch him?"

Zethan's knuckles went white from clutching the steering wheel hard. "Cut off his cock and make him choke on it for what he's done to those women. Rape him with a molten hot crowbar—" He shut down quickly when he realized he upset me.

Tears broke out of my eyes, and I slammed them shut. Danny hurt so many people. My mother. Me. The Wolves. Innocent women. The Jackals. I didn't want him to die. He was my brother. But if he murdered our father, he was dead to me, literally and figuratively. And I'd be the one to put the bullets through his back like he did to Dad. Only, I wouldn't let him escape like Slade. I'd make sure I finished the job. Hell, I'd use my damn powers to end his life if I had to. I suspected if I had the powers of life that I also possessed some control over death. One way or another, my brother would not walk away alive, so help me goddess.

Zethan's control broke and he shuffled over the seat to embrace me. "Don't blame yourself for what's happened."

"I don't know what's gotten into him," I sobbed into his arms. "He's always been a hothead. Always competing with me. Trying to outdo me and get Dad's attention. But he was never sadistic. Never cruel."

Zethan lightly stroked my back. "Well, something fucked him up."

## CHAPTER 14

*A*aliyah

"Jerry!" I threw myself into my uncle's arms and hugged him inside the shelter's entrance. He looked so much better than when he first came out of the cell. Fatter, faded bruises, and only wary eyes instead of fearful ones. "How you doing?"

Slade permitted Jerry to assist in the shelter after I bargained his ass off for my uncle's freedom from the cell. The president didn't want Jerry anywhere near club business, so he put him to work, cooking, cleaning, washing, and anything else Zethan needed. Under constant guard, of course. Always driven to the shelter with a blindfold and by different routes so he never memorized the directions. Protocol to protect the shelter's location and the women within it if he ever slipped away and returned to the Wolves. I doubted he would. He loathed what Danny was doing as much as I did. We talked about it the last few days we'd worked side by side together.

"They're keeping me busy and on my toes." Jerry patted my back and let me go, smiling, the tension gone from his features and body. If I didn't know better, I'd have thought he was enjoying himself surrounded by all the women. "The Jackals do good work here."

"Yeah, they do." I rubbed Jerry's arm.

Zethan stood a close distance away, always guarding me. Cautious in case Jerry tried to hurt me and use me as leverage to get free. The Jackals weren't sure of his loyalty and warned me not to get close to my uncle, although I had no doubt of where his allegiance lay.

Danya, Lesley's little girl, raced up to Jerry and flung her arms around his leg, sobbing into his jeans. "Mom says we've got to go, but I don't want to, Uncle Jerry." She gripped him tightly and slammed her eyes shut. "Tell her we have to stay here with Uncle Zethan and Slade."

Her mother, Lesley, waited patiently behind her with a suitcase stacked with new clothes supplied by the shelter to get them through the next two weeks. The Jackals had endless generosity, fueled by their need to balance the good with the bad.

"Oh, honey." Jerry sank to his knees with a loud crack, holding onto her shoulders, his dark brown eyes gazing deeply into hers. "You've got to get back to school. Make new friends. Your mom's got a new job waiting. Uncle Zethan bought you a new car and house. Isn't that exciting?" She sulkily shook her head, and he brushed her light hair. "Trust me, in a week, you won't even remember old Jerry and this place."

"Yes, I will!" she wailed, throwing herself around him and hugging him tighter. "You make the best sandwiches. Don't tell Uncle Slade. He's nice and gives me candy when no one's looking."

Zethan and I exchanged a grinning glance. Uncle Slade.

Danya took a real liking to him after they bonded over cheese and salami sandwiches. Every time he visited, which was every few days, she was all over him, following him around.

"Who will tell me bedtime stories and watch for kangaroos on the porch?" Danya and I settled into that daily ritual when I stayed at the shelter. Didn't take her long to move on with Jerry.

I hid my smile behind my hand. Seeing the little girl's attachment to my uncle stripped my conversation with Zethan from my mind and shoved it to the back where it belonged. The past should stay there and not be dredged up when it threatened to ruin me.

Zethan approached Lesley with the stack of papers. "Look after yourselves." He, too, had built an affectionate bond with the precocious, adorable child, taking her out for ice cream, or buying her a pink teddy.

"I can't thank you enough." Lesley clutched the papers close to her chest.

"It's nothing." Zethan smiled. He was humble, simple, uncomplicated, said only whatever was necessary. "You've got my number programmed in your phone. Call me if you need me for anything. If he finds you, contacts you, let me know straight away and my team will get you out."

"Sure." Lesley threw an arm over his shoulder and dragged him in for a cuddle. He made a surprised sound as if he hadn't expected the gesture, which shocked me because I'd have imagined he'd get this reaction quite often.

Lesley smiled, patted him on the shoulder and moved to me, throwing an arm over my shoulder and dragging me in for a cuddle. "You take care of yourself, Aaliyah."

A weight hugging my leg told me Danya joined in, making it a group hug. "I'll miss you, too, Aaliyah. Don't let Uncle Jerry steal all the jellybeans."

"I'll have to hide the jellybean jar from him, won't I?" I looked down at her and tickled her chin. "And not as much as I'll miss you. Who will make kookaburra noises with me now?" One of our favorite pastimes.

"Zethan." Danya not so subtly pointed at him, making his brows rise and his gaze drop to her. "He likes you."

"Does he?" I grinned at him.

"Yeah. I can tell," Danya said it with the absolute certainty of a child. "He looks at you all the time with gross love eyes." She poked out her tongue.

"Ewww. Boy germs!" I pretended to wipe them on Danya's shoulder, and she giggled and squirmed, trying to get away. I bent down and caught her in a hug, poking her, making her squeal and wriggle more. "He's too grouchy and rides a bike!"

"Yuck!" Danya scrunched up her face. "Don't let him kiss you. He eats stinky tuna and pickled onion sandwiches."

I burst into laughter at her honesty. "Ewww! Stay away from me, Zethan," I teased, and he blew me a kiss, making Danya giggle even harder against me.

"Danya, that's not nice." Lesley clasped her daughter's hand and dragged her away.

"Your ham and jam sandwiches are gross." Zethan stuck his finger in his mouth and pretended to puke.

Danya broke free of her mother and rushed at him, beating at his legs with her palm. "No! It's the best sandwich ever." Zethan made a vomiting noise, prompting her to hit him harder, and then they both laughed.

He crouched beside her and hugged her. "Be good, okay, and look after your mom. Protect her from the monsters under the bed."

"I will." She wove her arms around his neck and hugged him back. "I've got the monster-slaying sword you gave me." She let go and pretended to swish the invisible weapon.

My body vibrated all over watching him with the child. Nothing gave him more joy than interacting with her, protecting her, giving her a second chance. Gentle, caring, and friendly were words I'd never have associated with this brutal, complex, haunted man. A side I rarely saw, unless he comforted one of the women. Otherwise, he just grunted, barely saying two words. At the club, he was subdued, withdrawn, saying his piece when required. In that moment, I was drawn to him more than I ever was to another person. I didn't want to feel this way, but couldn't shut it off, and it felt deeper than the mate bond. Soul-level shit. Like we were meant to be beyond all the curse bullshit. It made me want to run away screaming.

"Okay, you better get going." Zethan gave Danya a gentle nudge. "You've got a long drive ahead of you. Uncle Jerry made your favorite sandwiches."

"I even saved some jellybeans and put them on for you," Jerry threw in, lifting Danya's sorrowed face instantly and she squealed.

With a last wave, Lesley led Danya by the hand from the entrance, concluding their time at the shelter. We saw them out, watching them drive off and waving.

"C'mon, let me buy you lunch." Zethan jerked his head at me. "Jerry, you want anything?"

The Jackals treated him fairly by allowing him to work at the shelter and free him of his confinement. I could never repay them for their kindness.

"A meat pie from the bakery and a vanilla slice would be good, thanks, Zethan." Jerry clapped him on the shoulder, showing a comradery I hadn't observed before. "A Coke, too."

"Sure thing." Zethan trusted Jerry because he trusted me, and that gave me extra peace of mind.

Instead of driving to the bakery though, Zethan pulled up outside of Machete Park. From the center console, he grabbed a plastic bag with birdseed in it. Something told me we were making a side trip before grabbing lunch.

"Coffee?" Zethan asked outside the van as I crossed my arms to fend off the winter morning's chill.

"Vanilla latte, please." I tagged behind him to *Crema*, the little hole in the wall coffee shop that Castor took me to.

A few minutes later, we wandered across the road, coffees in our hands. We fell into a natural ease, not needing to say much but enjoying each other's company. Being with him had an innate quality about it, like we were old friends who had known each other our whole lives. But I felt a weight on his heart that sat like a dark shadow slowly choking him to death. Zethan stopped outside a gated pond inside the park's grounds where ducks and a few geese roamed the water's surface. Beneath the water, giant, bright orange and mottled fish squiggled in search of food.

"I used to take Dylan here every weekend," Zethan started, tossing some birdseed through the brown fence and into the water. Ducks scrabbled to the pond's edge to gulp down the food. "This was his favorite place."

Sorrow pricked at me, and I picked absently at the crack in the coffee cup's plastic lid. "Do you still come here? Every weekend?"

"Occasionally," he admitted, gaze locked onto the water. "More so lately. It's peaceful. Time away from all the bullshit with the club." He hung his head, making his blond hair dangle over his eyes. "It was his birthday last week."

Hell. Anniversaries like that were the worst. Pain like nothing else I ever experienced. Gut-wrenching guilt. Heart-crushing sadness. Absolute loneliness and grief. I'd give anything to go back in time to correct my mistake so I didn't have to take my daughter's birthday off work every year to lie in a ball and cry.

"Happy birthday, little man." I gestured to the bag of seed in Zethan's hand. "Can I?"

He gave it freely, and I slid my hand inside, pulling out a palmful of seed. Tossing it to the birds eased the stranglehold on my heart. I imagined my little girl with me, laughing gleefully as she chirped excitedly at the ducks pecking at the food. Begging me to open the gate so she could pet the duckies. Giving them names based on the spots on their feathers. Missing out on such events in her life made my heart crush, and I pressed my hands to my ribcage.

"I'll never get to learn what my little Mia liked." I tucked the bag of seed under my arm and picked harder at the split plastic lid. "Her favorite color, animal, or food." Details I should have known. Fuck, I should have known everything about her.

"Have you ever tried tracking her down to meet her?" His question was like a sucker punch that tripled the pain in my chest.

"I think about it every day." It hurt to get it out with the grip on my chest. "But I don't want to confuse and upset her about who her parents are. Maybe when she's older." The crack in the lid widened just like the one in my heart. "I don't know if her parents will agree to let me meet her anyway."

"I would do anything to see Dylan again." Zethan took the lid off his steaming black coffee and swallowed some.

This man didn't hold back on me. He was as open as a book to me now. A book I contemplated closing if it brought out too much pain and anguish. The nurse within me still wanted to heal the pain buried in his heart. Something told me he might be the key to healing mine.

Two quick steps brought Zethan crashing into my arms. "I didn't mean to upset you."

"It's fine." It wasn't. Devastation hit like never before.

Tears burned down my cheeks. My drink fell to the ground. I was an idiot and should never have let her go. Every damn day since, I regretted it. Worst decision of my life, seconded by healing my brother from Slade's gunshot wound.

"Let it all out." Zethan's fingers sifted through my hair. His lips brushed the skin of my forehead. I melted into the hard wall of his chest. Clenched my fingers over his biceps, needing every part of him flush to my body to ward off my heartache. "She's still alive, Aaliyah. There's still hope. Don't give up."

Hope didn't exist when I couldn't be with my daughter. When I failed her as a mother and did the unforgivable.

Joint pain made my grip on Zethan slacken. The ache in my belly threatened to topple the pain in my heart. We had to separate, but I didn't want to when this man was the only thing keeping me standing. Zethan made the choice for me, letting me go gently and stepping back to collect my drink for me, placing it in my hands.

Topic change needed, and fast. "Did you and Liz ever consider kids?" A can of worms I shouldn't have opened, but this pain was easier than discussing my daughter.

He stared into his dark liquid, his entire demeanor closing off from me, turning detached, hard, distant. "Nah, it was too soon for me. She and Slade tried IVF, and she got pregnant twice ..." Oh, fuck. She lost them. He didn't need to say it. The downcast expression said it all. "Once naturally to Castor, but she lost it. Same with Slade."

"I'm really sorry to hear that." I swallowed hard at my drink, desperately needing the heat to melt the solid mass of ice stuck in my throat. "Are kids still off the table with you?"

"I don't know." He scrubbed his stubbled jaw. "I don't think I'm meant to have anything good in my life."

Fuck. He didn't really think that, did he? I interpreted the angst crippling our bond to mean that he was just down because of missing his son.

Zethan looked up at me with eyes that burned with pain. "Do you wish you could just walk away from it all? All the god bullshit and just live a normal life?"

I wasn't sure what he was getting at. Did he blame the gods for all his agony and torment? Blame them for taking everyone he loved?

"I do too much good work for Isis to walk away," I whispered.

"I'm tired of it all," he admitted. "Running the Underworld while I sleep is exhausting. Dealing with all that death..." Despair fused in his eyes. "The bullshit with the club. Losing Abigail, Dylan, then fucking Liz. Sometimes I wonder if Osiris has affected me more than just scarring my body. That death has bled over from the afterlife into my world and intends to consume everything I hold dear."

Oh, God. He blamed himself for all his tragedies. "It's not your fault."

"Not my fault." His voice came out hard like steel. "Osiris'."

"I understand why you might think that, but tragedy hits a lot of people, Zethan." I moved closer to brush his chin. "You're not alone."

Wild, raw torment ripped through our link and chilled me to the bone. "Aaliyah, I need to protect the shelter. It's the only thing that keeps me going most days. The only good thing in my life."

"What about the club?" I wanted to say *what about me*, but we weren't a thing, and I worried he gave up on us before we even had a chance to begin. That he'd keep his distance not only because of the curse, but because he worried that anything between us would mark me for death too. My heart cried out with devastation, and he felt the reciprocal effect, closing his eyes.

"I don't know anymore." He rubbed at his pinched brow. "All I know is that I want you, but I don't want to hurt you. And it terrifies me to think of what fate you might suffer because of me."

# CHAPTER 15

## Slade

HEADS WERE GOING to fucking roll if I didn't acquire the cash the club needed for our debts. I was sick and tired of all this bullshit. Underhanded moves to screw us out of the market and take the Jackals down. Whoever the coward was, he'd regret messing with us when I pulled every damn tooth from his jaw, broke every bone, killed him, and revived him. Then I'd do it all over again, ending with a perfect crescendo of burning the fuckwit to a crisp.

This waiting game to prove our enemy's identity and connection was killing me. Cat and fucking mouse. We were the damn mouse, sneaking around, avoiding our foe, hatching plans to better it. While those fucks were the predators, with everything laid out to fuck us up the ass over and over. We didn't have a shred of evidence to connect that fucker Danny with messing with us. Blindfolds were placed over Castor's ability. Our enemy knew how to get past our defenses and strongholds. I hated feeling vulnerable and under attack when chaos and destruction were my goddamn domain.

"Prez?" Castor's voice brought me back to the moment.

I released my hands from my handlebars, which were twisted metal about to snap off the frame. Fuck. I'd need a new set now. And we'd lost Tank, our mechanic, so I'd have to send it down to our shop for replacement.

"You okay, Prez?" Castor ran a hand over the metal, using his magick to unwind the kink, returning it to its original form.

"Fine," I growled, not wanting to get into it.

I set my boot on the ground and flung my leg off my bike. Pressure in my knuckles made them ache, and I freed it with a crack of each hand. I thumped my palm on Castor's shoulder in appreciation.

"Ready?" he nudged me for our meeting.

Dread coiled in my gut. I scrubbed at my jaw, not looking forward to this. The outcome would make or fucking break us.

"Yeah." I left my bike in the parking lot and took the lead, letting my enforcer cover my back.

"Slade! Castor!" Tony greeted me inside his establishment with an extended palm, the classic Italian smile backed with wary brown eyes. His cheeks looked a little puffier and redder than last time.

We were late on our payment of Pharaoh by a week. Never been late a day in our business relationship, and I hoped Tony would consider that and cut us some slack. Give us another few weeks to round up the cash to settle our debt.

I threw my hand into his and shook. Tony switched to Castor and gave him the same treatment.

My throat dried and I coughed out the first few words. "Tony. About this month's bill. Any chance of an extension?"

Wariness in Tony's gaze flicked to worried. "Sorry, Slade." The smile fell from his lips. "I gotta put food on my table. Pay for my wife's grandiose lifestyle. Woman costs me five thousand a month with her hair, nails, massages, psychologist. Don't get me started on the clothes."

Fuck, here we go. The family speech. Heard it before. Out of respect for him, I listened to it, hoping he'd take pity on me. I had twenty-something men employed in the club to pay, too, goddammit.

Tony's gaze jumped to the ceiling, and he pressed his hands together in prayer. "Heaven help me, the damn kids' school fees. Do you know how much those bastards at Saint Stanislaus charge me per term? Four thousand each. For three kids. Gives me fucking heartburn just thinking about it!"

I scratched the back of my neck. Time to come clean. "Here's the thing, Tony—"

"What's going on, Slade?" Tony crossed his arms over his meaty chest, highlighting his beer gut. "You've never been late. Two weeks, a reminder notice and no sign of payment. Now you show up here asking for an extension." His scraggy brows came down hard.

My hands clenched at my sides, wanting to tear Danny fucking Heller's throat out and drink his damn blood. Burn him on a goddamn pyre to satiate my lust. "One of our shipments was hijacked, stolen, and sold to competitors."

"Fottimi," Tony swore in Italian, cupping the sides of his jaw with thumb and forefingers. "Who? Who's the bastard?"

Reluctance pulled the bond tight on Castor's end. He didn't want me to give away too much information. Neither did I, but I wasn't sure how much longer I could draw this out.

"We don't know," I admitted. Waves drew back from the shore within me as a tsunami began to build.

Castor yanked harder on our link in warning, and I listened, cutting off further explanation. Tony didn't need to know that we couldn't sell his product, that the thief had worked out how to copy the formula and majorly undercut us. We'd be too much of a liability, and he'd fucking quit on us.

"We're in the process of offloading two of our assets to repay the bill." The tsunami swelled, dragging the water to it, absorbing its energy, ready to smash the coastline and devastate it. "We just need a little more time to get the cash to you."

"Fanculo, Slade!" Tony threw his hands up like a dramatic bitch. "How much time? I thought you were rolling in it."

Fuck. We were. Until Aaliyah arrived.

Castor squeezed harder, like he held me on a goddamn leash, and I wanted to grab hold of the line, wrap it around his throat and tug. See how he liked being choked. I glared at him over my shoulder, but my eyes fell to the fading bruises over his nose. Bruises I caused when I lost the fucking plot. Marks I promised I'd not make again. If I touched him again, Aaliyah would never speak to me, and I'd fucking regret it.

Tony's hands fell to his hips, and he shook his head decisively. "Sorry, Slade. If the Jackals can't afford to pay, then we can't conduct business anymore. I run a tight ship."

Fuck, just what I needed. I couldn't afford to lose Tony's services. Or worse, him going to work for one of our competitors. He had our goddamn recipe and could sell it off to the highest bidder regardless of the contract we drew up. Criminals rarely stuck to agreements when it came to money. They stabbed each other in the back and screwed them over.

I moved closer, hovering over him, my shadow blocking out the light from behind my head. "You'll get your fucking money, Tony."

Castor reined me back with a heavy hand on my shoulder, reminding me to bring it down a notch. Heeding his advice this time, I spun on my heels and marched out of there before I could incinerate that fat Italian fuck for being such a tight-assed cunt. We'd been business partners for two years and paid on time every time. Yet this prick couldn't cut us some slack just once, after everything I'd done for him. Raised him from a small-town food chemist working for the local food packager to a multi-million-dollar businessman. I wouldn't let this slight from Tony slide. High time I began looking elsewhere for a new business partner. Someone more cooperative and flexible. Loyal. Steadfast. Someone who wouldn't dare fuck me over in a time of need.

The tsunami stormed for the shore, promising to leave nothing untouched.

I took off on my bike so fast I left scorch marks on Tony's pavement. Closed gates approached as I gunned the throttle, charging through the metal and smashing them from their hinges. My bike took a nasty hit, mangling the front tire and frame, but Castor repaired it instantly and got me roadworthy. I didn't slow down the whole way back to the club. Caught the attention of three highway patrol cops that Castor redirected. One of his powers that actually worked.

Back at the clubhouse, I stormed across the club's acreage, destined for somewhere remote and private. Half a mile away, I paused in a thicket and unleashed the mounting destruction. Grass flattened as if rolled over by waves. Two gum trees toppled to the ground with a thud. Fire kindled in the bushes and exploded with flames. Winds picked up, carrying dirt and leaves in every direction. Ice cracked on the ground at my feet, and a blizzard whipped at my hair and cut. The release did nothing to satisfy my need for destruction. Rage blinded me to anything else but the need for devastation.

"Slade, we'll figure this out!" Castor yelled behind me.

"Just listen to me."

To what? Radio fucking silence on his end? Meanwhile our enemies destroyed us. No, I didn't want to listen. I wanted to wreak havoc on the world. Tear buildings and structures apart with wind. Spread famine, plagues, and disease to end civilizations. Burn the debris and people with fire. Flush away the stink and crap with floods. Finish with punishing blizzards and bring new meaning to the words *when hell freezes over*.

"Get the fuck out of here!" I shouted at him, not wanting to hurt him, unsure if I could contain the chaos and protect him.

My flames encircled Castor, and he shielded his eyes from the heat. "Slade, I'm not leaving you here… you know I can't do that."

Fuck duty. Fuck the club. Fuck Tony. Rain down fucking hell. Destroy everything around me. Imagine I was doing it to Danny fucking Heller and his cowardly partner.

"Slade, you're gonna get yourself killed." Castor grabbed hold of my arm and dragged me back.

"Don't stop me from finishing what I started." I meant to push him back, warn him not to interfere, but my chaotic magick lashed out with flame instead. He hissed and clutched his burned flesh to his chest.

"Fuck, Slade." Castor knew better than to try again and backed away.

The loving brother in me watched in horror at what I'd done. It was too late. Set had full control. He wanted to punish and destroy and fed off my rage. It had been too long since he unleashed like this. Molten steel flowed in my veins, fueling my wrath, leaving me no chance of stopping.

A panicked SOS went down the mate bond calling for help. Worry replied in a call to action. Fuck, they were coming, and they planned to talk me down.

Fire consumed all the air around me, and my lungs couldn't get enough oxygen. Fury, flames, and ash fueled my god and me right then. Clouds darkened the sky as a storm front built overhead. I called them down, circling them, crashing to the ground, suffocating the fire. Dust kicked up from the wind, scratching my skin, coating my face. Lightning crackled everywhere, including over my body. If it wasn't for the god power within me, I'd be dead along with all the grass, bugs, and foraging animals.

Sparked with greater power, I went on like this, torching, scarring, destroying, tearing apart the land, ready to end the world. Set smiled with gratification as the reason for his existence conquered.

Several voices called my name. "Slade!" My brothers. I ignored them.

"Go away." My voice crackled like fire.

"Slade, what are you doing?" I knew that voice. Soft, heartfelt, concerned. The silkiness in the bond. Vanilla and cherries scent. The soothing caress of my mate. Her fear and worry for her safety, mine, and that of the avatars. I'd not hurt or lose my brothers and mate. Castor was an accident.

She approached me, low and cautious. The way a snake handler would treat a venomous serpent he tried to collect. Zethan snagged her arm, but she shrugged him off. "Slade, you need to stop. You're going to hurt yourself or someone else."

I couldn't stop when I was on a bender. Nature needed to be destroyed. Chaos must reign. Vengeance exacted. Fire, blood, and ash—my legacy must be fulfilled. Someone must pay for what was done to my club. Rebirth came from destruction, and I was that force. Electricity crackled over my skin, jumping off me, sparking another wildfire. Thunder shattered the air between us.

"Go away, woman." I didn't want her here.

"Slade, baby, please." I blinked at her words. She never called me baby. Woman tried to trick and coax me, but I wasn't so easily fooled when she hadn't forgiven me.

Fire roared hotter and higher at my growl. "I'm not falling for your tricks."

She tried another tact with me. "Slade, talk to me." Her soothing lilt made me twitch. I burned too bright and hot to calm down.

"Leave now, woman." I scorched the ground black in warning at her and my three brothers. Faces strained and eyes narrowed from the heat of the fire.

"Don't growl at me, Mr. Vincent." Fierce. Feisty. Ferocious. My mate. A force of nature just like me. The fertility goddess within her could give and take where she saw fit. Piss her off, and she'd starve and destroy a civilization with the ease of Set.

Mr. Vincent. That was more like it. I blinked again. Aaliyah's words chipped away at the anger holding me hostage. My muscles spasmed and I jolted. The fire and passion within my mate beckoned me closer.

My body burned like coals. "Say my name again." I wanted to hear it burn on her tongue and shoot all the way to her pussy.

My nurse crept closer. Slow. Hesitant. Hands raised. "Come to me, Mr. Vincent." She gestured to me. "Kiss me. Touch me."

Tempting. Not as tempting as melting everything down. I couldn't be contained and controlled. My coals burned so hot that the heat had to escape somehow. I wanted to break shit. Tear the fucking club and everything around it down.

She didn't mean it anyway. Manipulated me with promising words. Tried to control my fire. Lies. Deception. Decoy. "Stop playing with me, Nurse A."

"I meant it when I said I wanted all the destruction of

your god, Mr. Vincent." My brave little mate came right up to me, cupped my jaw with one hand, looping her arm around my neck, drawing me down to her. "Give it to me. Now."

Her kiss made me forget everything, and I sank into the sweetness of it, the silk of her lips, the curl of her tongue with mine. Drowned in the heat and languidness of her. Hardened at the little whimper of pleasure she made. Distracting little minx. Wild and primitive magick within me responded to the call of her inner darkness. A darkness I'd love to give to the world.

But then I snapped back to reality, realizing what she did. That this wasn't real. It had nothing to do with wanting me and everything to do with calling me back from the brink of destruction.

Frustrated, I growled and withdrew from her, licking my lips, stealing one last taste of her. "Stop it, Nurse A. I don't want you like this."

"Like what?" She grabbed me with two hands this time, lowering me to her. When she kissed me again, harder, demanding, she claimed ownership over me. My mate was every bit my equal and she knew it.

My jackal responded, growling deep in my chest. Taking charge was our territory. He nipped at her bottom lip to teach her a lesson. We wanted to own her, dominate her, control her. But she couldn't be owned. Not by me or the others. She was a fighter, a savior, independent like her falcon shifter. Trying to cage her, force her into a relationship with us would just encourage her to leave, and we'd lose her forever.

"Goddamn it, Nurse A," I groaned. "Don't say that shit unless you mean it."

Truth snapped the bond, like a slap to the face. This wasn't an act. This was all her. Wild and raw. All for me. Woman wanted me as much as I wanted her. She just needed time and space to forgive me. Then she'd be mine, if only I was a patient man.

I clasped the back of her neck and lifted her by her ass. She wrapped her legs around my hips and clung to me tighter, possessively, and fuck me if I didn't love it. Our tongues battled for dominance, flicking, swiping, tangling. Her fingers dragged through my hair, yanking, making me smile at the pleasant sting of my scalp. The hunger she summoned from me was primal, an intense wildfire that burned out of control and left nothing but ashes in its wake. She bit me back, her teeth leaving indents on my lip, the pain swelling. I claimed her several nights ago, and now she returned the favor, claiming me. Finally, she gave into me, giving herself to me. I melted into her, her kiss stealing my will to destroy.

"I told you I was all in, Mr. Vincent." Her hot whisper in my ear went straight to my cock. "Now come the fuck back from hell and be with me."

This woman would always choose to help others, her priority the safety and health of those she cared for no matter the cost to herself. It was who she was. In her damn blood. Selfless, caring, and pure, unlike the avatars and me, who took what we wanted, when we wanted it. We were born to break the rules for our gain no matter who we hurt in the process. She'd be there to pick up the fucking pieces afterward.

Whenever I lost control, my mate would always be there to call me back from the brink of madness. Aaliyah didn't give up on a person, no matter what. Even when I was a downright cunt to her. Locked her up. Interrogated her. Frightened her. Threatened her life. Yet she saved my men, twice. I didn't deserve her, but I'd damn well keep her. The woman made me want to be a better man. To use that chaos for good instead of destruction, the way nature destroyed to give rise to new life. A wildfire that encouraged seeds to sprout and grow. No other woman ever persuaded me to change. That was the power she held over me. In this moment, I'd do any fucking thing she asked of me. Even lower myself from magnitude ten earthquake to a zero.

I linked my fingers in her hair and jerked it. My other hand cracked down over her ass. Hard. Painful. Nerves along her bond crackled with pain and pleasure. I rubbed the area I just spanked to soothe it just as she calmed me. Her body shuddered at the pleasure and pain I inflicted on her.

"If you ever risk your life like that again, I'll do more than this, Nurse. A." The growl in my voice told her that sexy, round ass of hers would be red-raw for the stunt she pulled. I could have really hurt her. Killed her. She was reckless, dangerous, and I'd punish her for that.

"Do it," she goaded me. She knew this was the only way to get to me. To call me back from the wilderness I got lost in. "Punish me."

I brought my hand crashing down on her backside to prove my point. Then I slammed my mouth to hers, assaulting her with a hard and demanding kiss. My fingers tightened in her hair, making her whimper. Her lips scraped over mine, feeding on my chaos and desire, ending with a harsh, quick nip.

She came back to her senses quickly and pulled her face away from me. "Shit, Slade. I want a happy ending," she whispered, stroking my cheek, then glancing over her shoulder at my three brothers standing guard close by. "But I can already tell you four will be my worst fucking nightmare."

I croaked out a laugh. "Got that right." I stroked her beautiful, caramel face. "I can't promise fairy tales or happy endings, Nurse A. But I can promise you the best damn time you'll ever have."

## CHAPTER 16

### Castor

I NEEDED THE DAMN ANSWERS. Needed to find a way to get past the dark magick wards marking the Wolves' properties. Bypass the sigils on Danny and his men's skin to remove their demonic protection, leaving them weak to our attack. The longer it took me to find the spell, the worse things would get for the club. We'd lose ground in the drug's market, lose clients and business partners. Essentially, the Jackals would be fucked.

I rubbed absently at my stinging arm where Slade had burned me. Aaliyah sent her healing powers into me, leaving a raw, pink scar with fresh, sensitive nerve endings. A reminder not to get close when he lost his shit. I couldn't risk Slade losing control again. Next time he might do more than accidentally burn me. He might hurt us all. Burn the damn clubhouse down. Set the town of Bathurst on fire. I'd not let him injure our mate.

My focus returned to the book in my lap. A heavy, brown leather tome. All the letters blended together, and my brain couldn't process the hieroglyphs morphing into an incoherent jumble of figures and animals. I rubbed at my tired, aching neck, needing a break. My neck developed a damn crick from the angle of reading.

Zethan ordered me to take Aaliyah back to my place to keep her clear of Slade. No hesitation there. What happened with him this afternoon rattled her. Today was a close call, and she resorted to practically fucking him to lower his storming emotions.

Our president didn't get like that often. The last time I saw him lose his shit was when the Winter's Devils killed Liz. None of them lived to tell the tale.

I kept watching her, cued in for any change in her body language. She chewed her lip, flicked the page of the ancient spell book, her glazed eyes skimming over the material and not absorbing it. That wouldn't do us any good. We needed to be on our game to disable our enemies' protection, but that wasn't happening tonight while her mind was elsewhere. On him. What she said to him. She gave herself over to him completely. Surrendered to the mate bond. There was no going back now.

Aaliyah and I weren't at that stage yet, even though we should have claimed one another first. My past held me back. Held me captive. Forever chained to it, it messed with my head so that I couldn't let it go. Couldn't give myself entirely to her.

Woman didn't help the matter, leaving me a confused, tangled mess, with her reluctance to fully commit to me or my brothers. Intentions leaked into the bond indicated she planned on having fun with me while our time together lasted, but once it ended, she'd return to her normal life and be done with us. Fucking crushed my damn heart with the promise she made Slade this afternoon, claiming him, sealing their bond. That should have been me. A bevy of emotions assaulted me. Rejection. Turmoil. Fear. Jealousy. I reverted to my dark shadow on the bond to conceal my fluctuating reactions. Didn't need her to see how she affected me.

Distracted, she flicked another page without reading it, possibly skipping over a precious clue we couldn't afford to miss.

I climbed out of my chair and moved to her, snatching the book out of her lap and slamming it shut. "That's enough for today."

She jolted and looked up at me as I set the tome down on my coffee table. "Hmm?"

"Let me make you dinner." I held out my hand, but she didn't take it, the sting cutting deep. "What's your favorite meal?" I disguised my trickling feelings by pressing my fingers to my temples. "No, don't tell me. Let me guess." I paused, grinning. "Longhorn beef sirloin, pickled walnut salsa verde and tropea onions."

She snorted. "What is that? All I understood was beef, salsa, and onion."

"Come and find out." I jerked my hand at her, and this time, she accepted it, squeezing it.

"Anything with cheese is my favorite meal." She lifted to her feet so easily with my help. "Mexican and Italian. My ultimate fave is lasagna."

"Lasagna, it is." I put everything into my smile despite feeling hollow.

"Castor." She tugged at my arm to keep me standing beside her. "You're hiding from me again." Fuck, the woman didn't miss a thing. Her nurse training taught her to be vigilant and sharp to any changes of a patient. Only I wasn't her patient. I wanted to belong to her and her to me.

I gave her everything she needed physically, but there was

still a reluctant side to me that guarded my affections. The part that feared rejection. Her claiming of Slade today triggered me, and I retreated behind the six-inch steel walls that fortified my heart fiercely. Only she was like a tree root that burrowed her way beneath those defenses grown around my chest and penetrated it. Pretty soon she'd dent the metal and penetrate the shield I defended for four years.

I let go of her hand, moved to the fridge, piling ingredients in my arms and setting them on the counter. "How does cheesy garlic bread sound?"

She worked her lip between her teeth again. "Delicious." She said it with as much enthusiasm as I could muster after my dick had been sent packing to the depths of winter.

Pre-empting me, she collected a grater, cutting board, knives, and other implements we'd need to cook. We danced around each other, grabbing more vegetables, a lasagna dish. Comfortable with each other, we anticipated each other's moves. We were practically a damn couple, yet she didn't commit to me. I didn't reciprocate, and maybe that was why she held back on me.

Aaliyah's gaze went to the spell books on my coffee table as she peeled the carrots. We liked lots of vegetables with our meat. Call us the healthy ones of the bunch. One could only survive on canned soup and noodles at the club for so long before needing fresh meals.

"I don't understand how Danny survived four bullets to the back," she voiced, her statement catching me off guard. How did we go from me hiding from her to this?

I chuckled as I removed the skin from the garlic. "He had a little help from his friends. The demons protected and healed him." I was kicking myself for not noticing it at the first ambush.

Her back straightened, and she dragged her hand through her hair.

"This whole time he's been messing with dark forces."

I went to kiss her lightly on the top of her ear but stopped myself at the last second. Fuck, we were getting a little too comfortable with each other, and it troubled me. I didn't want to fall into a pattern with her if she didn't want to get serious. I couldn't shake the feeling that she'd leave. She admitted it through our bond. Knowing this held me numb and detached.

I cleared my throat and said, "I think I've found a way to bypass the Wolves' protection."

She noticed my resistance and set her hand over my wrist, stopping me from crushing the garlic. "Are you okay?"

"Fine." I hid behind a smile and put aside the garlic to grate the carrots she'd peeled. "It's a rare spell to coax the demon away from the Wolves with an incentive. We capture them in a demon trap, negotiate a new deal with them to abandon the Wolves."

Aaliyah's concern probed at the bond and she stared at me, assessing me, trying to figure out what was up with me.

I didn't want her to dig any deeper and didn't give her the opportunity to say anything. "I'll attach them to me, drown the bastards and cleanse myself in the sea."

"You're not doing that." Her eyes widened. "What if you get possessed?"

"It's not a possession," I explained. "I bind them to me so they can't harm, then get rid of them for good. It's an ancient African voodoo practice."

"Sounds dangerous." She started to chop up the onions.

"It's the only thing I've found to disable the demonic protection." I hadn't tried the spell yet because of various distractions. Jaxx's execution being one. Searching for the new competitor, a second. Then having to deal with Hellfire MC on top of that. My schedule was cleared though, leaving me space to test my hypothesis.

She dabbed at the corner of her eyes, wet with onion-burning tears. "Can't you bind them to an amulet or a stone or something?"

I brushed her collarbone to reassure her. "They won't abandon the Wolves for something as insignificant as a stone. They'll want something substantial. Something that can feed them. They're vampiric in nature and sustain themselves off human fear, anger, cruelty, and all the dark emotions."

"Danny has that in spades, huh?" Life threw her a curveball, but she ducked every one, and her fight and determination to never give in continued to impress me. "You sure you're juicy enough for the demons?"

I chuckled, and she shivered at the sound. My dick twitched at the way my voice did that to her. Had her puddling at my feet when I brought the daddy out with his dark, undeniable timbre.

"You don't think I'm tasty enough?" I gestured at myself up and down. A joke disguised as the truth. I was paralyzed by fear. Held back by it.

"Oh, you're tasty." She grabbed my shirt with both fists, dragging me to her, and laying a kiss on my lips. Gentle, probing, still trying to crack the mystery that was me.

Fuck, I'd gone from wary and hesitant one moment to unable to resist her the next. In the week that she stayed with me, we instantly settled into a routine, and I could get used to this. Cooking with her, feeding her, licking the taste of the food from her lips, fucking her at the dining table because I couldn't wait to get to the bedroom. I wanted it all with her. But I couldn't shake the feeling that she'd leave, and it held me numb and detached.

"Castor, I'm drawn to you all in a way that I've never been to anyone else before." She curled my hair over her finger. "I don't want to feel this way, but I can't shut it off, either. I don't want to hurt anyone or be responsible for your hearts if I decide to return to my life. It's only a curse. It isn't real."

She still didn't fully accept the mate bond. Accept us. Want us. My walls closed around me as my defenses shot back up. The thought of being without her prompted my throat and stomach to tighten.

The primal side of her made promises to Slade that she didn't entirely understand. They were bound whether she liked it or not. She wasn't walking away from that, and he would never let her leave. Curse or no curse, she was ours, and I refused to break it if it meant I'd lose her too.

A fierce possessiveness overtook me, Dark Daddy rising to the surface. He never let go of his toys. She was ours, and we'd make her see it.

"It's fucking real, Aaliyah." I seized her hand, holding her so tightly she whimpered. "The curse binds us together. Connects our hearts and emotions. But it doesn't force us to love one another like a love spell."

"If I go back to work in Sydney, away from you all, I won't feel any of this," she argued, attempting to jerk free, but I wouldn't release her.

"Dull the mate bond then," I challenged, a swipe of my hand finishing the business in the kitchen, assembling the lasagna ingredients, setting it out in the dish and tossing it in the oven to bake. "Go on. I'll do it too. See if you still feel the same way." I'd prove my point.

I felt her retreat from me and did the same. Lust, respect, and attraction for her remained just as hot and bright as it ever had. She clenched her thighs together as she felt it too.

Selfish, greedy, and wanting to punish her for daring to threaten to leave, I dragged her to the wall and swiped my hand over the spell, exposing the basement doorway. I threw open the door and dragged her downstairs. If she thought she could leave the daddy, then she had another thing coming. I flicked on the light at the bottom of the stairwell. Dim lighting illuminated the red walls and selection of toys. Daddy dragged her to the bed, threw her on it and called to a binding, which snaked out and secured her wrist. She yanked at it, breathing hard, glaring at me. We didn't stop and had her bound within seconds.

Heat banked in her eyes. Her heart thumped in time to her desire. Moisture flooded to her core, wet for me. No mate bond tricking and confusing her.

"Use your magick and get yourself out of this if you want to leave." I crawled over the bed to her, straddling one of her legs. "Go on."

Nothing held her here when she could get out of this if she wanted to. I taught her to use her power to free herself of rope, manacles or handcuffs if she was ever kidnapped and held captive.

She jerked at her bindings but made no move to escape. Just as I thought. She lied to herself. Made excuses. Tiptoed around her feelings for us and refused to dive into them and explore them. She cared for us. Wanted us. Used the bond as justification to run from her feelings. I was not just a lover to her. Some fuck buddy to waste time with. It wrecked me that she regarded me like that, and that she considered leaving me.

Daddy picked me up from falling apart as he stroked her leg. "I'm going to make sure you want no one else but us ever again."

"Castor," she said breathlessly, fighting the mate bond and me.

"Escape if you want to leave." I leaned down to kiss her thigh. Trembles ripped through her. Lungs pumping hard to get air, she gasped.

My magick dragged her legs wider for me, and I skimmed my palm along her inner thigh. She panted at my teasing touch. "You enjoy it when I control your pleasure. Your body betrays you. It wants more. Quakes when I command you. Makes you beg when I deny your release. Cries out when I dominate you."

Her eyes narrowed, sharpened on me, watching every little move as I traced circles along her legs, getting higher, closing in on her sweet spot. She loved the way I touched her. I was clued into her every motion, sound, and feeling. The way her eyelids fluttered at my caress. The soft moan she gave when I kissed her skin. The pop of bubbles along our link like she soaked in a frothy bath. She could tell herself she felt nothing until she was blue in the face, but it wasn't the truth. I'd show her the truth.

"I'm going to fuck you hard and fast. No foreplay." I stripped off her clothes with my magick, leaving her bare, her wet, pretty little pink pussy exposed to me. "My cock is going to worship every inch of your pussy. Make you beg for the release I'll deny you for refuting our real connection."

She fought against that, her wrists pulling at her binds, tightening them. I didn't let her get a word in sideways and grabbed the overhead chains, tugging them, sliding her legs over her body so her knees pressed against her arms. She squeaked but still made no move to escape. Silky ass cheeks met my touch as I skimmed across her flesh. I cracked my hand down on her ass hard, and she hissed as the sting traveled straight to her core and turned her to molten liquid.

"I'm going to show you what it's like to be cherished by me." My cock ached to be inside of her, and I rubbed it against her exposed pussy, teasing her. "Brand your soul and entwine it with mine. Make you remember me forever, so you'll never think of fucking leaving again."

I placed my hands either side of her arms and lowered my mouth to hers to stop the argument bubbling on her tongue. My lips asserted ownership over her, sucking and sliding.

Demanded she sink into the kiss and give herself to me, just as Daddy liked it. He was in charge here. She could tell us to stop, and we would. But she didn't, not even as I poised my hard cock at her entrance, seeking her permission to enter. My little baby would not have the pleasure of foreplay for what she did.

"Last chance, dark sorceress," I whispered in her ear, making her convulse with arousal, her nipples pebble, and her core ignite even hotter.

"Fuck me, Castor," she begged. Just as I'd predicted, she didn't want to leave. She wanted this as much as I did.

Giving her what she wanted, I speared her with my cock, and she took every earth-shattering thrust.

"You are mine and you will never leave," I communicated every word with a hard plunge into her sweetness, conveying my need for her, my desire for her to stay. "I will tie you up here and do this to you every night if you ever consider it or try it." I slammed into her to pound the message home.

"I'm yours," she whimpered, delirious, thrashing her head because it was the only part of her that could move from where I pinned her to the bed.

I kept hammering into her, building our release, thumbing her clit to heighten her pleasure.

"Oh, God." Her eyes rolled back in her head as she approached the pinnacle, and I slid out of her and removed my slick shaft.

I clapped down on her ass again and laughed, enjoying controlling her pleasure. "Tell me that you won't leave. That you'll stay. That you're mine."

"I can't do that," she panted.

Have it her way. She wouldn't be getting release. I sampled some of her juices from my cock and enjoyed her musky flavor. Punishing her, I stroked my thickness, building up my own pleasure.

"Castor, please," she begged me.

No. Not until she gave in to me all the way. I crawled back off the bed still pumping my length, torturing her. She trailed every motion, moaning, writhing what little she could. Pleasure escalated in her from watching me and the sensation seeping into our bond. That little minx was going to come if I didn't stop her. But I couldn't bring myself to deny her. I threaded my cock through my hand until orgasm cracked through us, and we both lost our breath.

I waited until my breathing steadied and told her, "If you don't want to be my mate, then that's the last pleasure you'll get from me."

"What?" She thrashed at her bindings, and I released her, flipping her to her knees, making her rock forward and brace herself against the bed. "That's blackmail," she snarled at me when she righted herself.

"No, it's not," I whispered. "You don't want to lead me on. But you're the one who's afraid to get hurt." Pot calling the kettle black. "I'm not going to lose myself in you if that's the case."

I left her there and marched up the stairs. Asshole. I gave her a fucking ultimatum. I wasn't that damn guy. But I wouldn't let her break my heart, either.

## CHAPTER 17

### *A*aliyah

WHO WAS the man standing before me? Transformed from a biker into a sex god with tan trousers that showed off his fit legs and an illegally tight, navy buttoned shirt. A warm, pleased smile greeted me. Glow about his gray and golden eye. Coconut hair gel and spicy aftershave teased my senses and I wanted to lean in and lick him. Damn, he looked so different. His face had lost the whole dark, haunted vibe, transforming him into a relaxed, poster boy for the Air Force. Alluring. Disarming. One hundred percent lickable.

"Glad you came." Alaric ushered me inside, his hand going to the small of my back as I stepped into the threshold. The old sparks shot from my spine to my toes and head, leaving me giddy and my knee strength failing.

When he leaned down for a swoonworthy kiss to my cheek, my body went into meltdown mode, everything dissolving into molten liquid gold. Smitten.

Wary of being sucked under his spell and forgiving him completely from that gentle, teasing slide of lips, I didn't return the kiss, giving him a coy smile instead. "Thanks for inviting me."

Truthfully, I was glad to get away from Castor's for a night, especially after the awkward way we'd ended our sexual encounter last night. Pissed at him, I'd skipped dinner, gone to my room and slept, suffering the guilt that spilled over into the bond. Both mine and his. The small part he let me see. On one hand, he wanted me to pledge that I was his, promise not to leave, yet we both weren't ready to fully commit. We still needed to get to know each other better … not that I planned on promising him any more than what we had. His trepidation and reluctance betrayed the secrets he hid from me. The guy gave me whiplash with his conflicted emotions. At least with Slade, he was as easy to read as a playbook. Castor was puzzling and shadowy.

Today, we'd both avoided each other, barely saying two words. He'd dropped me off without a kiss or an impish tap on my ass, leaving my heart wanting our banter and natural playfulness back.

"Hungry?" Alaric offered his hand in my direction, and I was glad for the distraction from Castor. To fill the hollow void in my chest.

I tucked my hand in my jeans pockets. "Starving."

Rejection flickered in his eyes at my rebuff. "This way."

Guilt scratched at my stomach as I trailed behind him, taking in his homey place. Polished wooden floors so shiny I could see my reflection in them. A lamp on a stand provided dim light for the hall. Olive green walls that brought out the amber hue of the wood. Photos, both color and black and white, of family members covered one wall. Cute. He took pride in his family.

"Big family," I remarked.

He stopped by a wedding photo of a young couple. "My dad had three brothers and sisters." That was huge by my standards.

I drifted along the line of photo frames, admiring what I assumed was his grandfather and father in squadron pictures from their service in the Air Force. "Where are you?"

He scratched the back of his neck. "My photos are in my den." His answer made me wonder why he didn't display them and take pride in his contribution to his generational service to Australia.

"Show me them later?" I stroked the photo of his grandfather, then his father, noting their striking resemblance with sharp jaws and noses. "I want to see how handsome you are in your uniform."

My heart circled a lasso and tossed it outwards hoping to catch his while my mind cringed at flirting with him. Tonight was about connecting and making a fresh start, not misleading him. *Fuck, Aaliyah!* Being around these four men made my mouth lose and my pussy even loser. Damn ho!

His grave smile as he nodded and rubbed his palms together struck me in the chest. Prickling on the bond conveyed his disapproval, and I let it rest, wondering if it triggered him.

Standing stiffer, he moved onto a family crest for the Hawk family, which, of course, was an eagle with a scepter in its mouth. "Mom's obsessed with tracking genealogy."

Topic change. Got it. Alaric wasn't like the other men, and I had to handle him with care and patience. He needed comfort and safety and rewarded it with trust. I'd treated a lot of abused patients like that and just needed to build rapport. The only problem was, he wasn't a patient, he was my mate, and that brought with it a whole other can of worms.

"So's mine," I replied. "The Hellers descend from Thomas

Heller, a clerk who was instrumental in abolishing slavery in England in the 1700s." I quoted from my mom's proud declaration.

Alaric's eyebrows hiked, and he tapped his family crest. "Descended from Scottish royalty."

I chuckled and hit him in the arm. "Damn, you win."

I swore I heard the shriek of a hawk in my head. The flutter of silky wings on my cheek. Light scratch of talons on my arm. Caress of a hard, sharp beak on my neck. I rubbed at the spot, left warm and golden.

Alaric watched me with curious eyes. "That's my hawk."

I stroked my neck. "He can touch me?"

"Psychically, yes." This shifter business was both strange and comforting at the same time.

His fingers twitched, and I felt his deep ache to take my hand. I was torn whether to encourage him or not by extending mine. We agreed on a fresh start between us, nothing romantic, even though he wanted to take it there. Hell, I did too, but I remained guarded. Creating another damn romantic connection would make leaving impossible. Nope. Had to steer clear of that territory. Tonight was strictly for getting to know him, passing the time while I stayed with the Jackals, and determining if I could alleviate his PTSD symptoms. Nothing more.

Music playing softly in background speakers immediately set me at ease. Scented candles burning on the table smelled like coconut and lime. Lotus flowers decorated the center of the table, my favorite. He'd remembered. Bonus points. I hiked my eyebrows at him. At dinner the other night, Slade declared that Alaric would bring me flowers to every dinner. Damn. He went all out to set a dreamy mood. Must have been the romantic, doting one of the bunch. A nice change from what I was used to. I smiled as I trailed behind him, relieved that at least one of my mates was sweet and amorous.

Bikers weren't exactly known for their sense of romance. Least, the ones I'd known weren't. My dad's idea of a date was to take mom for a weekend of riding or to a biker rally. My ex, Jimmy, took me to biker parties, concerts, and dive bars. Never got me flowers. Barely remembered my birthday. Hardly romantic.

"Gone all out to impress me, huh?" I teased with my words, parted lips, and raised brows.

Shit. There I went again, getting all mushy over another avatar. My heart and mind swayed back and forth like the pendulum of a grandfather clock.

*Fuck, Aaliyah, get it together!*

Alaric's gaze dipped to my lips, and his tongue snaked out, licking his. "Why wouldn't I want to treat my mate like a queen?"

Queen. Why did he have to say that? I had no doubt he'd be the one of all my mates to treasure and pamper me. Goddammit, he wasn't making this any easier. Neither were my raging hormones, smoldering pussy, and lassoing cowgirl of a heart. Because if I was honest, I *really* wanted to be adored by my man. All four of them. How many women were lucky enough to be worshipped by a harem of men?

I clamped my hands on the back of the dining chair. "Smells good."

*Nice diversion, Aaliyah. Like a pro!*

"Hope you like creamy garlic salmon." Alaric went to the oven to remove two dinner plates with salmon, white sauce, and vegetables laid out on them. Smelled divine.

The candle flame flickered as he set them on the table. My heart went all gooey when he sat me down, set my napkin over my lap, his fingers lingering a little longer than necessary, and poured me a white wine. Wine! Not beer or whisky.

"To fresh starts." He lifted his wine to toast with me, and I repeated the words and clinked glasses with his.

My taste buds nearly died and went to heaven as I sampled his meal. "It's incredible."

Cream dribbled down my lips, and he reached out and wiped it away with his thumb. Taken aback by the move, I froze. Anticipation had me expecting him to lick it and smile seductively the way Slade would. Instead, he brushed it over his napkin. I swiped nervously at my mouth with my own. After the disastrous way things ended last night with Castor, I didn't want to incite further affections and lead Alaric on with any untoward moves.

I desperately clambered for something to move the conversation along. "Did you cook this or get help from Castor?"

Castor was the culinary man of the group, whipping up multicultural meals and delicacies from other countries. Not a wasted question either, since I knew little about Alaric besides that he served in the military, suffered PTSD, and he now worked as the road captain for an MC.

"Believe it or not, Aaliyah, I'm a skilled cook." It was strange to hear Alaric tease me when he was always so dark and serious. "Mom made my brothers and me learn."

Extra bonus points. The bikers in dad's club weren't known for their culinary skills. Dad mastered the barbeque and that was it. My last boyfriend, an ER doctor, perfected macaroni and cheese.

Alaric seductively lifted his wine glass to his lips. "Mom said it would make us good husbands."

*Husband.* Goddess, why did he have to say that word? It set me on edge. I didn't need any reference to queens, mates, husbands or anything remotely romantic if I planned on leaving here without kissing him. Worse, ending up in his bed. I'd already bedded two of the avatars—best sex of my life—and if I lost control, I'd add a third to my tally.

He laughed at the memory and sipped at his wine. The bob of his Adam's apple lulled me to stare at him, captivated. "Dad was very traditional. Yes, sir. No, sir. Mother stays at home to raise the kids. But my mom was a feminist and raised us boys to share the load when he wasn't looking."

If his dad was traditional, then I didn't imagine having his son in a biker club would go down well. "Do your parents know you're in an MC?"

We both went to grab the wine at the same time and our hands brushed. Sparks flew. Worlds collided. Stars burst. Goddess. I stuffed my hand in my lap and squeezed it between my thighs to dull the sensation. Did it go away? Hell, no! My lap heated hotter than a damn sun.

Alaric rubbed at his forehead. "Dad's not too happy about it, but Mom's always been supportive. She knows I need the brotherhood."

Whew. We ignored the whole jolt of electricity thing.

I cleared my throat. "My dad wasn't thrilled when I left the club to study nursing. I didn't want to stay in the family business."

"Guess we have that in common," Alaric mused as he finished up the last of his meal. "What else do we have in common?"

I tapped my lips. "Let's see. I practice yoga four times a week. I already know you don't." I winked.

He laughed. "Gym man and jogger all the way." I bet. He had to keep in shape for his military service. Served him well now. He had a damn fine body. Strong. Broad. Very fit. Not as big as Slade or Zethan. "What else?"

"Every month I abseil with the Blue Mountains Rock Climbing Club."

"Impressive. My turn. Dad and I sail his boat in summer." Speaking his name made a pang hit my chest. "Not anymore."

Alaric reached out to take my hand and stroke it with his thumb. Heat spiked in my body, and I dragged my hand away.

"I crotchet and watch TV."

"Crotchet?" Alaric leaned back and barked out a laugh. "Are you ninety?"

I stretched over to hit his arm. "Hey! I'll have you know it relieves stress. Medically proven." I winked at the last part.

He twisted to face me, and my body temperature went up. "Liar."

"Tease me again and I'll crotchet you a nice little beanie." At my threat, he frowned and scrubbed his hand over his styled hair. "Pink will bring out your eyes." I blinked mine to tease him.

"Yes, Nana." I hit him again for that reply and giggled.

We both smiled, lost for words as we gazed into each other's eyes, the pull magnetic. The pupil in his gray eye had dilated and the golden one turned liquid like molten gold. I noticed it did that when the bond went taut with longing and desire. It was one of the most beautiful things I'd ever seen. Knowing I affected him like this made my breath hitch in anticipation of him leaning over to kiss me. The rest of my body stiffened with unease.

"Hope you like apple and rhubarb crumble," he said, breaking the moment, as if he sensed my disquiet and wanted to put me at ease.

He'd just said the magick words. I loved apple crumble. Up there with my top dessert of cheesecake. The man knew the way to my heart.

But I was feeling pretty full and rubbed at my stomach. "Mind if we take a break and star watch? Give me some time to digest." I sipped the last of my wine to wash away any food left in my mouth.

"Sure." He smiled and removed the napkin from his lap and set it on the table. "My observatory is outside. Need a jacket?"

"Love one." I couldn't help the words that tumbled from my mouth.

I remembered all too well the last time he lent me his jacket, how it curled around my body and filled every sense with his intoxicating smell. I wasn't able to get his scent out of my mind afterwards. Nature, pine, loam, fresh linen, and soft spices. It clung to my hair and sweater.

Draped in one of his winter jackets, I followed him outside to his telescope setup. A huge, dark thing standing on a tripod.

"This is a Takashi Refractor." Alaric rubbed the telescope like it was his baby. "It's got dispersion glass that eliminates chromatic aberration that gives a violet glare you see on some cheaper telescopes. It has a four-inch focuser, fully multi-coated optical surfaces with extra layers of anti-reflection coating."

I giggled and hit him on the arm. "Nerd alert."

His golden eye glowed, hypnotizing me with its depth and beauty. "You would be too, if you had the Sky god in your head."

I laughed and felt his hawk ruffle its feathers at the sound. "I have no idea what any of that means."

He twisted a knob and adjusted the lens direction, pointing it skyward. "It basically means it provides high magnification and astrophotography."

I crept closer, eager to see what he planned to show me. I only ever saw images of stars and never a real one through a telescope lens. "You take pictures of the stars?"

"Yeah, I'll show you some later." He grabbed my hand and

tugged me closer, maneuvering me so I leaned down to look into the lens. His hand failed to move and rested on my back. "See that?"

I kept my hands to myself, unsure whether to encourage any affection, even though every nerve in me screamed and begged for me to touch him back. It took everything I had not to return the simple gesture, and my fingers ached from squeezing the telescope so tightly.

Looking at the glitter of swirling stars distracted me, and I marveled at them. Pink, purple, blues, and a golden center. "It's beautiful. Does it have a name?"

"That's the Orion Galaxy." Alaric didn't move his hand and I enjoyed the comforting weight of it. How natural and right it felt resting on me. How I wanted him to move it all over and rub the hollow of my back and set off that spark from head to toe again. "Let me show you another."

I moved back to allow him to adjust the angle of the scope. When he finished, he gestured for me to peer down. A circling mass of gold and brown that reminded me of his bright golden eye exploded in view. "That's spectacular."

Alaric's hand traveled to the curve of my back as if he read my mind. "That's the Andromeda galaxy."

I used every ounce of concentration to admire the stars and not lose myself in his touch. "Does it have any planets?"

Alaric adjusted the scope again. "Currently they've only found the planet they named PA-99-N2. But ..." He brushed his hand over my head. My vision changed, sharpening, clarifying, zooming in to see so much more detail. "That's the gift of Horus."

"Goddess," I breathed, taking in all the detail. Four suns burning brightly, one violet, one gold, one red like our own and another greenish. Hundreds of stars twinkled on the outskirts of nineteen planets that I counted. "Nineteen?" I confirmed with Alaric.

He twisted another lever. "There's one hiding behind the golden sun." His other hand never left my back and started to move in slow circles.

I bit back a moan and examined the edge of a dark blue planet beyond the sun. "Incredible." He let me study it for a while, leisurely stroking my back until I moved away from the scope and looked up at him.

His golden eye glowed hotter, darker, like pulsing fire on the sun's surface. Redder with lust. Beautiful. Nothing like it. "One day I'd like to show you the stars, Aaliyah." His husky croon weakened my resolve about one hundred points and spread heat to places it shouldn't have.

"Stars?" He just showed me them, so I frowned, unsure what he meant by that. He was too much of a gentleman to be crude. Suggestive, yes. Behind my eyes when he fucked me? Nope. From the heartfelt warmth spreading along the bond, I assumed he meant sharing his love or making love. Hell, the man knew the way to get me smoldering all over with his sweet promises.

I found out the meaning when Alaric brushed the side of my face with his knuckles then he leaned down to claim my mouth in a soft caress. "The stars in your eyes." He pressed a hand over my chest right below my neck. "The stars in your heart. The stars in my love."

Goddess, how romantic! I didn't know how to respond when he put me on the spot with a comment like that. What I should have done was slam a lid on it. Ignored it. But I'd be dammed, it set off a glow in my belly that radiated outward to my fingertips and left me floating, lost in space somewhere in the damn Andromeda galaxy amid the starlight. And only he could rescue me and bring me back to Earth.

"Whoa, we got a romantic here!" It was safe to say he made me all girly and nervous with his poetic words, and I just blathered like an idiot. Made my girly parts steam up, too.

"We do." His hot murmur pierced right through my heart and sent a bolt of lust to my pussy. Steady, warm arms wrapped around me, pulling me closer, and I stopped breathing the moment our chests connected. One hand moved from my back to cup my head, tilting mine so our gazes locked. "Got a problem with that?"

My body responded to the challenge, and I let out a breathy whisper Marilyn Monroe would have been proud of. "No problem here."

Fuck, I was in a losing battle here. May as well quit while I was ahead. Surrender to these men and the promise they held for me. Or run like hell and never look back. I was caught between the two, unsure which direction to go.

"Good." He released me, grabbing my hand, and setting one hand on my back, swaying me around in circles. Part of me groaned at losing the contact. The other swung the lasso faster and higher, screaming *fuck me, we were dancing*. Not just any dancing. Slow dancing. The kind where he tucked me back against this wall of muscle, so close that my lips almost kissed his neck. "Cause you're going to be swimming in the stars once I'm done with you."

## CHAPTER 18

### *A*laric

MOVE OVER FRED ASTAIRE, Alaric Hawk was in the house! My boldness shocked me. Normally that was Slade's domain, whereas I was the respectful gentleman. But something about my new mate brought out a whole new side to me. Confident. Courageous. Forward. She also quieted the demons, and I needed the fucking relief.

My mate let out a soft sigh at my words, her eyes leaving a burning trail up my chest, neck, mouth, until they finally settled on my eyes. Stubborn, tenacious woman resisted my advances, wedging a cockblock between us. I examined the bond for a reason, putting it down to her resenting me for the way I'd treated her. Surprisingly, I found no resentment, and an enormous weight lifted off my chest. Her reluctance stemmed from something else I couldn't decipher. Maybe she saw me as a patient, a lost cause because of my demons. Either way, I wouldn't give up just yet. Her resistance weakened with every touch, gaze, and promise. But I'd never overstep her boundaries when I respected rules. Although, once she forgave me and said the word, we were on and there was no go back!

Besides, we didn't have the smoothest path in our relationship, and I shouldn't expect her to instantly forget it and forgive me, kiss me and get into my bed. My mate needed time and patience and I'd give her whatever she needed. Space, a hundred bouquets of flowers, romantic whispers, shy little kisses, touch her at every opportunity, and show her what she meant to me. I'd not leave things unsettled between us when I needed my mate by my side. Two years without her was agonizing. I hadn't had anyone since. Craved her touch and nothing else on this world could satisfy but her.

I stroked her cheeks and made her eyelids heavy. She squirmed in my grasp and the desire to break free dropped in our bond.

"Am I ever gonna see you in your uniform?" Classic Aaliyah stall tactic. The woman wanted my mouth on her, making her moan my name, but she stubbornly refused to let me. I respected her wishes and released her even though my fists curled to keep her trapped in my arms.

"This way." I straightened and took her to my den.

The room smelled dusty, and I considered opening a window to freshen it up. Hadn't been in here in a while. Lately it set me off. A few minutes in here to let Aaliyah see my Air Force photos should be okay though. She'd keep me tethered to sanity.

Overhead light made the mushroom-colored walls a shade or two darker brown. Pictures, service medals, and framed qualification certificates decorated the east wall. My grandfather's antique oak desk hugged the north corner. A bookshelf with games, non-fiction editions, and

Star Wars figurines from my childhood rested along the west.

"Look at all this," Aaliyah cooed as she took it all in, her eyes lightening from the deep aqua to lighter blue. "So many medals."

Awards I didn't want. But the Air Force had to reward me for what happened. Stuck a fucking medal on my damn uniform like it took away all the horror I endured.

"Oh my God. Aren't you strapping in your uniform?" She traced my picture of the proud, smiling young man who joined the Air Force to make a difference and fulfil his family's legacy to serve our country.

A man medically discharged, broken and beaten down, scarred mentally and physically. Flashbacks hit me at immense speed, the jolt of them rocking our bond. His face appeared in my mind's eyes. Taunting smile. Cruel eyes. Sadistic mind. My body twitched and I slammed my eyes closed. Drums thumped in my ears as my pulse sped up. I needed him gone.

"Alaric." Aaliyah hesitantly reached for me. Concern registered through our connection. She knew something wasn't right, but she remained distant and wary after I strangled her.

I blinked the vision away. "I'm fine. It's just a bit of heartburn."

She gave me the bullshit eyebrows but let it go and turned back to the frames. I couldn't fool my little nurse.

"Is this the plane you flew?" She glanced back at me with eyes wide with wonder. "It's huge. How did you get that beast off the ground?"

"With a lot of practice." I glanced at the picture of my co-pilot and me with our arms over each other's shoulders. Good times. "Three years of pilot training. Ups. Downs. Failures. A lot of drinking with my mates."

Aaliyah turned to me and smiled. Warm. Home. My mate. "Do you think Horus came to you because you were a pilot or that you became one because of the god? I sometimes wonder if that's why Isis chose me?"

"We all contain some facets of our god's character," I replied. "That's why they chose us. I signed up for the Air Force because it was expected of me, not for a love of flying. That came after they accepted me as a pilot."

She nodded and chewed her lip. "You said you hadn't flown planes in a few years. Do you miss it?"

Talking about the aircraft made his face sharpen into view. Sweat beaded my forehead and I shakily swiped at it. *You're dead. You're not real.* I clenched my fist tight to my side. But he appeared as real as Aaliyah did in front of me. I shook my head, fighting off the vision.

"I can't do it anymore," I replied, my voice taking on a hoarse edge.

"You don't enjoy it?" I wish she wouldn't keep asking. "I don't think I'd ever stop loving nursing." She might if she'd been through what I had.

"It reminds me of a time I'd rather forget." My agitation scaled and I twitched again.

"Shame. I would have loved to have gone flying with you," she mused.

Recollections returned with haunting vividness. An explosion in my left engine. Warning alarms as the mechanics failed. Lights on the flight instruments flashing. Dials on the engine instruments hitting critical. The plane's nose tipping down. My knuckles going white as I gripped the steering throttle. Trying to adjust the throttle levers to no use. Sweat dripped down my face and I wiped it away. I didn't want to go back there. Not with him.

"Alaric, are you having an episode?" Aaliyah's voice grew

distant as if she'd been ripped away from me or I was thrust back there.

In the cockpit. Smoke stinging my nose. Alarms hounding my ears and rousing me. Radio crackling with a transmission. My leg broken in three places and me screaming. I blinked the memory away and sucked in air. Fuck, I needed to get out of here before he came to take me there.

"Alaric!" My mate's distant voice called to me, but I couldn't find her. She vanished. Somewhere in the darkness she found me, her palm connecting with my arm, tugging at me gently, drawing me back. "I'm here. Come back to me. You're safe. Nothing's going to hurt you."

My mate. I fought to get to her. Lungs screaming and burning for air, I caught her shoulders and clung to her, snapping out of it. I gasped as I sucked in air. My body shook everywhere. My damp shirt stuck to my back.

"It's okay, Aaliyah," I ground out. "Put some jazz music on. I need it."

She scanned my CD collection but didn't find anything.

"No," I growled, breathing hard. "The records."

"Shit." Her hands trembled just as much as mine, which surprised me, given her profession. Surely, she was used to patients panicking. She flicked through my father's collection of records. "Some of these are vintage. They

must be worth an absolute fortune," she stuttered nervously. "Shit, I have no clue if this is jazz or not, but here goes."

She set a vinyl on the record player as I fought the next wave of flashbacks. The dial scratched and the scape made me wince. A few seconds later music commenced, soft, mellow, growing in beat. Fluidic guitar broke out and hushed drums and piano. Soothing. My grandfather used to play it to me. Grandma said it was the only thing to calm him after an episode. Seemed PTSD ran in the family.

My twitching reduced in tempo and the memories faded into the background. "I need a drink," I rasped, heading for the door, but she blocked me, setting a firm hand on my chest.

"Alaric, will you try something with me?" I blinked at her question.

The PTSD wormed at the back of my mind, ready to surface if something set it off or I descended into panic again.

*You'll never be rid of us,* the demons hissed.

"I need whisky," I rasped.

Aaliyah slowly took my hand and ushered herself into my arms, clasping one arm on my lower back. Her other hand held mine out to the side, the way I'd held it out earlier when I danced with her on the porch.

Alaric, I'm going to ask you something personal and I won't be offended if you don't want to talk about it, okay?" She budged me to move in shuffling motions.

*She'll never heal you,* the demons snarled.

I gripped her hand tighter, staring at her, waiting for the question, desperate for her to silence the voices.

My mate gently swirled me in circles. "Have you sought professional help for the PTSD?"

"Yes." My jaw flexed and I ground my teeth. "It didn't help."

"Oh." Her brows worked into a crease. "One of the therapists at my work ... ex work," she corrected herself, reminding herself that she had no job to go back to. "She recommended a therapy call breathwork. Have you heard of it?"

"I'm not doing some pansy-ass meditation," I scoffed as the demons croaked with laughter.

"It's not mediation," Aaliyah replied, rocking and swaying us to the mellow beat of the jazz. "And breathing has been scientifically proven to be beneficial. It lowers blood pressure, stress, and many more problems."

"I don't want any of that shit." *His* face emerged from the shadows and the demons screamed louder, welcoming him.

"Okay then. It's your decision." Aaliyah's hand circled my lower back, drawing my anxiety down a bar. She was like a drug. My own personal Prozac, and I was addicted. Like a junkie, I needed more of her.

I pulled her closer and leaned down to whisper in her ear, hot and shaky. "I need you to soothe the demons."

"Let me in, Alaric." Her big aqua eyes studied me with worry set deep in them. "Let me see what my gift can do." Her hand on my back skimmed up my arm to my shoulder, rubbing me, reassuring me, seeking my trust and permission to treat me.

"Take it all away." I closed my eyes, focusing on the sway of our bodies, the melody, the feel of her in my arms. Soft, mesmerizing, soothing.

While I kept hold of her, she let go of me, letting my hand fall to her hip. Both of her hands came to my temples, and the instant she connected with me, the memories surfaced. The crashed plane with me injured and trapped in the cockpit. Our Afghani enemies finding the crash site and hauling me from the wreckage, taking me to one of their underground bunkers where they kept other prisoners of war, starved them, taunted them, tortured them, broke them. Aaliyah gasped as my mind relayed my torture in hers. Where my torturer carved out my eye and broken all my bones.

"Alaric," she whimpered, her body jolting as if she felt all my pain. Her eyes slammed shut, she bit her lip, her back arched, and she released an agonized cry. Nails clawed into me as she suffered through my horror.

"Aaliyah." I shook her, but she was lost to the visions.

Multicolored lights trickled along her wrists and arms, up her neck into her head. Memories stretched and twisted as if she sucked them from my mind into hers. Hooks binding them to my consciousness refused to let go, and I shrieked with pain as they sank deeper. My demons hissed louder at the threat of losing me as their host. Aaliyah gave another cry and terror and dread flooded my system as she agonized through it all. Horrified, I lifted my hands to her wrists to break her connection from me, but she was immovable, solid, and stuck to me. Blood trickled from her eye and nose as if they'd carved hers out and broken her beautiful face.

"Aaliyah, no." I clutched her limp body in my arms, not wanting her to have to go through that harrow when it had broken me.

She screamed, her grip of my head breaking hold as she collapsed to the ground. I dropped beside her, dragging her onto my lap, clutching her to my chest, stroking her forehead, whispering to her.

"Fuck, what have I done?" I rocked my mate in my lap.

"Alaric, what did they do to you?" She moaned, somewhat lucid, as if she awoke from surgery, eyes firmly shut. Her fingers clawed into my arms, holding on as if I was her anchor to stop her from falling back into the pits of hell. "Your eye. Your bones. Your body." Shudders ripped at her body.

Fuck, she saw it all. Suffered it all. My heart shattered into a million pieces. Now she knew the extent of how broken and damaged I was. I'd rather have endured a lifetime of torment than put her through that. But I didn't know what would happen when she touched me.

"Don't worry." I stroked her sweaty hair from her forehead and kissed the top of her head. "Horus gave me a new eye. I see one hundred times better than before. He saved me."

I wiped the blood from beneath her eye, smudging it on her face. Was it mine or hers? Terrified that she suffered the same fate as me, I went ballistic for my injured mate, and I tapped her face.

"Aaliyah, look at me, baby." Tears that were threatening brook loose. I shook with all the fear welling inside of me, falling apart for her. "Show me your eyes."

"What?" She roused and cracked open her eyelids. Both precious treasures remained in their sockets, and I strummed her cheeks.

"Fuck. Thank Horus." I pressed my nose into her cheek, nuzzling her, wetting it with my tears. "You're okay, baby."

"What they did to you was horrible." She reached for me, her touch sparking another flash of memory. Her power had attempted to remove my pain but wasn't successful. My torment and distress too much. Shocked and horrified her to the core. "You're such a strong, brave man. I would have done the same things to escape."

Fuck, she saw that too. My rampage to escape. Murdering all my captors, even the kind soldiers who showed me mercy. Leaving no one alive as I gunned them down, slit their throats, and unleashed the powers Horus bestowed on me. Saving four lives of my fellow servicemen from the Australian and US Armed Forces. If the Sky god hadn't come to me in the cell after they took my eye, I would have perished in those dungeons. I owed everything to Horus.

I shrunk away from her on the bond and loosened my grip on her, frightened she'd see the monster stalking inside of me.

Aaliyah's constant sweep over my jaw and cheeks eased the traumatic burden on my mind and soul. "You did what you did to stay alive. Don't blame yourself." She always knew the right thing to say. Encouraged me. Built my confidence. Eased my damn guilt.

"Shh, baby." I cradled her tighter, kissing her forehead, cheeks, and nose, wanting her to forget everything she saw. "It's okay. When you're ready, we can get desert. Your favorite, remember."

"I want to try again," she whispered. "Draw the memories from you. I know I can. I just have to push aside my emotions next time. Be objective, like I am when I tend to patients."

"No fucking way. Thank you, but no." She flinched at my harsh response.

Fuck. I swore at my woman. Dad would have cracked me on the side of the head for that. Remorseful, I took her hand, lifted it to my mouth, and kissed the back of it, sending a rush of heat to her chest that soaked into our link and warmed me, chasing away the demon's touch on my soul.

"I just need you to hold me, talk to me, and soothe the demons. You're the only thing besides the alcohol that keeps the memories at bay."

She cupped my jaw. "You need release, Alaric. To be set free. You're a caged bird with a dampened spirit."

I buried my face in her hair, curbing breaking down again. All this time I was trapped with my demons, and I longed for freedom like my bird.

"Fuck, no, Aaliyah," I grit out. "I won't let you go through that again." No matter how much I needed liberation, she wouldn't suffer because of me.

"Alaric." She nudged me to lift my face to meet hers. "I agreed to help you. Let me." Her darkened eyes pleaded with me.

I shifted her into my arms and climbed to my feet. "Help me by eating dessert with me. Stay the night. Lie in my arms. Chase my demons away."

"I don't know if that's a good idea after what happened," she whispered as I set her down, holding her steady.

No, it wasn't. I hurt Liz one time when I experienced an episode during one of her sleepovers. There was a good chance I'd have another attack in the night, but I couldn't bear to part with Aaliyah when she calmed me and attempted to absorb some of my trauma. That shit would mess with her head and she shouldn't be alone tonight. She could go back to Castor, but he didn't know what she or I went through. Tonight, we needed each other.

"I'm not asking for you to sleep with me." I caressed the side of her face. "I'll sleep on the floor it if makes you comfortable. This is for your sake as well as mine. I don't want you to be alone with that haunting shit." I never swore or raised my voice at my woman, but all manners were out the window.

She thought for a few moments. "Just for the night then." Relief coursed through me that she agreed. I thought I'd have a fight on my hands like Slade always did. "No touchy feelies. No kisses. And no poetic whispers!"

I kissed her forehead as my hawk shrieked his approval. "I wouldn't dream of it." I raised my palms. "I like my balls intact, thank you."

# CHAPTER 19

## Aaliyah

I HATED to do this to him. Hated myself for being a fucking snitch, especially after last night, but Slade needed to know what he was dealing with. Alaric was a ticking timebomb waiting to go off and the president needed to deal with him before someone got hurt. I paused outside of Slade's office, hand raised, knuckles ready to knock.

Oh, God, last night. After I'd witnessed all the horrors Alaric endured, we slow danced a little more, and eaten all the damn apple and rhubarb crumble over a series of hours. We curled up on the sofa together, my legs on his thighs, him massaging my calves and feet and vice versa. Heaven. I threw all my no-touchy rules out the window, sensing he needed the contact. Who was I to deny him the care he needed? Hell, I needed his warmth and the comfort of his arms after what I'd seen. Fuck. I felt like the world's biggest traitor for using his pain against him. When he found out what I did, he'd be crushed, our relationship burned to a cinder with no hope of resurrection.

This damaged man amazed me how he handled everything the world threw at him. His captors might have broken his spirit, but they didn't break the man despite him thinking himself a lost cause. He was one of the strongest persons I ever met. Not many people would have handled what he went through and come out alive. Many military vets committed suicide from their experiences and not being able to cope with the world to which they returned. Yet, Alaric came out the other side, found a new purpose, a new brotherhood, and coped as well as he could. Drinking his demons away through a different bottle each night.

If it weren't for him, I wouldn't have handled my shit last night. Alone in my bed, I would have been haunted by the visions, disturbed and unable to get sleep. It wasn't like I couldn't have gone to Castor for comfort after the strain between us.

Hours swept by as Alaric and I talked, laughed, soothed each other's troubled minds, then fallen asleep on the couch. This morning, I woke up in his arms, protected, respected, and adored, and I couldn't bring myself to move away. I was tired of being strong, tired of doing what was right, so tired of fighting everything. Alaric was so wrong and oh, so right, and I thought to hell with it, and just went with the flow.

This morning, he made me breakfast, a smorgasbord of food and endless tea. Eggs, bacon, hash browns, tomatoes, sausage, mushrooms. The man could cook like Castor. Alaric also remembered how I liked my tea, perfecting the right amount of cream and sugar, making me want to stay overnight with him every night. I could get used to being spoiled like a queen. His queen.

The door to Slade's office flung open, jerking me out of my daydream. I righted myself from the shock to look up at the sexy, rugged Jackal's president. His disheveled hair, wrinkled shirt, and dark, puffy eyes suggested he had slept at the club and not very well.

My body flushed with the raw, brutal need seeded by him every time we were near each other. The very reason I avoided him the last couple of days. Oh, that and the whole claiming thing by my damn shifter. Cheap hooker. I felt fucking awful for luring him down from a meltdown by reinforcing my promise of accepting all his god's darkness, only to leave him high and dry by hiding from him. Talk about leading him on. I needed to get my hormones in check, and fast, because every time we were together, my body betrayed me. Made me cave to his dirty promises and touches. Bringing him back from the brink of destruction had left my body wild, electric, and humming with his dark power, desperate and aching for him. Staying away had been best for both of us. It kept me balanced and not mad with lust.

I knew I wouldn't be able to steer clear of him forever. The seriousness of Alaric's condition brought me to Slade's doorstep. The Jackal's president deserved to know what he was up against. Alaric's mental health put the club's member's safety in jeopardy. What I was about to do went against patient confidentiality and kicked me in the damn gut for betraying Alaric's trust, but I had an oath to uphold. Protecting patients against personal and social harm meant I had to consider the bigger picture. Safety of all the men, not just one. Otherwise, I failed the Jackals in my role as temporary club medic.

"Mornin', Nurse A," Slade's voice dropped into an alluring octave, more upbeat than his low grunts and stiff posture, indicative of the stress burning him to the end of his fuse.

My organs burned with a fever bordering on lethal. This

man was going to be the death of me. I absorbed every sinfully sexy inch of him.

Today was a whole different story, though. Armed with his classic, dimpled smile, Slade seemed more relaxed, leaning in the doorway, his body tension unwinding as he crossed his massive arms over his chest. Oh, yeah, my eyes went to his forearms, the smattering of light hair, the muscle, strength, and brutality of them. They may have also wandered up his magnificent biceps, lingering in buff town, before moving back up to the light beard covering his rough jaw. My reluctant, heavy gaze complained as I dragged them over his rugged face to settle on his sexy damn indigo eyes. Fuck, if I wasn't careful, I'd cave like I did every time, jump him, and drag him to his desk for another three-orgasm round. I licked my lips, debating it. Every time he touched me, I lost myself. Damn wild, primitive sex god of a man.

Slade flexed his muscles, tempting me to take another peek. "Like what you see, old lady?" *Yes, yes, I did. Don't mind if I admire you.* "Look all you want. I'm yours." His mood had lightened with my presence. Seemed like I was a drug to more than one person.

I rolled my eyes at his flirtations. Devil couldn't help himself. Not that I was complaining. I enjoyed it, I'd just never admit it. The avatar of Chaos already had balls as big as space and I wasn't boosting that huge ego.

I cleared my dry throat to return the moisture he stole from it. "Got a minute?"

Slade's bottom lip curled up in protest. "Onto business so soon?"

"It's important."

"Drink important? Deep and meaningful important? An itch that needs scratching important?" Damn flirt.

"The first two." I shoved at his chest, pushing him into his room.

"Hit me, Nurse A." He crossed to his desk, sitting on the edge, stressing the massive size of his strong thighs in his molded-on jeans.

I clawed a hand through my hair, trying to figure out the best way to say it.

"Hey, what's wrong, sugar?" Slade swept me into his arms and ran a thumb over my cheek. Heck, he needed to stop that. Right. Now. "Brix giving you trouble? I'll fucking knock his teeth out."

That made me smile inside. Brix could do with some missing teeth.

"No." I caught Slade's wrist and held on, needing his strength to deliver the speech I'd prepared. "I had dinner with Alaric last night and he had an episode. I think the frequency and intensity are getting worse."

Slade made a disapproving sound that I wasn't sure stemmed from jealousy that I wasn't with him or because his road captain bugged out again.

I swallowed the painful lump stuck in my throat. "He's a risk to the club in his current state. If he has another episode on a mission, he could get himself or another member killed."

Slade's neck and shoulder muscles bunched, and he rolled his neck as if the stiffness gave him grief. "This is the last thing I fucking need right now. Hawk Boy's a critical asset to the club." He scraped the back of his neck before setting his huge paw on my waist. "What do you suggest, Nurse A?"

Kindling ignited in my belly, warming the cold mass. Slade damn Vincent wanted my opinion rather than forcing his will onto me like he had with dressing me and hounding me into a date.

"Since Alaric won't let me treat him," I said, my voice hoarse, "I recommend that he gets psychiatric treatment."

The president's thumb left a blistering trail across my

skin. "The club's all he has after leaving the military. Benching him will destroy him." He glanced behind him out the window with a heavy, glum stare. "What do you think? Should I pull him from duty?"

Slade damn Vincent respected my opinion, and I wasn't even a patched-in member or his fully convinced mate. Massive turn around in the trust factor. A smile split across my face.

The urge to tease him rose up but I let it slide away due to the gravity of the matter. "Alaric dreads that. I think it would be detrimental to his state of mind, but I honestly don't see another way."

Slade leaned his forehead to mine for support. "Fuck. I hate to be the prick to sideline him, but I won't have another Jackal lying in a grave." The bear of a man scrubbed harder at his neck, conveying his back tension and pain.

"Sit down." I clasped his hand and drew him to sit in his chair.

"Oh, God, right there, Nurse A," Slade moaned as I worked his tight muscles. Huge muscles that my small hands could barely grasp and knead. "Fuck, you're strong for a little thing."

"Years of practice restraining unruly patients." I smiled against his ear, making a bolt of his lust tap the bond.

"Tie me down and massage me any day, Nurse A." This probably wasn't the time or place to banter, but with the tough decision he just made, and the tension weighing him down mentally and physically, he needed a moment of peace. I let him have it and dug into his tight body harder. "Fuck, that's good."

I glowed under his praise and rubbed deeper to break up his knots.

Slade stopped me by tugging one of my wrists, dragging my arm over his shoulder and wrapping it around his neck.

"Thanks for coming to me with this. I value your medical opinion."

I leaned my chin on the back of his head, making him groan with approval. "I'm sorry you had to make this tough decision."

"Call of fucking duty," he grunted, kissing each knuckle, branding my skin with fire. "I've got to be hard on everyone's ass when it's ours on the line."

I wanted to scream and hit him for what he did to my body. Tell him not to do that. Not to work me into a burning frenzy of lust. Turn me into an aroused beast that wanted to bite, scratch, kiss, fuck, and shriek as he filled me. Now wasn't the time. We had to work together to take down my brother and ensure we survived the hell he started. I channeled my frustrations into breaking up the cluster of knots in Slade's back.

"I know what it's like for Alaric," he admitted, brushing my hand along his cheek, eliciting electric shivers all over. "My dad tried to bench me when I lost my shit at hearing his terminal cancer diagnosis."

I stroked his hair and listened, eager to hear more of his past.

"Zethan tried to bench me again after Liz died and I couldn't fucking function." Slade brushed my hand between both of his when I prickled and tensed. "I know you don't like to hear it, but she's a part of me. I'll never mention her again if that's what you want." He let go of my hand with a final kiss, letting me work his neck and back with both hands.

"It's fine." I might have pinched his muscle hard enough to make him grunt. It wasn't that I bristled at the mention of Liz. Her name brought back hostilities from a week back that I'd rather put behind me.

Thinking about it rationally, this was a big fucking deal

that such a hard, gruff man like Slade showed me his weakness. Emotions got the better of him. Everyone had a vulnerability. Bikers rarely showed theirs. The fact that he had laid himself bare conveyed his trust, his willingness to share with me as both his medic and mate. I'd be lying if I didn't concede that I wanted to know this man better.

"You admitting that means a lot to me." I applied a bit of magick to dissolve a stubborn bunch of knots, releasing his pain and flooding the bond with his relief. "I like hearing about your past."

"What do you want to know?" Slade's tossed back his head. So. Fucking. Sexy. "I never learned to read or write because of my disability. I was a monster in school because I hated it and couldn't follow the lessons. Always in detention."

I giggled and lightened my touch, rubbing his skin, making him groan with pleasure. "Oh, I bet you were a hellraiser."

"Fucking right, old lady." Slade grinned wickedly over his shoulder, melting me a little more with his sinful smile. "Don't expect anything less."

My inner vixen howled for this demon, and I think he heard the call, smirking at me roguishly. *Shit. Stop that.* The fire in his gaze and the glow of his dimples beckoned me down to his mouth. I held firm and resisted.

"I joined the club at sixteen as soon as I left school." He grazed his palms together and my body awoke with need to have them skimming over my shoulders and neck. "Prospected for two years. Worked my way up to VP underneath Dad. Old bastard never let me get ahead 'cause I was his son. He said I had to earn the right to be president. Toughened me up a lot. I was a reckless fucker in my twenties, boozing, partying, running wild with Set's help." His grin weakened me.

"My dad was the same with me." I used my elbow to really

get into a tight hoard of muscles in Slade's shoulder blades. "Tough on me. Tougher than he was on Danny. I think he knew how hard it would be for me because I was the only woman in a boy's club."

"Fuck!" Slade's back arched. I wasn't going easy on him. "You turned out okay. A pain in the ass, but okay." Asshole. For that, I ground my elbow into him, showing no mercy. "Fuck, I'm gonna spank your ass hard for that." He twisted on his seat and followed through with his threat.

Pleasant heat soaked into my smarting ass cheek. Lust speared me to the spot as he caressed over the smoldering glow. He gave me another light spank and set me on my feet.

I kept him on track with more questions and a lighter knead in between the torturous ones. "When did you take over the club?"

"Twenty-six," Slade grunted as the pain eased. "When dad got too sick to manage it."

"So, the club's been your life?"

"Pretty much."

"What do you do to take a load off?"

"Party!" Slade shouted. "What else?"

I ground him harder. "I'm serious."

"I like to kick back with my VP and smoke a fine Cuban." Slade reached behind him to stroke my hip. "Treat my woman to all the fine things in life."

"Hobbies?" I chuckled.

The intensity of his hip rub deepened. "Sex, bikes, whisky, breaking shit, and barking at people. And in that order!"

I hit him for his smartass response. "Be serious."

"I'm a simple guy with simple tastes." Slade curled his arm to rub behind my knee and along my calf. "Dad and I used to go camping and fishing, but I haven't been in almost two years. I love riding my bike on a big trip, but the club's been crazy busy since we brought out Pharaoh." His other hand bent back for a cheeky squeeze of my ass. "I savor every moment with my woman. Weekend getaways on yachts, the beach, skiing trips, penthouses, helicopter rides. Whatever you want, baby."

Slade was a generous man and lover. He'd deliver me the world if I asked it. But I was a simple girl too and didn't ask for much. His company was enough. Although, I was partial to the whole boat getaway idea.

"Good thing Dad and I used to sail, then, 'cause you're in good hands." I ran my fingers through his light, Mohican-styled hair.

"Captain Nurse." Slade gave my ass another squeeze, and my body pooled with wet, luscious heat. "Beautiful, sexy, stubborn, smart, and aeronautical!"

I giggled again, loving the easy flow of witty repartee between us.

Slade twisted in his seat again, this time to grab me by the waist, drag me onto his lap, and cradle me in his arms. "I'm always in good hands." He kissed my cheek. Spicy and backed with heat, but respectful. "So, when am I gonna see your sexy ass in your cut?"

"Stop it." I shoved my palm into his shoulder. At his disheartened flare on the bond, I added, "It was a sweet gesture. Thank you."

Slade's arms secured around my back. "I meant what I said about wanting you to become part of our family. Things with us won't be like what it was with the Wolves."

"I know." A topic I didn't want to venture into when I planned to leave. I sensed Slade was about to club me over the head and beat me into submission until I agreed to stay.

Instead, he left a trail of kisses down my jaw that I allowed and swallowed my pleasured moan. "I can already tell you're gonna leave a trail of broken hearts, Nurse A."

Fuck. Why'd he have to say that? I tensed in his arms. "But you'll be breaking yours in the process."

I thumped him again. "Cocky much?"

He grinned, those lickable dimples on display. "You wouldn't expect anything less, would you?"

Slade Vincent was a heartbreaker, all right. The kind of guy you didn't walk away from unscathed. I'd crawl on bloodied hands and knees from him, heart burned and turned to ash. That I could count on.

# CHAPTER 20

## Slade

FINALLY, a fucking clue in this dark mystery. Castor came through after his channels were dark for a week. A little slip-up on some cockhead's part, and we had a clue to investigate on our slimy new competitor's runner. After dead ends and nonstop mysteries, I didn't put much stock into the lead. Hope faded fast in my mind, leaving me nothing to cling to. Shit was going to hell in a fucking handbasket. But I'd hunt down every damn lead until we got our man or men.

My crew assembled in the garage, Castor and Aaliyah gearing up on my left, Alaric pulling on his riding gloves on my right.

Castor kept his distance and his hands to himself for once. Strain on the bond indicated a falling out between him and our mate. Fuck, another headache to deal with. I didn't need more goddamn drama. We couldn't afford for cracks in our relationship to chase our mate away. I'd sort out these two when we got back to the club.

For the first time in a week, it didn't hurt to push my shoulders back. *Thank you, old lady.* Woman sure knew how to massage out the kinks and pep me up with her little visit yesterday. Reprieve from my aching back allowed me to get my first good night's sleep in days.

Dread sat like a lead weight in my gut at addressing my next task. Last night I was on too much of a high after my little nurse's visit to drop the news on Alaric. Crushing his heart was the last thing I wanted to do when his mental state was fragile. I didn't want to be the asshole that pushed him over the edge. Eyes burned into the side of my head and I turned, catching Aaliyah's expectant gaze. Fuck, I just had to get it over with.

The outcome of our dummy drug run could have been a hell of a lot worse if Zethan failed to snap Alaric out of his episode. Both my men could have been dead, and I'd not lose another man on my fucking watch.

I zipped up my jacket, ready to bite the bullet and get it over with. "Hawk Boy, get over here."

Alaric's grip dropped from his handlebars where was about to roll out his bike. He maneuvered through the parked bikes to stand beside me. "Yes, sir?" Fucking sir. I would have ripped him one for calling me that but one shitty order was enough for one day.

My brow tensed hard enough to cause an ache as I set a heavy hand on his shoulder and stared a goddamn hole in the ground.

"What?" Alaric chuckled nervously. "You look like you're gonna ask me to marry you or something."

Fuck. Not funny. I pinched at the corners of my dry mouth. "There's no easy way to say this, but I've decided to bench you."

Shock flinched along the bond and his expression. "Why?" Alaric jerked back and my hand fell from his shoulder. "What for?"

"You nearly got my VP shot on the dummy rug run. I can't afford for you to jeopardize the crew or yourself if you have another panic attack." My tone was like the toll of death. Somber. Serious. Grave. "You need to get your shit together. Seek professional help and deal with your PTSD."

"Fuck." Alaric rubbed at his creased forehead, the fire of betrayal striking our attachment. "Aaliyah came to you, didn't she?"

"This is my decision and I've been debating it since the dummy drug run," I growled, trying to leave her out of it. I didn't want to deal with discord between those two on top of all the other shit I juggled.

Putting out multiple fires at once was bogging me down in little shit and preventing me from dealing with the bigger picture. Nailing Danny Heller to the sabotage on our club so I could launch offensive moves.

Alaric shook his head in disbelief. "I can't believe this."

"You knew it was coming, Alaric." I slid out of concerned friend mode into leader. He'd respond to my seniority. Accept the order. Obey it. "I've given you chances to deal with it, but it's getting worse. I can't have another man in the grave. I won't go through that again."

"We're fucking outlaws!" Alaric shouted, capturing the attention of Castor and Aaliyah. "Some of us are bound to die in the process."

My jackal snarled at his lack of respect, but I ignored it, knowing he out of all my men showed me the most esteem. I'd not have him make fucking excuses for himself and his behavior. Excuses would get us killed.

"You're not coming with us until you can prove you've got this under control. Am I making myself clear?" I snatched his helmet off his bike and flicked my hands, signaling at him to hand over his keys.

Alaric fished them out, slammed them in my palm, and gave me a *'fuck you'* salute. "Crystal, sir." His boots thudded on the concrete as he stormed off, muttering curses under his breath about trusting Aaliyah.

Fuck. Not the way I'd hoped that would go. I knew it wouldn't go down well, and now I worried this might unhinge Alaric further, that he might harm himself or do something stupid.

Aaliyah shrank away on our link as Alaric glared murderously on his way past. She made the right decision to come to me with her recommendation. I saw firsthand how dangerous Alaric was when he lost control of his mind.

Castor's gaze jumped between Aaliyah and me, but he said nothing. I liked that he kept his trap shut and respected my decision. Orders were orders with him. He respected the rule and law of the club.

I went to my nurse's side and touched her back. "You okay?"

"Fine." She didn't sound fine. Sounded like she carried the same weight of guilt as I did.

"You did the right thing. Alaric will get over it," I reassured her with a rub of her lower back, stealing one on her ass on the way down to cheer her up. She smiled and smacked at me. "That's my old lady." I grinned and winked at her and returned to my ride.

She sighed and dragged her helmet down over her head.

"All right, Bird Boy," I called to Castor, setting astride my bike. "Lead the way and let's get these cunts."

***

. . .

We rolled up in style, riding through the suspected drug runner's warehouse amid workers, machinery and stock movement, interfering in their operations. I parked at the rear of a truck being loaded by a forklift, making a fucking statement. *Fuck with us and I'll fuck with you.*

Looked like an everyday warehouse, aisles of eighteen-feet-high shelving, pallet racks, crates of product, hydraulic lifts, forklifts, and employees milling about, dragging service carts.

Cunt in the vehicle tooted and shouted at me to move. I cut his engine to silence the annoying beep assaulting my ears. A snap of my hand at my side twisted the key to the off position and another broke it in half. I finished with a glare and growl as I alighted my bike that shut him the fuck up.

Castor mustered at my side with Aaliyah behind me. I mentally checked in with my woman and found her heart beating faster, her adrenaline spiked, her shifter loving the thrill. Woman craved adventure and danger. We'd make a Jackal of her yet. She had a taste for it, she just didn't know it yet.

"Who the fuck's in charge here?" I asked the fat prick with the gorilla-hairy chest on the forklift.

"Office." He pointed a limp finger to the south. "Ask for Larry."

Larry needed to fire this cunt's ass and hire someone who didn't squeal at the first sign of danger. If one of my employees did that, his ass would eat concrete on the way out.

"Touch my bike and I'll feed your balls to my pit bull," I barked at the crowd of confused warehouse workers, who stared with worried expressions and edgy body language.

A few of them backed away, looking to make themselves busy elsewhere. My jackal remained on high alert, sniffing, listening for anything out of place. Any one of those assholes could pull a gun and start shooting. After my woman took a bullet for me, I was on high alert, keeping her tight to my side.

I gestured at Castor to leave us. "Check the warehouse top to bottom." He strode away, uncertainty and disapproval pricking the bond at separating from his president and mate. It wouldn't be for long, and we'd be right behind him, separated by a few aisles.

I signaled at Aaliyah to follow me. We swept through the rows, searching for the drugs. Castor's whistle called my attention to the west, and I claimed her hand and dragged her with me. My enforcer awaited in the third aisle, flicking his switch knife open. He jerked his head at the left shelf, prodded the open box to expose packaged plastic bags full of grey pills. Fucking grey. They didn't even try to copy our golden pills. Gold, like the Egyptian gods. Castor's knife pierced one of the bags, slicing it open, and he closed his knife and pocketed it. He removed a pill from the packet, broke it in half and tasted the powder inside.

His mouth scrunched up and he spat on the floor. "A poor knock-off. They've substituted some cheaper ingredients and it reflects in the quality. It's bitter compared to ours."

On top of knowing every little fucking detail of every book on the planet, my enforcer inherited his god's ability to detect flavors and ingredients. Made him a pretty good cook, too.

Satisfied with his assessment, he glanced at Aaliyah, and said, "Call it out of me. I don't want to chance the side effects of this crap."

While Aaliyah used her magick to remove the drug from his system, I tried out the grey powder inside the capsule to confirm it. Yep, that was a shitty excuse of a copy all right.

"Trace any purchases of the ingredients," I ordered Castor and he nodded.

Pleased that we found our enemy's product before it went to market and ruined our business further, I grabbed two bags and carried them down the aisle and through the center of the warehouse. Confused warehouse workers parted from the center crowd still gathered, muttering to each other about our intrusion. I marched through them to the group of administration buildings at the north.

"Got a lock on some shipments," Castor informed me from my rear.

"Good," I grunted.

Inside the mezzanine structure, we navigated two corridors until we came to a reception desk manned by a young bird in her twenties. Dolled up to the max, and wearing an inappropriately low-cut top, she stopped mid conversation, eyes widening at me.

Aaliyah was a stunner compared to this creature. Didn't need an ounce of makeup to look smoking. I pulled her beside me, setting my hand on her waist to show her off.

The receptionist's body stiffened as she assessed me and hung up the phone. "Can I help you, Mr.—"

"Looking for Larry." My voice came out low and menacing to match my mood at finding the product produced by our competitors.

I scanned the reception area for movement. My jackal was vigilant after the last time we burst into a warehouse and the Wolves jumped us. Castor shielded both Aaliyah and me from the rear. I should have brought more men.

"Just a moment." The woman picked up her landline and dialed a number. "Someone here to see you." She nodded, her gaze nervously flicking up to me. "They didn't say." She paused to listen, her grip on the handset tightening. "You should get out here and not keep them waiting."

Aaliyah softened into my grasp, leaning into me, giving me hope we were on our way to forgiveness. I examined the bond for reinforcement, finding her willing and receptive to my hold, but on edge with the confrontation.

Larry staggered out a few moments later, a thin man about five eight, greying hair and fuzzy beard. He wore brown chinos, a buttoned, collared shirt and a cotton sweater over the top.

"I usually don't see people without appointment," he announced, clutching a black leather compendium to his chest.

"I don't give a fuck." I tossed a bag of pills hard at his gut and he caught it with an oof and stumbled back three steps. "Where'd you get this?"

"That's my business," the skinny fuck dared tell me.

I removed my cigarette packet from my cut's pocket, selected a pre-rolled cigarette and lit it. "You've got three seconds to talk," I said blowing out a trail of furious smoke in his face. "Before my enforcer here starts unloading bullets in your chest."

I heard Castor slide his pistol from his cut and unclick the safety.

Aaliyah backed him up with her weapon, although I knew she wouldn't use it for a deadly shot like we would. Woman wasn't a killer. Upheld her medical oath. My inner demon rose to the challenge to make an outlaw of her.

Larry's chest reddened and his neck muscles corded. "Who the fuck do you think you are, coming in here, threatening me?"

A god motherfucker. This cunt was less than ten seconds away from perishing if he didn't provide answers.

"I'm the man your client ripped off with this cheap-ass knock-off of my product." Castor pressed his weapon to Larry's temple to back up my words. "And I wanna know who made this shit and delivered it."

"No idea who made it." The fact that he sweated bullets

said otherwise. "We've been instructed to deliver it to the runner for distribution to the market."

"Not anymore," I said the words slow and threatening to hit home my point. "This will be your very last shipment. Got it?"

"You gonna pay for the lost revenue?" This cunt had the fucking nerve to hustle me. Hunger rose to let my beast sink its teeth into him to drink him dry then piss on his corpse. "This client paid pretty well to deliver his shipments."

Aaliyah's disbelief and shock stained the bond while Castor found it amusing as usual, his smirk lighting us both up.

I ignored the fucker Larry and ordered, "I want all the paperwork on your client and CCTV footage of the courier."

Larry got all huffy about this and the end of the barrel of Castor's gun dug harder into his forehead. "Cynthia, call the Sin Vipers and get them down here to sort out these jokers." Bluff was clearly a big part of his strategy.

My eyebrows hitched at the gall of his asshole. The overly made-up receptionist lifted the receiver to dial the number.

After I burned all of Hellfire MC's stock and they interfered in our operations, I didn't want to fuck over another club. But if push came to shove, I would.

"Yeah, call them, Cynthia," I goaded the bitch to see how far she'd go. "And you'll be joining Larry here in the afterlife."

The handset clunked on the base. She kept clicking the button of her pen, agitating me.

"Smart girl, Cynthia," I told her. "Now get me the paperwork I requested."

She slunk away to hunt it down. Bitch better come back with something good, or I was about to raise hell on old Larry here.

Larry grabbed his cell phone from his pocket and tried to dial a number. Probably the Sin Vipers. Castor disconnected the call, leaving Larry confused and punching in numbers repeatedly until he swore, gave up and stuffed his cell back in his pants. Dumb fuck tried the landline, forcing me to go and grab him by the collar and drag him away from the phone.

I was about to punch his lights out for bitching when Cynthia returned with the paperwork and provided it to me. Unable to read it, I passed it to Castor.

"Says it was delivered by private courier, no return address," he informed me. Of course, it was. Our enemy wouldn't be stupid enough to get it registered and tracked. Mark my words, we'd trace the fucker. Investigate every little lead until we found the cunts and destroyed them.

I shook Larry, releasing the bastard with a shove, sending him stumbling. "Get me the CCTV footage of the delivery." I pulled my gun on him, aimed and jerked it.

Larry straightened his shirt, scowled at me, and led me to his office where stale air with the smell of Doritos hit me. My stomach growled, wanting to be fed. Only my jackal and I wanted blood, not a cheesy fucking corn chip. Computer keys clicked as he accessed the warehouse's security footage, which wasn't hooked up to outside internet lines for Castor to trace.

"What day do you need to access?" he asked, and Castor gave him the date, prompting the skinny fucker to pull up the footage.

My shifter sight zoomed in on the courier truck, a small haulage Toyota, committing the number plate to memory. "Find that goddamn truck and its exact movements," I ordered Castor.

Castor gave a stiff nod. "Yes, President."

"That all you want?" Larry bitched, as if he had better shit to be doing.

"Thanks for your cooperation," I snarled. "If I ever hear

about you doing business with these fuckers again, I'll be making another visit, and I won't show you any mercy."

Larry grumbled something but I didn't bother to listen as my body temperature soared with the intention of destruction.

Seated back on my bike, I turned to Castor. "Find anything?"

"It's your fucking birthday, Prez." Castor smirked deviously, spurring my dark chaos to thunder. "Found where the courier collected the drugs from."

The best news we'd had in weeks. To celebrate, I sent out a pulse of magick to incinerate Larry's shipment of Pharaoh.

"Lead the way, asshole." I smiled back like a fucking demon ready to raise some fucking hell.

CHAPTER 21

## Zethan

I CLINKED my beer with Slade's then Castor's, celebrating their win today. "Good work, brothers."

The club had its first success in weeks, locating and destroying our competitor's product and burning the premises of their assembly service. Our enemy wouldn't be able to get back into production on the market for weeks to a month. By then, we'd have located them and annihilated the pricks fucking with us. If we couldn't afford to repay our debt with Tony and get our drug back online, then we'd be damned if some sabotaging prick stole our spot.

Victory put my president in his best mood since Aaliyah's arrival. "Bird Boy is my fucking savior." He grabbed Castor in a headlock and kissed him on the head. "We're gonna party tonight, thanks to him!"

"Sorry it took me so long, Prez." Castor fuzzed up Slade's

hair, eliciting a bark of laughter and my president to let him go.

I smiled and swallowed some of my beer, grateful for the win after blow after shitty blow. Cool, malty liquid soothed the worried burn of the last few weeks. What a fucking relief.

Retaliation was anticipated for impairing our enemies' plans. But fuck 'em. They started this shit. We'd be ready. Hopefully we'd find the bastards before they had the chance to strike and deal them the crushing, deadly blow, ending this bullshit once and for all. Nothing would please Slade more than killing Danny Heller. I'd enjoy watching him choke on his severed cock and being punished in the same ways he abused the poor women he kidnapped and brutalized for his porn and snuff operation.

Aaliyah swept past me in a breeze of intoxicating cherry, coconut, and vanilla haze that drew my gaze down to her bouncing ass. At the stereo, she put on some music—one of Slade's heavy rock playlists—and it thumped through the speakers.

Despite his benching, Alaric stuck to himself in the corner, sullenly sipping at his whisky, observing everyone. He hung out here because he had nowhere else to go. Our link soured with aggravation from the serious stink-eye he aimed at Aaliyah. I supported Slade's decision one hundred and ten percent. Our road captain was a walking fucking liability. Almost got me killed back at the dummy drug run. We couldn't afford to lose more men or have anyone injured. He was welcome back to full duty once he got himself sorted. We wouldn't abandon him in his time of need. As his brother in arms, I'd go check on him and offer my support.

Aaliyah got in first, grabbing a beer and approaching him, testing the water. "Hey. Everything okay?"

"Fine," he answered with a scowl, topping up his whisky and downing it.

*Real nice, asshole.* Club medic, regardless of whether she was our mate or not, had a duty to watch out for everyone, not just him. Far as I was concerned, she did the right thing, recommending Slade bench him.

Slade slammed his drink down, railroaded through the room's center to grab Aaliyah by the waist with one hand, and drag her away from Alaric. He swung her in a circle, dancing. "And my little nurse deserves applause too." He drummed her ass as if clapping, and she laughed and smacked him. "Do it again, I love it!"

He nuzzled into her neck, kissing her long, tanned flesh, weakening her knees. Slade tried to worm his way back into her good graces with flirting, charm, flattery, and sexual advances, but she wasn't having any of that. She wanted more from him than shallow shit. I huffed. Good luck trying to crack an apology out of him. Our president apologized for no one and nothing. Aaliyah would have to bend and break his will to triumph there.

"Oh, come on, Nurse A." Slade tapped his cheek with a finger, his eyes bright with wickedness. "Not even a celebratory kiss?"

I laughed and shook my head at the extent he went to drag a kiss from her. She sighed and gave in, rewarding him with a chaste peck that made him grunt with approval.

"Better than nothing." He captured her by the waist again and claimed her mouth in a dominant kiss, not letting her go until she submitted to him and returned it. "Now that's better."

She hugged his massive shoulders, grinning and shaking her head. "You're impossible."

He cracked her on the ass and leaned down to whisper, "Don't take any shit from Alaric. If he's got a problem, he can come to me." He thumbed her jaw and she nodded before he let her wander away.

Brutal longing hit the bond at watching them and she glanced up at me from by the bar where she nibbled on Doritos. I hated being left out of her affections. Hated being apart from her. I wanted to go and talk with her, but Alaric needed my attention more than my solitude.

I carried my beer over to the sofa he reclined on, interrupting his game of shooting our mate daggers. "Want to play pool?"

He glanced up at me, pupils dilated and dark. "Thinking about heading home soon."

"One game won't kill you," I said. "That's an order."

"Fuck." Alaric clamored out of his seat, snatched the bottle of whisky he cradled, and trudged to the billiards table with it and his glass.

I set my beer down on the side of the billiards table and racked up the balls. "You 'doin okay?"

"Good as I can, for being benched." Hot bitterness stung the bond that I could relate to, and perhaps offer him some comfort from my experience and as VP.

I reminded him of an event almost two years ago, where Slade withdrew me from duty after I started a bar fight to defend a woman being preyed on by her boyfriend. Beat the asshole black and blue and put him in hospital for a month. Got arrested and threw light on the club. The club's lawyer got me off, citing emotional distress and triggers from my sister's murder.

"It's just for a little bit while you clear your head." I thumped him on the shoulder, grabbed a pool cue and handed it to him, letting him break the balls. "You'll be back before you know it. Benching me was the best thing Slade did for me. Cleared my head, got me back on track, and I haven't drawn the attention of the cops since."

Alaric also had to keep his nose clean since the cops

planted drugs on his bike and arrested him. Poor bastard was facing double the criminal charges.

"Holes," Alaric grunted, picking which ball he'd play with for the game. He smacked his cue, slamming his ball into the group in the center of the table, sending them skittering in all directions. His yellow ball sank into the pocket. Asshole was really good at this game. Nearly always kicked our asses.

I grabbed a pool cue to take my shot. "Have you booked in to get medical advice?" I had my turn and missed landing any balls in the pockets.

Alaric glared at Aaliyah with narrowed, suspicious eyes intended to maim. "I'm speaking to someone from Department of Veteran's Affairs tomorrow. They'll give me a referral to a specialist."

I put a palm on his chest, warning him. "You leave her out of it. We went through hell with her to ascertain her allegiance. She's on *our* side. *Your* side. Keep that shit up and you'll chase her away for good."

Alaric brushed me off and leaned down to take his shot, scoring another hole. Lucky bastard. Unforgiving prick.

I wanted my mate more than anything. More than the fucking air I breathed. Having her with us and not being unable to do a damn thing with her was torture. Losing her would be a miserable nightmare. If Alaric was the cause of that, I'd give him something to fucking cry about.

"I confided in her." He rolled his shoulders. "Sort of, and she went straight to Slade the next day and I got fucking sidelined. I have a right to be pissed."

I could see where he came from. He confided in her as his mate, not his medic. That had to hurt. "Did you tell her the information was confidential?"

"No," he growled and swiped at his drink, swallowing all of it. He instantly poured another. "She touched me and witnessed my visions. I wasn't exactly in a good state of mind to lay down rules."

"Fuck." I rubbed at my wrinkled brow, trying to find the words to comfort him and not get him offside. "She's in a difficult position as your mate and the club medic, and was forced to choose between you and the safety of the club. What would you have done in her position?"

Alaric's shoulders slumped and he pinched the sides of his face with his fingers. "Fuck. I knew it was coming, I just didn't think it would be her to send me there. Especially after we agreed on a fresh start."

Spiny situation. No wonder he was bitter. But she was hurting too, evident by the remorse on her face and wrecking our bond.

"I'm sure she feels like shit too, for making that choice." I rubbed his shoulder.

"Maybe." Alaric dumped his whisky and glass by the nearby bar. "I'm gonna get out of here. Have a good night, VP." He shook my hand as he always did, and I clapped him on the side of the arm and said good night.

Aaliyah came to stand with me as I watched him leave. "He okay?"

"Not really," I replied.

"Fuck. I feel shitty for what I did." She picked at the beer bottle label, a habit I noticed her do when worried or thinking.

I wanted to sweep her into my arms and cradle her, tell her not to worry. Instead, I offered her words of wisdom. "It was coming, whether you instigated it or not. Don't let guilt consume you."

Her pinched hand rubbed at her forehead. "He opened up to me. We had two perfect nights. And what did I do? Broke his trust. Again."

This was cutting her up. Woman was too compassionate for her own good. She needed to take a step back and see things objectively. Alaric needed help, the kind his brothers couldn't provide, the kind a bottle worsened, the kind his role in the club exacerbated. She made the right choice.

To hell with it. I brought her in close, cradling her to my body, brushing aside the hair that fell across her face. "Alaric would have gotten worse if you didn't step in. You did him a favor. Did us a favor."

She chewed her lip, agreeing, but still torturing herself. "I don't feel like celebrating. Can you take me home?"

I wouldn't have been in the mood to party either if I was her. I jumped at the chance to be alone with her again. Like hell I was leaving her alone in Castor's house, unprotected.

I massaged the back of her neck and snagged my keys from my pocket. "I'll stay with you until Castor comes home."

The solemnness in her eyes as she glanced at him told me something went down between those two. A disagreement. Asshole usually had his hands all over her. Hadn't seen them interact all night or for a few days. I didn't pry. None of my business. She could tell me if she wanted to.

The moment we headed for the door, Slade shouted after us, "Where the fuck are you going? We're celebrating!"

"Got some shit to do," I called back to him.

Slade huffed and marched over to us. "Always got shit to do. You're getting boring in your old age. You never party with us anymore."

Why would I want to hang out with him when my woman wanted to go home, and I was waiting to spend time with her?

"You're not cool enough anymore." I knocked him on the front of his shoulder.

He grinned and hit me back. "Asshole." His gaze shifted to Aaliyah, his brows dropping, eyes dilating. "Night, Nurse A. Dream about me." For once, Slade held back on the flirty ass slap.

She didn't manage more than a grim smile and didn't meet his gaze.

My president remained respectful and leaned down to peck her on the cheek. "Don't worry about it. He'll get over it." His gaze twisted back to me, and he jerked his head. An order. Get the fuck out of here. Look after her.

"Night, brother." I urged Aaliyah forward with a light touch on her back before he changed his mind and tried to persuade us to do vodka shots.

I drove her to Castor's place and got her settled onto the sofa, making her a tea, me a coffee, and sinking down at the other end of the seat.

My dick hardened at the way her lips pouted, blowing on the steaming mug. "Thanks for bringing me home, hellhound dick."

A crack of laughter escaped. I didn't expect that. A warm relief hit me that she maintained her sense of humor despite feeling shitty about Alaric.

"Anytime, hellhound bitch." I smiled and sipped at my blistering coffee. Just the way I liked it, like the fires of fucking Hell.

Her smile lifted a fraction. "I need to take my mind off today. Wanna watch a movie or something?"

"Fuck, yeah." I wanted to snuggle up with her in my arms and drift to sleep on the sofa. Actions I might never get to do unless Castor could find a solution.

"Don't worry about Alaric," I said as she got up to load a DVD into the player. "He'll come around." Probably should have kept my mouth shut, but she needed to hear it one last time to ease the guilt stamped on her forehead.

"He hates me." She flicked on the TV and came back to the sofa and collapsed in it, always out of my reach. "So much for our fresh start." Regret scratched at the bond. It took everything in me not to scoot over and throw her over my lap and crush her to me. Unable to touch her, have her, taste her, that was my personal hell.

"It was for the best." I croaked back my fucking regret. Solid and heavy, blocking my fucking throat. "He nearly strangled me on the last run. Could do a lot worse on the next. Fire his gun at a brother. He took a bullet to his wing. Next time he might not be so lucky."

She stared at her mug and nodded. I bet she never got so twisted about one of her patients. People in shitty predicaments that interfered with their lives. Serious illness and injury preventing them from being able to work, care for their family, mounting their medical bills. Stress that came with it. Seen it with my uncle. We pitched in where we could and helped keep them afloat.

No, this good, little nurse followed the doctor's orders. Remained objective, scientific, and did all she could within the confines of her job. Just like I did as a police officer, trying to make a goddamn difference in a world of shitty darkness.

Except Alaric wasn't just her patient, he was her mate. That threw a whole new complication into the mix. Hard to remain neutral when you cared about someone. All she could do was support him, be an ear for him, answer his questions, get him back on track, as we would do for him as his brother in arms. The rest was up to Alaric. We couldn't force him to change.

"Anyway, I don't want to talk about him." Aaliyah jammed her finger on the remote control, and a blue light flickered as the TV activated.

And I didn't want to watch this fucking movie. I wanted

time with my mate, the stream of sunlight piercing the clouds of darkness. My mug clunked on the coffee table as I set it down. I reached over to grab her legs, hauled them off the floor and swung them over my lap.

"What are you doing?" she squeaked, splashing her tea on Castor's leather sofa as she squirmed to get her leg away. Too late. Down went the zip of her boot.

Fuck the curse. Fuck the pain. My fucking mate needed me, and I'd be the one to soothe her. I was tired of running from her. Tired of staying away. Tonight, she was all mine.

"What does it look like, hellhound bitch?" I released her foot, tossed aside her boot then began to massage her foot. My hellhound leaked a pleased groan at her sexy sigh and the pleasure stretching across her face.

Reality must have dawned on her, and she squirmed again. "Zethan." Her cautious, breathy warning went straight to my dick. I wanted my name on her tongue again and again, all husky and dripping. She gave up when she realized I wasn't letting her go.

"I'll stop if it gets too much." I dug my thumbs into the arch of her feet, and she jolted, back going ramrod straight. Most people carried tension there. I lightened my pressure and she slumped back.

"God that's good." Her encouragement fueled me, and I swept my thumbs over the ball of her foot.

Scratches launched in my gut, the first sign of the curse. Eager to prolong our union, I pressed on and applied a little more force, only willing to move away when it got too much.

"You're not at the shelter tonight?" She cupped her tea, elegant fingers curled around the mug. Fingers I wanted wrapped around my straining cock.

"Nope. I can't remember the last night I had off." I dragged my fingers from her heel to her the start of her toes.

"Slade promised to shoot me in the nuts if I didn't celebrate with club. One hour at the club saved my balls."

"Workaholic." A saucy smile stretched across her lips, and she nudged my thigh with her foot, teasing me. "Not that I can talk. I take any shift I can get." She groaned, not from pleasure, but because of what she said next. "Does that make us losers with no lives?"

I coughed a laugh. "No, you don't, hellhound, bitch. This asshole wins the ultimate loser crown." I tickled her foot and she giggled, doing her best to steady her mug and not spill it on her jeans. "Shittiest pick of gods sees me lose my dick at random intervals and sucked to the Underworld in my sleep to work a shift there too."

The scratching in my gut got more insistent but I pushed it down to burrow my thumbs deeper into her soles.

I think she felt it too and rolled her neck. "Really? Damn, that's unlucky. Don't suppose Slade gives you leeway?"

She sipped her tea, and damn, did I want nothing more than to be that hot fucking liquid caressing her tongue and throat.

"Nope." I gave her soles a break to stroke up and down her pads.

Her second nudge of my lap had my dick kick up, and me yanking her closer. "You work too much, loser. You need a life." The last bit came out as steamy as her cup.

The scrape in my abdomen turned into a dull ache. Pretty soon it'd get too much, and I'd have to move away. Not until I had my fill of her. Lavished her damn body with my massage. The last two weeks had been hell and she deserved to be treated like a princess.

"That a challenge?" I jerked her knees over my thighs and her breath hitched. "Dad drilled it into me to work hard. Be responsible. Guess I broke that rule by joining an outlaw MC."

"You sure did, hellhound dick." She needed to stop using that nickname because my hound begged to be let loose from his leash.

"Yeah, well, that asshole laid into my mom with his fists," I said.

Aaliyah reached for me with one hand, warming mine on her leg. "Oh my God, that's awful."

"It was hard." I felt helpless when I was small and couldn't defend my mom. "I learned early to protect my sisters and mother, taking his fists."

That was probably why my youngest sister, Abigail, sought out an asshole of a husband who beat her. She never knew any better. Signed her death warrant the moment she got together with him.

"Fuck, I'm sorry." Aaliyah curled one hand behind her knee.

"Divorcing the prick and remarrying was the best thing Mom did." My stepdad was a good man. Never touched her. Taught Carlie and me the value of strength and honor. He was more of a father than my own. "Enough about that." I didn't want to talk about those dark times when the memory of Abigail threatened to break me in two.

Time ticked down on our curse clock as the ache in my stomach concentrated, moving from my gut to my legs and chest. Game time. Get to know everything about this woman in the shortest space possible before I had to move away. And I didn't want to be apart from her when she chased away my darkness.

"Start talking, Nurse A, or I'll tickle you." I advanced from her foot to her calf, and she let out a stuttered groan that pulsed through my cock. "Hopes, dreams, fears, favorite color. All I know about you is that you're a nurse, live in the big smoke, you're good with people, and one hell of a firecracker when it comes to my president." She smiled at the last part.

Woman locked eyes with me drawing me into her crystal blue depths. "Demanding for a hellhound. Only if you reciprocate."

Fuck, I loved it when she flirted. Tension crackled between us, frenetic and bursting to be explored deeper. My hands possessively kneaded her legs, desperate to have all of her on top of me. Thighs straddling mine. Pussy grinding my crotch.

"Deal." I worked a knot out of her calf.

"My favorite color is dark green." She smiled over her mug and drank from it. "Your turn."

"Blue, like your eyes."

She snorted and hit me. "Who would have thought gruff, old Zethan was charming?"

I really dug into her leg for that. "More flirting and more talking."

Her laughter made Hell flames lick along my hound's coat.

"Hopes?" She made a humming sound that pulsated in my balls. "To serve my goddess in the best capacity."

"Honorable, but boring." Where did I fit into that equation? We served gods that were soul mates, and we as their servants, were also destined for each other.

"Shut up!" She hit me and I caught her hand and nipped the tip of her index finger. "What's yours, then?"

Fuck. Here came the darkness again, but it had to be said. "That no more women end up like my mother or sister."

"I wanna change mine. It's lame in comparison to yours," she whined. "That no one ever gets sick again."

I tickled behind her knee. "Then you'd be out of a job."

"Dreams." She leaned back on the couch, her sweater and

shirt rising, exposing her caramel skin, and I stroked it before she hid it. "Front row tickets at a Metallica concert."

Muscles in my gut clenched like my bowels wanted to discharge violently. We'd have to split apart soon, and I dreaded the loss of her. One touch was not enough. Nowhere near it. I never wanted to break this curse more than this moment.

"Babe, I've already bought you tickets."

"Good, hellhound." She patted my thigh and lightning bolts chased up my leg. She left off the dick, and good thing too, because mine was practically smashing through the denim. "And good taste in music, too. Hope you like *Tool*, *Nine Inch Nails*, and *Soundgarden*."

"Can you be any more perfect?" My grip weakened from my cramping muscles, and I know she felt it too by the tightening in her mouth and jaw.

"Dreams." She hit my thigh.

I grazed her thigh with the back of my knuckles. "To walk the Kokoda Trail like my grandfather."

"Nice. Okay, fears." She paused, gaze dropping to her tea, nails tapping the ceramic. "Immediate—what happens once my brother is dead. Will my mother and I be safe? Will the Wolves want revenge against me for siding with the Jackals, killing their president, and come after me?"

Protecting her at all costs was my number-one goal besides the survival of the club. "I'll kill every last Wolf if there's the possibility of that."

Her weak nod told me she wasn't reassured. "Long-term —that you four have ruined me for another man."

Despite the agony in my limbs, I dragged her onto my lap for a kiss. "Oh, I'll ruin you completely, and you'll never want another man. You'll never want to leave. And if any man so much as looks at you, I'll kill him."

My answer left her a little breathless and she croaked, "Fears?"

"That I can't protect everybody I love." I'd failed to protect my sister and she paid the ultimate price. Ditto for my previous mate. Fear burned a hole in my gut that I'd also fail Aaliyah.

## CHAPTER 22

### *A*aliyah

CASTOR'S LIPS MOVED, but words failed to register, my mind occupied by something else. *Someone else.* Echoes of Zethan's touch on my foot, ankle, and calf haunted me. Ghosted whispers of his touch spread across my flesh, and I wanted his touch back on me. Everywhere. For longer than five minutes. This damn curse played havoc on us all, in more than one way.

A magick textbook slammed closed, jolting me from my thoughts.

Castor's brows hung low over his eyes, matching his dark glare. His hair had circled into tighter curls from a rough night's sleep, if any. "If you're not going to listen, I've got other matters to attend to."

I kicked my feet up onto his ottoman. Shit. *Take your magick lesson seriously, Aaliyah.* My time remaining with the

Jackals ticked down, and I didn't know how much longer I'd have to learn from my counterpart, so I shoved aside all thought of Zethan. Sit back. Concentrate. Absorb as much as I could while it lasted. Never know when the knowledge might come in handy.

I removed my tea mug from the side table by Castor's favorite armchair, a leather recliner. "Sorry, what did you say?"

Castor scratched at his forehead like an impatient teacher about to lose his shit. "What didn't you hear?"

I squeezed my lips together. "Everything."

"Fuck, Aaliyah." He rubbed his drawn, red eyes with the heel of his palm.

"Someone's hungover and cranky today." I grabbed my water bottle and tossed it to him. "How many shots did Slade make you do?"

"Too many," Castor groaned, uncapping the bottle and guzzling it down. "I feel it everywhere." One hand skimmed his abdomen, which I estimated roiled and ached for punishing it last night.

I was glad I left when I did, or I would have been in trouble with Slade forcing drinks down my throat. "Got any electrolyte drink sachets in that impressive drug cupboard you're packing?"

Castor scrubbed at three days' worth of dark stubble. "I think there's some in the pantry."

"Wait here." I went to check, dodging the mess in the main room of the club. Crushed beer cans, strewn bottles, cigarette butts, smashed glass, and dropped pizza crusts. "Pigs!"

The Wolves expected me to clean up after them, and as someone desperate for recognition, I did it. Not happening with the Jackals. I didn't care if I was a prospect and that was my job. Screw that. Slade and I could go toe to toe on that matter. He wouldn't win.

Shaking my head, I continued, finding the sachet packets where Castor said they were. I tore one open and emptied the pale orange powder into a glass. Water hissed from the tap as I filled the tumbler and carried it back.

"Thanks, Nurse A." The first time Castor called me that. He slugged it down like a man who'd been lost in the desert.

Too much alcohol would do that to a person. Seen one too many drunks in the ER coming in with cuts, broken limbs, and burns because they lost their footing, got into a fight, or got carried away and hurt themselves. Then there were those who drank one too many in a short space of time, shorting out their liver and poisoning it.

It also didn't help things that he went cold and retreated from me these last few days, hiding in his study at his place or *working late* at the club. Explained his snappiness. It hurt to be at odds with each other when things had been so good between us. Worst of all, it was my fault. I deserved this.

I leaned on the desk next to him and rubbed his shoulder. "Want to take a nap and pick this up later?"

"Got too much to do," he muttered.

The weight of the club buried him deeper in the ground. Pressure to find evidence to link my brother to the stolen shipment of Jackal's product, find the murderer of their drug runner, my father, and identity of the behind-the-scenes player. Responsibility to find a spell to withdraw the demonic protection from my brother's club so the Jackals could launch a full-scale takedown. Burden to break the curse on us and our gods.

"Okay. Gimme a quick recap then." I grabbed my mug and sank into his desk chair, one hundred percent attentive this time.

Castor made an 'o' of his thumb and index finger, also holding up the remaining three fingers in a gesture that looked like the A-Okay hand sign. "Using this hand symbol can coax a person into spilling their guts." He sounded about as enthused as a teen working a shift at the McDonald's drive thru. "But it only works on those with a weaker will."

Guilt scratched at the back of my throat, and I threw on a smile I didn't feel, trying to lighten the mood. "Like a Jedi mind trick?"

"Something like that." His voice fell flat, mouth devoid of the usual sexy grin that ticked up at the corners.

My heart screamed, in tatters at the bottom of my ribcage. The dark, mysterious, sexy man had retreated into his shell. One step forward, two steps backward. We'd gotten too close, comfortable, and I'd fallen a little. The closer we got, the more my feelings built, I got scared, denying what we had and ran away. He took it as rejection and retreated.

I wanted to shout at him for letting me go. For not grabbing hold of me and saying *fuck it, you're mine, I'm not letting you go*. Direct and dominating, like his alter ego Dark Daddy. Hell, I'd even take sweet and romantic like Alaric. But no, Castor slid away, hiding with his ghosts. Nobody to blame but myself. My hesitancy triggered something in him, a buried wound, and he'd rolled up the defenses again, blocking me out. Anticipating the train was about to crash, Castor cooled things, slammed us into the friend zone, leaving us at odds once more. Strangers. Rivals. He wouldn't let me in again.

Heat flushed my chest and neck. I didn't know what he expected of me. Why he ... dammit ... the four of them ... were so insistent on me staying when I gave up this life seven years ago. Club life was dangerous and only brought heartache. I lost my boyfriend and father to it. Given up my daughter to shield her from it. Count my asshole of a brother in that tally, too. Greed and lust for power consumed him and he would pay the ultimate price once the Jackals were through with him. I refused to lose anyone else I loved, and if that meant protecting my heart from these four men, then I'd fight it with everything I had.

"Can we talk?" I needed to set the record straight. Explain my side of the story and make Castor understand.

The enforcer glanced at his Rolex. "I've only got an hour this morning to go through this with you. It's important. You might need it if you're coming along on rides." Straight to business. Zero affection. Hardened, cold eyes. Strictly professional tone.

Regret, anger, and sadness kept him trapped. Someone broke him, and he withheld fragments of his love. On the outside, he kept his levelheaded mask firmly in place. Behind it, anger burned and grief twisted him, and it drove a wedge between us. My hesitance and retreat were the catalyst here, throwing the fucking fuel on the fire.

Goddess, I was messed up. Stuck between not wanting to let him go and needing to move on, and I hated myself for it. A hypocrite. Goddamn cock tease. A sharp sense of ownership snapped into place between us. The more I pushed away, the more I wanted him. Wanted all of them. Resisting was becoming futile with my budding feelings, my reluctance to hurt them or myself. The time was approaching to make a decision and stick to it. The most difficult decision of my life, and I was afraid to make it.

"Can we do something else?" I blurted, frustrated and unable to concentrate, in desperate need of something that would help me forget about these men. Break the curse binding us. Let us move on without the manipulation of our hearts. "The spell you bought from Gable's shop?"

Castor put the brakes on that one. Delayed on purpose, I

suspected. A ploy to keep me with the club for as long as he could. But I wanted out, wanted to get away from the men who tugged on my heartstrings, wanted to be free of the constant back and forth that exhausted me.

"It'll take too long."

I wasn't having any of his stalling bullshit. "Show me how to do it and I'll finish it."

I grabbed the damn ingredients from his bookshelf and slammed them on his desk. Worming out of it was not an option when we needed to end this vicious cycle and put our hearts out of their misery. Move the fuck on. Make it a hell of a lot easier for everyone involved without the weight of the curse strangling us, confusing us, deciding for us.

Castor snatched his bowl, making a point of letting it clunk heavily on his bench. He ripped open the spell bag, tipping it upside down and unleashing the contents, and they pattered in the ceramic, like my damn mind in anticipation of being emancipated from these men.

"Crush these." The enforcer shoved the pestle in my direction and a bag of herbs. Black sage, myrrh, frankincense, and juniper. I recognized them from previous lessons. "Add some oil. A few drops. Not too much." Three-word sentences. Great.

I did as instructed, a nervousness eating away at my gut. Was this *really* what I wanted? Did I really want to make it harder on myself by making it easier to connect with Zethan? Fuck, there might come a time when he needed me to heal him, ride with him, carry a broken woman from his van, and the curse would make that difficult. No. The curse needed to be broken. I finished with the herbs, adding three drops of oil, combining them, then glanced at Castor for my next instruction.

"Light the candle and pour two drops of wax into the

bowl." Castor passed me a lighter and two red candles. "One for you and one for Zethan."

"Okay." The nurse in me followed his direction to the letter.

"Good. Tie the string around the cassia." Castor moved to his shelves, plucking a bottle of liquid in a light-sensitive amber jaw and returning. "Add about one hundred mills of this and let it sit in the mixture."

"What next?" I asked when complete.

"Let it sit for five minutes for the cassia to add its flavor and power." Brows dipped low, Castor shoved his hands under his armpits, sticking to the opposite side of the table.

Rejection stabbed at me, slicing my heart to shreds. Awkward silence stretched between us. This was more than a hangover. I hurt him, and I didn't know where to begin to apologize. I fought back the flush of shame that climbed my throat. Separation anxiety kicked in hardcore during the days Castor and I were distant. Causing him pain had shattered my heart. Smashed my own. I craved the reassuring comfort of his arms. Our flirty, fun banter to stave off the darkness hanging over me and the club. The ease of our scientific and magical conversations.

Our deafening hush coaxed him to keep busy, shoving the red candles in the tapers, flicking his lighter again, setting them alight. Guilt and pain that I held back seeped through, smothering the damn mate bond, forcing his gaze to me. Flames made his eyes redder and more exhausted. By all accounts, he didn't sleep at all last night. Hadn't come home, and Zethan crashed on the sofa to guard me.

Tapers dragged along the counter as Castor set them either side of the bowl. "These represent the two pillars of Egypt. King and Queen. You and Zethan. The power of the eternal flame burning on each stick will draw out the energy behind the curse."

A kiss of power hit my palms and crackled. It hung heavy in the air, flexing and waning, like fire fed air then deprived of it. The curse, gradually weakening.

"I think it's working. I feel it dwindle."

Castor rubbed his palms together. "Good. I'll watch this. You bring Zethan in here and we'll test it out."

## CHAPTER 23

## *A*aliyah

I WRANGLED my fraying nerves into line. *Hold it together, Aaliyah.* The finish line was in sight. I'd be free soon.

Zethan grunted his approval for me to enter and I spilled inside his office. He hunched over a club ledger, scrolling his index finger down the page, punching numbers into the calculator and scribbling down the total. Memories of last night flooded back, his firm caress digging into my tense muscles rising to the surface.

"Got a minute?" I interrupted and he glanced up.

"Anything for you, baby." Zethan flicked the pages of the ledger he read from. "I need a break from doing another audit of the club's finances."

"It's about the curse," I replied.

"Has Castor got a lead?" He dropped the ledger quickly and shot out of his seat, coming to join me at the door.

I scrunched my lips. "We want to try something."

Zethan closed the door behind him. "Should I be nervous that I'm about to be part of Castor's science experiment?"

"Only if you grow hellhound horns," I teased, Zethan cursing after me as I slid down the hall and back into Castor's study.

"VP." Castor paid his respect to the rank with a nod. "Drink these." He handed Zethan and me equal halves of the mixture in glasses. "I'm not promising anything."

Worth a try if it broke our curse. Then we'd be one step closer to removing the other, and we wouldn't be bound and slaved to one another. Maybe then it wouldn't be so hard to leave, and I wouldn't have to drag my heart from the floor.

"Bottoms up." Zethan's eyes burned with the longing for freedom of the barrier between us. He clinked my glass with his and we threw the contents down our throats. "Fuck, that's disgusting." He swiped at his mouth with his flannel sleeve. "Why didn't you warn me, you asshole?"

Castor chuckled and raised two palms. "Hey, I never said it would taste as good as whisky."

Zethan slammed his glass down. "Tastes like elephant piss."

Agreed. The potion tasted awful. Rum mixed with sour herbs. I stomached it. Barely. In my college years, I tried some pretty awful stuff. Wine in a box. Mixed spirits. Not pretty. But, hey, if this potion broke the curse and let Zethan and me interact, it'd make working in the shelter and club a hell of a lot easier.

Zethan took an assessing step toward me. Hungry, predatory movements that tested my instinct to run. Arousal went straight to my pussy like he touched me again. My body remembered him. Ghosted fingers skimming over my electrified flesh on replay all day. My mind shouted at him, warning him to stay back. That hussy known as my heart beckoned him over with a seductive finger. At the promise of his hungry kiss, she won out and my legs refused to budge.

"I should have done this last night." Zethan's rough, insistent grasp captured me, and my lungs forgot to breathe.

Blazing lips crashed down on mine. Bruising. Urgent. Desperate to make up for lost time. Worried that this might not last, and we'd be broken apart by the cramping in our bodies. The kiss stripped my legs of stability, and I went limp in his grip. Zethan cupped my ass, hefting me, and I wound my legs and arms around him to lock him there forever. Hard as a stone, he ground against me, desperate to release his month-long pent-up sexual frustration.

My hands were tempted to roam lower, searching for his belt, but the scars on the back of his neck captivated my stroking fingertips. Lines I wanted to memorize. Study. Caress with my lips. He shifted my hands to his shoulder. The bond immediately told me that the memory of his pain made him uncomfortable. I slid one hand behind his head, threading my fingers into his coarse, sandy hair.

Castor's victory soaked into the bond, closely followed by the sting of regret and longing. He wished it was him receiving the praise of my mouth and arms around his neck. I burned so hot from double the desire and longed for him to box me between them, his mysterious lips on my nape while Zethan's kiss punished the curse separating us.

Goddess, I was a goner. Lost to the men. Staying away was hopeless. Resisting them impossible.

"Fuck, Castor," Zethan growled, much deeper and darker than normal and the lost contact sent my lips and tongue wandering along his throat. "If this works, I'm gonna kiss you too."

"With tongue?" Castor teased, and a lightning bolt of lust struck my core.

"With my cock." Zethan's reply had me come up for air from the soft flesh beneath his ear.

"Fuck that." Castor huffed. "You can kiss mine."

They were into that? The concept of orgies with all four of them had me sopping below and shuddering with anticipation. I pictured them all surrounding me, attentive, demanding, setting fire to my naked flesh.

"I've got front row tickets to that," I murmured, head rolling back as Zethan nipped at my neck, marking me with sharpened hellhound fangs. A pleasant sting crashed in my flesh, jolting every nerve ending. Electricity crackled in my body, recognizing its mate, the man meant for me before the others who were also bound to my goddess and soul.

"You like that idea, baby?" Zethan swept hair off my neck, wrapping it around his fist, tightening it in his palm. "You wanna see me blow off Castor?" His guttural snarl encouraged my nipples to stiffen harder than steel.

"Yes." My voice came out throaty and urgent. Never in a million years would I have expected two hardened bikers to be into male-to-male business. Castor, maybe. He was into the kinky shit. Zethan, I didn't know so well, but his suggestion surprised me.

"Not until I've fucked my woman for a month straight." His grip on my hair sharpened, yanking my head sideways, letting his feverish lips heat me up hotter than hell.

Zethan maimed my mouth with an intensity that stole my breath. Like a man who was about to die and would never get another chance again. I clung to his shoulders as tightly as he crushed me to his body, unable to get away even if I wanted to. This was my forever. My everything. My mate. The wholeness of it exploded like a million stars.

"Feel anything?" Castor's scientific inquiry broke the moment. He watched the timer on his Rolex. "That's five minutes."

"Besides a raging boner?" Zethan snapped at him, threatening him to shut the fuck up and give us this moment. "Her nipples cutting through my damn shirt. Failing to resist the smell of her heat and fucking her on your desk?" An idea I was all down for the way he worked me into a frenzy. "Hell, no. We're all good, aren't we, baby?"

I loved the way he called me that. Possessive. Needy. Achy. "So far so good." A smile crept up my face.

"Excellent progress." Castor recorded notes in his book.

"Is the curse broken?" Zethan asked. "'Cause I want my woman riding with me to court tomorrow."

Fuck, that was right. The four avatars were charged with disorderly conduct at the Summernat Rally for brawling with the Wolves. My fault. I slapped my brother and aggravated the situation, causing one of his men to retaliate and defend his president, slapping me. Slade went nuts for the insult and threw punches. Tomorrow, they had to face the magistrate for a preliminary hearing for the incident.

Slade told me the appearance stressed Alaric because he didn't want to go to jail. The road captain had been imprisoned and tortured and the idea of facing three months behind bars for the charge terrified him. I ought to check in on him, even though I was the last person he wanted to see.

"It's looking good." Castor checked the time on his Rolex again, marking it in his notes.

My attentions from Zethan didn't make Castor uncomfortable. Curious. Assessing. Aroused, too. The bond indicated that he wanted his body pressed to my back, my tongue sucked into his mouth, while Zethan fucked me. Me screaming my pleasure into him while he fingered my ass.

Goddess. I beckoned for him to complete the circle, but he stuffed his hands back under his armpits, resolute. Distant. Hiding again. The shards of my heart shattered into smaller pieces.

Zethan must have sensed my twisting disappointment at being the cause of mine and Castor's damn estrangement. "Fuck, Castor, get over here and don't disappoint our woman. That's an order."

An order the enforcer couldn't disobey. Castor reluctantly crept closer. Not because he wanted too, because he had too, and it made me feel like shit. He framed my back, lightly stroking my arm, sniffing my hair. No kisses. No heated touches. Just contact. Not enough. Ever.

Zethan's heated gaze and touches erased some of my heartache. Fucking hell. This wasn't what I intended. At. All. I'd wanted to perform the spell to break the curse and eliminate the attraction and slew of emotions holding us hostage on the mate bond. Efforts that had done the complete opposite. Ramped up the lure one hundred-fold. Left my lady parts burning so badly that if I didn't get release with Zethan and Castor together, I was going to spontaneously combust and leave a burned hole in the enforcer's floor.

Castor checked his watch again like he had some place better to be. He used it as an excuse to inch away and scribble more notes in his book. "Try something for me. Leave the room, VP."

"I'm not letting go," he growled possessively, and a cascade of shivers went off like fireworks in my body.

We had to test this. I trusted Castor's instincts. Whatever reason he wanted us to leave had validity. A magical and scientific test of some kind. I dragged Zethan outside, and he groaned his displeasure. Pain instantly crippled me, as if it was masked by the spell, and I clutched my cramping stomach. He leapt away, breathing hard.

"Fuck, it didn't work." He scraped the back of his neck, expression murderous.

Not true. I didn't feel a single onset of pain until we broke from the pillared candles.

"Come back here," Castor called from inside.

"Fuck, man." Zethan pinched his waist, and if he was anything like me, the contractions relaxed.

"It worked," Castor explained. "The candles drew the curse from you, but when you moved away from them, their power diminished."

Zethan's brows shot up to his hairline. "You're saying we need to carry burning candles with us everywhere to be close? Fuck. Turn me into a pussy, why don't you?"

I giggled into my hand.

Castor rubbed at his chin, pleased with his progress. "It's something, asshole. Better than nothing. I'll keep digging until I can figure out how to break the curse completely."

"Thank you." I rubbed Castor's bicep and it stiffened beneath me.

Zethan grinned like he conquered the world.

Me, I was more lost than ever. Adrift in space. These men felt right to me, like we belonged, were a match. Home. Salvation. Welcome. Respected. Things I'd never been with the Wolves. I didn't have to hold back, filter myself, make myself tougher to win points with them.

Something told me that I'd never be able to break free of these men. They were my future, my world, my everything. The gods knew it. The avatars knew it. I was the last damn idiot to get the memo who needed to be convinced.

# CHAPTER 24

## Zethan

I WAS on a fucking high after yesterday. High from Castor's breakthrough in mine and Aaliyah's curse. Higher still being able to hold my woman for longer than a few seconds without the fear of killing her. Fucking her mouth had turned my world upside down. Long overdue, thanks to the building sexual tension from our texting.

Hardest thing to drag myself away from this afternoon. I could have kissed her mouth, roamed her body, raked her hair all goddamn night. Duty fucking called at the shelter, though. Always did. Every night. The tight budget we operated on didn't afford another manager to ease the load on me. That meant I had little time for a social life and zero luck in my personal life.

Club life… hell, yeah. Shitloads of growth with Pharaoh taking off, more companies under our belt, and the shelter expansion to service more women. Two incredible milestones that I was really proud of. But I put my everything into those two businesses, night and day, then ran the Underworld in my fucking sleep. I damn well deserved something good for a change. The gods rewarded me with Aaliyah, and I intended to enjoy her.

Numbers jumbled together as I went through the shelter's finances, combing for avenues to skim some money back to the club. I scraped a hand through my hair and took a sip of my cold instant coffee. My eyes ached from looking at the ledger for so long. I needed a goddamn break. Nothing was going to get done when my mind kept wandering to my woman.

I tugged out my phone and stared at the cover image of Slade and me, arms over each other's shoulders, smiling and standing in front of our bikes. Fuck I was lame. I needed a new photo. Maybe one of me and my woman to look at when I was busy and apart from her.

Unable to concentrate on anything but her, I flicked the ledger closed and sipped at the scalding liquid. Tonight's priority was convincing Aaliyah to stay. I had my work cut out for me. Losing another mate was not an option, curse or not. I was tired of being alone, tired of working so hard, tired of not having something good in my personal life. She belonged with us, and I'd work my ass off to keep her.

Missing my girl, I called up a message window and entered, *Thinking about your sexy fucking lips.* I hit send and set my phone beside my keyboard, waiting for her reply. Knowing Aaliyah, she wouldn't reveal her feelings, but would flirt like a champion. I was all up for that while I chipped away at her.

Time for a fresh coffee. By the time I returned with a roasting mug, she replied. Not just any reply. A goddamn selfie of her reclining on her bed, the pillows propping her up, pouting a kiss at me. Fuck me. Better response than I expected. I leaned back in my chair, and it creaked.

*How's the shelter?* she sent through a moment later.

*Boring without you.*

*Aww. Hellhound dick is sweet too.* She added to that text with a pic of her tapping her chin with her finger and folded her brows low. Hot. I couldn't decide which to use as my new screen image.

*What are you doing tonight?* I plugged back and sent it to her.

The bond pinched with loneliness. She missed Castor. Staying in the same house and being estranged hurt her heart. I had to be there for her and fill in the gap. He was not fucking this up for us or I'd fuck him up.

It took the longest time for her answer to arrive. *Reading about my goddess' history.*

She'd much rather be learning from Castor and his genius-level encyclopedia of knowledge than holed up in her room alone. Much rather be curled up with him than hurting. The enforcer and I were going to be having words. He was letting his past with his ex interfere in his relationship with Aaliyah. While shit between them was none of my business, it became my business if it discouraged her and sent her packing. I'd not stand for the others fucking things up with my mate.

*He's an asshole.* I couldn't help myself.

*Don't want to talk about that.* They had to address it at some stage. This was killing them both and we all got dragged along for the fucking ride on the bond. I hated to see my mate suffer, and I'd crack Castor in the nose if he kept this shit up.

I switched topics fast. *Been looking at bikes for you. Can't work out if you're a classic Harley girl, a sporty Ducati chick or old-school Chieftain babe.*

*Cruiser all the way,* she shot me down. *And you're not buying me a bike, sweet talker.*

Big fucking hint she planned to leave. Time to pull out the big guns.

*Oh, yeah, I am,* I teased her. *You like comfort over class and speed? Gotta make my girl comfortable when she rides with me.*

My heartbeat raced in anticipation of her answer.

*Yeah. It's a don't-take-shit bike. Kinda screams me, don't you think?*

I barked out another laugh. This woman got me.

Wasn't the answer I wanted, but I wore her down. Slowly. She never let anyone see how she really felt besides the snippets we got over the bond. Attraction and lust but not the life-long love we craved as shifters. Woman held back for some reason and I had to crack through that barrier.

*You're my kinda woman.* I typed back the compliment with a wink emoji to soften it. Didn't want to scare her off with admitting how I really felt. How I wanted her so bad it ached.

*You're getting a lot of work done, aren't you?* Another diversion tactic.

*Got better things to do. Like talk to you.*

Approval glowed along the bond. My girl like the praise. Bathed in it. Too damn proud to admit it. I had to break down some of that obstinance.

*I enjoy talking to you too, hellhound dick.* Finally, we were getting somewhere. A little piece of herself bigger than a fucking crumb.

*I'm a pretty chatty guy.* I took the piss out of myself to get her laughing. Let her see a lighter side to me than the broody, serious asshole I portrayed to the club. I wasn't always this dull and dark. The last five years were a trial. Changed me.

Wounded me deep in my soul. I couldn't find it in me to just move on, but maybe Aaliyah was the salve my soul needed to lighten the fuck up.

I felt a snort along our link at my joke.

*Snorter,* I teased, thinking her quirk so adorable.

*You are so riding bitch for that!*

*Don't tease me.*

*Tease? Innocent old me?* she hit me back with. *Excuse me, but someone keeps promising me dates and dick pics. Talk about a tease. Tenterhooks.*

I cracked out a chuckle and leaned back further, throwing my feet up on my desk. This woman knew how to make me laugh, and I wasn't much of a laugher. Too fucking serious for my own good. I'd been lost for so long in my pain. Haunted by it. Unable to let it go. Aaliyah was the light in my dark, brutal world, the one thing preventing me from turning completely dark with no chance of turning back.

She sent me a third pic of her with droopy lips. Pretend disappointment. Flirty demoness was goading me into sending her a dick pic.

Two could play at that game. *If I didn't know better, I would swear you were urging me to send raunchy photos.*

Another pic came through. Her with a devilish smile that rivaled Slade's.

I stared at her for a long time. God, she was a stunner. Silky, dark hair, eyes bluer than topazes, apple cheeks, slightly scooped nose, lips that would make models jealous. I never wanted to get her naked more than I did right now. My dick sprang to life at that thought.

These four pics were going into a special folder, and I'd take them to the bathroom later to get off. Hell, maybe I'd jerk one out right here. Lock my door so no one interrupted. Tempted, I tapped my jeans button.

"Fuck it." I was doing it. If she wanted a dick pic, then I'd give her one to rock her fucking world. Show her what she was missing out on if she decided to leave.

I unzipped my jeans and took my stiffening length out, fisting it, bringing that fucker to full attention. The scars slashing through it made me sick and my length deflated. I slammed my head back into the chair's headrest, looking away. Eventually she'd see all of me if we were to be mates. It wasn't like I could hide that shit with makeup. If she cared about me, she wouldn't care about superficial shit. I brought him back with a few hard pumps, thinking about her legs hugging me as I pounded into her. Angling myself just right, I caught him in all his glory and sent it through to her, gripping my phone tight, desperate for her response.

A picture of her with her jaw dropped shot through. *Now who's the tease?* she wrote underneath it.

Relief flooded me. She wasn't weirded out by my scarred dick. Arousal sweltered along our bond like a relentless desert heat. My girl liked what she saw. Made me feel like a man, not a mutilated freak. I hardened, emboldened by her encouragement.

*More where that came from,* I replied.

Another image came through of her in just her bra, smiling, eyes wide. A lacy pink thing that showed off all her delicious cleavage. Fucking hell. Sexy temptress. My throat dried and I fisted myself harder, imagining my cock gliding between her perfect tits. Balls tightening, I rubbed one out hard and fast, desperate to come.

*Fuck, baby,* I instructed my phone to type for me and send. *You're so beautiful. I want you in my bed. NOW.*

It was then my motherfucker of a cock chose to vanish, leaving me high and dry. Pissed more than I ever was, I beat my head on the chair's headrest three times and cursed under my breath.

I felt a strange sensation, like someone grazed my goddamn cock, and I jolted upright. My body froze, and I cupped the spot where my dick should be. What the fuck? My mind went wild, wondering who the fuck had found it. Oh, God. Not some random place around the shelter. Fuck, I didn't want to have to explain away a wooden cock to five traumatized women. Christ, I'd never be able to look them in the eye again.

A hand pumped my wooden cock and the impression between my legs had me bucking in the chair. Someone had my goddamn dick and was acting inappropriately with it. I had to put a stop to it before it swelled bigger and frightened the shit out of whoever played with it.

*FaceTime?* Aaliyah asked and I glanced at my phone, then my crotch. *Wanna chat?*

Chat? Shit, she chose now to surprise me. Woman probably stripped into her underwear or something sexy. Fuck, I was torn on whether to go rescue my molested cock or take the video call she patched through. Goddamn it. My cock grew another inch and my groin tickled with the pumping motion someone subject me to. I couldn't take a call like this, bouncing on the seat like I had ants biting my balls.

I answered anyway to get her off my back with the promise to call her back once I dealt with this mess. She strategically set the phone up against the headboard. Rested her head in her hand, elbow crooked on the bed, wearing a sexy AF teasing smile as she stroked my wooden phallus.

Thank fuck she had it. I breathed, relieved she had it and some dirty skank didn't find it.

Wait. She wasn't just stroking it. Her mouth slid down over my crown, taking me deep, and I bucked again. My wooden dick popped as she released it and smiled, lazily pumping it.

"Baby, did you just suck my wood?" I panted, trying to stay in my seat.

She bent over her arm and giggled, unable to stop, her shoulders bouncing with the movement. No, no, no. I wanted her to keep going. Take me in her sexy mouth and get me off. But then I realized why she laughed.

"Oh, fuck." I realized the pun and covered my eyes.

She lifted her head and licked me again, twirling around my head, roaming down the underside. "Yes, I just licked your wood."

"Fuck, baby, that's hot," I croaked, wriggling my hips, desperate for her to do it again. I hadn't had the comfort of a woman's mouth in two years. "But maybe that's not a good idea."

I didn't want to hurt her. We didn't have the Castor's spell or candles to protect us. This could be dangerous, and I didn't want to risk it.

"I don't feel a thing," Aaliyah replied. "Do you think the curse only applies to our flesh and not your wood?" She slapped her face and snorted. "We have to stop saying wood."

Fucking cute.

"My dick might be inanimate, but I can feel everything. Everything."

"Really?" She teased me with a lick from base to tip, and every nerve lit up as if my dick were still attached.

I almost came at the sight of her playing with me like that. So many times, I imagined us together, in so many positions, but *never* like this. Shame crept into me at my disfigurement. She glanced up and smiled, acknowledging me, and shoved it aside as she sank over my enlarged wooden shaft. That was it. I bucked again, gripping the edges of my desk to hold myself in my seat.

"God that's good. Keep going." I threw my head back, stroking the edge of the table, pretending it was her head. If we were in the same room, I'd have my fingers tangled in her hair, gripping tightly, helping her up and down my length faster rather than the agonizingly slow pace she tortured me with.

Aaliyah brought me to the edge, then stopped, her mouth popping as she came off me. Temptress smile on her lips, she inched her underwear down, spreading her gorgeous, long legs to reveal her sopping pussy.

"Oh, fuck baby," I groaned. "Touch yourself."

I didn't care that she left me high and dry. Seeing her naked was just as rewarding. It was about to get a hell of a lot more gratifying watching her get off. My naughty little temptress disobeyed my command and dragged my tip along her burning, slick flesh, and I moaned at how it felt exactly as if I were there with her.

"That pussy belongs to me, and I want you to touch it," I ordered her.

"Oh, I'll touch it good, hellhound dick." Her back arched as she flicked her clit once like she strummed a guitar and plunged my cock deep inside her.

I fell off the goddamn chair from surprise and how incredible it felt. "Jesus, baby, you're fucking yourself with my wooden cock!"

"Yes," she panted, dipping it in and out of her wet heat, flicking her bud. Her body responded with wild bounces of her hips and ass.

Fucking hell, that was the hottest thing I ever saw. Other women turned away from my scared dick. I never showed them my wooden version 'cause they would have run a mile. And, the whole god story. Fun explanations. Yet here was my mate fucking herself senseless on it. She didn't see the imperfections. Didn't notice or didn't care. Sexy temptress plundered her goddamn pussy, going buck wild, moans turning to heated shouts of my name that had me mindless with pleasure. I was already close before when she sucked me off, but now I straddled the line and was about to peak.

"I'm about to come, baby," I warned her, unsure what would happen when I did. Knowing my luck, that wooden bastard would spit splinters or some shit into her pussy and hurt her, ending any future sexual acts between us.

Mad with need, she kept driving my dick into her until she came, hard and shuddering, not stopping until I was there with her. Her face scrunched and she bit her lip, and I panicked that I'd hurt her.

"Fuck, are you okay?" I panted, squinting into the camera. "I didn't shred your pussy with splinters or some shit, did I?"

*Good one, fuckwit.*

She hiccup-laughed. "No. I'm all good. Languid. Jelly-legged. Fucked to oblivion."

Thank fuck. I let out the breath I held onto. That was how I wanted her to feel. I wanted to make our first time incredible for her. Blow her away. Now I wanted to do was drive over there, light those fucking candles Castor gave us for the spell to let us get close, and fuck her brains out all night.

Fuck me and my responsibilities. Maybe I could delay them for another half an hour. Go another round or two. Convince my mate never to leave.

"I suppose I should give you your cock back, huh, hellhound dick?" She waggled it in the air, and I barked out a laugh. "I kinda like this as a trophy."

She had me there for a minute. I was fucking glad it magicked to her and not some random place around the shelter.

"Keep it." I gave her a wicked grin. "I'm coming to get it later tonight and taking you to heaven."

My luck kicked in and the bastard blinked back on my desk.

"Fuucckk," I groaned.

"Awww." She made a sad face.

Her juices covered it, the scent toying with my shifter and I brought it to my nose, inhaling her sweet, honeyed perfume. Unable to resist, I tasted her, savored her, enjoyed her. God, she tasted fucking mind-blowing.

"You taste so fucking good." I cleaned up every last drop of her, with her watching, lids growing heavy and sleepy.

"Bet that's not how you expected your night to go, huh?" She slumped on her pillow, smiling at me through hooded, sexed-up lids that grew sleepy.

"Sure didn't." I smiled back, pleased it went this way when I worried it might go another, with her running from my disfigurements.

Aaliyah didn't make me feel like a freak for having a dick that magicked off to random places. She didn't judge me for the freakish scars all over my body. My weirdness aroused her, and of all the things to get her off, my goddamn wandering cock came through in the end. I scrubbed my face, relieved.

Aaliyah's eyes were barely open.

"You tired, baby?" I rasped.

"Yeah."

"Dream of me, sexy." I blew her a kiss and she sent me one right back. "Goodnight."

"Night." She ended the call, and my heart sank a little that we didn't talk, joke, and fuck a little more.

I clicked on the last photo she sent of her in her sexy AF lacy underwear, savoring the memory of tonight. Never in a million years did I expect our night to end like this. Best night ever. My wandering junk, the biggest surprise of them all.

Here I planned to joke, tease, throw in some serious texts, and get to the bottom of her heart, her hesitations. My dick jumped the goddamn gun and threw a spanner in that plan.

But it didn't ruin it altogether. My girl was coming around. I felt it under my breastbone. The deep, needy ache for all four of us that never abated. Tonight had given me hope to keep going, never give up, show her we were meant to be together. Because I had my sights on her and I didn't intend to let her go. Ever.

## CHAPTER 25

### Alaric

Slade's irritated hand signal in the rearview mirror indicated for me to pull into the roadhouse. Fuck, he wanted a piss or smoke break, and I was too lost in my thoughts to notice. Horus' eye helped me see minute details my human eye couldn't, down to the movement of an ant half a mile away, and normally I'd be all over that shit. Not today. More reason for my president to keep me away from the club when I wasn't on my damn game.

I didn't want to stop. Wanted to ride straight through, get this morning's court proceedings over and done with. My gut clenched with apprehension of today's verdict.

Obeying my president, I flicked on my indicator, my anxiety mounting as I pulled into the busy roadhouse, the three other avatars, Benny and Kill Bill behind me. Our bikes purred as we slowed and killed the engines.

Aaliyah rode with Slade this time, putting my president in

a good fucking mood despite the preliminary court hearing we were attending to plead not guilty for our disorderly conduct charges. After she dismounted, he jumped off his bike with a spring in his damn step.

I remembered riding with her, the pleasure it gave me to have my mate's arms banded around me, her legs hugging me, chest molded to my back. Three fucking hours of heaven, free of demons hissing in my ears.

"Allow me, Nurse A." He removed her helmet, setting it aside, rubbing her thighs, touching her at every opportunity.

Wish I was so fucking chipper when we were about to be slammed by the cops gunning to put us behind bars. Slade removed his cigarettes and lit one, sucking the smoke down and releasing it.

Benny and Kill Bill hurried into the convenience store to grab their usual junk food hoard. Sausage rolls layered with ketchup, packets of potato chips, candy bars, and a can of Coke. Assholes were asking for clogged arteries and a heart attack with the shit they ate.

As road captain, I should have patrolled the area, scanned for any threats and danger. But I couldn't hold my thoughts together. Couldn't stop fidgeting. I checked my Longines watch. 7:20AM. Our Magistrate's Court hearing commenced in three hours, and we left at daybreak to get there on time. Eager to get back on my bike, get this summons done with, I paced along the length of my bike. Standing around made me twitchy and I felt like I was about to lose my shit. Knowing Slade, he'd give us fifteen minutes to stretch and chill out before departing. I'd count every fucking second. Anything to hold onto my sanity.

Aaliyah stretched her legs and arms, glancing at me with a hesitant and remorseful smile. Resentment pumped hot and bitter through my veins that she held my heart. That she betrayed my confidence. Body tensed, I turned my back, not wanting to be tempted by the curves of her perfect body. I couldn't withstand my desire with her flexing her legs and bending over like that. Shutting myself off from her allure became my new goal.

She was just a liability to me that I didn't need, and I'd not encourage her to approach me and apologize. Didn't want to give her the time of day. I know I acted like an asshole, but she betrayed my trust. After what I went through, I couldn't have someone in my life that I didn't trust. Staying away was for the best. Right now, I only had two modes—pissed off and bitter. If she came over, I'd snap at her, and I had to be careful what I said in front of Slade when it could be used against me to keep me from the club.

I pulled out my phone and scrolled through emails to discourage her approach. Bills and advertisements. Psychologist appointment. Treatment for my PTSD. Review by the Department of Veteran's Affairs. I needed a clear head to focus on my hearing today, on getting my head right, and getting back to the club.

The week away from the club was hell. Banished, I laid low, fixing my bike, completing some repairs around my place, chasing up medical forms, attending doctor appointments, following up referrals, and trying not to go stir-fucking-crazy without anything to do. I drank way too much, slept in, ordered pizza, not gone out, pretty much turned into a hermit. Skipped viewing the comet three nights ago.

My duties around the club normally kept me pretty busy. Coordinating various rides for product, meeting new shipping contacts, and new dealers. Twice daily flights over the clubhouse to scout for trouble. Protecting the women at the shelter. Down to inspecting our bikes for bugs or sabotage prior to a major ride like today. Never could be too careful. Cops set tracking devices on the bikes of the Junkyard Dogs to trace their movements, build evidence briefs, and eventually busted them for drug trafficking crimes. The Silver Wolves sabotaged their enemies by messing with their bikes, causing twelve of the sixteen Dark Reapers to crash and injure themselves.

I felt lost without my brothers and the club. Slade and Zethan came over one night for beers and pizza, but it didn't feel the same. They treated me like a wounded fucking puppy and not their brother. I didn't want to be pitied.

Leathered head to toe, Castor and Zethan headed inside the rest stop diner to use the men's room.

Benny and Kill Bill took a cigarette break in between stuffing their faces. They came on the ride to protect Aaliyah while we were busy in the courtroom.

Heavy footfalls moving away from the bikes told me that Slade went to take a leak. Wild and untamed, he didn't give a shit about etiquette or witnesses.

Softer tread approached me, and my muscles seized and locked up, refusing to let me escape. Fuck. Aaliyah pulling me aside for 'a chat.' Last person I wanted to talk to, today of all days.

Our upcoming proceedings set my nerves on edge, and they were about to explode. Leading up to it was absolute hell. Late nights, no sleep, the nightmares coming with more ferocity, my anxiety scaling the walls. Bars slammed down around me, trapping me, and I slammed my fist on them, begging for freedom.

"Hey, Alaric." My bitterness weakened at the rusty contriteness in her voice. *Do not soften. Do not be lured by the siren to your demise.* "Today's a big day for you. How are you doing?"

Panic invaded every cell. It was only a pleading hearing, but I felt the noose around my neck, choking me, my feet dangling off the platform.

Why the fuck did she have to look out for me? Be so

damn caring? It'd be a hell of a lot easier to be mad with her if she was a bitch. Steel battlements clunked as they rolled up around my heart.

"Fine." I said the word, punishing her with my tone. This was not a door I wanted to open. Hellfire would enter and burn me if I did. I was already blistered by her.

I flexed my gloved hands in and out of fists. *Do not fucking look at her.* Looking at her would break my determination to stay away.

"I feel like shit for what I did." It came out as choked as I felt.

I kicked my boot at my tire. "Too late now. What's done is done." My words were smoky and dangerous, warning her to back away while she still could, before I said something I regretted.

She let out a stuttered breath that was like a bludgeon to my already pulverized heart. "Alaric, I know I hurt you. I'm sorry. I really am. I save lives for a living. One day, I hope you can see that I was trying to save everyone, including you from yourself."

Fuck. She was right. I was the liability, not her. The club had no stability with me in it. They were safer without me there to drag them into the pits of Hell with me. Someone could get hurt. Aaliyah was protecting them. Protecting me. I was better off without her. She was better off without me. I was too far gone. Fucked up. Dangerous. I'd only hurt her. Hurt the fucking club. I couldn't voice anything but a wounded grunt. Shame burned a hole in my throat, and I hightailed it away from my bike.

"I really hope we can continue our fresh start despite everything," Aaliyah called out behind me.

I stood on the edge of the highway, gulping in air. Trucks rocketed by, the turbulence and air pressure they pushed out swaying me. Bernoulli's principle. Same rule that gave aircraft their lift with wings when the air flowed faster over the smooth top and slower underneath.

Heavy tread and the smell of cigarettes clued me into Slade's approach. "Alaric, you good to ride?" Concern replaced his normal gruffness.

My eyes snapped open, and I sniffed and wiped my nose. "Yep. Just needed some air."

Slade came to stand beside me, gaze on the traffic. Non-threatening. Shoulder to shoulder. Brother to brother. "You worried about today?"

Flashbacks of my confinement in the cell hit like a hammer. *His* face leered and laughed at me. An image burned into my mind with no hope of clearing it out. A dark space in my mind that I couldn't go back to but might have to if the judge convicted us a few months down the track when he made his judgment.

Not the only conviction I faced, either. Bathurst cops planted drugs on my bike and provided false statements attesting to my guilt. Bogus charges. Motherfuckers. That hearing was scheduled for October, three months away. Charges that either judge could take into consideration for my sentences. The wait for determining my fate killed me. I thought I put my days as a soldier behind me, but now I fought wars on too many fronts.

I slammed my eyes shut, sucking in air, trying to cling to my last shred of stability. "It's been on my mind," I told Slade.

"Barry's gonna get us off." My president thumped me on the shoulder, attempting to reassure me, but the doubt lingered at the back of my brain. "Don't you worry. You're not going back to that dark place. Ever."

I nodded because it was all I could communicate. I really hoped he was right. The others might be luckier. Me, not so much. Eventually, the bomb dropped would land on me, and the law would catch up with me.

\*\*\*

I BOUNCED MY KNEE, waiting for our matter to be raised. The judge was running an hour behind due to delayed paperwork for a previous case, which pissed me off when I worked like clockwork. Sitting around shredded my anxiety to pieces. I wanted to be put out of my misery and get the fuck out of here. No chance of that when it put the club further under the microscope.

Architects went to town on the interior of the building, and not in a good way. Undulating panels on the ceiling reflected the rocky seas in my stomach. Holes perforated in the wall panels represented my broken mind and soul. The four of us sat to the right of the room in the accused dock, fifteen feet from the judge. Barry, the club's lawyer, would sit in the center with the counsel for prosecution—a high-ranking cop with legal qualifications—once our matter got underway. Empty seats along the far-left wall would house a future jury if the case ever got that far. The arresting police officers sat in attendance in the public gallery, eyeing us off and giving us disgruntled stares. We got that a lot from the police. It never used to bother me until I got set up and my and my brother's freedom was on the line.

I gripped the edge of my seat, going stir crazy from impatience.

The ACT Magistrate's Court dealt with summary matters, offenses carrying a penalty of two to five years or less. Castor ran us through the process beforehand, so we didn't get any surprises. Barry, the club's solicitor, had also briefed us on what to say if questioned by the judge. We all had our speech practiced beforehand. Except my mind had gone fucking vacant.

When the bailiff introduced the judge's next case, I snapped out of my thoughts and almost leapt off my seat. Anxiety caused my mind to blank out a bit on some of the words he used to introduce the case. Barry and the prosecution's counsel moved to their position at the desk straight in front of the judge.

"What are the charges?" The judge flicked through his brief, the scraping on the overhead speakers making my hawk shriek.

"Assault Occasioning Bodily Harm," the police officer read out. "Inflicting Actual Bodily Harm and Disorderly Conduct, your honor."

Fuck. Two additional charges. Dirty fucking cops never failed to stoop lower and lower. They must have been in contact with the Bathurst police to coordinate their bullshit approach. My brothers muttered under their breath. Sandstorms whipped at the edges of the bond. Slade was going to go off if this went downhill.

Barry adopted his bull-like glare, and I could tell he was about to deliver a serve. He'd had that same ferocity while representing my preliminary hearing before the Bathurst judge at the bogus drug charges. "Neither my clients nor I were notified of these additional charges, your honor."

"We apologize, your honor, we added them to the charge sheet yesterday," the prosecution counsel defended.

"It's common courtesy to notify the defendant's counsel." I felt better being under Barry's representation. They didn't call him the bulldog for nothing.

"What do your clients plead?" the judge interrupted, not tolerating the snark or further delay in his courtroom.

I sat on the edge of my seat, my knuckles aching from holding the lip so tightly. We were guilty, thanks to fucking

Slade for starting this shit. But the Wolves kicked it off by hitting Aaliyah and we would never tolerate that.

"Not guilty," Barry declared with all the authority of the courtroom. "I bring to the court's attention an Apprehended Violence Order against the defendant, Mr. Danny Heller, president of the Wolves Motorcycle Club."

What the fuck? No one said a word about an AVO. Seemed Barry had a surprise of his own. Was this a late submission like the police's?

Slade's face remained stoic as he punched a fist at Castor's arm. Right. I got it. Thoth's avatar had worked his magick behind the scenes, entering the fake AVO into the record to paint a different picture than the prosecution outlined in their submission to the court. Paperwork that could change the entire course of our charges. Castor must have worked on this while I was on a break from the club.

The judge flicked through it, reading through his half-moon shaped glasses. "These are some very concerning allegations, counsel for the prosecution. The sister of the defendant, Miss. Heller, accuses her brother, the defendant, of kidnapping, drugging, and assaulting her on a previous occasion."

He left out the part about her brother shooting her. Circumstances that would cast a dark shadow over the club if included in the AVO.

The prosecution counsel sank lower in his seat, telling me his case's chance of success lowered by thirty percent.

"Miss Heller is not present in the court today to protect her safety, but I'd like to call her as a witness in future hearings." The judge scribbled down what I assumed was a related note in his paperwork. "Miss Heller's statement to the court outlines that Mr. Heller's men backhanded her unprovoked at the Summernat Rally, aggravating my client, Mr. Vincent, who rushed to defend his girlfriend."

Not how the events transpired. Aaliyah had slapped her brother and his man had retaliated to protect his president. But Barry and Castor attempted to paint another picture of how the events unfolded. I was down with that if it got us out of the charges.

Barry went in for the kill. "Miss Heller will also testify, along with her surgeon, that her brother, Mr. Heller, shot her in the stomach three weeks ago. This resulted in serious damage to her intestines and bowel."

Fuck, they didn't just bring that up. I wanted to scrub my unshaven jaw but that would make me look guilty.

The judge crooked a challenging eyebrow. "Based on this evidence, do you still wish to proceed with these charges, counsel?"

"We would, your honor." The prosecution didn't sound so convinced.

Slade cursed under his breath.

Damn cops were gunning for us. They were probably paid by Danny and his mysterious buddy, all working in collusion.

"I must warn you," the judge said, stern and insistent. "That I don't like your chances of getting a conviction here based on a family dispute turned out of control."

"We'll take that into consideration, your honor," the prosecution replied.

"Good luck," Barry mumbled under his breath. Thank God for my hawk hearing to catch it.

"I'll schedule the next hearing for two months from today." The judge slammed his gavel on the block. "Dismissed."

I felt a sense of relief as we all piled out of the courtroom, following our solicitor out to the parking lot out back, standing by his Mercedes for a private debrief.

The judge leaned to our side by the sounds of it, but he hadn't heard the rest of the evidence yet. Barry just tried to crush the cop's confidence to get them to back down and withdraw the charges. Shakedowns sometimes worked, sometimes didn't. Anything could change in two months. New evidence produced by the cops. Fake witness testimony. I didn't trust the bastards one bit after the way they'd framed Slade for Aaliyah's father's murder or for planting drugs on me. After introducing new charges and expressing their wish to proceed on flimsy charges, they sounded desperate enough to try and frame us all. None of it reassured me and my nerves flared with apprehension.

"Alaric," Slade barked. "Check the car." Code for *check for trackers or listening devices.*

I performed my duty, scanning beneath the car with my hawk vision for any devices, not spotting any. "Clear," I called out, coming back to stand with the huddle

"What do you think, Barry?" Slade asked. "Do we have a strong case?"

Barry adjusted his tie. "You heard the judge. What do you think?"

"That's what I wanna hear." Slade clapped the club's solicitor on the arm.

CHAPTER 26

*A*aliyah

I couldn't believe I was here again. Eight months earlier, it was a nightmare, and none of the daunting horror or shock departed. Straddled on Kill Bill's parked bike, I picked at my black nail polish, willing myself to go inside. Test myself mentally and physically.

*Shit, I could do this. Couldn't I?*

Hoisted flags whipped above me, agitated on their poles by the cool breeze. The Australian flag joined by the red, yellow, and black Indigenous flag. Each snap of material felt like it flayed more of my broken heart.

Jagged mountains in the distance dropped off sharply, reminiscent of the steep, rocky decline my father took. A one-way ticket to hell.

"You going in, or what?" Kill Bill's impatience prodded me from the front of his Harley. "Don't tell me we rode down here for noth'n. We risked our ass with Slade for leaving and stepping foot into Wolves' territory."

Now he was spooked? Didn't hear him whine when he accompanied his president on the dummy drugs raid. Not a fucking peep. I'd only managed to convince them to accompany me by promising to fix Slade's murder charges.

"Don't worry about my brother or his men," I coolly reassured, dismounting Kill Bill's bike. "They won't be stupid enough to pull shit out front of the Katoomba Police Station."

I already cast a concealment and protection spell Castor taught me over Kill Bill, Benny, and me. Not that I could tell them that. God business and all that. Wherever we went, we just looked like a bunch of retired old-timers going for a ride in the mountains, all traces of Jackals logos hidden behind my magick. The protection spell would ward off any dark magick from the demons attached to the Wolves. It wouldn't deflect bullets. No Neo and *Matrix* magick shit here.

Prompted by the unsettled Jackal, I shrugged off my cut, seeming to restrict my air and squeeze around my arms. Couldn't walk into this place showing allegiance to the wrong club when these guys were on my brother's payroll. The assholes that planted bogus evidence to pin Slade with my father's murder. Charges I planned to get wiped with my next move.

"I'll be no longer than an hour." I didn't bother to ask Kill Bill and Benny to wait for me. Rank and file and all that. Prospects held little power in the club, and I didn't want to start a shit fight with the sweaty, hairy-assed senior members. They might call me their president's 'old lady,' but they wouldn't stand for me bossing them around like I owned the place. I buried my cut in Kill Bill's rear bike compartment. "I'll text you if I'll be longer."

"We'll get some lunch, we're starving," Kill Bill grunted. "Want anything?"

Hell, no. Couldn't stomach a damn thing. "No, thanks." I fist bumped the Jackal and he cranked his engine and rode off with Benny at his rear.

"Goddess protect them," I whispered, zippering up my bottle-green leather jacket, and taking my first step inside.

Fuck, this was a crazy gamble. I didn't know if it would work or backfire, but I had to try and clear Slade's name. I couldn't live with myself if he got convicted and served twenty years for a murder he didn't commit. The idea of a such a force of nature being caged behind bars hurt my heart. The risk was worth it if it paid off. Worth it if it saved the man who spared me my life, even after he found out I infiltrated his club. The Jackal's president could have left me bleeding and wounded after my brother shot me, but he didn't, he got me medical attention, antibiotics, and painkillers. Sure, he kept me a prisoner in his cell, but realistically, I'd be dead without him. This was the least I could do.

Beyond the debt and obligation, deeper motivation threaded through my ribcage. The fierce and wild need to protect my mate at all costs. A selfish need, fearful of being separated from him, of our future being stolen from us. Admitting this meant I had to acknowledge my growing feelings for him, and that frightened me when I didn't want to get attached to him or the other avatars. Brakes slammed in my own chest, attempting to put a halt to my heart running away with them before she got hurt.

Confused, I pushed my fingers through my hair. Maybe Castor was right. I was scared of pursuing our bond, and that was why I wanted to leave. Maybe a relationship with the avatars was worth fighting for. Maybe I shouldn't be so hasty and walk away from something good. Hell, if I was crazy enough to risk my life and enter Wolves' territory knowing what my brother could do, then I obviously cared for them, right? Who was I kidding? It ran deeper than that. Soul fucking deep. Aaliyah Heller didn't tempt fate for just anyone. My heart pattered in my chest. I must *really* like the guy. More than liked. By the end of this, walking away wouldn't be an option.

A disheveled man with crumpled clothes, greasy hair, and stinking of alcohol, swung the door open, almost collecting me in the face, crushing any fantasy thoughts of the avatars. Asshole looked like he spent the night in lock-up by the way he stumbled out the door and along the pavement, almost face-planting in the neat garden.

The young and fresh constable manning the desk went straight as a board at my approach. Recognized me. Knew who my father was.

"Can I help you, ma'am?" he asked.

I tapped my nails on the counter. "My name's Aaliyah Heller. Can I speak with Detectives Smith and Beatie, please, about Alexander Heller's murder?"

The constable's cheek twitched. I didn't know who was more nervous, me or him. "Let me see if they're available, ma'am." He picked up the phone and dialed a number, his jittery gaze flicking to me every few seconds, setting me on edge. "A Miss Heller is here to see you about the Alexander Heller case." He nodded and ah-huhed. "Yes, I'll let her know." He set the receiver in its cradle. "Detective Beatie will be down in a minute."

I gave him my best pleased smile. "Thanks."

Stomach twisting in knots, I wandered back to the wooden bench and took a seat, waiting for what felt like twenty minutes. Fuck. I promised Kill Bill I wouldn't be long. Man-bitch would gripe about danger if I took longer than an hour. I only came here for information that might help solve my father's murder, find his killer, absolve Slade and get the

Jackals the men who set them up. A risky gamble, one I hoped paid off.

Eventually, a jacked-up officer in tight, and I mean tight, navy trousers and pale blue shirt emerged from the nearest door. *Hello, Chris Meloni.* Ironic that this guy looked like the actor in *Law and Order.*

"Miss Heller?" he addressed me, clutching a manila folder. Polite. Calm. Prepared.

I jumped out of my seat, flicking my thumbnail with my forefinger. "Thanks for meeting with me."

"Do you have any new evidence to provide the investigation?" Sr. Det. Beatie asked. "A statement? Circumstantial evidence?"

*Hell, yeah. My fucking asshole of a brother orchestrated this! Are you blind? Arrest the right man. Take him down. Do your fucking job and protect the community from a murder in your jurisdiction.*

Sadly, they wouldn't. Dad had greased them up early on to get them off the club's back. They turned the other way every single time. Good little puppets. Loyalty that would have continued for my brother, the main reason they were gunning for Slade and the Jackals to aid the Wolves in ascending to the top five clubs in the country. Imagine all the cash the crooked cops could earn. Then what next? An all-out war against the other four clubs for dominance? Because that was where this was headed. Gang wars. Assassinations. Thugs. Ruined careers of police when they conducted an investigation.

"No, uh." I scratched at the back of my neck. "I was hoping you might have some new leads."

Detective Beatie crossed his arms in front of his chest. "We can't discuss an active investigation, Miss Heller."

"I understand." I feigned consideration. "I thought you might be able to give me something to ease my mom's mind.

She hasn't slept well since my father's murder, and I hoped to set her mind at ease."

"We're sorry for your loss, Miss Heller." The detective tapped his file on his thigh.

That wouldn't stop me from doing what I was about to do. Time to put Castor's lessons to the test. Experiment with my magical prowess and get any intel that might help the Jackals in their war against the Wolves and Slade's murder charges. I knew in my heart he was innocent of my father's murder. Sole responsibility lay at my brother's feet. Blood was on his hands. Maybe not literally, but he played a part in it, whether it was commissioning the hit or pumping the bullets into my dad's back.

Fuck. I felt like an intern nurse all over again, completing practical placement in one of my four clinical settings. Unsure and cautious, I deployed the hand symbol and mind trick Castor taught me to tease out information from the officer.

Det. Beatie's blue eyes glazed over, and he blinked a few times. Cords in his neck twitched and his head jerked to the right. He grunted and pressed a hand to his forehead as if beset by a sudden headache. Recognition flickered in his eyes. Shit, he resisted my hold, and I was losing him. I applied more pressure, slackening his hold on his face, his hand dropping to his side. The spasms in his neck calmed and all control in his eyes faded. Goddess, I think it worked. The mental lock inside his mind snapped open, and he scraped his jaw back and forth, glancing between the constable behind him and me.

The officer's face went from stony and unreadable, to pleased and victorious. "Maybe I could let you in on some good news, Miss Heller."

Shit. I did it. *Castor, you're getting a kiss when I see you next! Your dick sucked by me and Zethan!*

"Oh? Really?" I let out a relieved, watery laugh. "Thank you."

The detective inched closer. "We've got new evidence against a suspect."

My stomach soured. "Slade Vincent?"

The detective gave me a gratified nod.

My tongue thickened, blocking off my throat, swelling until it cut off my air way. Fuck. Slade was in trouble. I had to warn him. Coming here was the right choice. "What... what new evidence?"

The detective used this as an opportunity to get even closer, hovering way too close for my liking, his bitter coffee breath making my nose twitch and my stomach roil. "Bullet casings that match his 9mm pistol and receipts for purchased cartridges."

What the fuck? No shells were found at the crime scene. Now they suddenly showed up? Something fucking fishy was up here. The cops planted more evidence in their quest to take Slade and the Jackals down. I doubted Slade would be stupid enough to commercially purchase ammo from a licensed dealer when he could get them through his back channels, same way my dad did it.

"That sounds promising," I lied. My heart stung for speaking the words aloud. For going against the mate that claimed me. The mate that claimed my heart and would keep it hostage. "That bastard deserves to rot in prison." I added that for emphasis even though I didn't feel one bit of it.

The detective smiled like a fucking shark about to eat a damn seal.

Time to extract more information. "Do you work for my brother?"

The question seemed to snap the detective out of my hold. "I work for the New South Wales Police Force."

I wrangled for influence over his mind. Shit, I was an

idiot for trying this without much practice. I was going to do more harm than good. "Why are you going after Slade Vincent?"

Detective Beatie's face darkened. "He's a fucking murderer."

Only part of the story. I needed to know the complete picture. Why they wanted to take Slade and the Jackals down. What their plan was and when they were going to execute it. The Jackals needed to be ready with a defense for the war on all fronts. The avatars were mine and I'd not let them suffer.

"So was my father," I enunciated every world clearly and slowly. "Why the Jackals? Is this personal?"

Det. Beatie scraped the corners of his mouth. "Our time is up here, Miss Heller." Fuck, I lost control.

"Thank you for your time." Translation: *Fuck you. You're going down, asshole.* I watched him leave, waiting, hoping he changed his mind, or my spell turned things around. He didn't.

I raked my fingers through the sides of my hair as I left the police station.

Kill Bill and Benny were parked outside, chomping down on Burger King. They pushed a bag at me when I approached. Absently, I picked at the fries, trying to ease the curdling in my stomach.

Armed with the new evidence, it wouldn't take the cops long to descend on Slade, arrest him and put him behind bars until his sentence could be put to a judge and jury. I had to warn him. Protect him somehow. If only I knew how.

## CHAPTER 27

### Aaliyah

"I OUGHT to dismember you for being so stupid." Slade burned hotter than a space shuttle on reentry into the Earth's atmosphere, spewing his frustration at the two bikers and me inside his office. "What were you fucking thinking driving into Wolf territory?"

Fuck. I only wanted to help the situation, not make it worse. My fault for texting Slade when we left the courthouse to let him know where we were going and that we'd meet him back at the clubhouse. The instant his court hearing ended, he flipped out, sending cranky, aggressive messages, threatening death to Benny and Kill Bill. Not a fun ride home. The whole time, I wrestled with the fight I'd have on my hands to shield the bikers from blame, and the agony crashing in my chest. Slade's torment and fear of losing another mate, another important woman in his life.

When we arrived back at the club, Slade almost punched

Benny's lights out until Zethan broke it up. Now the three of us stood before the president and three senior members. Tension strangled the room. Benny gave me a foul look. Kill Bill stared straight ahead at the biker memorabilia on the wall. The three avatars stood by their president's side.

Damn Slade didn't let me get a word in sideways. "Listen to me, Slade," I interjected with a hand to his arm.

"Stay out of this, prospect!" he barked, shoulders hulking, arms puffing out as if he prepared to take another swing to punish Benny and Kill Bill.

Oh, we were going there, were we? Doctors tried to talk over me or talk down at me when I was fresh out of college. Demeaning me because I didn't know what I was talking about. My father's men constantly competed with me, trying to outdo me, forcing me to be better, smarter, faster. I didn't take their shit then and wouldn't take it now from the president. He wasn't my boss, he was my pseudo boyfriend, mate, hot, sexy fuck buddy… whatever… and I'd not let him dress me down.

"Slade!" I shouted to no avail. Wind swarmed louder that a plane turbine in my ears. Sandstorms lashed along the bond, scraping me. Punishing heat instantly dried out my skin and burned me.

"You fuckers are on night duty for the next month," Slade ordered. "Sentinel duty looking out for the intruders in our sphere."

"Fuck, man," Benny griped. "I've got my kid's dance recital next weekend.

"Bad luck, asshole," the president growled.

"Slade." I grabbed his arm again, but he jerked away. I deflected some of his heat, ready to unleash my own.

"Out! Now." Slade barked at Benny and Kill Bill. "I don't want to see your mugs for the next month."

"Last time I do you any favors, prospect," Kill Bill

muttered as he marched out, Benny hot on his heels, slamming the door behind them.

Fuck. I had to fix this. Make Slade see reason. The infuriating man was a shoot first, ask questions later kind of guy. He needed to hear me out first and make a decision second.

So, I matched him energy for energy. Storm for storm. Lion to lion. God to god. "I swear, old man!" I bellowed at the top of my lungs, drawing every eye to mine, including Slade's. "If you don't listen to me, I'm walking out of this club for good."

Surprisingly, the threat to leave didn't get him, but the words *old man* softened his end of the bond. His hiked shoulders lowered as he speared me with his glare. "You've got thirty seconds before I leave this room and kill them." I had to stop my fierce bear murdering one of his own.

"Please, don't punish them," I started, lowering my voice from a wild storm to a tempered one.

Slade crossed his hulking arms over his barreled chest. "Twenty seconds."

The man made me want to punch him and jump him at the same time. "They did as you ordered. They protected me. Nothing happened. This was all my idea. I talked them into it to protect you and the club. Punish me."

"Oh, I fucking plan to, prospect." Slade captured my arm roughly, twisting it behind my back, telling me I was in for one hell of a punishment.

In one swift move, he picked me up, spinning me horizontally to face the floor and I squeaked, surprised by the move. He sank into a chair, setting my torso over his lap, crushing the air out of me. Fuck, he previously threatened to set me over his knee to smack the stubbornness out of me the sassiness from my mouth.

"If you ever do something as reckless and dangerous that puts your life at risk or the club in danger, I won't be so kind next time." Slade's brutal words cracked like thunder.

He was wild. Feral. Unchained. The thought of me being hurt again unhinged him. He wanted to burn the whole world down but had to restrain himself after what happened with Castor. That energy had to be let out somehow, and I was his target. His hand cracked down on my ass, and my eyes watered from the sting biting my flesh.

Oh, no he fucking didn't. Prospects did not get punished this way. I was a grown-ass woman, not a child, and if he touched me there again, I'd give him a black eye.

Before his hand thundered down over my butt like his temper, I spat my words out, fast and burning. "The Katoomba Police are gonna hit you with fresh evidence in my father's murder case."

The chaotic energy flinging debris along the bond died down. Sawed breaths dragged out his mouth as he slowly calmed.

"That's my dark sorceress," Castor mumbled.

Slade cut him down with a glare.

"What?" Castor shrugged. "Proud mentor moment here. She used the mind trick I taught her."

The volatile Jackals' president kept one hand on my back, holding me down, the other scraping his bearded chin from the sound of bristling hair. "This is no time to praise her." I wriggled on his massive thighs, but he held firmer, pinning me. "Fuck, just what we need. More bullshit and setbacks. Another knee to the balls to devastate the club."

"Hit our mate again, and I'll knock your fucking teeth out." Zethan's growl set off a chain of explosions along the link. Slade went off first, followed by Alaric, then Castor. Thrills arced through me at Zethan standing up for me, to his president, no less.

I mowed down the other two with a glare for not

defending my womanly honor. They wouldn't defy their president. Alaric had been molded through rules and punishment through his military service. Castor supported it, given his sway to law and order.

Slade prepared to retaliate with a dark promise of his own, lifting the weight of his arm from my back, shifting me from his lap and setting me on my feet. He stood, intimidatingly slow, murderous glare challenging his VP. Fuck, they were going to fight over me.

But Zethan surprised me with an alternative move, sweeping me into his arms, curling his body and arms around me like a shield. I wasn't sure if he did it to protect me or dissuade Slade from swinging. Fury pulsing down the bond said he wouldn't tolerate his president punishing a woman. Ever. Not even sexually.

"You okay, hellhound bitch?" His knuckles brushed my red, angry burning cheeks, dispersing some of the heat.

I wanted to zone in on the use of *that* term of endearment, but I was too pissed at Slade for humiliating and degrading me. "I can't believe you just did that, you asshole. I was trying to protect you."

Slade stood to full height, towering over me, glaring like a devil ready to raze a town. In that moment, emotion blinded him, and he couldn't see past it to recognize the good intention in my motives. That I just wanted to protect him. Warn him so the club could make a plan if hit with more unrest. Panic, terror, despair that he might have lost me swirled in his mind. This was more than just the mate bond. He cared. If he didn't, he wouldn't have gotten so worked up and scared, and almost punched Benny and Kill Bill's lights out.

My chest stung for putting him through the needless distress. He was even more worked-up than he'd been after his visit to his manufacturer. Fire, ice, sand, flood, storms, winds, and plague begged for release if I didn't stop it.

"Pull that stunt again, Aaliyah." Fuck, first names. "And I won't just spank your ass, I'll fuck that sweet hole with no warmup."

A threat he was all good for. I should have been insulted that he threatened to punish me like that. But I'd be damned, a shudder of desire rocketed through me at his heated promise. I stuffed that bitch down quick, so he didn't catch on and follow through with it. Didn't need him to know it turned me on as all hell. That I couldn't stop thinking about the last time we were together. The raw, animalistic sex we had. How hard I came. Three goddamn times!

*Down, woman! Think about that later.*

Zethan refused to move aside, even though the curse kicked in, pinching my skin, sinking deeper to my muscles.

Emotions were still raw after Tank's death. Slade blamed himself for losing a man as much as I blamed myself for my brother's actions. The thought of losing another mate set Slade off. Triggered a damn avalanche. I caused this and it was up to me to calm this storm down.

Full of regret, I wormed free of Zethan and threw myself at Slade's chest, winding my arms around his neck. The president's chest rose and fell like rocky waves, but I clung to him, navigating the rough waters.

"I'm sorry. I didn't mean to upset you." I combed my fingers through his thick, dirty blond hair, gradually lowering the fired-up beast with silky strokes on his nape. "I didn't want you to go down for a crime you didn't commit."

Slowly, his palms surrendered, sweeping over my body. Ass first, for a firm squeeze of my stinging cheeks. Waist next, lingering there for a few moments, savoring me, soaking in my curves. He coasted up my torso, purposefully grazing the sides of my breasts, causing me to mewl and him to hiss. When he couldn't take it any longer without throwing me on the table and following through on his earlier promise, his palms jumped to my arms. Rough fingers possessively dug into my shoulders. Tight. Protective. Unyielding. Eventually, he settled his arms around me, leaning his face to the top of my head, nuzzling me.

Anger leached from his body with every second our bodies united, but it didn't lower his dread at potentially losing me or me being injured again. Me taking a bullet hurt Slade worse than if it had hit him. Physical pain he could deal with since he'd been stabbed, shot, and punched more times that he could count. Watching me suffer reinforced his helplessness and agony, and he never wanted to go through that again.

Slade's lips dropped a rough kiss to my hair. "Fuck, Nurse A. Don't you ever do that to me again." His low and dangerous voice carried his threat to spank the disobedience from me, but the caressing hand on my neck, the thumb stroking lightly along my pulse, told me he'd make the punishment pleasurable too.

"I won't," I whispered, raking my fingers through his coarse Mohican cut. "I promise." Once again, I brought him down from total destruction.

"Good." Slade was not the kind of man to say thank you. He took what he wanted, when he wanted it. Anticipation tingled in my belly knowing that he'd exact my punishment the next time we were together.

I might have doubts about staying, about these men and their profession, about the way they killed to protect their club and turf. But they weren't just criminals to me anymore. They were men who loved hard and lived harder. Brothers through thick and thin, and fuck knows things were getting really thin. They were a team until the end, and they wanted me to become a part of that. Our means of getting things done might differ, but we could work on that.

Fuck, I was so focused on what I didn't want that I didn't

see what I wanted. That Slade would have my back and never let me down. That with him, I was family—accepted, and welcome. I didn't have to be the fiercely independent girl who could only rely on herself. That he wanted to be the man I counted on. That he loved so fiercely, he'd burn the world down if anyone hurt or killed me. Go to war to protect, defend and seek justice for me. Leave nothing left but ash and tears. Even if it was against his own club. Who could say they had that kind of love? I sure as hell couldn't until today.

In his arms, I felt cocooned in a blanket of safety. Nothing could touch me or hurt me. After being the girl on the outside all my life, fighting for my place among the biker men, the doctors, my damn family, I just wanted to belong. Slade was my damn ticket to belonging.

Whether I liked it or not, we needed each other. I lowered the temper and chaos that overwhelmed him. Soothed the beast when it took hold. Provided peace and calm to the storm channeled by his god. He was a wild force of nature that battered the walls I shielded behind and freed the rejected, wounded beast running away from her problems. Much as I hated to admit, the man who was my damnation, was also my salvation.

"How about we go for that ride tomorrow? You and me?" I was already bound for hell. Might as well burn and go down with him.

"10AM. Meet me here." He cracked me on the ass to seal the date. Then he leaned in to whisper just for me, "You know how to wrap me around your little finger, woman."

"You'd expect nothing less from the avatar of Isis."

"No, I wouldn't," Slade murmured into my hair. He moved to sit on the table, pulling me to lean between his legs. "Now tell me about this goddamn evidence the cops have."

I rubbed over his calloused knuckles, enjoying the feel of

his arms encircling me. "They've found bullet cartridges that match your 9mm pistol."

"How convenient." Castor turned away to massage his forehead, muscles rippling in his back with every motion. "Initial reports said they never found shells."

"We'll be ready when they come, Slade," he growled, prompting the other two to move to their president's side in solidarity.

Castor set a heavy hand on Slade's shoulder and squeezed. "Barry said he's got mounting evidence of corruption, scandals, mishandling of evidence and harassment within the police's investigation. Enough to lodge a complaint. This will tie those assholes up in so much red tape they won't have time to go after you."

I hoped he was right.

Evidence. I needed to review the police's documentation somehow. Ascertain lies from truth. Real suspects from fake. Evidence from planted shams. The longer my dad's murderer remained at large, the antsier I got, the more my brother got away with it, and the Jackals crashed into dangerous territory. The man to get me what I needed was Castor.

Slade's neck broke out in a red rash. "Call him. Tell him to submit it before the shit goes down."

Yes. Slow down the police's investigation. Get the heat off Slade to give him and the Jackals time to exact justice.

"You got it." Zethan clapped Slade a few times and dropped his hand. Then he turned to the rest of us to address us. "Our president is not going down for that shit. We protect him. Send him into hiding."

"Fuck, no!" Slade raised his voice. "I don't cower like a coward. Let those cunts try their worst."

## CHAPTER 28

## Slade

I DIDN'T WANT to move. My woman was bundled in my arms, and after our heated exchange, I just wanted to cuddle her. Soothe the hollow ache in my heart and the worry over losing her.

But fuck me. My phone had to ring, didn't it? No rest for the fucking wicked. I put the call on speaker phone to let Zethan and Aaliyah in on it. I dismissed Alaric to go home and rest after the stress of our court hearing. Castor went to prepare us all a coffee.

"Tell me you have good news, Reg," I growled my answer into the phone, clutching Aaliyah's waist tighter.

"Better than good news, Slade." Reg sounded like a biker with a new ride. Thank fuck. I was sick and tired of shitty news.

"What is it?" Asshole shouldn't keep am impatient cunt

like me waiting when I squeezed my girl too tight, and she tapped my arm to ease up.

"I've got two buyers for the gold." Reg delivered the best news the club had in weeks.

My spirits lifted and the constant tight ache in my muscles eased. I rewarded my woman with a massage of her arms and belly.

"Good work, Reg." Asshole deserved some praise after I'd threatened to kill him if he didn't sell our stock.

Except, I had one small problem. The club didn't have another shipment once this stock sold, and we couldn't leave our customers in demand if the copycat cunts resurfaced with new product in a few weeks' time.

That ungrateful cunt Tony made it clear he wouldn't do business with us unless we paid our outstanding debt. Funds from Pharaoh production built his business into high-end, food-grade herbal oils—a cover for the drug fabrication. Disloyalty like that made him dead to me. Fucker could stick his goddamn business up his ass. The Jackals were in the market for a new player, and I'd put Castor on the hunt for one.

I loaded the asshole to the hilt with tasks. Breaking both the curses on the avatars. Tracking any connection to tie the Wolves to our stolen shipment and murdered business partner. Cracking the mystery of who worked behind the scenes with Danny and his mutts. And now, obtaining any documents that would help our solicitor deal with the dirty cops. Normally, he was fast and efficient, but with all the hurdles put in place by the shadowy cunt, my enforcer was slowed down, and that was never good for my raging impatience.

Aaliyah kneaded my thighs to bring the temperature down. The woman was the right amount of calm to my disturbance. Explosions of joy went off in my chest at holding her like this when she always kept me at arm's length. We ought to fight more often. Maybe then I could get into her heart and her in my bed. Period.

Castor entered my office, cradling three steaming mugs. Coffee. My veins needed caffeine after the early morning ride to Canberra. I nodded my appreciation and accepted the boiling ceramic.

"Hold up a minute, Reg." I put my distributor on hold to have a private discussion with my VP, enforcer, and woman. "How the fuck do you wanna handle this?"

Zethan sipped at his drink. "Offloading the drugs will fix our debt and ease the strain on the club."

Castor's heavy frown lightened. "The sales of the bar and tattoo parlor could be a down payment for more product with Tony."

"That cunt is dead to me. Insulted me by refusing us a payment extension. We're not using him." My earlier indignation returned, bubbling like molten steel, until Aaliyah rubbed it away with a few light strokes. "As for the sale of the assets, we might not see that money for a few months at worst."

"Can we dip into the shelter's funds?" Fuck, Castor's suggestion might start an internal war.

I raised two palms to placate my VP, knowing he'd get his back up about this. "Just until we get back on our feet. Then we'll pay back every cent." Choice was his since he ran the joint and did the club's numbers and he allocated the budget.

Zethan made a dead-set disapproving sound in the back of his throat. The answer I expected. "I'd rather not if we can avoid it."

Fuck, if things got really bad, I might be forced to be the asshole to shut the shelter down. Protecting the club came first. The gods would understand, and we'd make up for it later with all our good work. Balance would be met.

I posed the question that had to be asked. The one that

backed my VP and me into a corner. "Would you consider it as a last resort? We could divert incoming women to Carlie's shelter for a few months until money picked up."

Aaliyah tensed in my arms, as if she didn't like the question either. I ran my palms down my woman's side to get her to relax.

Zethan sighed and pinched the corners of his eyes. "Yeah."

I respected his decision. Didn't mean I liked taking from the shelter or compromising all the hard work Zethan put in. "Appreciate it."

One heavy question down, one more for my enforcer before I got Reg back on the line to finalize the deal. "How's your search going for new manufacturers, Bird Boy?"

Castor sighed at the warm coffee sliding down his throat. "I've got three potential candidates with good track records."

Hope flourished in my chest for the first time since Aaliyah walked into my damn life. Potential crackled in my veins at new business relationships and at the club setting things right.

"Book meetings with them for this week. I want to meet them. Suss them out." I had a good gut instinct with people. Could tell if they were lying or hiding something.

"Yes, Prez." Castor finished his drink.

I let go of my woman to remove Reg from hold. "You there, Reg?"

Gunfire pinged in the background. Horrified screams froze my blood. Bodies hit concrete with a thud that rattled in my bones. Someone shouted, grunted, and swore. Another shot went off and the grunting went dead.

My gaze flicked to Zethan and my arms instinctively banded tighter around my woman. "Reg? What the fuck's going on?"

The phone crackled as if someone picked it up. "Uh. Hello? This is Fred." A man. Voice strung tighter than guitar strings. I wracked my brain for that name. Reg's right-hand man. "Reg can't come to the phone right now. He was... was just shot... through the head. Five more of my staff got hit too, by the assassin, one trying to take him down."

Fred's reply made the cold in my body turn to ice. "Is the assassin alive?" I wanted to question the cunt while I tortured him.

"No. Alistair our security guard shot him. Fuck. Reg's not breathing. I ... I think he's dead. Oh, God. The police. They'll find the drugs."

Motherfucker better shut his mouth right now. Feds or the Katoomba Police could have tapped the line and listened in to get more dirt on me.

"Get everybody out of the warehouse immediately," I told Fred. "Do not call the cops, and don't let anyone go near the body. Got me?"

"Yes, sir." Fred sounded a little better now that I'd taken control of the situation. Didn't blame him. It wasn't every day an assassin wandered into your workplace and whacked your boss. Not everyone handled blood well. I was just lucky I served the god of War and Chaos, otherwise I might not have been so nonchalant about it. I sure as fuck wouldn't be offhand about this next round of sabotage on the club.

"We'll be there in a few hours. In the meantime, I'll send a crew to deal with it."

"Okay."

"Call me on this number if there's trouble."

"Yes, sir."

I hung up on him. My heart took a free dive into my stomach. I rubbed at my tired fucking eyes with the heel of my palm. Riding down to Sydney was the last thing I wanted to do after a day trip to Canberra and back. It was late afternoon, and we'd encounter sunset and kangaroos on the trip.

I shifted Aaliyah from my lap and paced the length of my

office. "This is the work of Hellfire MC. Those fuckers did this for busting into their titty bar and breaking their noses."

Aaliyah grabbed my hand, pressing it between hers as I restlessly marched. She struggled trying to keep up with my longer, faster stride, so I slowed my pace for hers.

Castor swiped my mug off the table, probably anticipating I'd smash it. "I haven't heard anything on my channels from Hellfire."

My VP rubbed his tired, red eyes. "Don't tell me they're working for Danny and his little buddy too?"

"Unlikely." Castor folded his arms over his broad chest. His eyes went out of focus the way they did when he searched his information channels. "There's chatter in the underworld. I think our mystery player is behind this."

I swallowed the tight band cinching my throat. Venom spiked in my veins. Fury sparked and surged. "Get the fuck back," I warned.

Wary, my VP and enforcer backed away. Assholes were used to my outbursts. They were getting worse lately. First, I torched, froze, ripped up, and electrified the land out back of the club. Burned Castor in the process. Almost harmed my brothers and mate. Chaos pulsed thick and heavy in my veins, needing expression. With everything possible going wrong, I was losing it and needed to get my shit under control, and I worried the day would come when not even Aaliyah could bring me back down.

"Slade, no." Aaliyah's words didn't sink in as my rage tipped my desk over and let it crash on the floor.

Except it didn't hit the floor at all. Her power caught it, holding it hovering off the floor. Magick lessons with Castor were paying off. Now I wasn't so pissed at her spending so much time with him.

"Dark Sorceress," Castor whispered.

"I ... I haven't done that before, have I?" She didn't glance away from the wooden desk as if she feared she might drop it if she did.

"No, you haven't." Castor moved to her side. "But I can teach you how to repeat it."

That was the first time they'd really talked in days. Something went down between those two that I didn't have a chance to dive into yet. Felt the schism down the bond, though. Now my temper broke that barrier.

I righted the desk and set it back in place. "Sorry to break up the touching moment." Now that I was done, I was fucking leaving. "Castor, you're coming with me to clean up this fucking mess. We don't need eyes on the club or anything tracing back to us."

"Yes, Prez." My enforcer went to leave the room to go get his shit.

Before he departed, I barked, "Get me a secure line for my next call."

Castor twirled a finger in the air. "You're safe."

I grunted my thanks. Venom pumped harder. I'd make sure to inject it into the veins of the cunts who screwed with me for the last goddamn time.

"Dial Sammy the Bull," I ordered my phone and it got to work.

Sammy answered in five rings, which had me jerking my knee, nervous that he'd not answer, leaving us in a tight spot. "Long time no speak, Slade. You boys been angels for once?"

I snorted. "We won't be after we find the cunts fucking with us."

"I'll expect more business then." I heard the smile in Sammy's voice, and I wanted to punch the cocky fucker for being right.

"I need a cleaning crew down to this address." I recited it. "Shells, cake." Regardless of the secure line, I used the code for bullets and blood. With the cops gunning for me, I wasn't handing them more evidence to ping me.

"Twenty thousand pineapples." Translation: ten thousand dollars in a briefcase made up of fifty-dollar notes.

Fuck. Money we really needed. Fifty Gs always remained in our safe that I'd have to take. We might even have to borrow from the shelter now that selling the drugs was off the table.

"We'll bring it." I ended the call.

Death was guaranteed. Blood certain. At this rate I wasn't sure if it was our enemies' or our own.

## CHAPTER 29

### *A*aliyah

IT WAS JUST ME, Slade, the bike, and wind. No club. No drama. No heat from outside forces. No bundled ball of rage from my frustrated and helpless mate.

My thighs squeezed around his, my arms banding across his stomach. Goddess, he felt good. Dangerous darkness raging beneath hard walls of muscle. His chest rumbled louder than the engine, approving of my tight grip.

Heat pumped from his body into mine, warding off the chill of the winter morning's air. Slade would always be my shield. My provider. My protector. I sank into the comfort his body provided, hugging him tighter.

Every muscle in his back and shoulders cranked tight from the last few days of stress. Tension that I contributed to, and shame climbed up my throat for putting him through his stricken, distraught terror. Haunted by his tormented gaze every time I closed my eyes, I tossed and turned last night, unable to sleep knowing I caused his aggression towards his men for taking me to the Katoomba Police Station. I deserved punishment as club medic—not a slap on the ass punishment—but I should have been on patrol with Benny and Kill Bill, not on the back of Slade's fucking bike. Something I'd rectify tonight after our ride.

The president's intense reaction made me see things from a fresh perspective. How much the passionate man cared for me and wanted to love and protect me. Would destroy anyone or thing in his way that threatened me. How much he worried about his men and me, how much responsibility he bore, and how much my brother's interference wore away at Slade's perseverance.

My only thought in this moment was to relieve some of that pressure before it exploded in a fit of rage and fire. Carrying it around the way he did was no good for his health. No good for the club or the member's safety.

In Castor's library texts, the ancient Egyptians were obsessed with death, disease, and health. They wrote about how emotions left unchecked or sliding out of control led to illness and death. Slade was a walking fucking heart attack with his drinking, smoking, and stress. I was really worried for him and needed to bring him down a few levels before he got sick and died like his father. One of main reasons I offered to go for the ride with him. Let Zethan and Castor take the reins for a bit to ease the pressure, even for just a day.

Wanting my fingers on Slade's skin to loosen some of his tension, I slid my hands under his shirt, sifting through the tuft of hair on his firm belly. Contentment zinged through the bond, encouraging me to explore his huge frame. Ridged planes of his abs rippled under my fingertips. Massive swells of his pecs curved under my palms. Sculpted marble made into warm flesh. Utterly perfect. Mine, if I wanted it. And I wanted the devil who tempted me to abandon my past for him. So. Bad. I wouldn't walk away unscathed from a man like Slade Vincent. He'd leave me burned, scarred, chained to his bed, begging for more.

He guided the bike off the main road into the turnoff for Bridal Falls at Govetts Leap, Blackheath, dangerously close to the edge of Jackals' territory and the border of my brother's. But that was Slade, living on the edge. If we got into a confrontation with my brother's club, I had no doubt the president would unleash that brewing temper and leave nothing but piles of ash.

I no longer feared Danny. In fact, I looked forward to another meeting, breaking through the demonic barrier protecting him and getting the truth from him with my new tricks. Payback for my father's murder and all the terror Danny let loose on the Jackals.

Yesterday, Slade's outburst of chaos awoke a darkness within me. The dark face of my goddess, the great mother, punisher of her wicked children. When the ancient Egyptians slighted her, failed to honor her, praise her, give sacrifice to her, she punished them with floods, lost crops, failed harvests, and famine. That same darkness resided in me, and boy was I ready to deliver to Danny.

The bike bumped over the rocky, dirt track, not a car in sight. Isolation made the engine rumble louder, probably chasing away every creature within a mile radius. Winter sunlight streaked through the forest, lighting the way for the two semi-gods to visit and relax on our picnic. Fuck knows we earned the time away from the club.

Slade pushed my left hand from his chest down to the bulge straining in his jeans. I knew what was on his mind the moment he parked his bike. Fuck first, picnic later. Every time we were close this happened. I couldn't resist the devil. Steely hardness grew under my denim massage. His chest purred like the damn bike, vibrating his ribcage and back, right into my breasts.

Eager to feel his silky length, I unzipped his jeans, freed his massive cock and palmed it. Fisting him, I enjoyed the surge of power from owning such a strong, dangerous man with just my touch. Rocking hips told me he wanted me to get him off and fast. Impatient man. Get him off, I would. I pumped his shaft—clearly not hard enough, as his hand clamped over mine—squeezing, working him fiercer and faster. Slade Vincent liked control and dominance, even down to shaping my moves.

The bike surged forward with his desperation to park and get on his knees with me straddled over his thighs. I met his urgency with quicker pumps that made him shudder rougher than the Harley. A sharp turn had us pulling into the empty parking lot, where he cut the engine fast and trapped my palm to his cock. He flung his helmet off and rested it over his handlebars.

"Every time we ride, Nurse A, you're gonna touch me like that." He pawed at my thighs. Rough. Grueling. Needing to be inside me.

I shook off my helmet with my spare hand. "Only if you ride bitch," I countered, stopping his pleasure, making him growl with disapproval, tighten his grip, forcing us both to do the work.

"I'm only riding bitch while I straddle your ass and fuck your pussy." He reached around to cup my behind the best he could in that position.

"We'll see, Mr. President." At my heated threat, he quaked his release,

shooting his load onto the speedometer of his Harley.

Slade slapped my thigh. "Get your goddamn ass off the bike so I can lick that pussy until the only sound coming out your sassy mouth is a croak."

I bit at my smile as I dismounted. "You don't want to eat first?"

We'd been riding for an hour and a half straight. I'd missed breakfast, knowing Slade would go overboard and bring a massive picnic lunch.

"Fuck, no." The bear of a man cast himself off his ride faster than he disposed of his helmet, fly open and cock bouncing for all the world to see. "I'm skipping the goddamn main course and going straight to desert."

His dirty words shot my pussy like a love arrow from Cupid himself.

Despite my best intentions to leave the club behind for a day and alleviate Slade's stress levels, I should have known we'd end up here. Things always heated up between the two of us, burning hotter than a wildfire. When we were alone, we couldn't keep our hands off each other, couldn't stop the animalistic pull toward each other. Around Slade, I felt wild, free, out of control. The heady combination had me both falling and frightened by the unfamiliarity of it.

Grin dark and devious, Slade unbuttoned my skin-tight, dark capri jeans. My legs trembled as he stripped them down my ass, over my thighs, all the way to my ankles, helping me out of them. Claiming my mouth with bruising force, he positioned my lacy butt on the side of his seat. He spread my legs to dip between them, kissing me, rough and panty melting. Bristles grazed my soft flesh, and I arched my back at the contrast.

Calloused knuckles ran along the gusset of my underwear. "This pussy belongs to me." One jerk had my panties splitting apart.

"Fuck, Slade I don't want to go commando on the way

home." I thumped him on the arm. My pussy would chafe on my jeans.

He sniffed my soaking panties and stuffed them in his back pocket. "I'm keeping these for when we're apart."

I laughed and covered an eye. "You're so crude."

"Why wouldn't I be? You smell fucking incredible." He sank to his knees, spreading me as wide as I could go. One swift move lifted my legs over his shoulders, almost dragging me off the bike, and I yelped. Strong hands supported my pelvis as he cradled my pussy to his lips. He smacked my ass and growled, "You kept me waiting too long for this." Greedy man sampled me with a long, hard swipe of his tongue. "Fuck, you taste good. Just like I imagined."

The bike rocked from my wild buck. "Oh, God!"

"Keep worshipping me, baby." Slade's eyes smiled as he gave me another slow lick with that long, thick tongue that rocketed me off the bike and deeper into his mouth.

He licked me like he fucked. Rough. Wild. Without mercy. His tongue attacked my clit, circling it, flicking it, quickly working me into a frenzy. *Oh, God.* I thought I was gonna come three times on his face. My fingers dug into his hair, gripping tight, and he grunted. He sucked so hard on my clit that I thrashed with delirium and quaked over his shoulders at my first climax.

Straightening his back, he brought the heel of his palm down hard on my pussy. "Don't ever keep me waiting for this pussy ever again. I'm not a patient man." He treated me to another blow, then cupped my sensitive flesh, easing the burn. "Not one to be tested."

Fuck. I wanted all his hard, rough edges. To be burned by his fire. Treated to his possessive, wild touch. Owned in the bedroom and have my brains fucked out until I couldn't walk or talk. Smolder in the afterglow with him as he dragged his rough hands along my skin.

"I'm not gonna go slow or easy on you, Nurse A," Slade warned, his grip on my thighs harsh with the promise of discipline. "Zethan saved you from a spanking yesterday. Consider this your punishment."

Meaning: he wouldn't give me a break between orgasms. He would deliver justice with his tongue until I was going out of my mind with clit sensitivity or numb from too much sensation.

"Fuck," I groaned as he fiercely dragged his tongue along my sopping flesh. I stared into his retributive gaze for a semblance of mercy. Nope. Not a scrap of it existed behind his dark eyes.

Then Slade was off again, burying his head between my legs, showing no signs of slowing down. It was like my body was made to come alive, set ablaze when he touched me, come apart when he had his way with me. No matter how much I denied it, argued with myself, I was his, whether I liked it or not. It was proven when he dipped one finger into my slick heat, pumping hard, bringing me to my second climax.

"Slade!" His name rocketed out of my throat in an uncontrollable scream.

"That's it, Nurse A." He stroked my g-spot and I bounced beneath him, unable to control myself. "Scream my name and come on my face again. Three times. Every time."

I couldn't get enough air into my lungs as he pleasured me. The need for him in that moment, primitive and violent, burned me like a fire out of control. Dulling the sensitivity creeping into my clit from being brought to orgasm twice in a short span of time. One final sweep of my inner walls had my release burst out as a strangled groan. If Slade Vincent taught me anything, it was that he didn't lie. The only thing coming out my sassy mouth was a croak.

My body felt battered and bruised, like a chunk of rock

amid the asteroid belt that had crashed into every single solid body with orgasm after damn orgasm. It took me a long while to come back down, whole and aware.

Back on planet Earth, rooted in reality, I found myself cradled in Slade's lap, him nuzzling my neck, his fingers laced with mine. Tender. Sweet. Intimate. Words I'd never associate with him.

He licked the last of my juice from his lips. "Worked up an appetite yet, Nurse A?" I was surprised he gave me breathing space and didn't spear me with his stone-hard length jabbing my ass.

I ran my hand through his crumpled hair, loving the rugged coarseness of it. "Yes." He understood through our connection that I needed to settle down before we did any more of that.

He helped me back into my jeans and zipped himself up. While he set out the tartan picnic rug, I unpacked the basket from the back of his bike and set the contents down. Yep. Slade went all out. Sandwiches—salami and cheese, of course. Dips, sliced carrots, ciabatta, smoke meats, brie, berries, and champagne. I flicked open the containers for us to pick at.

Seated on the rug, I shirked off my pine-green riding jacket and set it down as a little pillow in case we laid down.

"Wow, someone wants to impress." I fed the president a strawberry and he nipped at it, then licked my fingers seductively.

"Anything for my goddess." I could get used to him saying that. Could get used to this lifestyle with the Jackals where I was the central figure, adored by and taken care of by four men. I scratched at his bristly, sandy-blond beard, resolving myself to that outcome more with each passing day.

Slade beckoned me to lie beside him, offering me blueberries wrapped in prosciutto. The combination of salt with tart sweetness exploded on my tongue. Damn, this man knew how to win a girl over. I was slowly losing the war with him. With all four of the men. I hoped the same couldn't be said for the war brewing with my brother.

## CHAPTER 30

### *A*aliyah

THE DREAMY BUBBLE that Slade cultivated with the hotter than fuck sex burst pretty quickly when I remembered the danger the club was in. Weakened and at breaking point financially, the club would suffer more divide if Slade let this continue. Exacting justice came at a price. Retaliating against my brother demanded casualties, blood, more lost men, and possible irreparable harm to the club. Fronts Slade couldn't fight if he was imprisoned or distracted by a battle against the police.

Fuck, there I went again, thinking the worst. Today was about lessening Slade's worry, not mine. Screw my brother. I was going to forget about him and just enjoy this picnic with Slade before we returned to the club to prepare for war with the Wolves. Enjoy it while it lasted, before the heat was cranked up. Bombs launched on either side. One club left in ruin—that club being Danny's—because in the end, there was no way he could win against the Jackals when they were backed by gods. Led by a goddamn god of war and destruction.

"Here, sugar." Slade fed me more berries, making me suck them from between his fingers, and I groaned.

I enjoyed his punishment. Hell, I'd do it over and over again if I crashed like that from his tongue. But my punishment reminded me how I disturbed Slade to the point where he acted aggressively at his men and probably caused their relationship harm. That was on him to fix. But when we got back to the club tonight, I'd join Benny and Kill Bill on patrol duty. It was only fair. Hopefully, the gesture would go a long way to patch up things between them and me, as well as with their president.

I scooped the ciabatta bread in the dip and lifted it to Slade's mouth. "I'm sorry for scaring you yesterday." It had to be said. Again.

He shrugged and swallowed his food. "I'm extra cautious and protective since I lost my mom when I was six, then Liz two years ago."

Now everything made sense. Why he insisted I stay with the Jackals. Why he wouldn't let me go. Until my brother and his fuckwit of a mystery friend interfered with the Jackals, Slade Vincent had everything. Money. Power. Clout. But family and his mate were more valuable than guns or drugs, and he protected them as fiercely as a dragon hoarded gold. He'd destroy anything in his way that threatened everything he valued, and it gave me a strange, dark sense of satisfaction.

"I didn't know." Not about his mother, at least. I dragged him into my arms, kissing his temple and stroking his beard. "I'm sorry."

His palm skimmed my arm, fingers tracing firm circles on my ballet-pink sweater before digging in possessively. "I won't lose you, Nurse A. Ever." Anguish and dread at what might happen to me trickled along the bond. "I know you wanna leave us. That you don't think we're right for you. I won't lie, I want to chain you to my goddamn bed to make you stay."

I felt greedy with power, knowing how much he wanted me. The extent to which he'd go to keep me. Who he'd kill to keep me safe. Slade Vincent was stamped on my heart as much as I was stamped on his. We belonged together. In his mind, nothing would keep us apart. My heart was convinced of him and the avatars, but my mind lagged behind, needing time to catch up.

Slade rolled out of my grasp, twisting me to face away so my back rested against the hard wall of his stomach and chest. "I know you don't want to be with grubby bikers." The bond pinched at his admission of what he really was. "You deserve doctors, fancy cars, a mansion, vacation homes."

Slade understood the core of me. Knew the life I wanted to build, free of my past, my family's business and expectations of me. One where I saved people and did no harm. He also didn't hold anything back from me, and would give me the brutal truth. Fuck, I hadn't expected to be put on the spot, and after yesterday, I didn't want to cause him more anguish.

I craned my neck to look up at him. "Homes? How many are we talking here?" I tried to continue our light banter.

Slade smiled, forlorn, playing with two berries, crushing them between his forefinger and thumb, then letting me lick off the darkened mess. "Your husband is a specialist with a practice. Asshole can afford the vacation homes. One in the Gold Coast. One in Mexico. One in Europe." Sounded more like his fantasy than mine.

I didn't know where he got this idea that I wanted to marry a doctor. Hell, no. Arrogant, cocky ER doctors or specialists who didn't have time for a relationship or dated three women at once like the last asshole I saw didn't register on my radar. No amount of money could convince me to change my mind on that front.

"Damn. I'm looking forward to four holidays a year." I chuckled and popped berries in his mouth, hoping to shut the president up.

He dropped a kiss to my lips, parting my mouth, seeking the friction between our clashing tongues. When we came up for air, he croaked, "We can make you happy. Can he?"

Fuck. How did I answer that? A deep vibration in my soul told me I belonged with the Jackals like the stars belonged in the night sky. But I couldn't be certain it wasn't the curse making me believe that. I had to be sure before I made my mind up.

Now it was my turn to play with the food, jabbing a carrot stick in the dip. "What makes you think he can't?"

"He won't," Slade said with absolute certainty mixed with a little jealousy. "Not with his dick in his office manager."

I slapped Slade's arm. "Did you just ruin my fantasy husband?"

"He's an asshole." Yep. Definitely resentful of a make-believe man.

My indecision with the men made them all suffer. Castor had retreated because of it, Zethan told me he wouldn't let me go, and now I pushed Slade into possessive mode, guarding his keep like a damn monster. Their anguish at the threat of losing me was like another knife to my heart.

Curse aside, I questioned what held me back. The biker lifestyle... always on the road and never at home. Hustling and committing crimes for more money. Killing to defend their turf, exact revenge, or to take what they wanted. Playing up on the old ladies with mistresses and whores like my dad did to my mom countless times, like Danny did behind his wife's back, and Jimmy did to me before I decked out him and the ho. I wanted to be my man's one and only. No other. Ever. Fuck, yeah, I was as possessive as the avatars of my man's fidelity.

I ran away screaming from that life. The toughness and hardness of it. The uncertainty of whether my man would come home to me at night. I didn't need Slade to drag me back into that world, no matter how persuasive, sexy, and rugged he might be.

"Bikers aren't known for their loyalty either, you know," I voiced, letting indignation creep into my voice.

Slade's fingers clamped around my arm. Harsh. Forceful. Unforgiving. "We're shifters. We mate for life. Your scent is all we can think about. Other pussy doesn't even register. Doesn't even compare. If you left, we'd be broken and incomplete."

Fuck. His admission had me awed. Lost for words. Floaty and bubbly. Soaking in the truth that spilled through our connection. These men might be hard on the outside, brutal, violent, and ruthless when they had to be, but they would absolutely cherish me if I let them. All I had to do was open the door for them and admit them in. It creaked open a fraction right there and then, and I had no doubt Slade Vincent would shove it wide, rip the door from its hinge and never let me close it again.

These men never pretended to be anything other than what they were. I was the liar, the fraud, trying to escape my family history and past. The stubborn bitch who only fell into nursing to do the damn opposite of my father and brother. Saving lives instead of taking or ruining them. All because I never felt good enough and like I belonged in their world. That and I wanted to feel like I had ownership over and control of something in my life.

Goddamn it. That was the crux of my problem, wasn't it?

I still felt like I had no say with this situation with the gods and avatars, and that was why I rebelled against it. Except Slade and the avatars never treated me like my father's club members. To the Jackals, I was family. One of them, and always would be. I'd never have to work hard to impress the avatars for their acceptance, love, or belonging. It was a given. I was stupid to throw this gift away.

"If you don't want to be the club medic." Slade released the pressure on my arm, returning to tracing circles on me. "Would you consider a transfer to the Bathurst hospital to be closer to us?"

Appreciation welled inside me that he gave me another option. Bathurst Base Hospital was a hell of a lot smaller than Northshore Hospital and wouldn't have the variety of nursing positions offered by a larger-scale facility. I knew because I'd been researching it more and more lately. Positions in rural hospitals were competitive and preference given to existing staff. Meaning, I needed a stellar resume, to suck someone's dick or get Slade to ruffle up the Head of Nursing to employ me.

If, and it was a big if, I considered to stay with the Jackals, I wanted to know what they would sacrifice for me. Fair was fair, if I had to let go of a part of my life for them.

"How many vacation houses are you offering?" I teased, biting my lip. "And what are you gonna sacrifice for me?"

Slade's arms banded around me. "When we get back on track, as many as you want." The man was *too* generous. "I'll quit smoking, swearing, whatever you want. Except sex, whisky, and bikes."

"What happened to whatever I want?" I hit him and he grinned. "As many houses as I want is a big claim and will cost you a lot of cash."

"Fuck. How many homes do you want? Twenty?"

"I wouldn't mind one by the beach or a lake. I'm a Pisces and need water."

"By a lake, huh?" Slade folded his arms and tucked his hands behind his head, letting me smooth my palms over his bulging biceps. "I could swim, fish, hide dead bodies."

I tickled his armpits and he squirmed. "You love ruining my fantasies, don't you?"

"I won't ruin them, I'll make them for you." A bold statement from the president. "And our four kids."

"Four?" I dragged my nails along the insides of his folded arms. "Goddess, my poor vagina!"

"One for each of us."

"You've got it all planned, don't you?"

"I'm not getting any younger, Nurse A." Slade's expression shifted from mischievous to serious. "I want to start a family."

My ovaries whooped at his admission and my vagina clenched at the thought of passing four children through it, especially a giant one from this bear of a man.

"I've seen how beautiful our pack can be with my family together. What's wrong with wanting that? Wanting to make my old lady happy?"

Nothing wrong with it. At. All. The more he spoke about his dreams, the more it convinced me to stay with them.

"I want to claim you for life, Nurse A." Slade's gruff tone dropped to a soft, silky whisper. "Possess you. Own you. But I can't own you, can I? You're independent, free, have a career, a life, a future mapped out. One that's not chained to four bikers. Staying with us would condemn you to a life with the devil. Crime's in my blood. Violence in my nature. I don't want to take you down with me. But I want to know what you want. Whether you'll stay."

Fuck. For once, Slade Vincent asked me, rather than railroaded me. Gave me the choice my father never had. Something I never expected from him. A man who knew what he was. Who he was. The devil of the Egyptian pantheon. A man that would give me the world if I asked it of him. Burn down everything if I said the word. Provide for my every need and whim. Pleasure me senseless anytime I needed it. Protect me so fiercely and violently that nothing harmful could ever touch me.

But I didn't want anything from them. Gifts, home, and bribes weren't going to keep me there. Only my heart would. That bitch was already invested, lying back on her sunchair at her vacation home, watching her men swim in the lake while she sipped Piña coladas. The only obstacle in my way was my head. Last week, it was leaning toward leaving, but the previous three days, today included, turned that around.

"I want you, Slade." I fell into him and buried my face in his chest. He was my weakness and I hated it. Being in the circle of his arms stripped away my uncertainty. "But I'm frightened of losing myself. Of losing everything."

"Just give us a chance, Nurse A." Slade nuzzled into my hair. "Take a leap with us. We might be wrong, but what if we're right?"

Pain speared my chest at how he saw right through me. That was my problem—I feared I would regret it. That they'd be taken from me like my father, Jimmy, and Tank. I'd have no control over what trouble the club would run into. Cops pursuing the Jackals for crimes. Rival clubs wanting to take my men down. Accidents they might encounter on the road. Negative thoughts clouded my head and judgment. One too many accidents witnessed in the ER crashing my in my mind. Tears caught in my throat, and I let out a whimper, burying my face in his chest, my hair curtaining it.

Fuck, why did I throw so many barriers up? What was I afraid of losing? Maybe I was too bitter and damaged from my past to recognize something worth fighting for. I wished it would be easy to wipe my hands of the avatars and walk away but my heart was in play, and that bitch wasn't willing to give up on them. Not now. Not. Ever. I was starting to feel the same.

"Fuck, baby. I never beg, but that's how much you mean to me. To us." I loved the surge of heady power at knowing how much I affected Slade. How I reduced the man who took everything he wanted to a begging mess.

But this moved way too fast for my liking. I wasn't ready to go all in, pack everything up and relocate to live with them. Once, when I was young, immature, and sought my father's approval, I wouldn't have flinched to jump in head-first. Not anymore. Slow and cautious. Test, study, report, and make a decision.

After the battering my heart and confidence took from my time in the Wolves, I didn't trust quickly or give my heart away easy. Guess I could blame my dad for that. Sure, I didn't want ordinary. I'd let Slade gun-fuck me for crying out loud! I wanted exciting, all-encompassing love, but I also didn't want trouble. Trouble spelled as four D.E.V.I.L.S. The Jackals couldn't give me picket fences, roses, a four-bedroom home. But they could give me the ride of my life, and after living both lives, fast and furious versus quiet and cautious, I was beginning to want the thrill and unexpectedness of my daredevil life back again.

"Let me think about it." I thought I'd have a fight on my hands, but surprisingly Slade nodded, accepting it. "Two weeks ago, I was your captive. Now I'm your medic. I don't want to make a hasty decision. This is life changing."

Slade stroked his hand up and down my side, comforting me, letting me have my moment. "Don't make me wait too long, Nurse A. I'm an impatient bastard and will punish you harder, longer, more cruelly for each day you make me wait."

I barked out a pleased laugh. He rolled me onto my back,

letting me pay my penance with my mouth and tongue. I curled my legs around his hips, drawing him closer, fingering through his hair. Slade dragged me into a deeper, demanding kiss, sealing his promise.

He left my lips wanting and burning when he pulled away to whisper, "I've got a surprise for you in a couple of weeks."

I dragged my nails through his beard, loving the bristle of hair. "Oh, yeah? What is it?"

"You'll have to wait to find out."

I groaned, hating how he teased me with that little slip of information to keep me on edge.

"Keep your sexy ass away from the storage room. It's locked, so don't use your magick to pry it open, otherwise I'll know." He parted my legs to slap my pussy again. "This is what you'll get if you dare."

Damn. I wanted more of that. Right. Fucking. Now. "Doing that only encourages me."

Slade ground his growing hardness into the juncture between my legs. "Come here, my naughty little nurse. Time for another spanking."

## CHAPTER 31

### *S*lade

My war god senses snapped me awake. Something was wrong. Fireballs erupted over my palms as I launched off my back, sitting up in my bed. Thumping boots on wood accompanied the cops raiding the clubhouse. Cold kiss of steel to my temple warned me that Danny fucking Heller had a gun to my head. My motion to melt the cold steel knocked something onto the floor. Glass, clattering and spinning. Someone groaned and adjusted beside me. Fuck. One of my brothers. Tied up with me on the floor.

It took a few moments for my mind to clear away the sleep fog. The peach light of dawn crept through my window, and I blinked, scanning the room. Clothes scattered all over the floor. Bra, underwear, jeans. Champagne bottle slowing from a spin. The mother of all hangovers from the three bottles consumed. Candles on my bedside. Fucking candles.

No steel at my temple. No one in my room. No cops shouting orders outside to arrest me. Fuck. Paranoia was getting to me. I scraped the heels of my palms to wipe the sleep from my eyes.

Set sometimes warned me if something serious was going down. The last time he made my stomach burn like this, the cops were on their way to arrest for me for Alexander Heller's murder. Hence, the start from my bed.

A warm, solid body curled into my side, adjusted beside me. Aaliyah. Naked. Glorious. All fucking mine. Dark hair curtaining half her face. Long lashes fluttering over her closed eyes. Supple, soft caramel skin with a dewy glow from fucking her brains out. Her palms pawed the sheet, seeking me out.

Worried that I might hurt her with my magick, I extinguished the flames and scrubbed my tired face, the heat of my palms jolting me more awake.

Aaliyah's hand found my thigh, encouraging me to lie beside her. I fit my body around hers, draping an arm over her waist. Her scent dressed me, and I breathed her in. Cherries. Vanilla. Something new. Smoke. Ash. Whisky. Clove. My scent mingling with hers. She was mine now.

Our first night staying together. Yesterday was a real breakthrough. She showed me her vulnerable side. Admitted her fears and what held her back from jumping into a relationship with us. Woman was a tough nut to crack. Didn't trust in the mate bond or the gods. Held back her feelings and didn't give her heart away. Impossible sometimes, but I loved the thrill of the chase. Winning her over would be my greatest achievement.

When I wanted something, I went in all guns blazing, and I was ready to pack up her belongings and move her into my place. But Aaliyah wasn't ready to take that kind of step with us yet. Woman didn't like to be pushed around. Didn't take shit from anyone, least of all me. Putting more pressure on her would chase her away. Against all instincts, I dialed it down, declared my intensions, and left the ball in her court. Gave her the space she needed to make her decision. I hoped it would show her what it would be like for someone to always have her back. Show her she could be part of a team and not the outsider. Break down the barricades she kept putting between us. Show her we could love her the way she deserved to be. That was all I could do. I hated feeling so out of control and her so far from my grasp, but I wasn't going to fuck this up.

Despite her uncertainty, I had to be content that she was attracted to me, into the hot, brutal sex, that we were bonded and claimed as mates, and that she said she wanted me. Woman gave a little more of herself to me every day. No promises yet, but I worked my way under her defenses. Our conversation left me hopeful and confident that she'd finally come around. The day she said the word I'd spoil her fucking rotten with whatever she wanted. Danny fucking Heller was not going to ruin this for me.

For now, I had to be content with the small things. That she was with us, alive, safe, and protected. That she wanted to shield me from taking the fall for her father's murder, going as far as risking her life to do so. That we inched closer to forgiveness, with her taking the first step, going for a ride with me. That she let me fuck her again after swearing off it. That she stayed the night last night when she previously avoided it. Fuck, maybe my luck started to change.

Woman didn't want ordinary, didn't want a doctor husband, a Toyota, white picket fence, and soccer mom duties. She craved a strong, dominant man. The thrill of the open road, a ride between her thighs, and gun between her legs. Mystery of her goddess and magick. Freedom to practice medicine without the restrictions placed on her by bureaucrats and wankers in the system she worked for. She might hide behind her whole danger and risk excuse, but that was what her heart desired above all else. Where she started. Where she'd end. My girl was a wild force of nature like me. I just had to make her see it.

Her eyes pried open and focused on me. She sifted her fingers through the tuft of hair on my chest. Luscious lips arced into a smile just for me.

"Morning, Mr. Vincent." I'd never get tired of that name or the way it made my dick ache to be balls deep in her.

"Mornin', Nurse A." I kissed her forehead and tightened my arm banded around her waist. "Hungry? Want breakfast? I can go grab you something."

Fuck, listen to me. Eager to jump out of bed and get her whatever her heart damn well desired. Me and mornings did not mix. At. All. Oil and water. But I was up for making her pancakes if she asked me to. Pick her flowers. Sing some sappy romantic tune. Make my fucking bed.

She propped her elbow on the mattress and leaned her head on her hand. "How about you do me a favor instead and go easy on Benny and Kill Bill?"

Not this bullshit again. My palm came down hard on her ass. "Careful, woman."

Her lips twisted into the sassy weapon she wielded. "Or what? You'll send me out there too?"

Crafty woman was angling for it. Wanted to be out there getting punished like my men. To stand as one of them, and get punished like them. I should have been happy that she wanted to be one of them, but those assholes knew better and should have refused her request. I only went easy on her because I needed her to stay. Next time I wouldn't go so easy on her.

"Or I'll put you over my lap again." I cracked my hand on her bouncy ass to prove my point. Heat flared in her eyes at the threat. Blood rushed between my legs. I was all but ready to continue spanking her and roll her onto her belly to pound into her when my damn phone went off on the nightstand. "Fuck." Irritated at the intrusion, I snatched it up and answered. "This better be good."

"Hey, Slade, you need to come down here right away." I only got a call from Rusty when something was wrong at the bar. Some cunt who caused a fight and damage. Cops rolling up to arrest someone for drunken behavior or conducting random drug checks.

Pound town was not fucking happening anymore. "Fuck. What now?" I growled down the line.

A line folded along Aaliyah's brow.

"The cops raided the place." Rusty's warning turned my body to stone. "They're searching for drugs and illegal weapons."

Motherfuckers. The police needed warrants for that shit. No paperwork was served to the club or me, and I didn't receive a single call besides this one to notify me. I needed to get Barry on the line to get this sorted out. More money to drain the goddamn club.

My throat tightened from the grip around it. I was fucked. Putting out fires everywhere caused by *Danny fucking Heller*. All. The. Fucking. Time. Attending to incidents left, right, and fucking central. Never able to focus on a game plan to attack the fucking Wolves. They were fucking me up the ass with two fists instead of one. The instant Castor got me some goddamn intel on that mutt and his backer I was going to town.

Rusty normally shut the bar at 2AM and was back home at 3AM. I glanced at my Tag Heuer watch on the nightstand. 7AM. Bit late to be calling me.

"Why the fuck didn't you call me sooner?" I asked my bar manager.

"Those assholes confiscated my phone while they searched the place." Rusty sounded exhausted and exasperated and I didn't fucking blame him. "Just get down here, now." Asshole ended the call before I could chew his fucking ass off.

Fucking Bathurst cops were doing this on purpose. Retribution for Barry submitting a complaint to the commissioner for gross misconduct. Bastards committed their second act to ruin the club after planting drugs on Alaric.

Pissed that I had another problem to take care of, I climbed off my bed to take a shower and wash the sticky mess of sex and sweat off me.

Aaliyah cracked open the door to my shower and slid in with me to bathe. "Want me to come down to the bar?"

Hell, yeah. I needed my woman by my side to calm me and stop me from doing something stupid like punching the teeth out of a cop's mug and adding to my list of fucking charges. I also needed Castor with me to throw the law in the faces of the cunts invading my bar.

I finished showering, cleaning my woman from head to toe, leaving her wet, dripping, and steamy.

Dressed and ready to leave, I called Castor first, filling him in on the situation, cracking each knuckle to expel some tension. "Why the fuck didn't you see this coming?"

Normally, my enforcer got word of the law coming down on us and gave us the heads up to prepare us. We could have warned Barry and had him tearing the cops to pieces, waiting like the little bulldog he was. I didn't know what was up with Castor lately, but he dropped the ball and let the club down. Big fucking time.

"There's nothing on the channels, Prez." I wanted to give him a serious beat down the next time I saw him. "No search warrants, nothing."

Then the cops had acted illegally. Off their own damn

backs. Barry would have a field day with this. I'd certainly not forget it. When the heat died down, I'd deliver to every single cop involved.

"Nothing on the fucking channels?" I barked. "Obviously there was, because there wouldn't be a goddamn raid."

"I'll meet you at Bangers," Castor said and hung up.

"C'mon." I snagged my woman's hand and dragged her out to my bike.

I sped down to the bar, nearly t-boning a fucking Suzuki in my haste, going off at the idiot driver who pulled out on me. My tires screeched as I tore into the bar's parking lot. Aaliyah's locked arms loosened from my waist, and she dismounted first closely followed by me.

My woman put her slender hands on my chest to bring me down two levels. "Slade, please don't go nuclear."

I was going to go something, what level was to be determined.

Castor rolled up, clean shaven, perfumed with aftershave, smelling of soap. Fucker looked good for 7:30AM in the morning. I probably looked like shit. Felt like it too, with my thudding head.

"Morning," he said to us both, hanging his helmet over his handlebars.

"Hey." At Aaliyah's greeting, he gave her a solemn once over, recognition jerking on the bond as he clued in on what we'd been up to last night.

"Hey, dark sorceress." A least the asshole spoke to her, which was more than what I could say for Alaric.

Inside the bar, everything was turned upside down. Boxes of paperwork dragged from out of the office. Bottles, glasses, mugs upended and all over the bar. Food removed from the fridges and freezers. Beer kegs emptied and opened. Uneaten meals and half drunken glasses of alcohol. Thousands of dollars down the fucking drain. Not to mention the rest of the damage to our reputation if the cops raided in front of our patrons.

"Motherfuckers," I cursed under my breath, squeezing Aaliyah's hand so hard her knuckles cracked.

Castor flanked me on the opposite side, scanning the place, prepared to drop every law on these motherfuckers once I was done burning off.

That was when I noticed Marcus, our informant, a lazy, paunchy, crooked cop we paid to warn us of this sort of shit. Prick sat at my bar, drinking my fucking whisky, and smoking a cigarette like he owned the goddamn place. Smoking was banned at indoor venues, yet this goddamn fuck took it upon himself to break the law and none of the other cops removing documents and searching the place took any notice.

I marched right up to the cunt, dragging Aaliyah with me, who struggled to meet my pace. "What are you doing here? Why are your men raiding my goddamn bar and why didn't you give us the heads up?"

Marcus finished his cigarette and took out a blue packet of Winfield Blues and lit another one. Heat flushed my neck like the burning stick. Fucker made me wait for an answer, sucking the smoke down deep, blowing it out slowly. "We're shutting this place down. Suspected drug dealing."

"Under whose authority?" I growled, the heat inside me getting critical.

The cunt had the audacity to shove the paperwork at me. Writing I couldn't read. Thank fuck I brought Castor with me.

Aaliyah rubbed at my arm and clutched my hand, doing her best to keep me from tipping over and killing someone.

Castor read the paperwork then commented, "This doesn't have the owner's name on it. Who the hell is Junkals'

Wrist Motor Club? The proprietor is Jackals' Wrath Motorcycle Club."

No wonder he didn't pick up anything on his channels. Fuckers were playing games and misspelling shit to avoid alerting us. This stank of Danny and his mysterious buddy. Reeked of corruption within the Bathurst police force. But we already knew that from when they'd framed Alaric. Now they were after Rusty and me.

"Is this a fucking joke?" My voice sharpened, promising hell to pay. "You can't enter an establishment without a valid warrant." Been down this road one too many times. Knew the fucking drill. Marcus was going to burn for letting me down.

Castor backed me up. "That warrant is illegal, and you know it. It's not even signed by a judge. You have no right to enter this premises. What's your name and badge number?" He slipped out his phone to record the details.

"We can enter this premises and we did." Smart-assed cunt. Let's see how he'd like to go a round with Barry and his superintendent. Then, after the dust settled, I'd take this motherfucker to a field in the middle of nowhere and blow his fucking brains out.

"Not under the law you can't." Castor stared the prick down, unblinking.

"We're shutting the bar down until our investigation is complete." Marcus blew out a cloud of smoke in my face, and if I wasn't holding Aaliyah's hand, I would have smacked his balls up into his throat. "You need to leave. Let us finish our search."

"So you can plant more drugs in my bar like you did to my man?" I loomed over the arrogant cunt. "No fucking way!"

"Then you're leaving under arrest." The asshole smirked, unaware he was a few breaths away from death.

Castor restrained me, holding me back. "Don't make this worse for yourself. Worse for the club."

He was right. *Cool your jets, asshole.*

"What the fuck is going on Marcus?" I growled, leaning in close to whisper to him. "Thought you were on our side."

"My rates went up and your club didn't pay up." He jerked his chin at Castor. "Gave your buddy here the opportunity, and he failed."

Cunt always hustled us for more cash. Fucker didn't deserve another cent when he just bit the hand that fed him for not warning us. An act I wouldn't forgive or forget. Motherfucker just signed his death certificate.

Not the first time he fucked up either. Fucker failed to clue me in that I was the chief suspect in the Katoomba Police's murder investigation of Alexander Heller. That, and Marcus' information was less reliable than the other three cops on our payroll.

Three times he was investigated for letting perps go free. Perps with connections to shady business deals with him and his wife. Evidence went missing or was destroyed before it was tested. Witnesses weren't interviewed and leads not followed up. Crucial evidence that got his cases reassigned. Marcus' reputation took another hit when they investigated him for taking bribes. The last two years, we tried to distance ourselves from this dirty fuck, but kept him on the payroll to shut his goddamn mouth.

Whether I liked it or not, Marcus had me by the balls. The cunt still had friends in high places to make this go away if he shook up the right people. Bile rose up my throat that I had to lower myself to this motherfucker's level to make this go away. But I was desperate. The club needed the bar's income to keep us afloat.

I patted my cut for my cigarettes, needing a smoke to clear away the ice prickling my stomach. Fuck. I left my tobacco on my desk. That put me in an even fouler mood. "What'll it take to get the heat off the club?"

"Sorry, champ." Marcus took another long hit of his smoke. "It's too late. Bathurst police are onto you. They're taking you down."

"What the fuck?" Castor got in before me.

Smoke swarmed behind my eyes. Fires in my imagination spread across the bar, licking at the alcohol, going up in roaring flames, reducing my establishment to ash in seconds.

"Sorry, buddy." Marcus gave me a conciliatory clap on the shoulder in passing. "Nothing I can do." He flicked his cigarette on the ground, stomping on it with his boots.

Burning all over, I created a crack in the oil filter of his car. Goddamn vehicle would leak oil and not start next time he got into it. Fire would lick at the oil and let that baby go sky-fucking-high. While I watched from a distance. Barbe-fucking-q piggy, piggy.

"You should know something else, Slade." Stupid mug smirked. "You're under arrest for selling narcotics at your establishment."

Two cops approached, sliding cuffs from their uniforms, and I knew this was the fucking end for me.

## CHAPTER 32

*Castor*

"You've gone too far, Marcus." Slade's furious heartbeat stormed along the bond as one of the cops cuffed him. War drums thumped as soldiers marched for war. Fiery arrows rained down at the dirty cop's feet. Warning shots to back the fuck off. "We don't sell that shit at our premises. Ever."

Marcus' triumphant smile tempted me to wipe it from his face with my knuckle dusters. For my president, of course.

"Crime pays, my friend. Crime pays." The dirty cop took out another cigarette from his packet, lighting it, smirking as he inhaled the smoke. "We know you deal here and at all your clubs."

Aaliyah's body slid between my president and the dirty cop's like a barricade, pressing her tanned hands to Slade's thighs. "Who do you work for? Who's behind this bullshit?"

*That was my fiery woman.* Pride circled in my chest like the power in Slade threatening to destroy this scene.

Waves of desperate, sticky energy pulsed in the air. Extractive. Irresistible. Potent. My little dark sorceress applied her coercion magick to get this asshole's lips moving and secrets spilling. As a mentor, I glowed fiercely with gratification, longing to reward her with a long, commending kiss.

Longing hit me hard, and my lungs cut off my air. I missed her. Missed those plush lips sliding on mine. Missed her body plastered to mine in bed or sunken over my lap while we studied. Missed that inquisitive, analytical mind absorbing all the magick her brain could grasp, questioning it, testing it, employing it. Being away from her was like having my heart torn out, ridden over with a seven-hundred-pound bike, then tossed into the wheel and shredded by the spokes. Worse than my mate dying. At least in that case, she was gone, but having Aaliyah around was like being in hell. I finally appreciated how goddamn Zethan felt being unable to touch her.

Marcus' mind jolted and slipped into the crack she opened. Darkness swallowed his grip on conscious thought as her ancient power took hold. The same power she applied to the Katoomba Police seeking insights into their investigations on her father's murder. Valuable information we needed. If only Slade heeded her warning and went into hiding, none of this would be happening.

Katoomba and Bathurst Police forces were working together to besiege the club. Goal: knock Slade from his perch, weaken and strain our club financially to the breaking point, and leave us vulnerable and open for Danny to muscle in on our turf. Never going to happen. Slade, Zethan, Alaric, and I wouldn't let it.

Marcus shook his head, resisting my dark sorceress' grip. He dropped his packet of cigarettes at his feet. Strain played across her face as she lost control. Mind games required endurance and stamina, months of practice to master, otherwise the cop would dance in and out of her hold. Less questions would get answered as his mind caught onto her trick. She needed my help to lock his mind in place or risked losing him altogether. Combined strength to hold this dirty fuck in place why she plied him.

Credit to her, we only recently found this technique in Thoth's library, researching spells to break the demonic protection on Danny and his men. I was doing this kind of thing a lot longer and built up the tenacity needed for these exercises.

Backed with my power, she secured his slipping mind and probed deeper. "Who authorized this raid? Who paid you?"

Marcus burst into a childish smile, his smoke dangling precariously from his lips. "Danny sends his regards, bitch."

Tremors rattled from my feet to my knees, up my thighs, making my damn teeth chatter from Slade's whole-body growl.

The two cops gripping my president's arm warily watched him, hands securing tighter on him as if they sensed their prisoner about to go loco.

For that slur, I brought Marcus' mind to its knees, his eyes rolling back in his head, my dark magick squeezing his balls to the point of passing out. The burning stick dropped from his lips, rolling on the floor.

"Take it easy, Castor," Aaliyah hiss-warned, gaze dancing between Marcus and the cops restraining Slade. "You'll hurt him."

I didn't care. No one spoke to my girl that way.

Aaliyah broke my hold over the dirty prick. "What does my brother want?"

"Don't say another word, boss," the young officer on the left snipped.

The Wolves must have paid the cops a fortune. Way more

than we ever greased them. By the sound of it, the whole damn department were in on it.

"No, say it," Slade growled. "I wanna hear it."

Dark sorceress' magick wrung out the answer from Marcus. "To annihilate the Jackals and ascend their throne." He laughed as if this was a damn joke. As if my president's freedom wasn't on the line. As if our club future didn't hang in the balance.

I wanted to do worse than Slade's violent intent stabbing our link. Wanted to make this fucker suffer for weeks on end before burying him six feet under. My hands slid into my cut's pocket, fingering my knuckle dusters.

Marcus' smug smirk lifted higher in triumph. "Danny isn't gonna stop until the Jackals are bones and dust."

Destructive forces surrounded his heart, squeezing, cutting off circulation, stressing his organ to the point it stalled. Mouth gaping, the dirty cop groped at his throat, face flushed red from the strain of sucking in air.

"Boss?" Brows on one of the officers creased.

Aaliyah checked the dirty cop's pulse. "I think he's having a heart attack. Quick, call an ambulance!"

One cop let go of Slade to summon an ambulance.

"Shit, lay him down," Aaliyah instructed one of the cops. I stayed put. Once they lowered him to the ground, she crouched beside him and commenced chest compressions. "Grab me a defibrillator."

The paunchy cop groaned and frothed at the mouth.

Woman would always try to save anyone, even a dirty, rotten police officer. Not gonna happen. I poured dark magick into his heart to stop it from restarting. If they tried the defibrillator, I'd cut the charge to the goddamn device and prevent this prick from reviving.

The final rock of Marcus's heart echoed in my chest from our mind connection. One last pathetic attempt to remain pumping alive and blood. Finally, his heart gave out and he slumped to the ground.

I kept a cool mask over my delighted smile.

Slade flashed teeth, pleased with his triumph.

Aaliyah breathed heavy, working hard to restart the dead cop's heart.

One of the officers brought the defibrillator over, unpacking it charging it, but the thing wouldn't work. "Shit. I think the batteries are dead."

Slade grinned. "God mustn't be smiling on poor, old Marcus. Guess he took one too many bribes."

Irritated at my president's insult, one of the officers grabbed him by the arm. "You're coming with us."

As Slade got dragged away, he threw a devilish grin over his shoulder at us. Barry would have him out in less than a day.

Aaliyah's pumps of Marcus' chest slowed as she tired. The cop with her brushed her aside to take over.

I strengthened the dark magick in the corpse's body to prevent that sucker from reviving. He broke our pact and betrayed the club. Double crossed us by working for Danny. Unforgiveable. This was the kind of man I used to face on the stand. Corrupt, soulless, psychopath. Better off dead. Slade did the world a justice by stopping Marcus' heart. Saved another innocent from his degeneracy.

The dead cop's cigarette butt and pack of smokes caught my attention on the floor. *Winfield Blues.* Why did the brand name stand out to me? A scan of my memory banks found a hit in Alexander Heller's murder file. The type of cancer stick collected from the crime scene with Slade's DNA on it. Except my president smoked rollie cigarettes not Winfield Blue pre-made. If Marcus was behind this raid, it was possible he might be connected to old Heller's murder. A lead that must be investigated and eliminated or brought to bear in Slade's defense trial. I snuffed out the dying cigarette with my sole.

With everyone distracted by Marcus' sudden collapse, I crossed to the bar, snatching a couple of serviettes from behind it. I bent and wrapped both the butt and packet in the paper, stuffing it in the pocket in my cut. DNA evidence to get chemically analyzed at a laboratory and compare to the files kept by officers investing Heller's murder. I had a hunch my findings would clear my president's name, implicate the police in the murder, and trigger an internal investigation.

\*\*\*

BACK AT THE CLUB, Aaliyah and I found Zethan in his office, bent over the books, grooves sunken beneath his eyes, skin a few shades paler than his standard color. Shirt crumpled, suggesting little sleep and crashing at the club. Hair disturbed from repeatedly spearing his fingers through it. He absently rubbed at the worry lines in his forehead as if that would wipe them away. Exhausted from working overtime in the club, shelter, and the Underworld, he didn't hear us enter.

He was clearly oblivious to the news of Slade's arrest, otherwise he would have been all over it, contacting his associates in the police force, getting information on their case against our president and the club.

Zethan would need to assume leadership in Slade's absence, a task he looked too drained for. Something had to give, or he was going to snap. We needed to support him, so he didn't get overwhelmed. Except all our men were busy securing our territory from Wolf invasions. Hell, we might need Alaric back to assist in this instance.

Shit. There was no easy way to say this. Best to just drop the bomb.

Aaliyah slid her hand into mine to give me strength to get it out.

With my free hand, I squeezed the evidence in my cut and announced myself. "Got some bad news, VP."

Zethan glanced up with red eyes, waving at me to come in. "What is it?" His body creaked as he unfolded himself from his chair to come over to Aaliyah and stroke her jaw. "Did a spell go wrong?"

If only. I would have preferred that. Magic had parameters and could be controlled and guided. The fucking cops were a law unto themselves. Uncontrollable like nature. Every reaction had a damn consequence, one that couldn't be contained, redirected, or broken like spell work.

Zethan probed the bond for more answers. "You lost someone?" He folded Aaliyah into his arms. "I'm sorry, baby."

"That crooked cop deserved it." She buried her face in his broad, strong chest, inhaling him. That didn't stop her from doing her duty to try and save him.

Zethan's brows drew down hard, his expectant gaze bouncing to me, demanding answers.

"Slade was arrested by Marcus, our informant." My grip on the new evidence stiffened with worry that the cops might burst into the club any second to confiscate it. "Narcotics planted in Bangers. They raided the place before closing time and searched for hours. Tore the damn place to shreds."

Deep lines cut through Zethan's forehead as he drew our mate in closer, cupping the back of her head. "Fuck. Aaliyah, you tried to warn him, but he didn't listen. Asshole should have gone into hiding."

Hindsight was a bitch. We couldn't turn back time. Well,

maybe there was a spell for that in Thoth's library, some quantum mechanics manipulation of time and space.

Realistically, my efforts were better invested in examining the new evidence collected. Prove Slade's innocence and get the cops off our back on one front, then smash them down on the others. Easy. My plan: drag in a few bent politicians with dirt on them, bribe them into conducting an investigation on the police, and establish rife malfeasance and misuse of police resources within the force. Involved officers would be suspended, possibly terminating them for misconduct. No one would touch us then and we'd be free to go about our business to ruin the Wolves and anyone else for meddling with us.

"What are you going to do?" Aaliyah murmured into my VP's chest, and my body longed for her to cling to me like that.

Zethan tipped her head up to drop a smoky kiss to her lips. "I'll fucking call Barry. Get this shit sorted." She nodded and tucked her forehead to his chest, ignoring the pain nipping at the bond.

Time to unveil what I found and suspected. "I found this at the bar." I removed the wrapped cigarette butt and cigarette packet from my cut, showing it to him.

Zethan's frown deepened. "You taken up smoking?"

I barked out a humorless laugh. "Same brand of smokes found at Heller's murder. It might be a longshot, but what if Marcus is the perpetrator or involved somehow?"

Tears speared Aaliyah's eyes and they glistened with the promise of cold, hard retribution. Zethan wiped them away with a brush of his lips.

My heart crunched at not being there for her. For holding back. Fuck, I was an asshole, but I just couldn't bring myself to do it when she hurt me. Rejection had me frozen. I needed more than just her support for our president and club. I needed her to stay. To lose every single objection to us. Accept us, love us, even if she couldn't be one of us.

Zethan combed his fingers through her hair to soothe her. "Doesn't explain how Slade's DNA was found on the cigarette."

I addressed the possibility. "Unless it was planted."

Zethan clutched Aaliyah tighter around the shoulder. "You think the dirty cop is Hellhound's killer?"

My fingers curled over the evidence. "Yeah, I do."

"Get it investigated ASAP," Zethan ordered.

Aches intensified along the bond, prompting Zethan to release his hold of Aaliyah, and her to move back beside me.

I stuffed what might be crucial evidence in dismissing Slade's case into my cut. "Yes, VP."

"Your next priority is breaking the demonic spells on the Wolves," Zethan commanded, assuming leadership in our president's absence. "We're going to pound them into the ground for this. And anyone else they're working with."

Aaliyah shifted uncomfortably. She'd like nothing more than this nightmare to be over. We all would. I was terrified of what came after that. Her saying goodbye for good. Then what? We all take another woman as a partner? It wouldn't be the same, wouldn't fill the emptiness in our heart, and it sure as shit wouldn't be fair to the replacement.

Fuck, maybe I'd been fucking stalling things to keep her with us, hoping the longer she remained with us, she'd change her mind. Still keeping her captive. Dependent on us for protection. That wasn't fair to her. I was an asshole. Dark Daddy an even bigger one for not letting go of what belonged to him. The day might come where I had to set my dark sorceress free, and I dreaded it with everything I had.

My VP's hand closed around the back of Aaliyah's neck as he drew her close. "Go ahead and get stuck into the spell books, baby. Castor will join you soon. I want a private word." He set a kiss on her head and patted her on the ass to get going.

In passing, she glanced up at me through thick, dark lashes, and my heart stung again.

The minute she was out of earshot, Zethan warned, "You're being an asshole to her. Don't let what happened between you and your ex interfere with your relationship with Aaliyah. She's not the same woman. If you're the reason she leaves, I'll fucking kill you."

I had no doubt he would. Revive me and repeat one hundred times. Nothing I didn't deserve for the way I treated Aaliyah. Zethan was in extra-protective mode since Slade went down. Bearing the burden of accidentally killing our last mate, our VP would do everything in his power to keep this one alive and with us.

"I'll talk to her," I promised.

"Make this right, asshole." Zethan jabbed a finger at me. "We need her. We lose her and we lose everything."

## CHAPTER 33

### Alaric

*She doesn't want you. You're too damaged. Twisted. Scarred. You belong to us. She won't save you.*

Fuck. The demons were getting louder. Distinguishing imagination from reality was getting harder, and I was goddamn losing it. My appointment with the shrink couldn't come soon enough. Daily existence was a struggle, and I didn't know how I'd get through one day, let alone two.

I threw back my third finger from my second bottle of whisky to try and shut the demons up. Alcohol didn't cut it anymore. Nothing did. Nothing but *her*. I needed her touch like a lifeline.

*Call her,* the little voice in my head urged.

*No fucking way.*

Something thumped on the wall. My demons hissed. Dark shadows twisted on my chocolaty walls. Demons taking shape. Startled, I threw my tumbler at them, smashing it, and they laughed manically.

"Leave me the fuck alone!" I shouted, fighting my rising panic.

My heart pounded out of control. They were finally coming for me. I dragged my palms down my unshaven face. I couldn't take any more of this. I needed something to help me sleep. A pill. Anything. Her. I needed her.

The front door burst open, smashing against my wall, and I jolted. Footsteps rumbled inside and my adrenaline peaked. An army of demons. Or Danny and his men here to finish me off. Served me right for failing to perform my perimeter checks. Fuck, I just welcomed death into my damn door.

I whipped my Sig P226 from my cut and aimed it at the doorway, not very firmly. My gun wobbled all over the place. Two demons stepped through the threshold, smiling, all sharp teeth and distorted faces. They'd come to take me with them. A one-way trip to Hell.

"Easy. Put that away, Alaric." The demon reached for me with dark, clawed fingers. "It's just me. Zethan."

Zethan? The demons had never imitated anyone before. Fuck, they sounded like my VP, even smelled like him, and when I blinked, the demon flickered to look like him. A copy. A good one. But I wasn't fooled.

I went to fire off a shot to knock the demon down when the gun flung from my hands as if torn by an invisible force. They were strong. Growing stronger, feeding off my anxiety and taking form. I snapped to grab my backup gun from a sheath above my boots. Too much alcohol in my veins slowed me down, and I fumbled for my weapon.

"Shit," I muttered.

"No, Alaric!" *Her* voice. Another demon forgery playing on my emotions and messing with my head. That wasn't her. She wasn't here. Neither of them were. "Oh, God, you're a mess." The fiend approached me, but the imitation Zethan seized her arm, scanning the mess in my lounge room.

Bottles of whisky and cans of beer sat atop my coffee table. Pizza boxes piled high and scattered on every chair but the one I sat on. One of the demons crunched on broken glass from my tumbler.

"Stay the fuck away from me, demons." I sloppily unlocked the safety on my pistol, waving it around.

"I think he's hallucinating. His pupils are slits. Eyes are droopy. Sleep deprivation." Fake Aaliyah diagnosed me, and I snorted. "He's in a bad way."

"Alaric. Buddy? How long has it been since you last slept?" Demon magick snapped the pin in my gun and killed the firing mechanism. Fuck. I wouldn't be able to fight them off. Two against one with dark magick. Possibly the demons that Danny and his men used to protect themselves.

"Fuck." I dropped the gun to my lap. Fighting them was futile. One way or another, they'd win. "Just kill me. Be done with it. I'm tired of your bullshit."

Shadows drifted across my floorboards, and I flinched at the demons' approach. My body shrank on the sofa as warm hands padded my face, stroking me. I expected dry, harsh alligator skin and claws but was met with silky flesh and short nails.

"Get off me." I tried to push it away, but it clung to me, brushing back my hair, wiping sweat from my clammy face.

"Alaric, come back to me." Her voice sounded so damn real and convincing, every touch alluring and soothing. This demon was good. Real good. "Shit. I shouldn't have stayed away. I should have been here to take care of you. Helped you sleep. That's my goddamn job."

What the fuck? Now it was just toying with me. Aaliyah didn't want me. Broken goods didn't make a good mate. I pinched my closed eyes.

Cool, soothing magick poured into me, clearing away the anxiety, the shadows, teeth, and claws. The thud in my chest eased as my heart rate and breathing came down. Sweat stopped pumping from my pores and dried up on my forehead and the back of my neck. Fog dispersed from my eyes, and Zethan and Aaliyah's face came into sharp contrast. I felt light, floaty, giddy, and free. Hadn't felt this good in over a week.

No demon could do that. They only made me feel shitty and worthless, reminding me what a head case I was. I stared in disbelief at the woman holding onto my arm as if she feared that I'd drown if she let me go.

"Aaliyah?" I was so zonked out from not sleeping and drinking twenty-four seven that I didn't recognize her or my VP.

"Alaric, I'm so sorry I let you down." She curled an arm over my shoulder and tucked my head under her chin. "I'll never do that again." She rocked me in her arms, and I'd never felt anything so restful and blissful.

"Why are you here?" I encircled her waist, breathing her in. Vanilla. Hazelnut. Wild berries. The scent making my demons back away and hiss.

Adrenaline from my fright burned up some of the alcohol in my veins, sobering me up, clearing my vision and mind.

Her falcon called to my hawk, shrieking, whimpering, begging me to unfurl my wings and fly with her. Lose my caging and be free. I nipped at her neck, wanting to snuggle and nest. Build us a fortress of pillows. Sleep. Forget everything. Wake up a new man without the demons and memories.

Zethan came to rest on the sofa's arm and set a heavy hand on my shoulder. "Slade's been arrested. Castor and Aaliyah have broken through the demonic protection. We need you back for reconnaissance."

## LEGACY OF THE GODS

Fuck, a lot had happened in my absence.

"He's not ready, Zethan." Aaliyah protectively tightened her grip on me. "You can't send him out like this."

"Send me out?" I clambered to sit up, untangling myself from her hold. "You want me back on duty?" If there was the smallest possibility of being reappointed to the club, then I wanted in. I was ready. Needed out of this house, away from the goddamn demons holding me hostage. "What do you need?"

Aaliyah's tone dropped to that of a doctor telling her patient they walked before they ran. "You're not well. You're staying here with me. I'll get you clean and on the mend."

Unease prickled at the bond. Zethan didn't like it. He was desperate to put an end to the club's turmoil before it went down in flames.

I wanted my chance to prove myself. Prove that I'd taken the first step to recovery. Prove that I still had what it takes to be a Jackal. I'd take any offer to get out of the house. Out of my head. Far away from the demons constantly haunting me.

That said, I also wanted my mate by my side, nurturing me, sending the fucking demons packing, helping me get my shit together. Every night since Slade benched me, I thought about our date, how we cuddled on the sofa, talking all night long, holding each other. My woman was my salvation from the darkness, come to show me the light, and I wasn't letting her leave.

"I'll give him a few days to get himself sober," Zethan instructed. "Then I'm sending him up. I need intel, and he's the only one who can get close enough to get it for me."

"I don't like this at all," Aaliyah replied, her disapproval taut like a tightwire.

I locked my hand around her wrist, begging her not to ruin this opportunity for me. "Aaliyah, I really need this." I needed to be with my brothers, my support network, my team. Staying at home made me feel weak and useless, and that wasn't helping me get better. Being active, keeping my mind busy, contributing to my club, *that* was the best version of me.

Her eyes met mine, objecting, protective, sympathetic. "Alaric, I don't want you to sink into another episode. You could get hurt. I'd never forgive myself."

I pushed away from her. "Well, this is fucking killing me."

Fuck. I was an asshole. Hurt her. Got aggressive to a woman. If my gran were alive, she'd slap me behind the ears.

I rubbed at my aching, exhausted eyes. "I'm sorry."

"I'll go with him and make sure he's okay if it eases your mind," Zethan cut me off, reassuring her. "We need to know where the Wolves are hiding out so we can take them down."

My mate chewed her lip, considering it, the tautness on the bond not easing. "I'm coming too. I know their clubhouse better than anyone. Where they hide their money, bonds, licenses, everything."

"Absolutely not." Zethan's authority clashed like sword hitting stone. "We don't know if they'll be there. You can draw me a map, though."

That got her back up and she prickled like a hissing cat. "Fuck your map, asshole. I'm going and you're not changing my mind."

My fiery little mate. Shrieks from my hawk supported her courage. I settled my hand over her knee and squeezed, drawing her gaze back to me, softening her fierce glare, and stopping her from talking to our VP like that. Respect for authority was paramount.

Zethan sighed and conceded to her. "Fine. But not until we assess it's safe to raid their clubhouse or launch an offensive."

Aaliyah lost her fiery heat and dropped into nurse mode.

"By the way, who's club medic here? Isn't it my job to determine if Alaric's not in the right frame of mind to go on a mission? 'Cause if it's not my role, what do you want me to do? Sit here and look pretty?"

I puffed out my cheeks, thread my fingers behind my head and sank back into the couch, letting those two go at it. My mate wasn't one to challenge. She'd fight, all claws and beak, to stand as one of the men. A quality I really admired even though it served against me getting back into gear with the club. Confrontations like in the Air Force wouldn't fly, and I'd be penalized for it. That was why I preferred club life where I had input and a vote.

"Fuck, Aaliyah. I don't like this any more than you do, but the club needs him." Zethan loaded his massive arms with five pizza boxes that had been piled on my coffee table. "You've got three days to get him better. Then I want an assessment and he better be ready to fly."

Aaliyah huffed at his ultimatum. Pressure through our connection showed their level of stress from Slade's arrest. Zethan had big shoes to fill, not that I doubted him, but he felt the strain of making the right decision for everyone. We couldn't sit back and keep taking the hits. Offensive action was needed instead of responding to every strike the Wolves launched.

He dumped the boxes on the kitchen counter, flung open my fridge, scanning it and muttering to himself, then slammed it shut. He hunted through my cupboards as well.

"He's got nothing to eat." Zethan bundled the boxes and moved to the doorway. "I'm gonna grab him some shit. Be right back." His footsteps retreated down the hall, and he slammed the front door.

"Come on." My mate tugged me to my feet. "You stink and need a bath."

Moments later, she had me stripped down and in the

bath, where she washed my hair. Her fingers worked my scalp, massaging away my anxiety, silencing the demons, providing my first moment of peace in over a week. This simple act pumped me with hope that I had a chance to get better.

"Lean back," Aaliyah ordered gently, and I did as she commanded, letting her rinse the shampoo from my hair and thread her fingers along my scalp.

I loved the way she took care of me, how my body sang, soared, floated, electrified. How I came alive again at her touch like a dead motor restarted. How she dragged me back from hell and put me back together.

She paid attention to every little detail, cleaning me thoroughly, leaving nowhere unclean. Except my cock and balls. She respected those parts, and I took care of them myself. I studied her, the way she absorbed everything, every cue of my body, every telltale sign that I needed treatment and to be handled with care. Not like me, sizing up threats and dangers, unable to relax.

In moments, my high was overshadowed by the darkness rushing in like an ocean tide. Vulnerability and shame that she saw me at my worst, broken down and a mess. That she pitied me and regarded me as her patient to fix.

Raised in a military family, I was taught to be strong, proud, and tough. Never to show weakness. Men didn't need shrinks. They dealt with their problems by holding their heads high and staying silent. During my darkest times, I relied on my Jackal brothers for support, but lately, it wasn't enough to get me through. I thought I could handle my PTSD by ignoring it, drowning it out with a dampener, thinking it would go away with time. It got worse, to the point where it started destroying me, and Aaliyah showed me that.

Therapy and drugs were my best bet to treat this damn

disorder. Love, reinforcement, and encouragement of my woman, too. I just hoped she stuck around to be my pillar of support. Hoped she shorted out the mess in her heart and mind to make the choice to stay with us.

When she finished washing me down, I clasped her wrist and looked deep into her eyes. "You're my saving grace, angel." I thumbed her jaw and cheeks, relishing the silkiness of her skin, the flutter of her eyelashes, closure of her eyes, her leaning into my touch. "Recommending Slade bench me was the best thing for me. I owe you my life for it."

Her eyes snapped open, and she froze as if taken aback by my admission. Tears glistened her eyes and she swiped them away. "No, it wasn't. I broke you and made you hit rock bottom." Sobs choked her throat, and I shifted my hand to the back of her neck, forcing her head up to look at me. "We should have gone together as a team. I didn't have your blessing or permission. I went above my duty."

"Doesn't matter anymore. You're here now, angel." I leaned over the tub to bring our lips together in mating. Her mouth was the sweetest thing I ever tasted. I drank her in, the warmth and calm she pumped into me. Medicine that brought me back from the brink of destruction. "Get in with me. I want to hold you," I murmured in her ear. "No funny business. I'll be a gentleman." I wasn't up for any of that shit anyway.

She worked her lip in that cute way she did when she thought things over. I half expected her to climb to her feet and leave the room, set a clear boundary that she was my nurse and not my mate. To my surprise, she stripped off her sweater, her blouse, exposing her silken, honeyed skin.

"Replenish the water." Her husky voice went straight to my cock like a jolt from a defibrillator that revived him.

I never drained the bath so fast and refilled it as I did then. Fuck me. She had me mesmerized, hypnotized, my eyes never leaving her. Her swelling bust bounced in her hot, little, lacy black bra as she peeled off her jeans. I licked my lips, aching for her as she slid free of her underwear. My gaze drank her in, memorizing every perfect line of her body, every curve and swell, the small tuft of dark hair over her pussy. Apricot nipples stiffened into peaks as she shed her bra. Despite my gentlemanly intentions, my dick hardened, bobbing for her, desperate to be inside her. She stepped into the burning water, sliding between my legs, and I clasped her waist to steady her as she sank into the heat with me.

After all the adversity, we were bare to each other. Soul to soul. Bird to bird. Mate to mate. This was the woman destined to be mine. Forever. Now that I had her, I was never letting her fly away. If she ran, I'd scout the world to locate her and bring her back to us.

I drew her back to lean on my chest, and scooped water into my palm, letting it dribble over her shoulders. Soon I had her torso wet and slippery.

Wanting to nurture her as she did me, I picked up my bar of soap, sudsing my palms. Her body trembled as I lathered her everywhere I could reach. Rapid breaths dragged in her mouth and her pulse pounded on her neck. Seeking me out, she tipped her head back to kiss me and I met her, tasting her spring flowers, warm rain, and sunset. I left no place untasted. Mouth, neck, ears, jaw, cheeks. My cock ached with desperate need, and I wanted to lift her up and surge into her, but it didn't feel right. Right now went beyond the physical, a connection on a deeper level of intimacy and trust. I finally had her where I wanted her. Where I'd always keep her.

The romantic in me rose to the damn occasion. "I fucking love you, Aaliyah Heller," I murmured against her swollen lips, and she lifted higher to grind her mouth against mine and moan into my kiss. I waited what felt like an eternity, my hawk dropping altitude when she didn't respond.

At last, she put me out of my misery, shifting to face me, coming to rest between my legs. She cupped my jaw, stroking my three-day stubble. "I didn't understand it until this moment. That you rescued me from harm and nursed me back to health." I ground my teeth at her mention of the mugger who hurt her. "That the four of you took me under your wings and protected me, even after I … kinda betrayed you."

I perked up at her admission of infiltration. "So, you admit it now?"

She squeezed my jaw. "Tell anyone and I'll have to kill you."

I chuckled and raised two palms. "Yes, ma'am."

"Smart man." She kissed my nose and my hawk shrieked with delight.

"Dead man if I don't obey my dark goddess." Aaliyah had the power to heal or damage. Infect a person with illness, make their immune system explode with cancer, or their dick drop off from gangrene. I might joke, but I wasn't messing with her if I wanted to get better.

"Don't you forget it." Her teasing eyes hardened with gravity. "Seriously, though. The four of you woke me up from a long sleep, blasted the loneliness in my heart, and sent me into such a lusty, confused spin." She caressed my lips in a tender kiss and held my head firm. "But I finally recognize you. My mate. My hawk. My god."

It wasn't exactly the fucking declaration of love or reciprocation I hoped for, but it would do for now. Because Aaliyah Heller didn't give away her heart easily. Didn't admit her feelings. Kept her cards close to her chest. I'd break down the last remaining wall between us and take my mate. Nothing was holding me back now.

## CHAPTER 34

*A*aliyah

WHAT THE FUCK was I doing stripping naked and bathing with Alaric? Pouring out my heart to him. Telling him that he was my mate. I kept a tight leash on my heart. Guarded her like she was the last tub of chocolate fudge ice cream in the freezer. No one was claiming that bitch.

I didn't expect the guarded, haunted, broken man to declare his love for me. Not so fast, at least. Hell, the words still smoldered in my chest, like the last coals in a fire. They swept me up in the heat of the moment and accompanying emotion.

Did I regret confessing to him? Not one bit. It was the truth. But it had changed things between us that couldn't be undone. That frightened me because there was nowhere to hide now. I couldn't pretend we were two adults insanely attracted to each other, but not right for each other. We went from acquaintances into mate territory, and the leap was staggering and fast, and tripped me out. I wasn't able to hold out on these men when they kept drawing me in. My heart stumbled and fell, and this time I was right there with her, refusing to run any longer. I longed for Alaric's quiet, vigilant, defending presence and his gentle, romantic touch. I was here for him, and I didn't want to leave until he was the best version of himself. The man he wanted to be but didn't know how to when he was broken and in pieces.

Alaric murmured in his sleep beside me, and I reached out to brush his long lashes, the planes of his sharp face, the curve of his plush lips.

My brave, tortured soldier who suffered so much. I wanted to weep for him, hold him and make this all go away. But it had to be on his terms. I needed his permission to erase his memories, and he made it clear he didn't want to put me through that, always defending and protecting me.

Zethan helped me put Alaric to bed because he needed the rest after almost three days of being awake. Sleep deprivation sent him into a sharp, manic spiral. Irritability, increased drinking, and anxiety. Hallucinations of his demons from poor cognitive function. I used my gift to coax him to sleep but didn't need much after our intimate bath relaxed him.

Hours passed as I lay beside him, checking to make sure he didn't stop breathing, didn't choke on his vomit, didn't devolve into an episode. I must have fallen asleep some time before dawn, waking with a start, fearing I lost him and groped for him. He lay where I left him, flat on his back, snoring, sleep free of nightmares. Watching him so peaceful gave me the utmost joy. Seeing him so broken down nearly destroyed me. I never wanted him to sink that low again. He was ready to make a turnaround, he just needed a guiding hand, and I was that for him.

The next morning, he woke early, 5AM, like a typical

military man. He sat on the edge of the bed rubbing his eyes, startling me awake. Light edged at the curtains; Ra's rays of sunlight waking the world.

Oh, no he didn't. He needed more rest. A three-day bender was not getting fixed with eight hours of sleep. "Come back, you need to rest."

He glanced over his shoulder, armed with a handsome smile, looking like a completely different man today. The grin stirred a flutter in my belly. Shadows fell from his features and he had a bit of color.

"Yes, nurse," he said sarcastically to tease me. "Just going to the bathroom. I drank a lot last night."

Twenty or so cans of beer and five bottles of whisky on his coffee table attested to that. God knew how many were consumed last night alone. He reeked of alcohol before I hauled his ass into the bath and scrubbed him clean. I hadn't seen him so unkempt before. Normally he was the image of orderliness. Shined boots, ironed shirt, and clean-shaven. By giving him space, I let him fall through the cracks, and I'd never forgive myself.

Slade rubbed off on me, and I felt protective and possessive over Alaric, not wanting him out of my sight.

"Come back here when you're done." I patted his pillow.

He pointed to his grey t-shirt, then to the thin strips of dawn filtering through the curtains' ends. "I'm afraid I can't. Soldier body clock at work."

Not a problem. I was used to early starts at the hospital. But bed rest was on the menu after three days awake and a manic episode. Nurse's orders. A scan with my powers while he slept told me his nervous system was alert and not functioning optimally, his cognitive function impaired, and cortisol levels high. None of which helped his anxiety, and I needed to avoid him having another bout of hallucinations.

I tried another tactic with him, wondering if enticement

might work. "I'll make you breakfast after you get more sleep. You need it."

"Uh-uh." He swiveled on the edge of the bed and wagged a finger at me. "I make breakfast in bed for my woman. Not the other way around."

Aw, fuck. Could he get any more perfect? Pity I had to park that idea. Wasn't happening while I was in charge of getting him well.

I adopted the voice I used on unruly patients. "Whatever I say goes for the next three days while you're under my charge. Food. Drink. Sleep. Medicine. Got it, soldier?"

His brows popped up. In his world, the male ruled the household, despite his mother teaching him some tips to be a better husband.

"Aaliyah you're my—" he growled at me.

"Alaric, you've been strong for so long." I scrambled out of the sheets to crouch at his back, massaging his neck. "Let me take care of you. It's my duty to get you well if you want to return to the club."

He flinched at my referring to him as a patient. Shit, I didn't mean to make him feel like a headcase, and I slid my arm around his neck, pressing my chest to his back. I didn't see him like that. At. All. Unwell, yes. Depressed at being separated from the club, highly anxious from the court case, prone to PTSD triggers in his environment. Nothing some therapy couldn't fix. He just had to surrender and let me get him back on the straight and narrow. Get him ready for his medical appointments in two days and give him the best chance of recovery.

I leaned my forehead on the side of his head, sifting my fingers through his hair. "When you're better, you can make me eggs and bacon, but not before. Okay? Nurse's order." I softened my voice on the last one.

"That's a promise, angel." He cradled my head in the

crook of his elbow and kissed my head. "Every time you stay over, I'll make you breakfast in bed. Fresh juice, scrambled eggs, bacon, mushrooms. Whatever you want."

I choked up at his pledge because I imagined myself propped by pillows and treated to an enormous plate and him making sure I was well fed.

"I'll hold you to it," I croaked in his ear.

Each day, I was leaning toward taking a risk, staying with the Jackals and making a life here. The longer I stayed with them, I just wanted to fall into their arms. Life with them would be blissful, and I'd be treasured, pleasured, adored, and pampered by four bad boys. I stood on the edge of the mountain, scared to take the leap, needing a nudge to summon the courage. Something told me Alaric, of all my mates, would be the gentle prod I needed to take flight.

I nudged him. "Go on. Get in the shower and clean yourself up. I'll have breakfast ready when you're done."

"I'll agree on one condition." He crooked a finger and lifted my chin with it. Fire kindled in his eyes and began to burn for me. "You sit on my lap and feed me the bacon."

He smirked and lowered his mouth to mine, silencing the argument bound to happen. His kiss scorched me inside, branded me as his, leaving me breathless and struggling to pull two thoughts together. When we came apart, I was ablaze, burning for him right back.

I nudged him harder. "Now you're pushing your luck, buddy."

He groaned as he climbed off the bed. "You play hardball, Aaliyah Heller."

I slapped his ass. "Don't you forget it."

Shivers hurtled through me as he leaned down for one last kiss. I watched him all the way to the bathroom before dragging my smoldering body off his bed.

Twenty minutes later, he sat at his dining table, shaven,

buttoned up in pressed clothes, and smelling like soap. He looked so handsome, so much better than last night, even though I dug the stubble on him. Sexy.

I laid out his breakfast and coffee. Probably shouldn't have given him caffeine after a heavy three days of drinking. Diuretics would dehydrate him and stimulate his adrenals, which he didn't need with his anxiety so high. But it was more a comfort than anything, to make him feel normal, reassure him he wasn't just my patient.

I cupped my mug of tea between my palms to warm them. "How are you feeling today?"

"Better." He ripped at a piece of bacon like a hawk would shred a kill. "Hungover as hell. My shifter will take care of that in an hour or so."

"You seem more like yourself today," I complimented him. He needed to hear it, be reassured of his progress.

"You're a calming influence on me." He took my hand, threading his fingers with mine. "You ground me like the skin of an airplane in a lightning storm."

My eyebrows flipped up at his analogy. "Explain?"

His throaty chuckle stoked the embers inside me. "The skin allows a current like lightning to travel through it and exit at a point where it doesn't interfere with the aircraft's flight."

"Oh." My chest purred like it had a motor in it. I loved knowing the effect I had on him. Loved it even more than he gave me the comparison through his pilot lens of thinking.

He broke apart his bacon but didn't eat it. "My demons also hide when you're near me."

A comment that needed a deeper dive. "Demons?"

"Voices in my head."

Fuck. He heard voices. I hoped he didn't have schizophrenia. "Real or imaginary?"

He shrugged, dropping his food. "No clue. They've been with me since Afghanistan."

It was probably too soon to ask this, but the moment came up, and I couldn't pass up the opportunity. "Can I try and erase the voices and memories?"

"We spoke about this." Alaric's stance hardened. "I don't want to hurt you and infect you with my memories. What if they haunt you and you can't get rid of them?"

"I'll do it for you." Stupid answer.

"No," he growled fiercely, reaching out with the speed of a hawk to clasp both my wrists tightly and pin them to my sides. "I've got this."

I wasn't frightened by his intensity. In fact, I was moved by his tenacity to protect me at all costs. The consummate soldier.

"If you change your mind…" I played it casual, left it up to him, leaving the topic be for now. We'd revisit in a couple of weeks, maybe.

He let me go, and we sat in silence for a bit, not eating, him staring at the olive-green tablecloth.

Shit. I'd gone too far. Uncomfortable, I nibbled at my bacon.

Alaric sipped at his coffee, and I mapped the muscle of his jaw and throat. My stomach clawed with the urge to be closer, closer than we'd ever been. Earlier, he tried to bargain with me to feed him bacon. Tempted to feed my hungry mate and fulfil his request, to turn things around, I shifted off my seat, claiming his waiting lap, going well beyond my duty as nurse. I wanted to give him some small semblance of happiness in a world shadowed by nightmares. Encouraged by his pleased rumble, I brought the strip of meat to his lips, prompting a warm smile. He licked at it and nibbled at the edges, but the best bit was that he saved some for me like his hawk feeding and nurturing his mate. Ridiculously sweet!

Fuck it. I didn't care anymore. Last night alarmed and frightened me and I never want to go back there again. He needed to know he wasn't just my patient, that I didn't cozy up to him because I pitied him. I wanted to be in his arms, reviving the damaged man, breathing new life into him the way only Isis' avatar could. He already came a long way since last night, showing signs of the man who took me for a ride up the mountain. A few days wouldn't make him whole, but it was a start, and therapy combined would help him handle his inner demons.

I scooped some scrambled eggs onto his fork and fed him, enjoying the simple pleasure it gave me.

"New rule." Alaric tapped me on the butt. "I cook and you feed me like this. Every. Single. Time. No ands, ifs or buts."

I leaned my head on his shoulder and laughed. "Deal."

He didn't exactly get his wish. Every time I fed him, he did it back to me, ensuring I was satiated too. We kept that ritual up until both our plates were empty. Then he circled his palms on my back and I caressed the hair at the back of his head. I wanted to kiss him, but felt it might be too soon, and gave him the space he needed.

While I couldn't sleep last night, I planned out activities to keep his mind busy, to stop him from drinking, fretting, or succumbing to his demons. That all went out the window with his distracting, deep gazes into my eyes. Of all my mates, he was content with silence, our bodies doing all the communicating.

"What do you want to do today?" I dragged my nails along his nape. "Home-based activities." I set the ground rule. No riding after his heavy drinking and lack of sleep. I wasn't putting us in danger. "Want to watch TV, play cards or dance a little more?"

"Strip poker," Alaric said it so deadpan that I spat out a laugh.

"You're for real, aren't you?"

"Yeah." He gave me the cutest smirk.

Strip poker could lead to naked bodies, touching, more kissing, and sex. As much as I wanted to know what it was like to bed him, the timing wasn't right, and I didn't want to lose the ease we had with each other by moving too fast when he wasn't well. But … maybe it might get him to relax, tire him out and I could get him back in bed. Worth a shot. Plus, if he enjoyed it, if it took his mind off the last week, then I was up for it. I just had to be wary of the winning streak Zethan warned me about.

My body groaned as I jumped off his lap, instantly missing our connection simmering with his heat as I moved away. "Get the cards and I'll be back."

## CHAPTER 35

### Aaliyah

I RUSHED into Alaric's room to throw on a few more layers of clothing that Zethan brought around for me last night, knowing I was staying a few days. *Hah. Let's see Alaric beat me now.* I wasn't normally a cheater, but I didn't trust that he couldn't see through the cards with his Horus eye. I mean, he could see a hidden moon in the Andromeda galaxy with his powers!

Alaric shuffled the cards as I came back out, and I was tempted to shove them aside and go back to sitting on his lap and curling up there all morning.

"Oh, come on." Alaric shook his head and chuckled as I sat opposite him, hands and fingers clasped, waiting for him to deal me my hand. "How many shirts are you wearing?"

I answered with another question. "How do I know you don't have x-ray vision with that eye?"

He shook his head again and finished his last shuffle. "You're a cheat, Aaliyah Heller."

I loved the way he said my name. Like a prayer on his lips.

"Cunning, like my goddess." I winked, setting my hand on his knee, needing the contact. "I saw the way you play billiards. You kicked Zethan's ass. I need all the head starts I can get."

"I'm gonna kick your ass and get you naked for this." He laughed, husky, warm, and content. It was the most beautiful sound, and my falcon responded with a call to his hawk, and I felt it graze my cheek with its wing. With each passing minute he returned to the man I'd first met, and I know I had everything to do with that.

I flicked my fingers at him. "Less talk. More dealing cards, mister."

He dealt the first hand, and I gathered my cards, trying not to frown at the shit hand he allocated me. Four, six, ace, and two.

I must have had the worst poker face, or the bond betrayed me because he laughed, and teased, "Want to fold already?"

"Hell, no." I didn't surrender so easily. I gestured at him to hand me another card. He hit me with one. *Shit.* A ten. There went my hand. I folded my spread and took off one layer of clothing, tossing it on the floor.

Alaric snatched it off the floor, swirled it over his head, and rubbed it up against his chest, pulling some dance moves. Ginuwine's song *Pony* started to play in my head. The other avatars told me he could be quite the party boy when in a good mood. That part of him started to shine through, and it pleased me that he felt better already. Another scan of his body told me his cortisol levels were much lower, his heartbeat steadier, his mind clearer. Not out of the woods, but good signs so far.

"Yeah, yeah," I said, smiling. "Quit your sexy, distracting moves and deal the next hand."

He tossed the shirt on my head and winked. "Be prepared to lose and strut around naked for me, Heller."

An hour later, I'd lost the next five games and he had me down to my bra and jeans. Strategy on my part to distract him and regain a little ground. Didn't work very well. Sure, his gaze dipped to my breasts, my naked torso and belly, and he licked his lips. But my plan worked against me. The man was a machine, and I should have known better. He was a pilot, a hawk shifter goddammit, with unbeatable concentration. Lives were at stake when he flew soldiers, and he couldn't afford distractions, and nothing topped his laser focus. My ego bruised with every game I lost, even the ones he tried to throw so I didn't feel so bad.

"See." I poked him in the chest. "This is why I wore extra layers. I knew you'd win! Nothing can break your concentration, Sky god."

He grabbed my hand, lifting it to his lips, leaving a sweltering single kiss on my knuckle. "Had plenty of downtime in the Air Force."

I bet. Plenty of time to hustle his fellow serviceman.

By the time he had me down to my underwear, he graciously threw his hand down, tapping out.

"Admitting defeat?" I cracked up a cheeky eyebrow.

"Truce." He gave me the sexiest, easiest grin, and I lost my breath at how it changed his edgy face. Seeing him guard down, without his natural vigilance, filled me with pure pleasure.

I tapped my nails on the table. "You went too easy on me."

"I can't slam my mate." He packed up the cards into a neat deck and shuffled them. "The rest of the club, yes, especially for money."

I chuckled and shook my head. "I'm rusty and need practice. Haven't played since the Wolves."

He bundled me out of the chair and cradled me in his arms, preserving my modesty, despite having seen me naked last night.

"We can rectify that, angel," he seductively whispered into my ear. "Make a poker champion out of you."

I playfully shoved at his chest. "Yeah, then I'm coming for you. Getting you in your underwear!"

His smile lit up the room, a complete change from the haunted, dark man last night. I squirmed closer, closing the space between us, wanting no more to exist. His earthiness called to me, and I sank into it. This man, the lost, broken soldier, needed me to shine my light to steer him out of his darkness. The trapped bird longing for freedom. I would lead him to safety and rescue him as he did for me.

"Get your clothes on, angel, before I get you completely naked and on your back." He patted my ass.

Tempting, but not happening. I climbed off him to get the pale pink shirt and throw it over me. Dressed, I stood by him, playing with his hair, gliding along his smooth jaw, behind to his nape, wanting to touch him everywhere.

He dragged me into his arms and carried me to the couch, setting my legs over his lap, where he caressed me. Hell, here he was looking after me, when he needed to be cared for. He made me feel the safest that I felt in years.

I wanted to curl up together and talk, share secrets, break him open and discover all his mysteries, and give him mine. Fall asleep together and wake up next to him. Heck, I wanted him to be my man. Not yet though. Not until he was ready. Because I was sure as hell ready.

"Will you come with me to the shrink on Thursday?" He rubbed the top of my thigh, and I held back a moan. "I'd feel better with you there. In case I have an episode."

I'd already seen him at his most raw and vulnerable. But exposing himself to a complete stranger was a whole different ball game. Appreciation melted me a little more that he wanted me by his side when he peeled back more of the layers to his trauma. I was sure there was more he didn't show me in his memory. When I'd touched him, I'd seen the worst of it, not the half of it. Many layers of the onion needed peeling back and shedding.

"Sure. Whatever you need." Whatever gave him comfort. I traced his jaw, his throat, the line of his muscled shoulders, desperate to caress every inch of him.

"Good. That eases my mind." One set of fingers locked tighter on my thighs, the other coming up to the back of my neck, lightly kneading.

He leaned across me to kiss me, his lips straddling the line of gentle yet teasing, making me slant in, chasing more. His hand rested over my hip with a comforting weight. Flicks of his tongue along my bottom lip sought entry and I parted for him. Slow, sensual motions explored every part of me, tasting me, pleasuring me. The contrast of his firm mouth on mine was completely different to my other mates, plunging their tongues into me, fucking my mouth. Delicate teasing brushes worked me into a wild heat, and I locked my arms around his neck, my thighs over his. Arousal built as our tongues locked and played, my pussy hollow and aching, needing to be filled.

The moment I dreaded came when he pulled away, panting. "Not yet, angel." He captured a handful of hair, gently tugging. "Not like this. When I'm better, I'm all yours."

He was right. This wasn't the right time. He needed to channel all his energy on getting better and not consummating things with me. I nodded, lost to the memory of his tongue gliding over mine, yearning for the next time.

His fingers worked along my neck and lower scalp. "I

don't know what would have happened if you and Zethan didn't bust in last night and save me. I can't thank you enough." He rocked me in his arms gently. "Angel, you're my rock, my stability, my anchor when times get rough. I don't want to lose you. I need you so fucking much."

I clutched his arms, leaking out a whimper from his admission. No one ever needed me this much. I felt buzzed to be the one to bring him back from the edge. I got the same thrill treating patients, but this was different. Special. More meaningful. This man was beginning to mean a lot to me, and I wanted to be his support as much as he was mine. And, shit, I didn't want to lose him either. Our journey together was just starting. We hadn't had much time together and I was lapping up this precious moment with him.

I know I should have played it safe, not jumped into his arms, fed him bacon, encouraged these affections, because it could impact my ability to mend him. But spending time with this man made me happy, and I hadn't felt this way in a long time. He looked at me like I meant the world to him. When he smiled, my body sang, floated, and I felt giddy under my breast.

We cuddled for ages, my heart elated that we broke through our difficult start and moved into this natural, comfortable rhythm. Breakthroughs were happening today for more than one person.

Sometime later, Alaric lifted me off the sofa and set me on my feet, taking my hand. "C'mon, you're going flying again." He towed me to the back door, opening it for me like a true gentleman. "You need the practice for what's to come. And you never know when you might need to get away in a hurry."

God, he was always thinking of me. Protecting me. He was right, though. War was coming and I should be ready.

We never knew what Danny and his cohort were up to, so we should go in with surprises of our own.

"And I want you in my arms again the next time we're airborne." He sealed that promise with a searing, sweet kiss. "Not yet. I'm not feeling a hundred percent and my navigation is off."

A shudder pulsed through me. Urgent. Needy. My falcon wanted to launch herself and get up there with him. Right. Now. But I respected his need for space and time when last night had been difficult.

He lifted me vertically, carrying me to the center of his yard, a neat space with groomed grass and a modest garden.

"Stretch those wings," he instructed, setting me on my feet. "They get stiff if you keep them locked in your back for too long."

I thrust those babies out of my back. God, it felt good to release them. My back had started to ache, and I thought it was from tension, but the minute I released my wings, the ache went away.

"Up you go." He gave my ass a gentle tap. "Not too high. Neighbors. Just get familiar with using your wings."

My falcon wanted to stick to his side, fly by her mate, not understanding why he couldn't come with her. I let her go, drifting across his manicured backyard, careful not to topple over his barbeque, chair, and tables.

"Good." I basked in his praise. "Try spinning. We'll tackle swooping another time when we can get higher."

I wasn't quite sure how to do that and edged my body sideways, knocking over his clay bird watering stand.

"Shit, I'm sorry." I landed and crashed a palm to my forehead.

"It's okay. It didn't break." Alaric righted it and urged me to keep going. "It's easier to spin in the air. Follow the currents. Let them guide you. Tilt the wing on the side you want to twist to."

Yeah. Okay. Natural for a Sky god, not me. And what currents? I was too low for that. But I took the lessons where I got them.

I twirled awkwardly, my feet hitting the grass, Alaric never straying from my side, arms out to steady me. Just like he did in the air. Every time I crashed landed—not very hard due to my limited height—he was there to pick me up. He positioned his body like a weapon beside me, poised to ward off any threats. Protector, soldier, and mate. His touch kept sending me into a tailspin, and I struggled to get airborne. He folded me into his arms, releasing his own wings, tucking us both in the safety and comfort of them.

Several things became startlingly clear through this exercise. He'd always catch me wherever I stumbled and fell. In the Wolves, I was on my own, and I wasn't used to having someone support me, watch out for me, willing to work together. As a hawk shifter, he understood the value of letting me leave the nest, learning to fly on my own, encouraging me to fly away, knowing that I'd always return to him. In that moment, I knew with blinding clarity that I didn't want to flee. I wanted to stay and be with the four of them. Have the love I deserved. Because this bird wanted a nest, a home, a family.

Alaric must have sensed it and kissed the side of my face and whispered, "Say you'll be mine, angel. Don't go."

"I'm yours." I kissed him back, soft at first, growing with heat, unable to get enough of him. "I'm not leaving. Ever."

He crushed me to him and peppered me with kisses everywhere.

\*\*\*

THREE DAYS LATER, Zethan returned to Alaric's house for his report. Alaric stood straight to attention, sober and clean, feeling better than he had in months.

"How's he doing?" Zethan questioned me.

"Much better." I smiled, closing my fingers over Alaric's, drawing his hand to my side. "His thoughts are clear and positive. Reactions agile and fast. He's slept every night with no nightmares or episodes."

"That's great news, buddy." The VP clapped Alaric on the arm. "How do you feel?" What he really asked was whether Alaric was up to going out to scout for him. Whether he could handle it without losing his shit.

"I'm not entirely there yet, but I'm headed there," Alaric replied. "Had my first sessions with the shrink and I go back next week."

"Good." Zethan stroked his stubbled jaw.

"I'm ready to get back to duty, sir," Alaric admitted. "Ready to locate the Wolves' hideout."

My grip on his hand tightened with reservation. We'd talked at length about this. Risks. Perils. Consequences. He had to do this for his club and brothers. For me. To protect us all.

The Jackals had returned fire by burning the Wolves' drugs and manufacturing premises. Retribution shots returned with the murder of our distributor, Slade's arrest, and the raid of the Jackal's bar. Explosions that wouldn't be the last. Hunting down the Wolves' hideout was critical to winning the war between the clubs and ending it. Alaric wanted to serve his club as he'd served his country. Protect and defend. It was what he was born to do. The reason the Sky god chose him. The pilot who shifted into a hawk, scanning the sky for danger, providing the warning we needed.

"I'll wait for you outside." Zethan moved in to steal a quick kiss from me, then gave us space, retreating to wait by his bike.

My mouth locked with Alaric's. Desperate. Urgent. Needy. Worried this might be our last kiss. My arms bolted around his neck, and he lifted me up to meet him, never wanting to let go. In the last three days, my mate was torn apart and put back together by me. Rescued. Brought back to life. He would have been dead without Zethan and me. He poured all his gratitude into his kiss, the palm he caressed my side with, the licks and nips of my neck, the fingers he knotted in my hair.

In that moment, I felt his heart torn on what to do. Stay with his mate in our little nest versus getting back on duty with his club. Too much was on the line, including our safety, and he'd do anything to protect me.

He smiled when he released me. "See you when I get back, angel."

## CHAPTER 36

### Zethan

I DIDN'T FUCKING like this one bit. Hated using Alaric for my selfish gains. With Slade gone, I made the goddamn call as VP, since we didn't have anyone else for this job and it had to be done. For all our sakes. Otherwise, we were going down with this sinking ship. Destination jail, death, fucking extinction.

Alaric rode ahead of me on his Chieftain, snaking along the narrow, winding roads. Castor took up the rear, guarding me and maintaining his protective spell. Misty, dark magick swarmed around us, concealing our group from vigilant eyes as we moved into Wolves' territory in the Blue Mountains.

The temperature dropped the higher we climbed into the mountains, biting through my leathers and sinking down my neck, nipping at my chest. Heat from my bike's engine combated some of the chill, but not enough, and I thickened my skin, adopting my hellhound's hide to keep warm.

Cars, buses, and bikes drifted by in the single lane opposite us. No sign of the Wolves so far, but Alaric was alert and cautious. Sliding into their territory uninvited and unwelcome could go very badly. A risk worth taking if it saved our club. No war was won without danger.

Our whole club operation was one big gamble, our drug production, murder, and bribery potential downfalls if the cops obtained evidence to convict us. All they'd been able to produce so far was fabricated bullshit, and that wouldn't stick in court, unless the judges were in on it too. We had to make sure they weren't, getting Castor to dig up dirt on them and deploy bribes, or go in heavy as an enforcer, ensuring a favorable judgment.

Alaric flicked his indicator on as he took the turn we'd mapped out, two miles from our stakeout point where he'd shift into his hawk and sail over Wolf territory, hunting them down. Aaliyah had worked her magick on him, giving him a complete turnaround. He was more alert and on the ball than ever. The lack of alcohol cleared his mind and sharpened his senses.

Wary of surprises around the bend, I edged my bike closer to his with Castor right behind me. Nerves crackled on my end of the bond and Castor remained on edge.

Not Alaric, though. Grateful waves lapped at his edge. Our road captain was glad to be back on his bike and serving the club, where he thrived and belonged. I was happy to have him back. Things weren't the same without him. With the band of avatars a man down, we felt incomplete, the way we felt before Aaliyah came into our lives with screeching, burning tires.

Slade should be here with us. Things were a lot quieter around the club without him, his dominant authority and banter sorely missed. Asshole would be dirty about missing out on scoping out the Wolves. He'd get over it, though. In three years.

Seventy-two hours later and my president was still being held in detention by the cops, despite the club's solicitor's best efforts to get him out on bail. In my time with the police, they could only hold suspects for six to twenty-four hours, unless granted exceptional circumstances by a judge to extend the imprisonment time to collect more evidence. That left them with a maximum of one more day to hold him until they released him on bail.

Critical time the club didn't have to waste. Each moment squandered gave the Wolves another edge over us. Motherfuckers were probably partying and celebrating my president's downfall with their shady buddy. With Slade gone, I had to take offensive action to strike back. Locate the new goddamn Wolves' lair, smoke them out, and ice every last one of them. Payback they deserved for what they did to the Jackals and the women they abused for their porn operation.

Miles ticked down as we inched closer to our destination, a sheltered spot on the east of Katoomba, where we'd park and safeguard Alaric while he scanned for our enemies. I'd not let him do this alone in his vulnerable state. Aaliyah reassured me that he was doing better, and I valued her opinion, but the slightest thing might trigger his PTSD. If that happened, he had his brothers to extract him and drag him to safety.

Alaric pulled into the remote area, parking his bike on a dirt road off the main beat. Isolated enough for him to strip naked and shift into his hawk and get airborne. He disappeared from view quickly as the forest concealed his ascent. Normally he would have pulled out his whisky flask and swallowed down half before he went up. Time with Aaliyah changed him. He was a new man. Refreshed. Restored. Renewed.

"Let's settle in," Castor said, removing a whisky flask from the back of his bike, and uncapping it. We toasted Alaric, swapping the canteen, taking the edge off our nerves.

"Slade was right. We should have made a move against the Wolves sooner," I admitted to our enforcer. "Saved ourselves from the catastrophe we're fucking in."

In typical Slade style, he wanted to annihilate the Wolves for attacking us, show our strength and menace. Teach other clubs not to fuck with us or die. In hindsight, maybe that was the smarter move. But Castor and I talked him out of it, convinced him that it was safer to get proof the Wolves were behind this. Fuck that shit. Enough was enough. The dirty cop Slade offed admitted the Wolves were behind this. It might not be concrete proof, written or photographic evidence that a cop would process and investigate, but it was enough for me.

"Hindsight's a bitch, man." Castor took another swig. "None of us could have predicted the extent to which they went to fuck with us. By all accounts, they've been planning this awhile. Possibly since the police targeted Slade as a suspect in Heller's murder."

The longer we let this shit go on, the worse decimation the club faced, and that would not happen on my watch. I'd take full responsibility, and Slade could take it up with me when he got out on bail. If he wanted to smash my face in for disobeying an order, bring it. I'd be happy to rearrange his face for slapping our woman's ass.

Rocky, forest-covered mountain landscape snapped into my vision as Alaric shared his hawk vision with us via his Sky god gifts. The township of Katoomba below with its rolling, steep hills, and picturesque views overlooking *Ngula Bulgarabang Regional Park* and the *Three Sisters* lookout. Traffic poured in from Sydney, tourist buses and visitors visiting the sightseeing town. Observations we asked him to share with us so we could keep track of him if he got in trouble.

His Horus eye honed in on the town, scouring it for any signs of the Wolves. Patient and focused, he searched for almost an hour, not giving up, until he found a lone Wolf riding through town. He tracked him as he went from business to business, walking out with packets of cash. Extortion money. Dirty, rotten motherfuckers were squeezing local businesses.

Angry heat flashed along the bond like a detonated bomb. Alaric wanted to swoop the prick and slash out his eyes and throat. Return every dollar to the hustled business owners. I wanted to capture the Wolves' territory hardcore. Protect the citizens from criminals like these.

We never did that kind of shit in our town. Never shit in our own backyards. Slade's father started the Jackals to fight a bunch of corrupt councilors that banded together to pressure farmers to sell large tracts of land to the council to subdivide and sell off, giving them kickbacks. Our original president gathered men into his club to protect his town and residents against the corrupt officials breaking the law. Disillusionment with local politics encouraged him into the outlaw side of the club, trading in guns to raise money to fund legal battles against the assholes in town. As the club got bigger, more powerful, better funded, we ran those pricks out of town, saving all but three farms. We never looked back since.

Slade was the ambitious one in his family, wanting to expand the club, our presence, territory, and stature in the Australian league. God complex, following his patron Set, who screwed over Osiris to ascend to the title of King of Egypt.

Another hour later, the lone rider headed west into the

neighboring town of Leura, where he pulled off the Great Western Highway, into the back streets.

"We're getting closer. I can feel it prickling over my skin like claws," my enforcer murmured.

Nervy, I paced alongside my bike, waiting until Alaric dived closer, stumbling on three more bikes parked outside a bar, and another ten out back. Ten minutes away from their clubhouse. Out in plain sight. Not even concerned about hiding from us. Ballsy goddamn bastards.

"He found them." Castor fist pumped and chuckled darkly.

Two of the Wolves emerged from the bar, jostling to carry a square, grey device that looked like a spotlight.

"What the fuck is that?" I snapped.

"I don't like the look of it." Castor's eyes flicked back in his head as he performed a scan of his communication pathways. When he came to, panic scolded the link, and he barked, "Fuck, Military tech. Get him out of there!"

What the fuck were the Wolves doing with that kind of gear?

"Return to base," I communicated to Alaric and threw myself on my bike, waiting for his return.

Alaric's bond wound tight as he looped away from the Wolves' bar.

To Castor, I ordered, "Check for whatever other tech they've got. We need to know what we're going up against."

Castor nodded and his eyes rolled back as he performed further scans.

Fire seared our connection and Alaric let out a shriek. Every muscle cramped and burned, and he dropped altitude as he struggled to maintain his low course. The Wolves hit him with another blast that melted him from the inside. Nausea, headaches, contractions hit with more intense force. Our road captain crashed to the pavement and rolled, losing his feathers and hawk, shifting back to his naked, human skin. Blisters weeped and raged on his flesh.

"What the fuck happened?" I shouted.

"Direct energy weapon," Castor whispered as Alaric's hawk glanced up at the barrel pointed at him. "Designed to scramble riot crowds, confuse and muddle them, make them sick, burn them. Fuck." Helpless and distraught, he wiped his jaw.

Christ. The Wolves were onto us. Ready and waiting, guns aimed and deploying advanced tech on my men. And they had Alaric. He'd already been captured and tortured once. I'd not let that happen again to my fragile soldier.

"Block that fucking thing. We're going in," I told Castor as I swirled my finger, calling on an Underworld portal, golden light tearing through the space in front of me. I lunged through the window to rescue my downed man.

Drums pounded in my head, my thoughts jumbled, and I lost all sense of direction. Contractions gripped every muscle in a painful stiffness that held me on the spot. Bitterness hit my gut and it swirled, angry, hot, and sour. Fire raged along my skin as if the sun were right above me. Intense pain sent me screaming to my knees.

Castor thudded beside me, clutching his head, barely able to lift his arm and deploy a dark magick spell.

Alaric moaned and rolled on the ground twelve feet from us.

I crawled to him, scraping my skin open, scaling the pain. More energy waves hit me, and I stumbled to keep upright. A knee came out of nowhere, knocking me in the chin and I rolled to my side. Blood gushed from my nose. Black dots blinked in my vision.

"Tie 'em up and get 'em downstairs," another Wolf ordered.

Two more men stomped to my road captain, bound his

hands, stuffed a black hood over his head and dragged him away.

A safety clicked and I blinked, trying to find the barrel to disable it. I managed to kill the mechanism a split second before the prick pumped a bullet into my brain.

"Fucking prick." I crawled to my hands and knees, fighting the urge to vomit. Fog descended on my brain, and I lost my thoughts. I needed to kill that goddamn machine so I could think fucking straight.

Two Wolves bundled Alaric into a dark van and slammed the rear door shut. Another punched Castor's cheek and bound his wrists.

*Osiris, if you can hear me, do something,* I called to my patron.

Clarity snapped in my mind as my god blocked the effect of the weapon.

The dick restraining Castor started to choke, grabbing his throat. Dark sparks flew off him as if two forces clashed. Hazy symbols painted the air between Castor and the Wolves. Fuck. They were fighting our magick and protecting the Wolves. Raising a damn shield that my enforcer's magick couldn't penetrate. Demons snarled in my head and whispered dark thoughts. Convincing, lulling, hypnotic growls that aimed to deter me.

Castor tapped at the side of his head as if impacted too. Then he staggered to his knees, releasing a mass of dark clouds. The device crashed to the bar's steps. Metal crunched and glass smashed.

"Fuck, Viper, you broke it," one of the Wolves snarled. "Danny is gonna make you pay for that."

The lapse in attack from their weapon boosted my strength and mindset. I climbed to my feet and death choked the bastard. My hold didn't last long. The demons turned their full force on me, redirecting my magick at me. My throat closed off and I gasped to breathe. The more I tried to fight them, they deflected or absorbed my powers, tightening their grip on my throat. I cut my magick and my airways opened up.

Fuck. I had to give Castor enough time to deploy his spell and separate them from the Wolves. Then every last one of those mutts would die at my hand. I tried to drain the demon's power with my death powers. Dark, misty hands clamped around my neck and choked.

"They're too powerful." Castor snagged my arm. "Open a portal."

We hadn't anticipated this move. Didn't bring Castor's spell with us to tackle the damn demons. Our mission to scout for the Wolves' location turned to shit when they fired at my road captain and taken their first casualty. If we left him, we left him to die. Not on my fucking watch.

"No, I won't leave him," I croaked, amping up my magick, fighting the force holding me.

The demon wrangled on my neck, crushing it, the tendons snapping from the pressure. I called on more Underworld magick, weakening it enough to get free. The vapor that grasped me shrunk and hissed like water boiled to steam. Its dark power throbbed within me, and I kept draining it until it crackled and vanished. That one act sapped me, and I hunched over, straining to breathe and stand.

"If we don't get out of here and get the spell, we're dead too." Castor hiked an arm under my shoulder to steady me.

Fuck. We had to get the spell and reinforcements. I cranked open a portal and Castor dragged me away from the scene. Away from my man. I hated leaving him behind. Running like a fucking coward. But if we stayed to save him, we'd both be taken too, and the club wouldn't stand a chance to rescue any of us.

*Aaliyah, forgive me for doing this.* I should have listened to her. Never should have come.

As Castor and I burst into his office, leaning on his desk for support to recover, I prayed to the gods Alaric was still alive by the time I returned.

# CHAPTER 37

## Aaliyah

ZETHAN AND I CUDDLED, stony-faced, distraught, waiting while Castor performed a location spell for Alaric. The Wolves removed him from the bar and hid him somewhere else when we returned with more might to disable the demons deflecting our magical attacks.

Candles and herb potions from Castor's spell enabled me to curl up on Zethan's lap. He ran a palm down my spine, sparking my unraveled nerves.

Fear needled down my spine at how Alaric was coping, *if* he was coping at being held captive. I felt sick to even consider what my brother did to my fragile, damaged mate. If he tortured and hurt Alaric, then I wished the same fate for Danny. Slow, drawn-out punishment over weeks, using every device the Jackals had on offer.

Every muscle in my body ached and cramped. Bile churned in my hollow stomach. Frayed nerves sparked with worry. Anguish sank into the depths of my soul. I sucked in a shaky breath as I searched the bond for him. Beaten unconscious. Bleeding. Aching. He needed me to save him. Needed his brothers to free him. *Fuck.*

"I shouldn't have left him." Zethan kept beating himself up over the turn of fate. "I should have done everything I could."

"He's not dead yet, asshole," Castor threw back. "Let's focus on finding Alaric, getting him out, then punching ourselves in the face."

I already went off my head at Zethan, my throat still burning from screaming, sobbing, and cursing him and my brother. Zethan asked too much of Alaric. He wasn't ready, no matter what he said. None of them were prepared by the sounds of it, the Wolves always one fucking step ahead.

The prospect of returning to the club thrust Alaric out of his darkness. That, and being with me. Endless hours of soothing, cuddling, nurturing, massaging, and rehabilitation lifted his spirits, curbed his alcohol intake, encouraged him to open up more. Massive signs of improvement. Attending his first psychological appointment was another milestone on his road to recovery. With his kidnapping, my mate took one step forward to be thrust two back by the fucking universe and gods.

When Zethan returned after giving Alaric space to heal, I didn't have the heart to crush Alaric and deny him getting back to what he loved. I already cut him off from his support network and sent him spiraling into depression and helplessness. Blame on his kidnap rested on me, and I fucking hated myself for it. Tears burned a path down my cheeks as I scraped my hand over my forehead and stinging, aching eyes, red from all the crying.

Castor added one of Alaric's hairs that we pulled from his pillow to the candle, and the flame soared, absorbing his energy. He tipped the wax into the bowl, mixing it with other ingredients I hadn't kept track of because my brain was skittish and glitchy.

Lost to my thoughts, I picked at my nails. Goddess, I did everything to keep these men at bay, battling off every attempt to let them into my heart. At every turn, they fought me, weakened and broke through my battlements, sneaking inside to claim their queen trapped in the castle. I wrongly judged them as heartless, ruthless killers. But they showed me their compassion, sense of community and family, their resilience in disastrous times.

Mysterious, dominant Castor caught me first, showing me kindness, patching me up after the mugger beat me, then again during my captivity. Slade used his devilish charm, his family values, his desire to protect me to win me over. Zethan hooked me with his passion to protect and support battered women, giving them an opportunity to rebuild their lives.

And Alaric, the most difficult of my mates to bond with. We had an up and down ride together. Bumpy. Stormy. Untrusting. Conflicted and damaged himself, he sensed the struggle in my heart, knew when it was all too much for me. Took me for a ride up the mountaintop to bring me back down. Kissed away my worries and made my heart beat again after being dead for so long. The loyal, steadfast soldier and defender.

Being with Alaric these last three days, starting with the steamy, intimate bath, melting into him, being present with him, naked, bared, open, changed everything. Our relationship evolved into something so much more than patient and nurse. Friend, confidant, and lover without the sex. We agreed to wait until he was better for that step. Just as I accepted him as my mate, he was taken from me. No one took what was mine. Not Danny. Not the mystery fucker. Certainly, not the gods.

Castor dripped the ingredients onto a map and rubbed his hands. He waved me over and Zethan lifted me to stand, tugging me over to the bench. The waxy liquid swirled on the map, shaping into an arrow that tracked along the map, stopping on a location.

The enforcer slammed his forefinger on the spot. "That's where they're holding him."

Zethan slapped him on the shoulder. "Get the crew ready to go in there and send these fuckers to their maker."

As Castor moved to the door and opened it, Robbie was waiting on the other side, carrying a FedEx package.

"Boss, this got delivered for you." Robbie progressed into the room and held it out for Zethan.

My stomach turned over and I clutched it. Fuck. This was a warning from Danny of what would happen if we went up against him.

Zethan's face whitened as he clutched the box to his broad waist. Apprehension dragged grooves through his forehead as he ripped open the box and plastic wrapping. Red writing that could have been blood scrawled across a small card.

*You're not welcome in our territory, Jackals. Bring back my men before yours dies.*

Beneath the card, a gray, bloodied, severed finger promised our undoing. Alaric's finger. They'd hurt him. After everything he went through, he was the last person to deserve this. I sent him to his damn death.

"Oh, God, Alaric." My stomach tipped and I lurched behind Zethan's desk and vomited.

Castor came to my side to stroke my back. "He's still alive. We can save him. The spell wouldn't have worked otherwise."

Not much comfort knowing my mate was hurt, scared,

and triggered all over again. I had to do something. Call Danny and beg him to let Alaric go.

"Robbie, get the men ready." I suspected Zethan swiped Castor's mixing bowl off the table because it smashed on the wall. I jolted from the impact and straightened, wiping my chin with my sleeve. A fate my brother deserved. "Buy as much fuel as you can fit in the jerry cans. Make Molotov cocktails. Bring baseball bats."

Robbie twisted a fist in his palm. "It'll be my pleasure, VP. The Wolves have had this comin'."

Zethan didn't stop with his firm commands. "We're gonna split into two teams. One will go and burn the Wolves' clubhouse to the ground. Leave nothing but concrete fucking stumps. The rest will go in and rescue Alaric."

"Yes, VP." Robbie checked out of the room like a man ready to cause havoc.

Zethan dropped the box to the bench and thumbed my chin, forcing me to look into his brutal green eyes. "I'm gonna feed your brother to my alligators. Fucking alive and begging for death."

His cruel streak came out when he got all protective over abused women and his men. When he killed the mugger who beat me. I wouldn't want to be Danny right now. The VP would make him suffer in the worst ways before the alligators ended his suffering.

I nodded. Words wouldn't come. I didn't have any. At least not for Danny.

"Don't blame yourself, baby." Zethan's massive arms banded around me, locking me in his fierce embrace. "This one's on me."

"No, don't do that." I coasted my hands along his biceps. "You blame yourself for too much and it kills you inside."

"Fuck, woman. You know me better than I know myself." His lips descended on my forehead, warming it and casting off the numbness that settled over me. We stayed like that for a while, until he pulled back to explain, "I've got to take the box to the Underworld and preserve it. Flesh won't deteriorate there."

I clutched my wringing stomach again. "Okay."

Zethan gave me a searing kiss before he cracked open a portal in the middle of the room and disappeared through it.

"Aaliyah," Castor's solemn, deep voice called to me.

"In a minute." I didn't look into his grave, amber eyes as I dragged my phone from my pocket to make the most important phone call of my life. The one that might save my mate. The one I didn't want the enforcer to interfere in. The one that might change the balance in this war.

My chest contracted and burned for air as I plugged in Danny's number. He answered in three rings.

"Give me the recipe to Pharaoh and we'll let your man go." My fuckwit of a brother thought it was Slade because he didn't recognize the burner phone's number.

"How about you take me instead?" I posed, pausing to delight in the slight suck of air on my brother's end. He didn't expect me. "I'm the traitorous whore, aren't I, for shacking up with the Jackals." I said the last bit to aggravate him into bargaining with me. Turn his anger onto me and direct it away from Alaric.

Castor's iron grip seized my upper arm, squeezing so tightly he cut off my circulation. He shook his head in warning, but I wasn't stopping.

"Trying to save your boyfriend, you slut?" Danny spat down the line. Good. Had him right where I wanted him. "He won't be able to touch that pussy after what I'll do to him."

Disgusting piece of shit.

Castor's chest quaked with a savage rumble.

Rage and the need to destroy my brother coursed through my veins so thick and hot, I almost passed out.

Darkness loomed in the back of my mind, a power desperate to bring my brother and his men to their knees. Isis' insult and wrath burning as hot and intense as Slade's chaos. They didn't call her the lady who called people to their deaths for nothing. She used trickery and dark magick to get power over Ra. Punished the people who didn't worship her. One thing was certain—absolute annihilation was coming for the Wolves, and the Jackals and I were going to deliver it.

"Do you want me or not, you cunt?" God. I even sounded like Slade. Aggressive and ready to tear my brother's throat out.

Castor's grip tightened, cutting off my circulation.

I avoided his gaze, the pleading in it that matched the despair along the bond. He wouldn't lose his mate. Not now. Not ever.

"Meet me at the clubhouse in two hours, you dumb bitch." Danny ended the call and my heart pounded hard from the confrontation and adrenaline.

My hands shook violently as I lowered my phone to my pocket. Castor took it from me and set it on the counter beside the sprawled map.

"You're not exchanging yourself for Alaric." His other hand came to my other arm, his fingers punishing and bruising. "If you try to leave, I'll lock you up in the cell and throw away the key."

I had no doubt he'd follow through on his threat. If he tried it, then it might come down to a battle of the gods of magick. We'd see who won. I'd go down fighting to save my mate, that was for sure.

"Fuck, dark sorceress." Castor released one of my arms and stabbed at his long curls. "I know you're too stubborn to listen to me." *Heck, yeah, I was.* "But just hear me out."

I yanked my second arm free. "Don't try and persuade me out of this with your wisdom and practicality."

"You can't go there alone." Castor splayed his arms wide, testing the fabric on his grey Henley. "This isn't about Alaric anymore. This is about all of us. We're a team and decide what to do together."

I snorted at the irony. "Funny, I didn't hear much deciding when Zethan grunted his orders."

"For God's sake, Aaliyah." Castor's harsh snap had me straighten to full attention. "He's our leader, and he makes the decisions. We execute them as a team. You need to come to the table and be a team player if you're one of us." His eyes and jaw hardened with accusation. "But you're not one of us, are you? You never were. You're just here to see this through."

Fuck. Castor always saw to the heart of me. Read my conflict like one of his damn books. Hearing it out loud was like a bike rolling over my heart, flattening it, ruining it.

I swallowed at the thick lump constricting my throat. "Castor ... I ..."

"It's all right, dark sorceress." He took my fumbled words and confusion as rejection and distanced himself again, jerking back to the map to take a snap of Alaric's location. "We asked too much of you from the start. The fated mates part wasn't an issue for us, and we accepted that you were meant for us. You didn't, though. You questioned it. Questioned whether we're right for each other. And you have every right to."

Damn him and his wisdom. The way he dragged my pain from me. Choked me up even more.

"You were different, Aaliyah." Castor's face pinched with grief. "We never shared club business with Liz. She couldn't handle it. Didn't like it. But we shared it with you."

Appreciation warmed the chilled bond, his admission, and the fact the Jackals trusted me enough to welcome me into their fold, touching me deeply. Dad gave me orders but never let me in his inner circle.

"We thought you understood us. Accepted us. That's what made you special. Our true mate. The one who wouldn't be taken from us."

My heart shattered at his heartbreak and loss. At how I compounded that. I had to make him understand why I was scared and distanced my heart.

"I've never known how to work as part of a team." My words came out strangled and weak. "My father pitted me against my brother and the other men to push me and make me strong. They always treated me like I wasn't one of them." I paused to adopt his voice. *"It's a man's world out there, baby girl. Don't ever show weakness. Don't let 'em push you around. Make me proud."*

I felt the sting between Castor and me. "My dad left when I was six. I never had a formative masculine influence in my life and wish I did. Even if it meant a shitty, competitive dynamic between us."

I hiccup laughed. "That's fucked up."

He scraped the back of his neck and stared down at me under his long, dark lashes. "Yeah, it is. Humans are weird like that."

A sob laugh bubbled out of my mouth, and he readjusted his position to return to me, keeping space between our bodies, stroking my arm.

My throat choked up again. "I'm sorry I'm not a team player." I clutched my forehead between my thumb and forefinger. "At the hospital, I got a reputation early on for being a smart-ass for using Isis' medical knowledge to question the doctor's diagnosis. They didn't like being shown up by me and treated me with contempt and put me down."

"Fuck, I'm sorry you had to go through that." The enforcer drew me closer, folding me to his chest, stroking my hair, sniffing it, resting his lips next to my ear. Fuck, I missed him, and clung to him tightly.

I sifted his shirt between my fingers. "They called me *Maverick*... you know, Tom Cruise in *Top Gun*. The lone, cocky pilot, who didn't take direction well." All the conflict of being made to feel alone and stupid came rushing back and I sobbed into his chest. "So, I shut up. Shut down. Did my own thing. Healing the patients behind their backs."

"Fucking assholes." Castor's large hands circled on my back and head. After a moment of soothing me, he cupped the back of my neck and caressed it. "We've let you into our world. Maybe it's time for you to do the same. Then we can finish this business with your brother, and all go back to our lives and move on."

Pain shot out in four directions of my heart. His corner blackened and bruised like a mishandled apple. He was letting me go. Breaking me free of him. Rejecting me as his mate. No. I didn't want that. Normally I was outspoken and fiery, but right when it counted, when I needed to speak up and fight, I couldn't get a fucking word out. It hurt too damn much.

Eventually I found the strength to get it out. "I don't want to go back to that. I want to work together." I shifted my hands to his shoulder and back. "I want to be part of the team."

He made an approving rumble as his hand drifted down my arm. But I still felt the pinch through our connection where he doubted me. "I'm sorry I've been distant. I've been wrestling with some demons. I shouldn't have put that shit on you. It wasn't fair."

No, it wasn't. But neither was the strain my hesitance put him through, inflaming old wounds, and pushing him away. My stomach locked with guilt for hurting him.

I leaned back to clasp his face. "I know someone hurt you

and you're scared."

He stiffened against me, body like stone, the quiet confidence and control he usually radiated stripped back. "It's a defense mechanism. I've done it all my life. When Dad left Mom and me. When my wife divorced me."

"I didn't know you were married." Shit. No wonder he backed off.

He shrugged, his maple eyes kissing my skin with every graze over my face. "I don't like to talk about it. I shouldn't have played out my insecurities on you when you hesitated and were unsure. You don't owe me anything."

Up until this moment, Castor was a mystery wrapped up in a bronze package. He stepped outside of his shield and unraveled the tightly constructed mask to reveal himself.

"Don't apologize," I said. "I'm the one who should be sorry. I wasn't completely honest about my intentions. But you read it through the bond, and you ran before you got hurt."

"I'm glad we had this talk and settled this before you leave." He still thought I was leaving? Obviously not everything was shared over our bond, because he didn't read my change of heart.

All my uncertainty faded after my three days with Alaric. I no longer saw the Jackals as adversaries or criminal bikers. They were men who grew on me, become important to me, proven to have my back through thick and thin. Men who possessed qualities I was looking for in a partner, and instead of being wrapped up in one package, they came in four, sexy, gruff, dangerous men. I wanted them. Every part of them. Good. Bad. Dark. Dangerous.

Why did I decide to stay after fighting it for so long? After the push and pull of my men? Fuck, I was a bitch to them. Drawing them in and out like the fucking tides, smashing and battering their hearts against the shore. I wanted to make this right with them. Be the mate they deserved. The great love to them. Fulfil the legacy I agreed to take up with my goddess Isis. To be a nurturer to Alaric. Healer to the club. Protector and defender of my men and team like the mother goddess I represented. Only then could I be complete and free off inner conflict and turmoil.

I started my path as a biker, drawn to the adventure of the ride, power of the bike between my legs, thrill of straddling the darker, criminal side of the club. Because, fuck, who didn't want to be a badass and rule breaker? That was why Isis chose me as her avatar. My goddess might be famous for being a mother, protector, carer and healer, but she never bowed to the male gods, a formidable force in her own right, standing strong and equal amid them. Like me, Isis never played by the rules, using her smarts and cunning to get what she wanted. Tricked Ra into giving her his true name so she held power over him. Duped Set to save her husband and help her son ascend to the throne of Egypt.

I was sick of playing by the rules. Sick of following rules dictated to me by corrupt hospital or medical systems when that bullshit held me back. I had so much therapeutic knowledge bursting in me that could be of use to patients worldwide. My way. My goddess' way. No bureaucratic crap standing in my way. The Jackals were my gateway to start my new path as club medic. Next step was up to me. The world was my oyster.

The loneliness I assumed Castor felt when his marriage broke down noosed around my neck. Culpability twisted in my belly that we were in this mess because of me. I needed him to give me another chance to make everything right. To be the mate he deserved. I didn't want him to hide or shield himself from me anymore. Didn't want him to fear that I'd leave. He was mine and I was his.

"I'm sorry I held back." It all came out fast and gushed. "I was a coward and didn't want to face my feelings. My fear of losing myself hurt you."

"I'm sorry, too. Sorry I played it safe." Fuck, he had to stop apologizing.

"I'm sure what I want now. I'm not going anywhere." I stroked his face and stretched up to leave a sweet, smoldering kiss on his lips that invited him to take more. "I'm staying right here."

"You want to be with us?"

"Fuck, yes."

Affection, attraction, and love trickled through our link, soaking me in warmth, silky softness, and the smell of damn roses.

Castor spanked me on the ass. "That's for using foul language." Another crack on my cheeks made me jolt. "And that's for tricking me into believing you were going to leave."

Fair enough. I deserved that. Thankfully, Zethan didn't see it or he'd have Castor pinned to the wall.

The enforcer's seriousness melted away, replaced with a softness and affection that took my breath away. "You don't know how good that is to hear, dark sorceress. Stay and be mine. Forever. I need you by my side."

"Always." These men were going to make me deliriously happy now that I finally let them.

"Now." Castor's voice echoed with all the dominating authority of his alter-ego. "I'm going to do what I should have done a week ago."

His lips slanted over mine, claiming me in a long, weighted kiss that enveloped me, lighting me up from head to toe. The kiss left me chasing more, and I dragged him down closer to me, seeking it.

When we broke apart, he gave me a villainous grin. "Now that we settled that, we have a brother to rescue, demons to unbind, an asshole to kill, and a club to smash."

## CHAPTER 38

### *C*astor

"I FUCKING HATE THIS PLAN," Zethan ground out like he wanted to tear Danny limb from limb. "I don't want Aaliyah anywhere near that prick!"

"How about we take a vote as a team to decide? Majority rules or winner takes all?" Aaliyah suggested, impressing me with how willing she was to work together, rather than for her own motives. She was integrating into the team. One of us at last.

My VP's brutal glare warned her to stop testing his authority. I'd lose my balls for challenging him like that. And I liked my balls intact. Only reason she got away with it was because she was his mate.

"Majority rules," I threw my vote in because we didn't have time to waste with arguing.

Zethan dug his fingers into his stubble. "Majority rules? You two assholes will vote against me."

That left Aaliyah as the decider. "Like you do with Slade." She winked and slapped him on the ass to warm him up, but the serious dick just grunted. "Sorry, hellhound dick, but I'm voting for majority rules."

"Fuck." The VP groped at both sides of his hair, losing his patience by the second. He itched to get to Alaric and rescue him, but we couldn't go in there unprepared. Not when the Wolves were always one step ahead of us and catching us off guard. This was too important to fuck up and we only got once chance, so we had to make it count.

Aaliyah ignored him. "What'll it be then? Hash out another plan or stick with my plan? I offer myself as a distraction while you two work your magick on the demons?"

"The latter," I threw my vote in, not liking to use my woman as bait, but needing time to set up my spell.

"Plan B and separate the demons from the Wolves," Zethan grunted.

Aaliyah spun on him, holding him to task. "You can't pick half an option, hellhound dick."

Zethan's shifter growled from deep in his throat.

Given the circumstances, it didn't feel right to sit back, smile and enjoy while they went at it. "What's your vote?" I interjected before they descended into a disagreement.

"Second option," Aaliyah pitched in.

"If Slade was here, it would have been a tie," Zethan grumbled his defeat, but got over it pretty quickly. "What's the fucking plan then?" His tone and face sharpened. "Because I won't stand by while you go to Danny alone. I won't give that prick the chance to put a gun to your head. We're not losing another mate. Period. I'll fucking offer myself as sacrifice if I have to."

"Agreed on the not going alone part." From the way Aaliyah ground her teeth, I could tell she struggled to concede on that front, fighting her natural urge to prove herself right.

Zethan's eyes narrowed like a suspicious beat cop. "You never agree and always fight us. What's the deal?"

Aaliyah went to reply, and I raised my palms to play the fucking mediator and avoid more squabbles. "Whatever. Just distract Danny while I break the bond tying the Wolves to the demons. Then we can smoke the fuckers."

Thankfully, Zethan dropped it, folding his massive arms over his barrel chest. "What do you want us to do?"

Time to run them through the plan to extract the demons. "If, for any reason, I get knocked out, shot, or can't perform the spell, I'm gonna need backup."

I showed Aaliyah and Zethan the spell-laced box I specially crafted for the occasion. A blackened, wooden box with a red satin interior with sigils carved into the outside and interior. Colors significant to the ritual I prepared to perform. Dark for the demons and red representing the goat's blood I laced the satin with to tempt them into it. Demons were all about their ritual symbolisms. One slip up and we were fucked.

"These words need to be chanted." I slid three pieces of paper with boxy, handwritten letters, one to each of them.

"Can we even pronounce this shit?" Zethan collected the note to read. "I don't want to get out there and have to read fucking Latin."

"I can help you if we get into trouble," Aaliyah said.

"I've got to prepare for every possible outcome," Zethan replied. "You might not be able to voice this."

I didn't want to think about that. About her getting injured or worse. I couldn't afford any dread or distractions. "Do your best. That's back-up if the demons don't play ball with my first plan."

Zethan clapped me on the shoulder. "That's what I want to hear."

He and I were both alike in that regard. Thought out every possible action and consequence, weighing them up for the best chance of success.

"We need to bargain with the demons to tempt them to abandon Danny and his men." I snapped the lid of the box closed. "Offer ourselves as new hosts. Say whatever lies we have to get them off the Wolves. Once they do, I'll trap them in this box and throw it in the ocean. It has to be saltwater to drown the demons."

Zethan wiped his face with disbelief. "Drown a fucking spirit?" Shivers made him twitch. Drowning made him uneasy since he didn't know how to swim. His god, Osiris, also drowned in a coffin. Double the dread. "Sounds like fucking fantasy."

"More fantasy than gods and avatars?" There wasn't anything to say to reassure him. "I trust what the books say. They've never let me down." I shoved the box into my cut, the spell and the rest of my demon enticements in my rucksack.

"Okay, lemme' tell the boys what to do," Zethan announced, crossing to the door. "Aaliyah, Team One and I will provide you enough distraction to do your job."

Meaning I had to find a private space to perform the spell out of witness range of the rest of the club. I gave a stiff nod to Zethan as he went to gather the rest of the team, dreading this. The demons wouldn't go easily. Ancient like the gods, I doubted they'd be fooled by cajoling and promises. They'd have to be magically torn from the Wolves and would put up a fight to avoid being trapped in my box. Hence, why I covered all angles.

. . .

\*\*\*

Team One and I were in place surrounding the Wolves clubhouse, at strategic locations to strike when the time was right. Men with guns patrolled the perimeter, showing off their clout. Robbie and Benny took out two, trying to strangle them with garrote wire that refused to puncture their necks, thanks to the demonic armor preventing their deaths. Blows to the head knocked them out cold and our men tied up the patrollers and dragged them out of view.

I motioned for Rusty and Kill Bill to move closer, and they proceeded.

That left me alone to recite the spell the instant the Wolves cleared the dark sigils scrawled on their walls shielding the clubhouse. I checked my pocket for the fiftieth time, confirming the wooden box in my cut. The rest of the spell ingredients were safely tucked in my rucksack.

Team Two was taking care of the bar where the Wolves kidnapped Alaric. Then they'd move onto the location where I magically tracked Alaric to ...that was, if the Wolves even moved him to their clubhouse for the exchange. I wouldn't be surprised if they planned to fuck us over again. Regardless, our aim was to destroy as much of the Wolves' property as possible. Return the financial strife and see how those fuckers liked it.

A hundred feet to the north, Zethan gripped Aaliyah's arm as they inched toward the Wolves' door. Fuck, my woman was brave, carrying forward, fearless in her stride, her only intentions to free Alaric and destroy her brother.

Danny emerged, backed with four men packing weapons.

I got straight to work now that they were in range. Ancient Aramaic poured off my tongue. Fiery light burned the sigils on the clubhouse, erasing the dark magick. Hisses cut through the chilly night. Demons detecting my magick at work. Inky shadows drifted across the space between us. I'd gotten their attention. Just a few more lines to deliver and I'd move to step two.

My shifter hearing picked up the click of tongue on Danny's cheek. "Looks like you're not that important to the Jackals after all, sis. Your pussy isn't worth shit if they're willing to trade you so easily for their man." Repulsive bastard tried to goad Aaliyah into biting, but she ground her jaw, staying silent, letting Zethan handle this as VP. "What a waste of twenty Gs."

Zethan's free fist curled as mine clutched the box so tight it creaked. Money Danny had spent to hire the mugger to beat Aaliyah. If only Slade was here to catch the proof we desperately sought to connect Danny to all our fucking problems.

Aaliyah wrestled against Zethan's grip. "You fucking asshole."

"Hand him over, Danny, or she doesn't take another step," Zethan growled, the vicious threat loud enough for the whole team to hear across the perimeter of the clubhouse.

Danny jerked his head at one of his men, giving the order to grab Alaric. The Wolf smirked and retreated inside.

Lumpy, dark clouds floated closer, and I raised a light magick shield to block them. They snarled as it burned them, and they withdrew. I kept up my speech, deleting the last brand on the clubhouse, rendering it dark magick-free and safe for the avatars to enter if we needed to.

I started on the second spell to separate the demons from the mutts. To the box, I added cigarettes, candy, and sliced fruit. I poured three shot glasses of rum and set them at my feet. Enticements to bargain the demons with if it got to that.

Murky clouds dragged out of our rivals as the spell weakened their bond. Howls pierced the night as the demons were torn like parasites from their hosts, deprived of the fear and negative emotion that fueled them.

"What the fuck is that?" I heard Robbie mutter from thirty feet to the west.

"Wolves howling, you idiot," Benny mouthed back.

I kept up the pressure on the demons. Three twisted shapes attacked my shield, destabilizing it, and I hurried my words to finish the spell. Fuck, I couldn't maintain the defense and break them from our rivals at the same time. One or the other. My priority leaned to separation and leave the Wolves without anything to hide behind. Then Zethan could suck the life out of them and end our crisis for good.

"Danny, what the fuck have you done?" Aaliyah's horrified cry echoed through the yard and my body stiffened with apprehension.

Just a little more, then I was done. I'd worry about my brother later. We each had a part to play. Zethan and Aaliyah's job was to free Alaric, mine to dissolve their Wolves' defenses, while Team One took care of the rest. If one part of the plan failed, we'd all be fucked, and none of us would get out of here.

Gunfire went off and men howled. I couldn't tell if we'd taken the hit or the Wolves had. Nearby, more men grunted, wrestled and beat the shit out of each other. It sounded like a fight erupted on the Wolves' porch as more of the Jackals descended on Danny and his men.

I delivered the last three lines. The black mass surrounding me reared back, hissing, howling, screaming at being sliced from the Wolves. I patched through a text to everyone, signaling go-time to take down the Wolves, seconds before clawed hands reached for me right as my shield broke. Cloud solidified into a coarse, bumpy grip that clamped around my neck and choked me. One of the fiends snatched the spell from my fingers. Fuck. Enchanted words I needed to speak to draw them into the box. My mind glitched with fear and I couldn't summon my photographic memory when I needed it the goddamn most. Now I was on my own. Plan fucking B.

"I've come to accord with you," I said in their native language scripted right from the spell books.

An icy voice that ended with a hiss responded in Aramaic. Seconds later the translation followed. "We don't wish to bargain."

"One way or another you're coming with me," I gasped, removing the spell-laced box from my cut and flipping the case open.

The mass of demons growled and snapped as if they recognized the spell. Some floated closer, drawn by the scent of goat's blood, unable to resist it. Others circled the shots of rum or tried to snatch the cigarettes and other goodies in the box. Items they couldn't get in their world and had to rely on the emotion and thrill from consuming it through their host.

"Let me go and I'll let you host on me," I gasped, growing desperate for air as the grip on me showed no signs of loosening.

All I needed was one to agree and I could hook them all. Otherwise, I'd force them off the Wolves with another spell.

"C'mon, you fuckers," I goaded. "I'm a fucking delicacy of fear. Daddy issues like Danny boy here. Mommy resentment, too. Divorced and fear of rejection. Dread of losing my mate. Bond with me!"

"I'll bargain with you." A misty shape emerged from the shadows and the hand on me released. "All these men do is whine, complain, and fuck. They're not ripe with fear like we were promised. Arrogant and cocky all the time that they'll win. Tasteless. Boring. But you smell appetizing. We could feast off you."

"Promised by who?" I prodded, desperate for any information I could get on who might be behind this. Because it sure as shit wasn't the Wolves with this kind of magick knowledge. "Who bound you to the Wolves?"

"The dark one." The long hiss prompted shudders through my body. My texts referred to the dark one, but I hadn't been able to work out who it was yet. "The one in the shadows."

"Who?"

The demon barked out a cold laugh and silenced itself.

Fuck. I needed to reel it in another way. "I agree to be your host."

Growls and barks accompanied the arguing demons as they fought for dominance and control. Figures in the murk slashed their claws and several of them shrieked and shrunk back. Smoldering burns dragged along the demons' forms as they were sliced up.

This went on for a few moments until the one who'd spoken to me said, "We accept your proposal."

I had them where I wanted them. In agreeing to parasite off me, they broke their pact with the dark one and had forsaken the Wolves.

Lifting the box higher, I shouted, "Come to fucking Dark Daddy!"

Summoned by the spell, the mass of inky shadow drifted to me.

Cool metal of the barrel of a gun hit my temple. "Drop the box, cunt."

The demons halted and let out a taunting, cruel laugh. Assholes tricked me and distracted me for the Wolves. Never trust a goddamn demon.

A snap of my dark magick disabled the gun.

Pages from my book flashed in my photographic memory. I flung out the start of a third spell, one that would force these bastards into my box.

The Wolf clicked the trigger, then swore when it failed. Cocksucker tackled me to the ground, and my face ate dirt as I came down hard. The box rolled from my grasp in the process.

"Fuck." I fumbled to right myself amid the tangle of arms banding my chest. I thrust my head back, connecting with the Wolf with a loud crack. He grunted and swore, releasing me, and I scrambled free.

Demons pounced on the box, lifting it, twisting it. "Maybe we ought to trap you in here, spell castor."

Fuck. I just had to hope Aaliyah and Zethan had shit covered on their end, taking down Danny. Otherwise, it was Sayonara fuckers.

## CHAPTER 39

### *A*aliyah

I FELT the dark magick shields on the clubhouse instant Castor broke through the spells. Followed by the snap of the bond between the demons and Wolves. The dark entities remained as their sickening, foul smell, and dark presence lingered, which meant the enforcer still had to trap them in his box. One spell down out of three.

Danny gripped Alaric by his shoulder as he kneeled at his feet. They'd dressed him in briefs and a tank top for his modesty but left him partially naked to degrade him. Bruises, welts, cuts, and burns covered his entire body. I couldn't breathe looking at him. Couldn't move an inch. His haunted face and shattered soul pinned me to the spot. Gold had drained from his bright eye as if all the life and god's power had been stolen from him. Shadows covered the sharp angles of his face. Partly conscious, his head lolled to one side.

Tornadoes swept through my body. Danny broke him all

over again. Left him an empty shell. My heart pitched a screaming fit, and I held back the weight of my power to get Alaric away from my brother before I unleashed the force of a nuclear weapon.

"Alaric?" I reached for him. "Come to me."

Danny jerked Alaric by his shoulder. "Give yourself up first, bitch."

I had yet another instance where my heart disobeyed my head, carrying me forward, when I should have executed my magick. All I could think about was touching my mate, pouring my healing gift into him, relieving his pain, and breathing life back into him.

Castor's apprehension struck the bond. A warning that something went wrong. A snap of magick followed, along with the corresponding howls of pain from the demons. He broke their bond to the Wolves.

Zethan returned my anxious glance. Go time. His hand whipped up and released the deathly powers of the Underworld.

Danny started to choke like a fish deprived of water. A sickly grey pallor leached into his face and lips. Luster drained from his eyes as all life was sucked from him. Skin around his face tightened as moisture dried from his body and it mummified into a corpse. Fuck, it was beautiful to watch. The perfect revenge that prompted the dark goddess side of me to rejoice.

Alaric slumped, almost collapsing without my brother to prop him up.

Vengeance pumped in my veins as I hurried forward, grabbing my mate, steadying him. "You're okay, my love. We're here to take you home. I'll ease the pain and get you healed." I staggered under his heavy, lifeless weight, but managed to drag him thirty feet away before dropping him against a wall.

I glanced over at Zethan as Wolves descended on him with weapons. His magick swelled as he depleted the life from them. Ratchet, one of the Wolves I knew from my time in the club, pistol whipped Zethan in the cheek as a last-ditch effort to survive. The VP sprawled forward, losing his grip on my brother.

"Fuck," I cursed, tossing out a bout of arrythmia that sent Ratchet's heart into cardiac arrest.

Jackals sprung out of the darkness, defending their VP and launching at my brother and his men, a brawl ensuing. Fists pounded flesh and men grunted and groaned. I flinched as a gun went off. A quick check showed a Wolf dead, taken down by Kill Bill. He took a bullet in the shoulder from an enemy and disarmed the man with a few punches.

Over my shoulder, demons snaked in Castor's direction as he battled them back with white magick. Too many of them to fight alone. Goddess, they had possession of the wooden box. We had to trap them and kill them.

My heart thumped heavily for both my mates, torn who to side with. They both needed me, and I wrangled with the choice of alleviating Alaric's pain or aiding Zethan and Castor to destroy Danny and eliminate the threat over all our heads. Both decisions were as dire and important as each other. This might be our only chance to defeat the Wolves, the demons, the shadowy player, and if Castor was in trouble, I had to think of them all. Be the team player I promised to be.

"Fuck, I'm sorry my love." I cupped Alaric's face then kissed his forehead. "I'll be back in a minute. Promise."

I headed for Castor first because Zethan looked like he could handle his own with the humans. The demons were another story altogether. Those supernatural fucks were deceptive and cunning, and I had to be careful how I handled them.

I passed Robbie and Benny. "Go help your VP," I ordered them, and they glared at me for telling them what to do. "*Now!*" I fucking wasn't in the mood to argue with these pricks.

They jostled away, muttering under their breaths. Whatever they saw in the next few moments would have to be wiped from their mind later.

I hustled into a jog, desperate to get to Castor, as the demons encircled him in a swirling, thickening mass of hostile cloud that hid him from view.

*Isis, hear me, great goddess,* I called to my patron. *Any advice?*

In all honesty, I didn't expect an answer, as she normally left me to my own devices. But this time she answered my call.

*Rob them of their source of sustenance, my daughter.*

Deprive them of fear? How the hell did I do that? Guess I'd make it up as I went, just like I did every other time. Palm raised, I cut off their food source, preventing the demons from absorbing the fear oozing out of Castor, me, and every fucking person at the clubhouse.

They snarled at me, red eyes flashing my way. Fire streaked along their silhouetted forms. Grass and dirt uprooted as clawed feet dragged through them, drawn by my call. Instantly, a block went up between us as they resisted. Pressure wound around my throat, denying me air, and I scratched at my throat.

Two could play at that game, fuckers. Isis, through her connection to Osiris, could tap into the Underworld powers too. So, I responded by exhausting their life, calling the evil from them, letting it burn out like a fire left overnight without wood. Demonic outlines crackled and sputtered before me, until their flames extinguished, and the cool breeze swept away their haze.

The reprieve exposed Castor, and I pressed forward, setting my hand on his arm, contributing my power. Applying my magick to such ancient, powerful beings weakened me, and I leaned on him for strength. There was only so much god power I could channel as a human before I tired.

"I can't destroy them all," I croaked. "They're too strong."

"Help me drag them in the box," Castor rumbled in his deep, dark voice.

I summoned the last of my quickly depleting power, combining it with my mate's, heaving the demons into the box. The inky mass poured into the receptacle, and I marveled how it all compacted in there despite the tiny space. When every last drop of cloud entered the chest, Castor slammed the lid shut and bound it shut tight by tying a red and black ribbon over it. The last element to complete the spell.

Castor bought me in for a quick hug and kiss on the forehead. "Great work, dark sorceress. You lived up to your name tonight." I grinned up at him relishing the praise. He slapped my ass. "C'mon, let's get back to our VP."

He took my hand and we collected Alaric, Castor throwing his arm under my fallen mate's shoulder and carrying him back to the clubhouse's front porch.

Zethan and the rest of the men had the Wolves surrounded, on their knees in front of him, weapons confiscated, lips and eyebrows bloody from battering. Clearly, the VP had laid off his deadly powers in front of the Jackals as our enemies were all very much alive and well. Disappointment sank in my gut at finding Danny part of that equation, albeit weak, woozy, sporting large bruises over his eyes a bloody gash on his neck.

"Don't have the protection of your demons now, do you, cocksucker?" Zethan smashed Danny's opposite cheekbone hard enough to break it. Instantly it swelled up, sealing his eye shut.

Benny and Robbie exchanged a *what the fuck is he on about* glance. Ugh. More shit for Castor to erase from the Jackals' minds. That'd keep my mate busy.

Finally, things were going right for us. We stripped the Wolves of their source of protection and left them powerless to whatever punishment Zethan and Slade saw fit.

Zethan ordered Kill Bill and Robbie to bring the vans to the clubhouse and the men to haul the Wolves into them. Prisoners. Dead men. Some former brothers that held no love for me. Not then, not now. They glared at me like I was a traitor. Fuck them. I loved my father and once loved his club too. They never reciprocated, never accepted me, and it was their loss that I'd found a new pack to belong to.

We returned to the clubhouse and Zethan disappeared downstairs with Team One to lock up the prisoners.

With Castor's help, I got Alaric set up in a bed, and he groaned, cracking open an eye. He startled and clambered up to the headboard.

I held out my palms in surrender, so he understood I wasn't a threat. "Alaric, it's just me. Aaliyah." I used my best soothing nurse voice to bring his alarm back down, because I couldn't treat him if he got aggressive and threatened my safety. "You're home and safe. Nothing's going to hurt you."

"Stay away, bitch." He kicked at me, almost getting my shoulder. "You told them we were coming. You did this to me." He held up his bloody stump where his finger used to be.

Accusation staked me through the heart and my mouth dropped open. Was that what Danny told him? Taunted him into believing throughout his ordeal to pit us against each other? Or did Alaric come to that conclusion of his own accord because of his natural suspicion and mistrust of people? This was so twisted and fucked up. Unable to get a word out to defend myself, I scratched at my aching chest, fearing he might never trust me after this. The stake deepened, and I whimpered, almost breaking into a sob.

"That's enough, asshole." Castor grabbed Alaric by the shoulders and held him down. "You don't talk to her like that. Show your mate respect."

"My mate wouldn't have done this to me," Alaric snarled, cold, distant, swollen eyes trained on me.

Every word hammered the air from my lungs. Fuck, we came so far in three days only to have a bomb dropped on our relationship, blowing it apart and obliterating everything. I didn't think we could come back from this. Ever. He'd never trust me, and I couldn't be with a man who always suspected me of ulterior motives. It hurt to breathe. Hurt to think. Hurt to fucking look at him.

"Shut the fuck up." Heavier and more solid in build, Castor leaned over Alaric, and my weak mate gave up his fight. "Aaliyah came to your fucking rescue. Nearly destroyed herself with worry when you were kidnapped. Offered herself to replace you as the Wolves' captor. Helped us take care of the demons to get you back here safely."

Spikes pierced deeper into my heart at the way Castor spoke to Alaric. Frightened and on edge, my wounded mate needed gentleness, compassion, and kindness, not bitter words. Especially not from his club. This wasn't his fault. Danny saw us coming and planned for it. Or his benefactor warned him.

"Don't. Please don't talk to him like that." I grabbed Castor's arm, hinting to let go and he did. "You're his brother, and he needs you."

"I won't tolerate him disrespecting you," Castor growled, inching backwards off the bed. "Now Aaliyah's going to heal you and you're going to stay still, aren't you?"

"Yes, sir," Alaric muttered, turning his head to look at the wall.

Pain clubbed at my cheat as my hands settled onto his arms and he jolted from my soft touch. His mind was scarred again, and it wouldn't be easy for him to forget what was done to him. I could heal him physically, maybe take his memories away, but I'd have to suffer every agonizing pain with him. Last time he stopped me from doing just that, because he couldn't bear for me to be hurt. Damn this man! I'd fucking go through hell and back for him if it meant he was free of his cage.

I waited until his arm relaxed to commence bathing and cleansing his stumped finger to ward off infection. Who knew when Zethan would get the chance to retrieve his finger from the Underworld? Until then, I couldn't attempt reattaching it. Alaric resisted a few times, jerking away, slowly realizing I wouldn't hurt him. With that finished, I pumped healing energy to sooth my injured mate's suffering and heal the bruises, cuts, welts, and burns on his body. I had to leave some marks on his face for show for the club. Couldn't give away my powers and identity, much as I hated to see Alaric looking so dreadful. Fatigue wrapped around me, forcing me to give up once I addressed those wounds. His finger would likely take more juice to reattach than I had right now, and I had to replenish first in preparation of tackling that.

"I'm sorry, Alaric, I need to rest," I explained, slowly removing my hands to avoid startling him. "My battle with the demons depleted me." I felt like a fucking warrior in a computer game needing to find a potion bottle to rebuild my strength and power.

He shifted his head to face me, his eyes softer, warmer. "Thank you, Aaliyah. For everything."

His response took me by surprise. After the way he

mistrusted me and accused me of betraying him, I didn't expect that at all. A glimmer of hope reignited in my chest that we might come through this in time. Lots of time. Whatever time he needed to be complete again. I'd be here, waiting, longing for him.

Words dried in my throat, and I didn't know what to say. I kept it strictly professional, nurse to patient, fearing anything else might be too much for him. "I'll try to reattach and restore your finger tomorrow." No need to tell him the whole story of where it was and why.

I didn't touch him, pat him, stroke him, kiss him, even though my heart begged me to. Baby steps. Rebuild trust first. Get him comfortable. Take it from there.

"Okay." He closed his eyes and leaned his head back, wincing as if still in pain. Shit, I hadn't given him complete relief. The nerves in his fingers were severed and would give him grief.

Castor patted Alaric on the arm, rewarding him for what I assumed was his calm and respectful behavior. "Need anything for the pain?"

"Got anything to put me to sleep so I won't wake up again?" I gasped at his answer. That wasn't the man I snuggled with and brought back to life. The man who opened up his heart to me. Soldier, defender and protector, Alaric Hawke was not a man to give up. Torture changed him. Ruined him. Broke him all over again. I couldn't bear to watch him give up and let go.

"Fuck, Alaric." I snapped off the bed to my feet. "You're a goddamn fighter. The defender of the sky." My voice scaled with frustration and desperation that my mate was so willing to capitulate to his despair. "What did Danny do to you that you're giving up this easily?"

He sighed and rolled onto his side, his mental pain too much to bear.

I should have left it alone. Should have let him rest. But he needed to know that I would fight for him, even if he refused to do it for himself.

"Give him a dose of sedative to sleep," I ordered Castor. "Arrange for someone to watch him round the clock. I'll take the first shift."

"Aaliyah, I don't think you should be alone," Castor started.

I raised a palm to silence him. "He's exhausted and injured. He won't hurt me." I curled up on the edge of the bed, turning my back on my hesitant enforcer. "And I'm not fucking leaving him."

# CHAPTER 40

## Slade

GOD, it was good to be free. Good to be home and back at my club. I strode through the clubhouse, feeling like a million bucks after my release from the shitty, cramped cell at the Bathurst Police Station. *Thank you, Barry.* Ten fucking thousand dollars later. One corrupt police officer's complaint lodged. Bullet dodged. Cleared my name, thanks to the CCTV cameras footage downloaded before the cops turned it off and confiscated the footage.

*Castor, you genius, I could fucking kiss you.*

The place was fucking empty but my shifter hearing detected movement and lowered voices in the next room. For safety reasons, we always had two members remain at the club to protect it, after the Winter's Devils raided us and killed Liz. Bones and Slash were on duty and should have heard Barry roll up in his Mercedes to drop me back at the club. Why hadn't those assholes greeted me at the fucking door? I was gonna kick their goddamn asses for not manning the club.

"Where the fuck is everybody?" I grunted, rolling my shoulder and neck, releasing the creak in my back muscles with a long, sharp crack.

In the rec room, it looked like a bomb had struck the rec room. Portable cots laid out in formation, my men resting in them, wrapped in bloody bandages, cuts, and bruises. Bloody shirts, pants, and cuts were thrown on the floor. Zethan and Doc Shriver tended to Kill Bill, wrapping up a wound on his shoulder. Slash and Benny patched up a bloody and beaten Rusty.

"What the fuck happened here?" I announced myself.

Zethan climbed from his crouch and jerked his head, signaling for a private chat in my office. When he shut the door, I crossed to my desk, desperate for a cigarette. My hands shook from nicotine withdrawal as I rolled a cigarette, listening in while he filled me in on what went down during my imprisonment. I couldn't light that damn smoke fast enough and suck down the hot fire into my lungs.

Relief teemed through me at hearing of Alaric's rescue, the capture of the Wolves, their three burned down assets, including their clubhouse. We were lucky we only came away with two shot and several injured. Could have been a lot worse if Castor and Aaliyah didn't break through the demonic protection. Wish I was there with my club for the victory. I'd make Danny pay for depriving me of that honor.

"You did good, Zethan. Real proud." I took a long drag and puffed out the smoke. "Shame I wasn't there to see that cunt Danny's face when he lost his demonic spell and realized he was fucked." I scraped my bearded jaw, fulfilling my dark, twisted fantasies, imagining how the shit went down.

"I know you would have loved to have wrecked some shit, Prez." Zethan set his heavy hand on my shoulder for comfort, and I chuckled. *Fuck, yeah.* My VP knew me too well. Couldn't win them all, though. I'd make up for it another time. "I kept Danny alive for you to kill him."

Good man. At least Zethan didn't steal that chance from me. I was fucking chomping at the bit to get to Danny. Had all sorts of torture planned for that cunt, starting with cutting off his balls and making him choke on them. Revive and repeat with my next sick fantasy.

"That's all that matters." I clapped him back, happy to be fucking home and out of my confinement. Pumped at the thought of paying Danny Heller a visit and cutting off all his fingers out of vengeance.

"How's Alaric doing? Can we save his finger?"

"Aaliyah reattached it this morning with her magick." Zethan wiped his bloodied forehead, earned from patching up Kill Bill's shoulder gunshot wound. "She stayed by his side all night, except for an hour where she tended to the others."

"Good. He needs her." So did I, but not just yet. I went to my alcohol tray and lifted the whisky in a silent question that my VP answered with a nod. I poured us a double. Fuck knew we deserved one for celebration. "What does Doc Shriver say? Is everyone else gonna be all right?"

I handed Zethan his whisky and he sipped at it. "They'll live. Pricks are strong like oxes. It's gonna take more than a bullet to put them down."

I chuckled and threw back my whisky, making a face at the burn down my throat. "Aaliyah didn't tend to them?"

"Nah." Zethan knocked back more whisky. "She hasn't left Alaric's side, except to stop the bleeding of Kill Bill's and Bone's gunshot wounds, and look after them until Doc Shriver got here. I ordered her not to use her magick to protect our aliases."

I huffed, knowing Aaliyah better than that. Stubborn woman wouldn't listen.

Zethan smiled and finished off his drink. "She actually listened for once."

"Holy fuck, pigs are flying." I poured us another drink.

"Aaliyah and I came to an agreement."

"I knew there'd be a caveat." Smoke curled off my cigarette as I waved my tumbler around.

Zethan chuckled darkly. "She's going to heal them slowly to avoid suspicion, to a point where they don't need for physical therapy and other specialist bullshit."

That was my girl. Kudos to my VP for wrangling her talent and stubbornness in. Asshole must have had a mean fight on his hands to win that battle. I was even more grateful that he got her to agree to stick around for a bit longer when she wanted out of here the minute her brother was dead.

Tentacles wrapped around my lungs thinking about the inevitable. Better to just rip it off like Band-Aid that draw out the pain.

I needed another sliver of whisky to get past that one. "Thank fuck things went our way. Things could have gone really bad."

Zethan scratch at his stubble, the serious bastard smiling for once. "I was beginning to think we were fucked for a minute, but thanks to Castor and Aaliyah's hard work reading the spell books, we got there in the end."

My throat dried at the close call and another mention of my mate. "Yeah." We almost were fucked. Almost lost our club and everything we'd built. But that wasn't what disturbed me the most.

I glanced down at my tumbler, the whisper of brown liquid remaining, dreading how empty I'd be when we lost our woman. That brought with it another lot of problems. Heartbreak. Separation. Rejection. Forced to choose a replacement if I wanted to have kids, knowing that she'd never be enough. Desperate to burn away that pain, I poured another double and refilled my VP's glass, despite him not asking for another one. I drained the rest of my drink and hissed.

"You don't need to drown away your sorrows just yet, asshole." Zethan grinned, clinking his glass with mine. "Aaliyah's decided to stay."

She did? Why? I had to go to her and find out what changed. Fuck. I guess none of it really mattered if she was sticking around. A giant weight lifted off my heart and let me breathe properly for the first time in weeks.

"Best fucking news all day." I wiped my mouth.

Fuck, I needed to bury my face in my woman's hair, inhale her, feel her skin beneath my palms, and give her a long, needy kiss. Four days apart was too long. I missed her fiery sass and the way she kept me in line. Woman deserved another good spanking for putting her ass in the line of fire with Danny. But I'd save that one for later.

Too tired for that shit. I hadn't slept well while in the police station. The bed was too small and uncomfortable, and I just wanted to crash once I checked on my woman and road captain. Punishing Danny could wait another day until I felt up to it. Let the fucker suffer not knowing when he'd die.

Zethan thumped me on the shoulder, sensing my itch to leave. "Go on. Go see them."

I plugged out my smoke, and patted his shoulder a final time before departing my office. Several strides carried me to the spare bedroom where Alaric was holed up.

I stood in the doorway, watching her patch up my man's restored hand in a compression bandage. Drawn and exhausted, her eyelids and the corners of her mouth drooped. Women didn't sleep while she observed Alaric's condition overnight. Once she was finished with him, I'd drag her kicking and screaming to my room for a nap. Tie her to my bed until she rested, if I had to.

Her gaze tipped up to mine and she smiled. "Welcome back, Mr. President." Croaky and tired, she still sounded like a sexy angel sent from heaven to tempt me.

"Hi, beautiful." I left off the Nurse A. It didn't feel right to flirt with her when my road captain lay battered on the bed.

My stiff back cracked again as I bent to press a kiss to her head. She cradled my wrist in her palm. I tucked her head against my thigh and stroked her, needing to feel her against me.

Alaric studied me through swollen eyes that Aaliyah left untouched for obvious reasons.

"How's the finger, Hawk Boy?" I stretched out a palm to him.

"Don't call me that, Prez." He shook my waiting hand out of respect.

Fuck. Poor bastard got hit in his hawk shifter. I should have kept my big mouth shut.

"I'll give you two a minute." Aaliyah tried to leave, but I kept her in place.

"Stay. Look after him. I want my best with Alaric." She nodded at my command. Fuck, either she was too tired to fight me, or Zethan was right, and she changed.

I liked this compliant side of her. Submissive women did nothing for me. Gave me a limp dick. But a fiery, witty woman like Aaliyah did it for me. Challenged me, kept shit interesting, stimulated the fire and passion in me. Then there was her other side... the caring, loyal, supportive, intuitive woman who knew what we needed when things got tough. A woman who was good with children and would make an incredible mother to our little pack and make me the happiest fucking man on the planet if she let me put my baby in her belly.

The bed groaned and sank under my weight, unable to take my size with theirs. I set a firm hand on his shoulder, and he flinched, shrinking back from me. This whole incident thrust him back to darker times and traumatized him all over again. He wouldn't get over this easily and would need more time away from the club to heal his mental scars. Asshole would hate me for benching him again, but it had to be done. He'd thank me later. Then we'd welcome him back with open arms.

I squeezed his hand, intent on addressing that later when he wasn't in so much physical pain. "Aaliyah did a good job on reattaching your finger." I looked back at her and gave her an appreciative nod.

She leaned her weary head on my shoulder, and I kissed her hair and brushed the back of her neck.

"It might take a few weeks for the severed nerves to regenerate," she advised, "but I'll work on it every day until it's as good as new or better."

Nerves. Fuck. I didn't think about that. I got shot in the stomach years back and hit a nerve. Pain was intense and unrelenting. Fingers had several nerves running through them, and to have them sliced? Fuck, Alaric would be in a world of pain.

"Need anything for the pain?" I asked.

He gave me a miserable smile. "I lost an eye, remember? It's no worse than that."

Aaliyah sucked in a hiccupped breath that made me want to push off the bed and take her in my arms, but my brother needed me more. His suffering was greater and long-lasting.

I scratched my forehead, wondering what the fuck to say to that. Asshole was getting pain relief even if he denied it. He didn't need to be a goddamn hero to impress anyone.

Before I got a word out, someone crashed into the doorway and groaned. Castor cradled his eyes as he slumped on the wood, mouth warped in pain. The bond crackled with warning. Stiff with alertness, I jumped to my feet, rushing to his side.

"Fuck, Castor, what's wrong?" Aaliyah leapt into action with me, taking the opposite side of him from me, the both of us guiding my enforcer to sit in the chair beside Alaric's bed.

Barely able to stand, he crashed like a heavy weight, making the chair rock and hit the wall behind it.

Alaric shied back at the noise and Aaliyah placed one hand on his chest and the other on Castor's knee.

I squeeze my enforcer's shoulder, trying to get answers. "What the fuck's up with your eyes?"

I swear to God, if one of those Wolves cunts hurt him I was gonna start a fire that never died out.

"Something went wrong." Castor's hands trembled as our mate shifted one away to inspect a nasty, dark burn and blisters over his eyelids.

My stomach sickened with dread. What the fuck caused that?

"Oh, God, you're burned. What did this?" She nudged his other hand away and placed both palms over his eye sockets to inject him with her healing gift.

"The light of Ra," he groaned, shaking from the pain as Aaliyah restored the burned, blackened skin. "It blinded me, and I couldn't defend myself from it. Too fucking bright and hot."

Dread twisted like a knife to the gut, and I snapped out of the chair with fire raging on my palms. "Ra's avatar was here? Is he the cunt helping the Wolves?" We had to go after him.

"No. It wasn't Ra." Castor's inflamed skin lightened, and his voice trembled with his discomfort. "It was someone else hiding behind his powers."

Horror sunk in as I realized the potential consequences

and complications of Castor being up here and not down questioning our captives. "Tell me the cunt didn't release the Wolves."

"They're gone." Castor bent his head, the bond stained with his regret at letting me and the club down. "Whoever we're up against is pretty powerful and can get past our wards."

Ice injected in my veins, dousing the fire in me. "Motherfucker."

"Who the fuck can use Ra's gift?" Aaliyah asked the question I couldn't get out past the icy anger formulating within me.

"The dark one the demons keep referring to."

"Who the fuck is that?' I growled, struggling to contain the lethal blizzard I wanted to strike this meddling cunt with.

"I don't know, Prez." Castor's shame burned a hole in my gut.

I gave him a conciliatory pat on the shoulder to show him no hard feelings despite being pissed as hell that we right back where we left off before I'd been thrown in jail.

"Stay with him and take care of him," I ordered Aaliyah, marching out of the room, and grabbing Zethan to come downstairs to the cell with me.

Dark grooves were scratched into the floor, through the center of the wards, rendering them useless. Fire had torched everything, including the stone, blackening it.

"Magick burns." Zethan scraped the floor with his shoe. "This prick knows spell work like Castor."

"Who do we know with that capability?" I growled, anger turning more murderous by the second, and I punched the steel of the cage, denting it.

I sucked in air, needing to get a grip on my aggression or I was going to smash someone's skull in.

Zethan scrubbed the back of his neck. "That's a question for Genius."

Fuck. Another job for Castor.

Now we confirmed that an avatar was behind this, we'd be paying the Egyptian Council a goddamn visit and sorting this shit out, demi god to demi god. Fist to fist. Magick to fucking magick. Attacking each other was against the covenant we agreed to, and I'd not sit by while one of our own fucked with us and hurt my men in the process. This cunt was going down, mark my words. And when he did, he'd be more than fucking sorry. He'd wish he never existed.

"Fuck, I completely forgot." Zethan croaked out a laugh and rubbed at his tired, lined forehead. "Danny might have won this round and escaped, but the prick isn't getting very far. I bit him and injected hellhound venom into him."

I snorted out a laugh and threw my arm over his shoulder, dragging him in for a hug. "Full of surprises, aren't you, asshole?"

"Sure am." I hadn't seen my VP grin that wide in a long time. "That prick's gonna die a slow, painful death until his heart gives out."

# EPILOGUE

## *A*aliyah

"I've got something I wanna show you." Slade's wolfish grin teased as he slipped his massive hand into mine and tugged at me to go with him.

I remained a solid weight in my chair by Alaric's bed, not wanting to leave his side. He just fell asleep after I administered some sedatives. Two days passed since I reattached his finger. His lungs and face were partially bruised, and I wouldn't let him out of the bed except to visit the men's or take a shower. Aided by the medication, he was sleeping with a few nightmares, but nothing bad enough for him to choke me. While he slept, I injected more healing energy into him, doing what I could to diminish the memories' hold on his mind. If he gave me permission, I'd erase them completely and set him free.

"Oh, yeah?" I flicked up an exhausted eyebrow at Slade. "Get a new tattoo in lock-up?"

"Smartass." His gaze slid up and down my body, ravenously taking in every inch as if his hands were caressing my skin, raking heat to every part of my body. Damn him. Every time I was around him, I was a puddle of need.

*No, no, no.* I was observing Alaric, making sure he mended, not getting hot and heavy for the president.

Slade leaned down seductively, gripping either edge of my chair, his lips playing against my ear. "Your keep sassing me, medic, and I'll be forced to teach you a lesson."

*Yes, please, Mr. Vincent.*

*Goddess.*

I glanced over at Alaric sleeping in the bed, reluctant to go anywhere in case he needed me. "Can it wait? I should stay here."

In typical Slade style, he didn't give me a choice and hauled me to my feet. "He'll live. It's only for five minutes, then you can come back. I wanna show you your surprise." He firmly set his hand in mine.

Right. The one he alluded to with threats to spank my ass if I snuck a peek before I was allowed.

"What is it?" I swung his arm, more than a little curious.

"You'll see." He ticked his head, encouraging me to leave, and I glanced back at Alaric, comforted by the fact that I wasn't far away if he needed me.

We moved through the hall to the end, where Slade put a hand over my eyes, holding me close to his rock-hard chest as he opened the door, nudging me inside. Anticipation piqued on the bond as he removed his hand.

I blinked a few times, taking in the set-up. Greeny-blue walls like a hospital. Wall braces holding medical tubs full of bandages, cleaning swabs, hand sanitizer, boxes of gloves, masks, needles, thermometers, everything in a nurse's toolbox. A locked glass medical cabinet containing drugs. Two long beds for patients to rest in or be assessed.

A large desk and a seat beside it with a brand new computer.

"What do you think, medic?" Slade poked at the bandages, grabbed a packet and tossed it at me. "Like your medicine bay?"

*My medicine bay.* The words danced on my tongue. Goddess, he'd created this for me. Gone to all this effort for me, providing me a space in the club. I never got this kind of welcome at the Wolves, even though I was the president's daughter. At North Shore Hospital, I didn't have my own space, a desk, an office to go when I needed a time out. I had to share with fifty or so other nurses. But this was all mine. Excited by the prospect, I crossed to the desk, running my fingers over it.

Fuck, this man knew how to win me over.

I covered my mouth with two hands and muttered through them, "Oh, God, Slade, you did this for me?"

"Fuck, yeah. You're a Jackal. One of us." He came over to me, encircling me in his huge arms, sparking a simmering glow under my breast. "Like it?"

I couldn't help the smile scrawling across my face. "I love it. Thank you."

"I knew you would." Slade smirked like the cocky devil he was.

He brushed my hair off my neck and leaned down to kiss my flesh with rough, fiery kisses. My body blazed with a need so hot and fierce that I feared he'd leave me in a pile of ash if he didn't give me his mouth.

Instead, he whispered in my hair, "What do you say, Nurse A? I know you've decided to stay, but are you in or out? Because I don't wanna play games anymore. And you promised this impatient asshole an answer."

Time to make my mate deliriously happy by telling him there wasn't anywhere else I'd rather be. The avatars were my mates, them and the club, my home, safety, and future. And I wanted to get to know every little thing about them more, fall deeper for them, let myself completely go and dive into the L-word with each of them.

I could barely get a word out as he nipped at my smoldering flesh and moved to kiss my mouth like he couldn't get enough. Blood flowed to my southern parts in a heated rush.

"I'm in," I replied huskily.

He leaned back to check my face, confusion playing at his tanned, lined forehead. "All in or just medic in? Because I want to give you everything you want, Nurse A. A space to heal. A house. Vacations. Babies. Boats. Bikes. Best sex. Bondage. Whatever you want."

I threw my head back and laughed at the last one. "That's a hell of a lot of Bs, Mr. Vincent."

"I was on a roll and couldn't stop." He cupped my ass and squeezed. "I want to give you the best of everything because you deserve it."

I wanted everything he had to offer. Wild. Raw. Passionate. Dangerous. Deadly. No more holding back. No more questioning what we had. No more hurting them.

"I'm all in. Medic. Mate. Old lady." I threw my arms around his neck and drew him down, drinking in his brutish, wild kiss. After a long moment, I stopped to lay it all out for him because I had one condition. "Medic, not your prospect. Been there, done that, and I'm not gonna get bossed around by Brix."

"That's my girl." Slade rewarded me with a hard spank that set off a soft glow in my ass.

"Old lady," I corrected him, kissing his nose.

He lifted me into his arms, and I curled my legs around his massive hips. Another crack landed on my ass, harder this time, making me smart with a deeper heat. "Still gonna have to punish you for making me wait so long. I'm not a patient man."

"I'm cool with that, Mr. Vincent." I dragged my fingernails through his scalp, eliciting a long groan.

"Fuck, woman, don't try and tempt me to lessen your punishment." He carried me over to the nurse's bed, setting my ass on it and squeezing my thighs.

"Wouldn't dream of it, Mr. Vincent."

Flashing his devilish smile, he backed away, snatching a packet of bandages, busting them open and unravelling a roll. He wrapped the length around his fingers, tugging at it to test the tensile strength. At his return, he wrapped it around both my wrists. Oh, yeah. I was gonna get tied up and punished until I was incoherently satisfied.

"How about I punish you right now?" he rasped. "I figure your office could do with a christening."

"Goddess, yes." My core flushed with heat. I could already tell I was going to enjoy my new appointment. On more than one front.

# JACKAL'S WRATH MC WORLD REFERENCES

Below is a list of names used throughout this series.

**Aaliyah Heller** - Avatar of Isis.

**Alaric Hawke** - Jackal's Wrath MC Road Captain & Avatar of Horus.

**Avatar** - a human embodied with the power and characteristics of their patron god i.e. Set is the devil of the Egyptian pantheon and his avatar Slade is made of sin.

**Bagman** - a person who receives payoffs.

**Castor Redding** - Jackal's Wrath MC Enforcer & Avatar of Thoth.

**Church** - Official MC meeting.

**Cut** - MC member's vest.

**Horus** - hawk-headed god of the Sky. God to Alaric.

**Isis** - Goddess of Healing, Fertility and Magic and consort to Osiris (wife). Goddess to Aaliyah.

**Little snack** - pay off or bribe.

**Osiris** - God of the Underworld and consort (husband) of Isis. Zethan's God.

**Patch** - Club logo emblem worn on an MC cut.

**Pharaoh** - drug made exclusively by Jackals' Wrath MC.

**Set** - Jackal-headed god of Chaos, Destruction, the Dessert. Slade's God.

**Slade Vincent** - Jackal's Wrath Vice President & Avatar of of Set.

**Stunt man** - fall guy set up to pin petty crime on to divert police attention when conveying a shipment.

**Thoth** - Ibis-headed god of Writing, Science & Magic. Castor's god.

**Zethan Stone** - Jackal's Wrath MC Vice President & Avatar of Osiris.

# SKYLER'S OTHER BOOKS

Are you curious to read the other novels by me?

**MYTHOLOGY UNIVERSE (GODS)**

**OPERATION CUPID**
Completed reverse harem mythology romance

1. Battlefield Love
2. Quicksilver Love
3. Awakened Love
3.5 Stupid Cupid - a Valentine's short story

**OPERATION HADES**
Completed fated mates romance

1. Lady of the Underworld
2. Lord of the Underworld
3. Rulers of the Underworld
4. Return to the Underworld

**OPERATION ISIS - Jackal's Wrath MC**
Reverse harem paranormal motorcycle club romance with shifters

0.5 Prophecy of the Gods - prequel exclusive to newsletter subscribers
1. Curse of the Gods

2. Captive of the Gods
3. Legacy of the Gods
4. Wrath of the Gods - coming 2022

**BLOOD DEBT MAFIA (Operation Anubis)** Paranormal mafia arranged marriage romance.

0.5 Falling for the Mafia (prequel) - coming 2022
1. Married to the Mafia - coming 2022

More gods series planned! Stay tuned.

**GUILD UNIVERSE - PARANORMAL ROMANCE**

**NIGHTFIRE ACADEMY (Guild of Shadows series)** Adult paranormal academy reverse harem romance

1. Darkfire
2. Wildfire
3. Crossfire
3.5 Hearthfire - available by signing up to my newsletter http://eepurl.com/dCOqkb
4. Hellfire

GUILD OF SHADOWS Box Set (Books 1 - 4)

**GUILD OF GUARDIANS**
Paranormal reverse harem romance with m/m

0.5 Witch Hunt (prequel novella)
1. Life's a Witch
2. Hindsight's a Witch
3. Witch Please
4. Karma's a Witch

5. Son of a Witch - coming 2022

**Fairytale Retellings:**

**WINTER QUEEN series (part of the Haven Realm Universe)**
Heart of Frost - a Snow Queen retelling with snow leopards

**DARK REFLECTIONS series (part of the Haven Realm Universe)**
Born into Darkness - a Snow White retelling with panthers

**STANDALONES**

Charmed- an Aladdin retelling
Claimed- a Little Mermaid retelling

**FALLEN STARLIGHTS - Shared World series**
    Orion (Galaxy Huntress) Fallen Starlights series

STALKY STALK LINKS

**Become a darkling and join my readers group** Skyler's Den of Darkness for exclusive content, latest news, and giveaways.

**Sign up to my newsletter here** https://skylerandra.com/index.php/newslettersignup/

**Stalk me on the Gram:** skylerandraauthor

**Give my Facebook Page a like** https://www.facebook.com/Skyler-Andra-Author-324882698294312

**Join my Street Team** https://forms.gle/eqjhuSb7EJ42X7o67

**Watch my videos on Tiktok** skylerandraauthor

**Check out my Youtube vids**, including book trailers and me reading chapters or sample audiobook chapters: https://www.youtube.com/channel/UC-MQvzm8R8MQEWVX2xd4v2g

**Follow me on Amazon** for notifications on my latest releases https://www.amazon.com/Skyler-Andra/e/B00JQTFBRI

**Follow me on Goodreads:** https://www.goodreads.com/author/show/8170388.Skyler_Andra

**Follow me on Bookbub:** https://www.bookbub.com/profile/skyler-andra

**Want to get free books?** Join my ARC team and leave a review within 12 days to stay on the team and keep up to date with Advanced Reviewer Copies

https://docs.google.com/forms/d/1woqywzG41qzpaXxA4ul02QWSmNYtDs83wzDcAO--TgY/prefill

You're a true stalker if you're following me on all ;)

Printed in Great Britain
by Amazon